NO GOING BACK. NOT UNLESS SHE DEMANDED IT.

Right then, however, the only thing she was demanding was his attention. She had unwittingly relaxed back against him, her spine tucked snugly up the center of his body as she became like liquid. Without even realizing he was giving in to the impulse, Magnus bent forward and brushed a kiss up along the slope where her shoulder joined to her neck. For a moment she went taut, her closed lashes lifting as she tilted her chin to look at him.

Daenaira quieted again, that liquid quality pervading her once more and her head drifting to sweep back against his shoulder where she remained resting with sultry blinking eyes that spun a knot of raw need in his belly. Not for the lust that fired his soul, but for that empty place that had craved the warmth and acceptance of her permission to touch and to hold her like this.

Also Available from Jacquelyn Frank

The Nightwalkers
Jacob
Gideon
Elijah
Damien
Noah

The Shadowdwellers
Ecstasy

Published by Kensington Publishing Corp.

RAPTURE

The Shadowdwellers

JACQUELYN FRANK

ZEBRA BOOKS
KENSINGTON PUBLISHING CORP.
http://www.kensingtonbooks.com

ZEBRA BOOKS are published by

Kensington Publishing Corp.
119 West 40th Street
New York, NY 10018

All Kensington titles, imprints, and distributed lines are available at special quantity discounts for bulk purchases for sales
promotion, premiums, fund-raising, educational, or institutional
use.

Special book excerpts or customized printings can also be
created to fit specific needs. For details, write or phone the
office of the Kensington Special Sales Manager: Attn. Special
Sales Department. Kensington Publishing Corp., 119 West 40th
Street, New York, NY 10018. Phone: 1-800-221-2647.

ISBN-13: 978-1-4201-0423-3
ISBN-10: 1-4201-0423-3

First Printing: July 2009
10 9 8 7 6 5 4 3 2 1

Printed in the United States of America

For Laura.
I know this one is your favorite, so it's all yours.
You're my very best beloved friend.
I don't know what I would ever do without you.

Vocabulary of Shadese Terms

Please keep in mind no translations are exact. These are meant to guide you to the general implied meaning.

Ajai: Ah-ZHĪ (The "j" is always pronounced as in *déjà vu*): My Lord, Sir, Master

Anai: Ah-NĪ: My Lady, Mistress, Madame

Aiya: Ī-yah: An exclamation of frustration or exasperation. (Oh my! Oh yes! Oh no! Oh boy!)

Bituth amec: Bih-TOOTH AH-meck: son of a bitch (or stronger)

Drenna: Drehn-NAH: Darkness (Heaven). The goddess of Darkness.

Frousi: Froo-SĒ: A sectioned fruit that grows only in darkness. It carries a great deal of water and plant proteins, making it a good source of energy.

Glave: GLĀV: A dual curved throwing weapon that folds for carrying and when extended (like a butterfly knife is extended) is in the shape of an "S." The blade has boomerang properties in the hands of an expert.

Jei li: ZHĀ-lē: (roughly) precious one, sweetheart, honey

K'yatsume: KĒ-at-soo-mā: Your highness (female), My Queen

K'yindara: KĒ-en-dah-rah: wildfire, firestorm (feminized)

K'jeet: KĒ-zhēt: a nightgown/caftan

K'ypruti: KĒ-prew-tē: Bitch! Whore! Derisive feminine insult.

K'yan: KĒ-yahn: Sister (religious)

M'itisume: Mmit-Ī-soo-mā: Your highness (male), My King

M'gnone: Mmig-nō-nē: Light (Hell). The god of Light

M'jan: Mm-*zh*an: Brother/Father (religious)

Paj: Pa*zh*: A pair of light silk or gauze cotton trousers with cuffs tight to the ankles traditionally worn under any skirt that flows away from the body with movement.

Sai: SĪ (sigh): A triple-pronged steel weapon used mostly for defense.

Sua vec'a: Swah VEHK-kah: Stop! Cut it out! Desist!

Names:

Guin: Gwin

Acadian: AH-cā-dē-an

Rika: RĒ-kah

Malaya: Mah-LĀ-yah

Killian: Ki*l*l-Ē-yan

Xenia: Zuh-NĒ-ah

Daer aira: Dā-ah-NAIR-ah

Dae: Dā (day)

Prologue

Magnus understood the nature of evil sometimes a bit too well. There were times like these when he felt as though he had become a mirror for it, his own soul a distant reflection now as other things crowded it out. It was a thick and unwelcome feeling, a little too much like losing faith. At the very least it was a jaded perspective, and because of who and what he was, it simply would not serve.

The priest took a breath and instead focused on the grim task at hand.

Magnus drew the sojourn blade he held in his scarred and callused hand over the carefully laid granite pentagons decorating the plaza. Sparks were shorn from its angular tip as he drew an arc of challenge before himself. Blade makers far and wide would have cringed at the rude misuse of the painstakingly crafted metal, but sometimes evil needed a special invitation. Magnus engraved this one in the granite before him.

"Anthran," he called, his deep-throated voice echoing in the empty air around him, the wells and hollows of the stone surfaces of the buildings toying with the sound. The stark, abandoned feel of the place was, to his mind, strangely apropos. "Where do you think you can go that I cannot and will not follow, except into Light itself?"

And even there I would follow you. I would consign myself to burn in that hell if that is what it will take to ensure you are forever destroyed and can never harm another living soul.

Magnus's voice built in power, the boom of it sending powerful echoes of intimidation out all around him. "What do you think you can gain from hiding when you can see the chase is clearly over?"

"Time, perhaps," a disembodied but familiar voice replied. "Follow all you like, priest, but at least I dictate the path. Nothing can command me now."

"Except me," Magnus replied with a feral glare in his golden eyes as he scanned the vast emptiness for a shadow, a sign . . .

"Yes, always you. A dogged little soldier in Darkness's doggedly righteous little army." There was a dramatic, put-upon sigh from behind him, but Magnus knew better than to turn around. Instead, he glanced down into the blade of the sojourn, looking in its reflective surface and finding it empty as expected. He could hear the tinge of frustration in Anthran's tone once his enemy realized his pathetic tricks wouldn't work. "You run yourself ragged chasing me down, priest, and you never stop to question it. What does it feel like, being a mindless little lapdog for a god you have never met?"

"I do not have to meet my gods to know They are with me," he reminded his Sinner.

"Darkness is just shadows, you fool! Light is just light! They are not heaven or hell, and not gods who are rule makers any more than I am a rule breaker. I am just like you, Magnus, a Shadowdweller, a being with special powers given to me by my genetics; powers I am meant to use to their fullest glory!"

"You, my unfortunate soul, are nothing like me," Magnus countered. "This discussion is pointless. Come out and face me. Force me to hunt you and I promise to make you regret it. I will relish the penance I will earn when I make you suffer, just as your victims have suffered."

"This discussion is for *your* benefit, Magnus, not mine. There *are* no victims, priest. I am just a dream. Whatever I do in this realm is made of fantasy just as easily forgotten as it is remembered. I am ether and mist."

"If that were true, then you would have no cause to fear me. My blade would never touch you. But you know it is a lie, Anthran. You have illegally crossed into Dreamscape. You have stolen into the dreams of innocents and become their worst nightmares. You have used your Shadowdweller gifts against your own kin and become the worst kind of Sinner. For that, I will make you repent."

"Blind faith is still blind, Magnus, and I don't believe in your faith or your laws. You think you have the right to regulate Shadowscape, Dreamscape, and all the others? You appoint yourself and the rest of your religious house as militant protectors. Why? Because of Scripture? Ancient scribblings of our forefathers who might have been diseased or madmen? Or do you do this for those twin dolls you prop up prettily as our king and queen?

"Ha! You fool!" Anthran spat in contempt. "Is this what you sacrifice the pleasures of the mind and body for? It is unnatural, the way you and your eunuchs and those frigid bitches live. Maybe if you had a few real, lusty women to ride your cock, you wouldn't be so quick to judge the desires of a real man. I have no wish to fight you, M'jan, only to guide you from the errors of your fanatical thinking."

"Ah, but I wish to fight you," the priest observed darkly, taunting his foe. "Come, come, Sinner. I will listen to your lecture so long as you give it to me with your sword in hand and sweat on your brow."

"Deal!"

Anthran came from nowhere, barely giving Magnus the chance to parry the ringing blow of his much heavier two-handed blade. The priest gritted his teeth as the feel of it reverberated into his bones, and then with a slide of metal on metal he shoved his opponent's weight off himself. Once they were separated, the circling dance began.

"Not bad," Magnus mused, "but not good enough."

"I am learning this environment," Anthran warned, curling a lip in arrogant mocking. "I am better than you think I am."

"Thank you for the warning. However, you are but a babe in these woods. I have known the ways of Dreamscape for centuries. You cannot think to defeat my experience." Magnus flung his blade around in a series of sharp sweeps, forcing his opponent into parrying at lightning speed. Once he'd tricked the other man into leaving himself open to it, Magnus booted him hard in the ribs. Anthran stumbled back, barely catching his balance and keeping himself from sprawling onto the granite and leaving himself completely vulnerable. He coughed, tossing back his black hair and grinning at the priest come to hunt him.

"Steel-toed boots," he noted, taking a moment to stretch out his injured side. "You think small, clever tricks like that will turn the tide of a battle in your favor? Those are linear tactics. Realscape thinking. This world is about power and magic and the vast reaches of the imagination!"

Magnus pressed his advantage, refusing to let Anthran buy recovery time with his chitchat. His lighter blade moved fast, like a treacherous razor, but it wasn't meant to parry a blade so much heavier. He was forced to use a great deal of strength to fend off his enemy.

"You might be fighting someone who is a perfect equal to you, M'jan Magnus!"

"Faith, Anthran! You ask me what makes me defend and fight so righteously, without proof of divinity? It is called faith! I believe with all of my heart . . ." He leapt in and crashed blades, dancing out of reach again with speed belying his impressive build. ". . . with all of my blessed soul that no universe would allow a vicious, low-born piece of filth like you to gain this kind of power and be allowed the freedom to glut himself on sin and wickedness at the cost of others. Not without providing the opportunity for balance. I am that balance. I am that covenant."

"Covenant!" Anthran spat viciously as he swung his weapon in a crushing overhead blow. "Magnus, you are a brainwashed fool! Your faith enslaves you and you praise it! It oppresses you and you celebrate it! Death is the only way you will take this power back from me!"

"So be it," Magnus stated roughly. He swung his weapon high, using the overhead swing of the blade to command all of his opponent's attention as he quickly reached for the bolos in the hard leather pouch attached to his belt behind his left hip. He held on to one end. The silver ball fitted into his palm even as the second ball flew from his fingers and spun out a length of connecting razor wire between the two. The ball and wire nailed Anthran, wrapping around his biceps like a boa constrictor hugging its prey, and Magnus yanked hard and mercilessly to commit the weapon to its place.

Anthran bellowed in agony as barbs cut and tore, the ripping sound of flesh echoing without mercy. Anthran's heavy weapon went flying, useless now that he had been caught with one arm crippled. The priest flung away the ball still in his hand and the freed end swung around Anthran's waist, digging in and essentially tying his arm to his side.

Anthran shouted in frustration and then resorted to his only recourse. He closed his eyes and focused as swiftly as he could while Magnus's deadly blade advanced. The priest sensed the attack a moment before it struck, and he hit the deck to avoid the swarm of throwing stars that whined past. However, despite his dodge, he felt two of them thump into his left shoulder, sinking into his flesh all the way to the bone.

Magnus ground his teeth together as he rolled back up to his feet. He had just lost full rotation in that shoulder, but it would not sway his course. He passed his blade to his opposite hand for the briefest moment and threw up his uninjured hand, using his fury to manipulate the power of Dreamscape to his will. Electrical fire jolted down from the sky in a bolt of jagged lightning, the strike hitting the granite right between Anthran's feet. The Sinner was blown back, flying several yards before hitting the ground. Regardless of the distance, Magnus was there when he landed, kicking the badly singed betrayer onto his stomach so he could grab him and yank him to his knees.

Once he was kneeling, the priest laid his blade against Anthran's neck, pausing only to draw a much-needed breath.

"Repent," he rasped, ignoring the pain and the blood rushing down his back from his wounded shoulder. "Repent and I will recall myself from this course. Beg for mercy and say you will seek penance and guidance back to the path of your people. We understand temptation; we believe in reformation."

"You are a concubine," Anthran choked out, his dark eyes like pools of oil as he looked up to Magnus and let them fill with rage and contempt for all the priest held sacred and dear. "You are a whore and a slave to your stupid faith and the idiot children on the throne. I am free!"

"You will die as the law demands!" Magnus ground out, showing his depth of frustration for the first time. "For *Drenna's* sake, Anthran, I beg you to come to your senses! Repent!" Magnus shouted as he braced his feet and swung up his blade.

"Fuck you and your law," Anthran spat.

Magnus swung down his blade, committing himself to his duty. There was the sound of air being sliced, and the smooth follow-through of a blade so sharp, nothing barred its sweeping arc. Not even the neck of a man gone mad.

Magnus strode through the antechamber to Sanctuary temple, hurrying across the vast space to the courtyard on the opposite side. He cut through the peaceful rock garden with its ebony fountain and serene statuary until he entered the women's dormitories. The students, who were the collective responsibility of all of the priests and handmaidens were separated to opposite sides of the complex according to sex, as wisdom and traditional sensibilities dictated. There were no males allowed here, just as no females were allowed in the halls of its counterpart. The teachers and guardians were, of course, the exception to that, although even then it was discouraged for propriety's sake.

But this was Magnus, the priest who stood closest to Darkness Herself and the most powerful and formidable defender at Her disposal. There was no corner of Sanctuary that could or would bar him.

He made his way to the next story and then back to the deeply secluded rooms in the rear reserved for students who, for whatever reason, needed to be removed from the rest of the population. Usually it was illness or injury or some extreme discipline problem that warranted this isolation.

Tonight it was something far worse.

Magnus did not bother to announce himself before walking into the room. The small area was spare and quiet, its lone occupants a handmaiden who quickly got to her feet from the chair at the bedside, and the young girl in the bed who did not so much as blink when he entered. She simply continued to stare blankly up at the ceiling above her, her covers tucked just as smoothly around her still body as they had been when she was brought there two nights earlier.

Magnus said nothing to the holy woman keeping watch, but she knew to back away into the shadows, leaving the priest alone with his student as best she could without exiting the room. Magnus quickly knelt on a single knee beside the bed and leaned over the vacant and dull child he had failed to protect in time.

"Miranda." He addressed her in the softest of whispers, believing that his message was the one thing in the entire world she would want to hear. "Your monster is dead, little one. The one who stole into your dreams no longer exists." Magnus raised his bloodied weapon above her staring eyes. "His head rolls upon the ground of Dreamscape even now, the hands that touched you in violence severed beside it. I speared his heart through with the tip of my blade until its blackness burst and was destroyed. He will never, never be able to harm you again."

After the longest minutes, for the first time since she had awoken from the ultimate nightmare, the vulnerable young girl blinked. She moved, only a single hand, and reached to grasp the sword around the middle of its blade. Magnus did not flinch or draw away, though he knew how sharp the thing was. Instead, he let her take the battle-battered weapon down against her chest and watched as she slowly embraced the steel, as if it were a sweetly treasured pet. She turned away from him and he relinquished his hold on the hilt. She drew her knees up, hugged the stained sword with all of her heart, and began the slight rocking that seemed to always go hand in hand with the keening pitch of first-shed tears.

Except she was perfectly silent.

Hugging her new best friend.

Chapter One

Two months later . . .

Daenaira blinked in surprise when the locks on the outside of her room tumbled open sharply. There was almost the sound of confidence to it, which was equally surprising, but then there was a long minute of silence, and that made her smile darkly. The door jerked open and the rotund body of her aunt filled the frame of it.

"Let's go, girl. I'm finally to be rid of you."

Dae didn't know how to respond to that news at first. Winifred had threatened her for years with everything from abandonment to hiring someone to slit her throat, so she narrowed her eyes suspiciously on the bitch.

"And don't try any of your tricks, you little hellion."

Winifred shook her chubby wrist, making the wicked cat she held in her fist rustle, the whip's nine tails giving off an almost musical tinkle as the metal tips clinked together at the ends.

Apparently, Wini was feeling benevolent today. Usually she was compelled to use the *hurish* to keep Dae in line. The cuffs of the *hurish* were around Daenaira's ankles and throat even now, rubbing and chafing them raw, especially so soon after the last dump of electrical voltage Winifred had used on her. It had been so powerful it had burned Dae's skin, which of course made the chafing even worse.

Winifred usually held the remote for it at the ready, though this time Daenaira could see the outline of it in her apron pocket. Still, Wini wasn't as fast as all that. She was being uncharacteristically brave; almost cocky, Dae thought, her eyes narrowing even further.

"I said get up!"

Dae shrugged and got up. She was still exhausted after their last go-around, never willing to sleep so long as she knew the household was awake and slithering actively beneath her. When day came and all Shadowdwellers went to sleep for those hours, then she knew she could rest a little easier. Auntie Winifred and Uncle Friedlow slept like two fat, dead pigs once they got started. Although there had been that one time when Friedlow had tried to trick her . . . so she slept light all the same.

She walked across the room, coming up short when her chains pulled her up to a halt about three feet from the door. Friedlow showed himself then and Daenaira immediately smelled a rat. She stepped back quickly, crouching and readying for whatever the pig had planned. But he rarely made his stupid attempts at her anymore. Too many knees in his soggy little crotch, she figured. When he held up the key to her wristlets, she couldn't help but arch a brow. His hands were shaking, making the key ring jingle tellingly, and she took satisfaction in that. Safe in the doorway, his wife sneered at Dae.

"We've sold you. You're someone else's problem now. Maybe they can get a decent night's work out of you for a change."

Sold. Gods. They had threatened it endlessly, but she hadn't ever thought they would really do it. They could be lying, but she sensed all too keenly that they weren't. Daenaira wasn't stupid enough to think the next place she ended up in would be any better. Her motto in life? Things could always get worse.

She thought about getting a last lick in as her slovenly uncle unchained her. But there was the cat and the *hurish* to consider, and she was really damn tired. Besides, she would probably need her energy when she got where she was going. Dae was surprised, though, when he took the entire cuff off each wrist, as well as sliding the chain loose of its loop. Usually they dropped the chain but kept the cuffs on to keep her readily available for lockup in case she decided to start trouble. Still, Wini had that remote, and she was already nervously fiddling with it. The stupid cow was going to set it off accidentally on purpose again, if she knew her.

Daenaira moved forward when her uncle backed well out of her way to let her pass. Just for the fun of it, Dae shouted in his direction at the last minute, making the idiot nearly piss himself. She paid for her amusement, though, when the nasty *k'ypruti* to her right sent the cat flinging at her with an arm that had gotten a lot of practice over the years. Thankfully, the bits on the end nabbed mostly the fabric of her dress as Winifred yanked back, but Dae caught at least two on her left arm in the back, the short sleeve abandoning little chunks of her skin to it. The sting of the lash she could handle, especially through cloth, but gods, did flaying hurt! Daenaira felt fury rushing through her like breaking daylight, and she rounded on Winifred with a snarl.

She stopped when the remote appeared quickly.

Flaying was one thing, but Winifred held death in her hand, and that was something else. Dae backed off quickly and even let the cow stick her foot in the small of her back and shove her out of the hall with it. What choice did she have?

As usual, none at all.

When she emerged to the front of the house, she immediately noticed two male strangers standing in the front hall.

They were uniformed, a livery of some kind fortified with leather. Like most Shadowdwellers, they wore black, but there was a distinctive violet embroidery on the edges of their coats. Probably the mark of their house. A noble house, by the look of it. *They* certainly weren't wearing a sari made of quilted-together pieces of Winifred's old outfits. They looked at her and she saw surprise register on their faces. They traded perplexed looks and she rolled her eyes and sighed. She was used to it, actually. She was the only redheaded Shadowdweller most people had ever seen. Sure, the red was so deep it was close to the usual black the women of her breed were born with, but not close enough. It was just enough difference to trigger Shadowdweller night-vision to read it as black-blood red. She always wondered what it would have looked like if she could have ever stood in sunlight. Or any light, for that matter. But no 'Dweller could bear any light other than moonlight. Maybe a single candle . . . but anything else and they would burn to ash.

That was what made the *hurish* so deadly. The higher the voltage, the brighter the arc of the electricity that shot around the metal delivery system. Winifred could have burned off her feet past a certain point, if she hadn't been afraid of killing her in the process. That much voltage and poof, there went a perfectly good set of cheap muscles and hard-laboring spine. Gods knew *their* lazy asses never did any of the work. They enjoyed the money made off the sweat of her brow as she did the laundry Winifred took in from the nearest high houses that couldn't be bothered to do it for themselves. It was a lovely convenience that freed up time for other things.

Lovely for them, at least. Lovely for her aunt and uncle. Not so lovely for her. Especially since slavery, she knew, was illegal. But their isolation from most of the city and the control methods they used on her allowed them to get away with it. They never let her off the property. Never told her about the outside world. All she knew, she had learned before she had fallen into their hands. That and what she had gleaned from the laundry she had done. She would know when someone had sex, lost their virginity, was wounded in a fight, or sometimes even what they did for a living. But it was a small cross section of information from a smaller cross section of the populace, so she supposed it wasn't all that important.

But this was completely unexpected. They must have gotten an incredible price for her, otherwise why give up the only source of livelihood they had? Unless she was going to be replaced by someone younger and cheaper to feed . . . easier to whip and beat into submission.

She had never been easy.

However, the fact that her newer owners were wealthy made her stomach knot with apprehension. A noble house willing to get caught owning a slave had a lot more to lose than a merchant laundress did. That meant they had more resources for hiding it out in the open, and far deeper desires for the use of their property than just making her wash clothes to keep them fed. It meant they weren't afraid of much of anything.

Daenaira quickly began to size up her competition. It didn't look very promising for her side. Both men were big and well developed. They were both armed in several ways that were obvious, and even a few that others wouldn't notice right off. They were trained fighters. Guards, if she had her guess. Still, if she was ever going to get out of this bright light, she was going to have to do something before she got to her new location.

And that was when Winifred hit the switch to the remote, getting *her* last lick in. The voltage was extreme, and Dae knew it right away. Her whole body seized with it, the skin around her ankles and throat burning even as the guards began to move forward to catch her.

Everything went numb and wild and then . . . blissfully . . . black.

* * *

Daenaira awoke to the sensation of being rolled over.

She tried to focus, her eyeballs feeling fat and swollen as they often did when she had been badly shocked. She saw the unmistakable silhouette of a man leaning over her. A really big man. She reacted before she was even fully conscious. She palmed out hard, catching softness and grinding it into the hardness of bone. She felt the answering spray of blood spattering against her and figured she'd gotten his mouth or nose at the very least. She would have preferred an eye, but she took what she was given.

She rolled out from under him, dragging her wobbling, uncoordinated muscles into something like a crawl. She didn't realize she was on a bed until she fell off it. She grunted and cursed when she hit the floor. *A bed! It figures!* Well, the perverted prick should have tied her ass up, because there was no way she was going to allow—

Strong hands wrapped around her arms from behind. He hauled her to her feet, for which she mentally thanked the moron as she got her vacillating strength underneath herself. It was probably only a matter of time before he jolted her into a coma, but she would be damned if she was going to be conscious for what he was planning. Grounding herself on braced feet, she windmilled back and around to the left, her elbows rising high and whipping out of his grip. One caught him hard in a cheekbone, and the second came full around to his lower jaw. She heard the harsh sound of teeth clacking together and an angry bellow of pain just before she swung her fist into his throat.

I'm dead, I'm dead, I'm so dead, she thought frantically even as she added insult to his injuries when she watched him fall gagging onto his knees and hauled back to kick him full force in his crotch. But before she could commit, she was grabbed from behind, whirled around, and belted hard across her face.

It was a good punch. Enough to stop her dead, seeing as how she was working on borrowed strength to begin with.

She felt blood explode out of her mouth even as fiery pain burned across her cheeks and sinuses. She'd be shocked if she didn't lose a tooth, she thought, even as her body flung back with the momentum of the punch's follow-through. Off balance and flying, she hit the floor in a skid. The smooth surface sent her skating several feet before she bumped to a stop against something.

"Sua vec'a!"

The roar burst into the room like holy thunder. Head spinning, stomach sick from it, half blind and half deaf from pain and worse, Daenaira knew she had never heard anything like the power of that voice in all her life. It was like the rising roar of a mighty lion, the power of which you never understood if you only ever heard it from a distance. But this was the voice of a beast who knew he was at the top of the food chain. He knew he was king.

She felt something move against her and realized she had come up against the feet of the voice's owner. In fact, they had stopped her progress across the floor. She curled her body instinctively, readying for the kick in the ribs or back that would follow, bracing as best she could even though she knew she should relax instead. It hurt less if she could make herself relax.

Remembering that helped and she let herself go lax, though remaining curled to protect her vitals.

"What in the burning Light of day are you doing?" the terrible voice demanded from above her. "Get out of my sight! Go before my katana meets my hand!"

The threat was clear enough, except she didn't know where she should go. Regardless, the way she was feeling, she didn't want any more trouble. Dismissal was just as good as winning in her book. She rolled onto her hands and knees and tried to crawl, but she couldn't support her own weight. Even a baby could crawl, and yet she couldn't drag herself an inch. Plus, she was drooling blood all over the place, and she had learned the hard way that bleeding on things was frowned upon.

She barely noticed the sound of receding feet, but she did hear the echoing clack of a shutting door that told her she was in a hell of a big room. She still couldn't move, so she was fairly close to the angry male above her when he crouched down. She saw him looming near her in silhouette only, details blurred completely away. She heard the creaking sound of leather from his clothing, and the telltale tap of wood against the floor. Hollow wood, with something inside it.

A sword. The threatened katana, no doubt. But on the plus side, she hadn't heard the sound of drawn steel, so she still had time to get her act together if she was lucky. Daenaira tried again to move, and again remained in a motionless pile.

She felt the heat of him as he leaned over her, reaching across her back. Dae should have kept still, just like she always should keep still and never seemed to manage it, but instinct made her grab the arm of the hand about to touch her, her nails gouging deeply into—

Holy Light, she thought with a mental gasp, *is all of that muscle?*

It was more like flesh made steel! She could hardly get her hand around the width of that thick bicep. Gods help her if he was left-handed, because if what she was feeling wasn't his sword arm, she was completely screwed.

To her never-ending surprise, she felt his opposite hand come to rest on the one she was digging into him. Winifred liked to cut Dae's nails off when she was out cold after a battle. She must have forgotten, because Dae made pretty good purchase. The thing was, instead of ripping her away from him, he simply held her fingers under his, keeping her from stripping his flesh but tolerating her injury to him.

This guy could be a bigger degenerate than she had anticipated. If he liked getting hurt . . .

She took note of the thick, hard calluses on the hand covering hers. There was years' worth of hard work at something; it was not soft and fat like her relatives' had been. Not in the least. Yet, she slowly became cognizant of the gentleness of his touch against her fingers. She suspected a trick, but for the life of her, she couldn't figure out what it was. Eventually she just let go, collapsing into an exhausted pile of panting, dizzy flesh. As if she'd never even touched him, he continued to reach for her, cupping her shoulder in his wide palm. Slowly he rolled her toward him, letting her flop loosely onto her back.

On the plus side, she could make out that he was in a low squat, his knees wide apart enough to give her a great shot at his vulnerable testicles.

"I am sorry for this," he said, the large voice spinning away into a kindness she could almost believe because it was so vastly opposite to the tone of earlier. "That will not happen again."

Wanna bet? She wanted to sneer at him, but her lip hurt an awful lot. Just wait until she got a second wind. All kinds of shit would be happening again.

Meanwhile, she was pretty much as dangerous as a ball of fluff under the furniture right then. Still, there was that rather attractive testicular target within reach. It could be fun. At the very least it could get her belted into unconsciousness. That'd buy her a few more hours, and she usually healed pretty fast, just like any other 'Dweller could. Provided she could go a few hours without shock therapy, that is. It tended to jar her healing molecules all out of whack or something.

She felt his hand slide up from her shoulder to her throat. Dae swallowed, feeling his fingers on the gold collar to the *hurish*. Not that she was a treasured pet or anything; the fortified gold was just the best conductor of electricity around. The built-in remote circuitry also had a delightful feature that humans used to keep their dogs within the bounds of an electrified fence—except it was jacked up to less than humane standards. Of course, humans called it something else.

Humans didn't even know Shadowdwellers existed, never mind that they shared technology. Well, lightless technology at least.

She felt him probing at the collar, trying to turn it or have it give way a bit more, she supposed. But she was swollen around it now, not that there was any leeway to begin with.

"What is this? Why do you wear your jewelry so tightly?"

She laughed, a sloppy snort that conveyed she was much less than amused. Her contempt mixed with her fury and the impotence of the moment, making things increasingly dangerous for the idiot touching her. The higher her temper spiked, the stronger she would feel. It was probably an adrenaline thing, but whatever worked . . .

"Please answer me when I ask you a question."

"Fuck you. I'm not your parrot, your dog, or anything else."

Daenaira had never learned when to keep her mouth shut, either. Apparently, she had a sucky learning curve. She felt those fingers come up to close around her face, his heated body closing in as he leaned closer and turned her malfunctioning eyes up to his.

"I do not consider you any of those things," he told her carefully, "but I do expect a level of respect in my house, girl."

His house. So he was her new owner after all. She had suspected as much, considering the way he had spoken earlier and the haste with which the other two men had left the room.

It didn't matter. He could be the president of the United States for all she cared. While humans found that to be an important person, Shadowdwellers did not. This male might scare the hell out of his other servants, but she was a horse of a different color.

She smiled.

Then she spat in his face.

How's that for respect, asshole?

She wished she could have seen it. She knew she was

bleeding really badly, too, because she was constantly swallowing the stuff. Dae would have paid good money to see some aristocratic *bituth amec* sprayed in red spit, and here the opportunity was, completely free. Served him right anyway. What kind of idiot would lean face-to-face with her after watching her kick his lackeys' asses all over the place? Now she was thinking she had to take that testicle shot just on principle. Then again, why blow all her tricks at once?

"That," he said very slowly, "was not only rude, but quite unhygienic."

Unhygienic? Was he kidding?

"Yeah? I've also been known to pee myself on command." She curled the less swollen side of her lip. "Might want to keep that in mind."

To her surprise, she heard him chuckle. And it wasn't some snide or superior mocking laugh either, but a rather genuine, good-natured sort of thing.

"I thank you for the warning. With consideration like that, I am certain we can work up to respect."

Then she felt him move to slide his hands under her back and her knees. Before she could respond, he had risen to his full height and was carrying her high against a chest made of chiseled rock. Dreading what would happen next, she tensed for any possibility. She was already in trouble, she knew, because he wasn't the least bit afraid of her. It had taken some time, but Winifred and Friedlow had learned a healthy fear of their caged pet, and she had worked it every chance she could to keep herself reasonably safe and alive. She had no idea how she could work the same effect on a man who seemed so blasé about owning a slave who threatened to leak on him like a baby doll. Also, there was the part where she knew she weighed a good sixty-five kilos, yet he was sweeping her up without so much as a grunt of effort. The muscle closed around her in the form of his chest, astoundingly broad shoulders, and those fearfully thickly developed biceps. There was no give on him anywhere. His belly was hard and flat against her round hip, and as he crossed the floor in a crisp, booted stride, he never so much as shuffled a foot under her added weight.

She was in big trouble. She knew it with that sinking surety she got in her gut right before the most dramatic events in her pathetic life took place. Daenaira was oriented to the room as she knew it so far, though, and she was positive he wasn't heading back toward the bed where this had all begun. However, without knowing what else was around her in the vast room, she couldn't say for certain if that was a good thing. She did understand that space in an underground city like this one was a scarce commodity. Once used for deep mining efforts, the caves and caverns the Shadowdweller city occupied were located in the far reaches of an Alaskan mountain range. The small sprawl of the city that existed aboveground appeared to the rest of the world as a wildlife and geographical survey post. Those buildings managed things like winter livestock and other city supplies or technology stations, all managed in a lightless environment, especially during the long, dark winters that gave her people respite from the dangers of daylight. Shadowdwellers migrated to the very edge of the Antarctic for the summer, following the darkness to a New Zealand winter that was far less harsh or dark than Alaska, but still less than eight hours of daylight in a day, which was much preferred to eighteen hours of North American summer days.

But here in the northern city, deep in the dark, it meant an entire culture lived in a slowly developing infrastructure, making space very, very valuable. If the room they were in was truly as large as it sounded, her new "benefactor" was as wealthy as they came. A Senator, she considered, although keeping slaves wasn't exactly politically savvy. Still, Senators were only useful in bringing the issues and needs of their people to the royals and arguing with them about progress, both for and against. But in truth, the Chancellors were the sole power of their government. Daenaira had once thought it would mean good things for their society when the twins had won the war and taken power about a decade ago. But since she had spent the past eight of those years washing clothes in captivity, she had no idea if it was working out that way. She didn't much care either. It had been hard enough worrying about how to keep ahead of trouble on a nightly basis.

Eventually they came to a stop and she felt him kneel to put her down on a soft surface. It was a sofa or a firm chaise, the satiny cushions sliding under her fingertips. She sat there tensely, trying to blink the persistent blindness away once and for all. It wasn't clearing up fast enough, and she needed her vision if she was going to have to fight. And she *was* going to have to fight, she didn't doubt that.

"Do you wish to explain to me why you were fighting with the guards?" he asked as he rose to his feet and stepped out of striking distance. She saw him squat again and heard the splash of water. There was a humid dampness in the air and she suspected they were at a hot spring.

He had a hot spring in his room? Or was it a bath? She watched him lean forward and realized he was washing his face.

Well, the urge to run up behind him and shove him into the water was just too strong. He had completely turned his back on her—she could make out the wide width of his shoulders and the dark fabric that stretched over them—and she was a lot faster than he probably thought.

Normally.

Daenaira sighed, realizing she'd just make things worse if she did it. Where would she run to afterward? She didn't have a clue where she was and where she could hide. She might as well save it for another day. She prayed there was another day to save it for. The thought made her heart race. She tested the strength of her limbs by holding herself upright and pushing her feet against the cold, smooth floor. Her new owner turned back to look at her over his shoulder, as if he could sense what she was doing and why. Dae went very still. He rose up and advanced on her, his enormous body quickly blocking out all of her vision.

"Why were you fighting with the guards?" he asked again, lowering himself into a vulnerable crouch with his knees parting around her shins.

Boy, is this guy stupid or what?

She tried not to warn him with a self-satisfied smile.

But then a gentle hand landed on her knees and a hot, damp cloth touched her face in soft, short strokes meant to cause her as little pain as possible as he cleaned her up. Dae realized his hand on her leg was just about as warm as the cloth he used. Heat was radiating from him and slipping under her skin, a swimming sensation that seemed to skip like free-flowing energy up along her nerves. She realized then that she could smell the scent of him. There was leather, from his clothing, of course, but it was more than that. He didn't reek of sweating armpits like her uncle did, offending her sharp Shadowdweller senses, but instead there was an appealing mixture of fabrics, the detergents used to clean them, the almost sultry scent of the soap he used, and . . . something else. There was a chemical scent, which she thought might be sword polish, but there was also this dark, toasted aroma, like when black fire burned at its hottest.

"He was on top of me in bed," she found herself saying truthfully. "If you woke up to find a man larger and stronger than you are on top of you, wouldn't you fight, too?"

His hand went still against her bruised cheek and she heard him draw a slow breath. "Yes, I would. Can you tell me, was he touching you inappropriately?"

"No one has touched me appropriately in eight years," she countered in a cold, bitter voice. "I haven't given my permission for so much as a finger to be laid on my person in all of that time, yet it happens quite frequently."

Daenaira was taken completely by surprise when he suddenly lifted his touch off her knees, clearly realizing he was doing the very same thing. Confused by his seeming kindness and the show of respect, she became suspicious of whatever game he was playing.

"You are right, of course," he said, his tone grim. "I am sorry. It was wrong of me to presume. Without excuse I will say I am used to touching others for my work and it is a habit. I will be more thoughtful in the future if it truly bothers you." He paused while Daenaira tried to figure out what in burning Light was going on. "What is your name?"

"My name?" she echoed. *Hmm. Girl. Bitch. Stupid. Idiot.* He could take his pick. She hadn't heard someone use her given name in years. "I suppose it's whatever you are going to want it to be," she said with a shrug. She'd keep her name, thanks. It was better than hearing it in contempt or in insult. She had a pretty name, actually, and she wanted to keep it that way.

"What does your family call you?" he demanded.

"Slut," she retorted sharply. "Or 'useless whore.' There are also combinations that include both."

He was silent for a long minute, and then the cloth was cleaning off her chin and jaw. "I see," he said, his low voice resonant with a hard sound that actually gave her goose bumps. She remembered then that, for all his tenderness of the moment, there was a deadly man in the form before her. How he reconciled the two was beyond her. Again, she suspected it was a tactic, meant to take her off her guard. "I could compel you to give me your real name," he informed her quietly. It wasn't so much a threat as it was a fact he was convinced of, and Dae caught another chill. This one raced down her chest, the sensation making her nipples tighten in painful response. She crossed her arms over her chest, knowing how thin the worn-out sari she wore was. "However, I would much rather you tell me for yourself. In the meanwhile, I think I need something to call you by. *Jei li* is too familiar for us at this point, and it would be an insult to use it when you do not trust me as yet."

"I am no man's *jei li*," she countered sharply. She might as well let him know that she wasn't the soft and cuddly type anyone could ever call "sweetheart."

"'Slut' and 'whore' are out of the question," he said firmly.

"Fine with me. Always did prefer 'you fucking bitch' anyway. It's so American slang."

"Gods, you are a little spitfire, aren't you?" he remarked as though both pleased and surprised. "No weeping or fear that you'd want to show, though I know you are feeling that fear. These snide, sharp retorts tempting trouble for you had I been of a different temperament. You pissed off the guards enough to make them forget themselves."

"No one fucks with me," she said through her teeth, the words colder than the Alaska winter above them. "I'll warn you now, if you think you're coming anywhere near my tits or my ass, you better be prepared to like it while I'm out cold, because so long as I am conscious it isn't going to happen."

Again there was that long silence, filled in by the stroke of the cloth along her throat and neck. He stopped at the edge of the *hurish* collar, and she was glad because it stung like a bitch.

"I see," he said once more, his tone just as cold as hers was now. Well, she thought, too bad if he didn't like it. Playing nice-nice with her wasn't going to win him any points. "It is my guess that this has been your experience in the past?"

"Is that your guess?" she asked sarcastically. "Wow. Bright guy."

"And who would try this with you?"

"My pig uncle, for one. But he got tired after a while."

She heard him swallow, but it didn't release the deadly danger she heard in his voice when he said, "Tired?"

"Of this."

She extended her leg forward, her foot catching him actually quite gently beneath where his scrotum would be. The top of her ankle fit snugly to his balls through his slacks, and her shin nudged against his penis. She was good at making as full a contact as she possibly could, making certain she caught all the goodies at once. Usually quite hard.

But this time she was making a point, so she just bumped him with a little slide to make him wholly aware of her positioning . . . and his. She had to smile when the automatic male reaction to grab hold of her leg to control her came over him. His grip closed tight around her calf and shin, but instead of pushing away as most would do to deflect her, he held her tightly in place against himself. Clever boy. He was taking away the power of her momentum this way, something most idiots never realized. She couldn't get up enough steam to castrate him if she was already in contact with him.

"Resourceful," he said, the sound of his smile in his voice surprising her just as much as the realization she could just about make out that smile. "But a kick in the balls has been known to simply piss some men off. To make them more violent."

"Is that a warning?" she asked, narrowing her eyes and trying to make out his features. Dark skin, dark hair, and a white smile described every Shadowdweller male alive.

Well, maybe not the smile.

"Yes. Not as pertains to me, per se—though I would be quite angry, I assure you—but I can teach you other ways that will take a man down in a single blow. Then you can run and get help freely."

"Freely." She snorted and flicked a finger against her collar, turning her foot so the ankle cuff pressed through his pants. "Oh right, because I'm so free."

She saw him shake his head and then realized she could see the shine of smooth ebony. It was long and loose, waved and curled to his shoulders. She looked up quickly and found his eyes. Under fine dark brows and the shelf of a serious-looking forehead, she found golden eyes. Almost as gold as her collar, but darker and deeper than that. Those eyes, and the strong aristocratic features they were set in, looked quite convincingly confused.

"What does that mean?" he demanded.

"Oh, please. Are you going to sit there and pretend I'm not a slave you just bought for gods know what? You can be all sweet if you like, but—"

"*What?*"

He surged up to his full height, which with her cleared vision Daenaira got to appreciate for the very first time. He was well over six feet, which towered over her as she sat. She hated sitting in front of a standing male. Too often they liked to try to grab her by her hair and try—

"I did not buy a slave," he ground out with a fiery affront and in a booming voice that gave her the chills. "I paid a bride price for a handmaiden. A dowry, just like any man who takes another man's daughter would do!"

Handmaiden?

Dae blinked and for the first time looked at what her new owner was wearing.

He was clothed in the dark violet uniform of a temple priest.

Chapter Two

"Well, somebody fucked up," she informed him with her usual snide attitude. "I've been a slave for the past eight years, and today I was sold to someone else. I assume that would be you. You can call it a dowry or what have you, but it's still buying and peddling flesh without that person's permission!"

Magnus wanted to reply, but he was so infuriated he didn't dare speak. He looked at the collar once more, as well as the anklets he had only just noticed under her skirt when she had pressed one to him. They were plain gold rings at first sight, but with ominous dread he looked closer, lifting her hair and seeing the circuit lock in the back.

No one has touched me appropriately in eight years.

That tidbit of information and others like it were beginning to fill in the picture for him. He realized he had touched her again without asking and quickly dropped her hair and backed off.

"Tell me that is not a *hurish*," he demanded of her. "*Hurish* are for controlling cattle. Livestock. Not people!"

"Well, it was all the same to my aunt and uncle," she spat back at him. "I guess they left it on for you as a gift. The remote is probably around here somewhere." She affected looking around herself. "No? Maybe the guards have it."

"They controlled you with electrical impulses?" Magnus had never heard of anything like it. Not in his society! The Nightwalkers were supposed to be advanced, sophisticated people. The Shadowdwellers were, unfortunately, considered the most juvenile of all supernatural species because their culture was still only a decade past picking themselves up out of the ashes of civil war. That, and they were tattooed with a centuries-old reputation of being mischief makers, causing a whole lot of trouble to the rest of the world. However, he and the reigning household had spent thirty years cultivating a newer and more ordered version of their society. They had dissolved the infighting clans, elevating good leaders into the renewed political body of the Senate. Everyone in the city was provided for. Education, shelter, heat, food, religion. As with any society, he knew things slipped through the cracks, but . . .

Slavery?

"No," she retorted tartly. "They used electrical impulses to keep me on the property. They used electro-shock to fry discipline into my ass. Ask your guards if you don't believe me. They watched Winifred do it to me right before we left."

Magnus didn't need to ask. If there was one thing he was knowledgeable of, it was the truth. Truth, in fact, was his special gift. With just a touch, he could compel the truth from anyone. It would replay in both their minds with impartial sight. Even those who didn't know they were lying to themselves couldn't hide from his power. Although he wasn't touching her at the moment, she was radiating the bald honesty of what she was saying in a rather beautiful sort of defiance that fed the truth into him with force.

He reached a hand toward her, saw her almond-shaped eyes narrow the tiniest fraction, and stopped to bend closer to her.

"Can I touch you to take these evil things off you?" he asked her softly.

"Are you really a priest?" she asked with suspicion as she looked over his uniform. She was searching for some kind of flaw that would reveal a deception, he realized.

"Yes. I am a priest. And you, little spitfire, are going to be my handmaiden."

That made her laugh. She started with a soft snort, but then belted out enthused amusement that might have made him smile if he wasn't so appalled by all he was seeing and learning.

"Okay, first of all, I am clearly not religious material, M'jan . . . um . . ."

"Magnus. M'jan Magnus."

He watched that hit her like a gut punch, and this time he couldn't help smiling a little when she giggled in a fit until her face flushed under the smooth cappuccino coloring of her skin. She brushed back the heavy length of her peculiar-colored hair with one hand while she waved the other in her face as if to help herself take in oxygen.

"Okay, baby," she gasped, still laughing so that her eyes sparked and glittered with her humor. "If you were going to pick someone to pretend to be, why in Light would you pick the head priest of Sanctuary? I mean, come on! Magnus is the most powerful priest there is, both politically and physically, I've heard. He runs everything and is practically married to Darkness Herself!" Here the humor stopped cold and she slowly stood up to give him a positively evil look of hatred, proving all of her laughter a lie. "And M'jan Magnus has had a handmaiden for two centuries. He certainly doesn't need another, and he certainly wouldn't want it to be some low-born piece-of-filth slave girl who never went to school in her life!"

So much rage.

Magnus had never seen so much anger in the blood and

spirit of a woman as he did when he looked into this troubled and magnificently powerful young girl. Slave? No. She had never capitulated, so slave was not the term for her. Captive, perhaps, but this woman was no man's slave.

Yet, she had offered herself to him.

"My handmaiden died six weeks ago," he said simply, feeling nothing would be constructive in elaborating on those circumstances with her. In fact, the less she knew, the more it would content him. At least for now.

"Died." She echoed the word, folding her arms under her breasts and creating a shelf that held her in enhanced shape. Magnus let his eyes drift briefly, but he took in the entirety of her curving body. He suspected she was thin for her generous height, but just the same, she curved like a back-mountain highway. There was a cut and sweep to her waist that accented her hips and, he suspected, her backside as well. He couldn't see at the moment. Between that and those rather hefty breasts, he realized this was definitely a full-grown woman he was dealing with.

He had thought she was younger.

"There's got to be—"

She was cut off when someone cleared a throat nearby. She jumped in her own skin, and without thinking, Magnus reached out to settle her with a calming touch on her arm.

"I asked not to be disturbed," Magnus snapped at the young guard.

"Apologies, M'jan Magnus," he said quickly, touching a spread palm to his heart and bowing with deep respect. "Chancellor Tristan has arrived, requesting an emergent audience with you."

Daenaira sat down hard, grateful the chaise was still right behind her.

Magnus turned to look at her, those strangely compelling

eyes of gold telling her so many things in one sudden jolt she felt as if her brain was on overload.

Truth. It was the truth. He really was M'jan Magnus, the greatest priest in all the history of Sanctuary, leader of the great temple of Darkness and Light. Her eyes dropped to the katana secured to his waist in a weapons belt. There was a pouch in the rear holding a set of bolos. On the opposite hip there were two other hard leather pouches. These, she suspected, held some sort of hand-thrown missiles like saw-stars or shurikens.

Magnus was also renowned in their world for being the most ruthless warrior protector of the 'scapes. Shadowscape, Dreamscape, or Realscape—any 'Dweller who violated moral law or the martial rules of those dimensions, he hunted them down and, usually, destroyed them. They were called Sinners, and the gods knew they deserved what they got if they did something to earn a warrior like Magnus on their trail.

But something had happened. She could feel it in a wicked, crawling sensation under her skin. Dae had no idea why she felt this way or what it really meant, but she knew that something had tainted the power of the man standing before her.

"Please, *K'yindara*, sit for a moment while I meet with Tristan. I will return as soon as I am able and we can finish our discussion," he said, a soothing hand gesture toward her seeming to be an aborted move at touching her with reassurance, but he remembered in time. For the first time, it began to sink in to Daenaira that things were not at all what she had thought they were going to be.

"K'yindara?" she echoed numbly.

"Well, it will do until you feel ready to tell me your name." He turned to the guard, who was staring at her with gaping curiosity. Magnus snapped his fingers to gain the guard's focus, the sharp sound reproving all on its own without the dark scowl that accompanied it. "See Tristan into my office. I will be right behind you."

"Yes, M'jan," the guard said respectfully before bowing

slightly and then hurrying out of the room. When he was gone, Magnus turned to look at her once more, his features shadowed with hard thoughts she wished she could hear.

"Take this time, *K'yindara*, to relax and reflect on the understanding that I am not here to hurt you. The details of your staying here will be our first topic on my return. Until then, try and rest easy."

She watched him hesitate a moment, and then he turned and left the room at a clipped step. Daenaira exhaled a long, slow breath as she slowly began to take in the room around her.

"Holy Light," she swore softly as she did.

The room was gigantic, really. Lined in dark maroon glass tiles with beautiful etchings, the walls and ceiling seemed to stretch above her and made her feel a little small in the middle of it all. She was in a bath. The floor that sprawled beneath her was patterned in a tight mosaic of maroon, jet, and golden tiles. The gold was an accent along edges of the surface wherever it was broken by objects or walls. Except for when it disappeared into the water of the enormous tiled bath sunk into the floor before her.

Bath was less appropriate than *pool*.

The huge expanse of water ran up to and then under the far wall, making her believe it was fed naturally somehow. She got up on her feet, wobbling in unreliable steps to the spot where Magnus had washed his face.

Holy shit! She had spit in the face of a priest!

"Oh gods," she groaned. "They definitely let you burn in Light in the afterlife for something like that." Not that she was a heavily religious woman, but she believed that much at the very least.

She shrugged it off nervously, realizing she couldn't change anything now. Then she looked down into the water. It was glittering gold. Gold tile lined it completely, except where she could see little lines of jet demarcating a set of stairs leading down into the steaming pool right next to her. A shelf of tile had been constructed nearby, a little above water level, and here there were bathing products like soap and shampoo. Fresh cloths stood ready, as did the towels to dry off afterward. All of that hot water and space . . . just to take a bath.

She looked around and saw no sign of the bed from earlier, or the blood she'd shed. But there were two alcoves on opposite ends of the room. Hurrying as best she could on persistently unsteady legs, she made her way to where her sense of direction said she'd come from. Sure enough, through the alcove was an archway leading into a vast bedroom, furnished and decorated in midnight blue and gold. The colors, she realized, of a handmaiden's uniform. The low bed was plush and beautiful, its coverlet made of rich velvet in midnight blue, intricate knotted designs embroidered around it in gold thread. Velvet and satin pillows filled most of the large surface of the bed, and she guessed she was supposed to fill the rest. There was everything else a woman could need. Vanity, dressers, a closet and clothing preparation area that included a steam ironing system and several bookcases. There was an adorable conversation area in front of a fireplace. A fireplace! Another one of those things only the wealthy could own because of the complications of venting such a thing in an underground city. Then again, if she was in Sanctuary, they were on the level just below the surface. Or, at least, they could be. Sanctuary was probably several levels on its own. The royal palace was also on the upper levels, as were the Senate and many of the noble houses and merchant services.

The city was miles wide and very deep, a convoluted arrangement of space, pathways, and everything a city needed. But every Shadowdweller knew that their entire society was run from this level. Religious, political, and financial. If it was key to their culture's survival, it happened here. The only exception, she supposed, was the hydroponics factory in the very bowels of everything. Since it was the only place where light was used, it was locked down and secured and only those brave enough to work close to that many lightbulbs were allowed in. Of course, not while the lights for growing the foods they cultivated were on. That would be the equivalent of an accident at a nuclear plant for their species. Anyone caught inside when those lights came on would literally be toast.

Dae noticed a lot of bare surfaces on the shelves and little tables in the room. This included large gaps in the books on the shelves. The mantel was bare of any trinkets or décor. Anything of a personal nature or touch had been completely removed. This, she realized, had been a dead woman's room. Magnus's previous handmaiden. Dead six weeks, all sign of her packed up and shipped off, and now . . . now here she was, supposedly to take her place.

No way. Nuh-uh. Not her. She was a lot of things, but a holy woman wasn't one of them. Besides, it was just the same as the past eight years! Handmaidens were servants to the priests they were assigned to. They waited on them hand and foot, as she understood it, like some sort of religious geisha, and were bound into that servitude for their natural lives. There was no leaving until . . .

She looked at those bare places again and felt a terrible sense of panic clawing up her chest. It was just a prettier prison, she realized. She'd been sold into slavery all over again, except this time it was publicly acceptable. Light, they even called it an honor and a privilege! Like an obscene lottery, women wept and screamed for joy when they were "chosen."

How in Light had she been *chosen*? No one had even known she was alive except Winifred, Friedlow, and their twisted friends who also had slaves and had as much to lose as they did if they ratted them out.

"This is insane," she whispered to the starkly lovely room.

She turned around to look at the exit on the other side of the bath. Shuffling and limping quickly across the room, Daenaira burst through the archway and into . . .

Whoa.

Three times the size of her large room, there was no mistaking that this was Magnus's bedroom. Not for a minute. Firstly, there was an entire corner filled with sword racks and weaponry displays, as well as everything needed to care for them. Like the metal polish she had smelled on him earlier. Sharpening stones, hammers, cloths, and more. The displays were artwork in and of themselves, made of rich woods or marble. However, none of it compared to the weapons themselves. Whoever supplied Magnus with his weapons was a true artist. From scroll-worked pommels and woven wrapped hilts to gleaming etched metal in the finest, minuscule detail, she had never seen anything like it. The sheer variety was breathtaking, and she didn't even know what half of the things were.

Checking if she heard anyone approaching, Dae figured it would be a while before he returned. After all, he was counseling the Chancellor. The very thought made her giggle nervously. Yeah, right. She was going to go out in public by the side of a man who counseled the royal twins. *Drenna,* what a mad idea! A handmaiden who cursed a blue streak, belched when she ate, and could sing bawdy limericks with the best of them, courtesy of the barroom her mum had run before her death. She'd practically grown up sitting on a bar rail and stool. She'd gotten drunk for the first time at the tender age of seven because some idiots had thought it would be funny to give her a drink every time her mother disappeared into the back room. Four years later her mum had died when one of the warring clans had decided to burn the place down because they knew they were losing the war and they felt like doing as much damage as possible on the way down. Then she had ended up with her "loving family," and now here.

She walked to a glass display cabinet that seemed reserved for throwing weapons. Sharp metal gleamed in everything from the plain to the intricate. Shurikens, saw-stars, bolos, glaves, arrow-stars, clockers, and about a dozen she couldn't even identify. There was even a boomerang, the inside edges of which had been made blade sharp, which meant you could only catch it on the outside edge or you'd lose a hand. Dangerous stuff. Deadly stuff.

She realized this meant Magnus probably knew how to use every single killing blade there. Light, there was even a case of handguns. The human weapons were deadly dangerous to use for their breed. The muzzle flash alone burned their retinas and blinded them, limiting how many shots they could get off with accuracy. It also burned if you didn't wear gloves, she'd heard. It was why blades were the weapon of choice for Shadowdwellers, even in this technological age. A decade after the end of the war, however, swords seemed to be mostly a show of fashion. For the common man, at least. For men like Magnus, it was a calling.

Dae moved to a velvet-covered tray and couldn't resist peeking under the cloth.

"Holy Light," she gasped, folding back the fabric and displaying the silver tray and the wicked set of sai and daggers on it. They were breathtaking and just about the most beautiful weapons she'd ever seen—and growing up a bar rat in the middle of a war, she'd seen a heck of a lot. Licking her lips, she picked up the heavy steel with a sense of reverence. The leather-wrapped hilts were brand new, showing no wear whatsoever. The counterweights in the pommels were round and just heavy enough to perfectly balance the triple-pronged weapons. The long center prongs weren't sharpened, although they weren't usually meant to be. The two shorter ones, however, were frighteningly sharp points. That was odd, considering they were meant for guarding or to catch a longer blade. She'd always been told they were a weapon of defense more than anything, but certain masters could do anything with them they set their minds to.

Dae turned one in her hand, her fingers fumbling a little since it had been so long. However, after a minute she was twirling the weight back and forth in a nimble touch, just the way Crazy Conrad had taught her day after day as he had played around with her through several beers. She actually smiled when she remembered him laughing at her when she'd been seven years old trying to manipulate steel weighing more than her whole arm. But she had grown. Fast. And because she had played with sai and other sharp toys to the amusement of the warriors kicking back around her, she'd grown strong.

"You need a lighter weight."

The sai dropped onto the tray with a crash and she whirled around to face the priest. Gods! He hadn't made a single sound! It was astounding someone so big could move that quietly.

And then she remembered to be insulted.

"I do not," she snapped. Then a bit primly, "I just need some practice."

Drenna, she was a proud little thing, Magnus thought as her stubborn chin rose and she tried to look down her nose and meet his eyes at the same time. Interesting trick, he mused, considering he was a fair eight inches taller than she was.

And he wasn't about to let her think she could get away with being stubborn unless she was right. She was going to need to defend herself in a great many ways in the future, and it was best she learned how to choose the best battles.

"A pound, at least," he corrected her as he reached past her to neatly rearrange the tray she had disturbed and then cover it back up. "Heavy enough to guard, but a bit lighter so you don't limit what you can do with it. You can use heavier ones to practice with to build your strength in your fingers and wrists, but for application, you will need custom made."

"Custom made," she echoed. She burst out in that snorty giggle and Magnus resisted the need to smile at the sound of it. "Yeah, I'll run right out and order that."

Sarcastic little thing, he thought.

"I will make them for you."

That seemed to shut her up. She gaped at him, open mouthed and silent as she tried to find a comeback. He was beginning to think her mouth was going to be her best weapon. He watched as she looked back at all the arsenal around her and then set wide eyes back on him.

"You made all of these?" she demanded.

Not asked, demanded. She was damn bold for a supposed slave. He dreaded to think of the kind of trouble she had caused herself because of it. Although all he had to do was look at the collar around her throat that he had mistaken for common jewelry to know the answer. He supposed, though, that was the point of the thing. If it looked like a necklace, no one would question seeing it on her. No one would realize they were walking past someone suffering under bondage. Magnus had since noticed the red chafing around her wrists, and he realized she had probably been chained up during daylight sleeping hours.

"Yes. There is a forge beneath the school. I will show you sometime."

"Yeah. About that . . ." She cleared her throat and wiped her hands nervously on the pitiful rag she was wearing as a sari. He'd never realized such a traditionally beautiful fashion could ever manage to look so ugly until he had seen this one. This city had its less fortunate souls, just as all cities did, but even their most impoverished people were finely dressed compared to this outfit. "Look, not that I want to go back where I was, but there's been some kind of mistake. I mean, surely you can see I'm not handmaiden material."

He folded his arms over his chest, leaning a hip against the weapons ledge next to him, and took his time perusing her tall, shapely young figure. She was lean and strong, her arms especially well developed for a woman, probably from some kind of hard labor. Her callused, rough hands supported that. She clearly hadn't owned shoes in years, her feet coarse and dirty, and he'd glimpsed knees just as toughened.

He was willing to bet she was sporting a few bruises as well, and not just from her tussle with the guards earlier.

The thought made him frown with dark anger. He owed that guard for hitting her. Oh yes, there'd be penance to pay for that. And if he found out that either of them had tried to mess with her sexually, he was going to have them castrated. He might even let *her* do it, since she seemed to have a taste for it. He grinned when he thought of the way she had made him aware of just how vulnerable he had left himself to her with the nudge of her foot.

"I see nothing of the kind," he responded easily, moving away from her in order to search his maintenance drawer for something to cut that damn collar off. Just looking at the thing made him feel surly and jaded toward his own people. He had already sent guards to fetch her miserable relations, though he fully expected they had hightailed it by now. Still, it was daylight for the next few hours, and there was nowhere they could go outside of the city. He would find them. And when he did, they would suffer just as she had.

He'd bet they had been damned shocked when the guards had come to the door offering a bride price for a girl they weren't supposed to have. Thank *Drenna* they had persisted. If they had left, he'd hate to think what those two would have been capable of doing in order to cover their tracks. The very idea made his stomach churn with righteous anger.

"B-but . . ." she stammered, showing insecurity for the first time, "I'm not . . . I mean, I can't . . . I'm rude! A-and coarse."

"Manners are learned, just like anything else. You are smart enough."

"No, I'm not!" she argued heatedly, her hands on her hips as she grew angry at the compliment. "I've never even been to school!"

Magnus dropped the cutters with a crash and turned to face her.

She smiled smugly, and for a minute he thought she was having him on. Then he realized it was because she thought she had won her point. Which meant she was telling the truth. She had said something similar earlier, but he had thought . . .

Again, he didn't have to touch her to know it was the absolute truth, although there was still that urge. Ever since Karri's betrayal, in fact, he had found it harder and harder to take someone at their word without reaching to touch them in order to verify the truth. However, she understandably didn't like to be touched, and he had already promised her not to do so without her permission. That would have to change quickly, of course, because priest and handmaiden came into constant contact with each other throughout the course of an ordinary day, but for the time being he was willing to take the time to earn her trust of touch.

"How old are you?" he heard himself asking.

"Twenty."

Gods. She was a child after all. Yet there was cold maturity in her eyes, and it probably just felt that way because he was . . . what? Fifteen times her age?

"Can you read?"

"Of course," she scoffed.

"Write?"

"Yes," she sighed impatiently. "My mum taught me. I have street smarts, just no real book smarts. I never came to Sanctuary before today."

"No. You were a slave before you came of age to go to school," he realized. Shadowdweller children were home-schooled until they came to Sanctuary for lessons at age thirteen.

That also meant she had never had any sexual instruction. At least, not the formal instruction every 'Dweller had when they came to Sanctuary. Their culture believed everyone should be taught in the ways and pleasures of the body, unlike humans, for instance, who kicked their awkward birds out of the nest to learn the hard way. This meant that, for *K'yindara*, anything she had learned had been likely done by back alley or by force.

Magnus had to turn away from her at the thought before she could see the rage in his eyes. Light, he couldn't remember a time when he had been so easily enraged. He knew it had something to do with his previous handmaiden's deceptions and the way the shock of her betrayal had struck him so very low, and that ever since then his emotions had been a stormy sea of unpredictability. However, he had been a priest of Darkness and Light for nearly his entire life, and he had spent centuries learning tolerance and forgiveness. He could overcome this jaded rush to fury he constantly felt.

"Are you a virgin?" he asked, grabbing the cutters and turning to face the shock on her half-swollen features. Despite her injuries, however, he already knew how pretty she was. He had seen her face over and over again these past weeks.

"I'm not answering that."

"Why not? It's a logical question. You had no formal education, so no sexual education, and you've been locked away since you were twelve. I am only wondering if your uncle got to you, or perhaps someone else." Though he doubted it, considering how hard and dirty she liked to fight. Still, as she had noted, there were always other ways.

And that was when he realized why she was being so defensive, why he could all but smell her anger and fear rising hand in hand.

She didn't know.

"You're not sure, are you?" he asked gently as he came close to her and showed her the cutters. She picked up her blood-black hair and hesitantly turned her back to him, watching him cautiously over her shoulder. "You think it's possible you were violated while you were insensate."

She was silent, and he saw her wince as he worked the cutters under the tight collar. With one strong squeeze, the cursed thing snapped off. But not before the broken circuit sent feedback through them both. She cried out and he cursed, but the necklace dropped to the floor destroyed. Magnus tossed down the cutters and quickly touched his fingertips to the slender length of her throat.

"Bituth amec," he hissed softly when he saw the blackened, burned skin that had been hidden under the collar. Yes, as a Shadowdweller she would heal quickly, except perhaps for a scar, but that didn't make this any less savage to him. "I have a salve for this. It will numb and heal. It will be gone by tomorrow evening."

"Thank you," she said awkwardly, trying to brush his touch away. However, Magnus caught her fingers in his and squeezed as he turned her around to look at him. There was vulnerability hiding in those tough, angry eyes of hers.

"Answer me. Do you feel it was possible that someone was with your body sexually while you were unconscious?"

"I'm not sure. I always thought I would be able to feel that, but we heal so quickly I—I'm not sure. I never came up pregnant and I was just thankful for that. Counted my blessings."

Magnus knew it was the truth because he had compelled it from her. In this, he couldn't be ignorant. He had used his power to hear her confess what she didn't want to talk about, and he was sorry he had to, but it was better for her if they spoke of it now.

"No one will do that to you here, *K'yindara*," he assured her softly. "If they try, they will answer to me, and trust me when I say people avoid having to answer to me." He gave her a wry smile. "Provided they survive answering to you first, of course."

That made her shoot him a sly smile, her quick eyes appraising him as though she were trying to figure out if he was all right. Magnus could see she wanted to believe him, but life had taught her to do otherwise. Then something occurred to her and she jerked her hand angrily out of his before stepping back from him. She was cornered, so she banged into a cabinet.

"That's total lying bullshit!" she hissed at him. "You said I'm a handmaiden! Handmaidens are supposed to have sex with the priests." She made a snarling sound, like a furious animal. "Oh, I get it. You're making nice to me so when you're in the mood later I won't say no! Well, forget it! No, in advance! Prick bastard!"

She shoved away from her corner and stormed out of his room, but he quickly caught up with her in the bath and snagged her arm. He had to react swiftly, though, when she whipped around to hit him. He caught her hand tightly before it struck his face, and then he jerked her up tight to his body and went face-to-face with her as he tried not to feel the sickness racing through his guts in the form of dread.

This is where it had all gone wrong before.

"No. No!" he said through his teeth, giving her a hard shake to get her attention. "First of all, no one here has to have sex with anyone. I could be your priest for five hundred years and you could say no to me every minute of every day of those years and I would have to abide by that. Do you understand?"

She made a huff of disbelief. Then she quietly studied him, those sly, sultry dark eyes of hers narrowing on him as she tried to pick out lies and deceit in him.

"But that would mean you couldn't have sex for five hundred years. I'm the only one you'd be allowed to screw around with, and if I say no, then you get nothing. For five hundred years?" She snuffled out that adorably sarcastic laugh of hers, and he would have smiled if he weren't dreading every inch of this conversation.

"That's right," he agreed tightly.

"That's bullshit."

"That's faith and religious law," he countered sharply. "I do not pay lip service to my faith alone. I am, you will find, an extremely devout man. I did not become leader of this religious house because I liked to fudge the rules. I am here because I do not tolerate insubordination and sin from my followers. I can only tolerate it from those who have not taken religious orders. I will forgive—I am always open to those who genuinely repent for their sins—but I will not forgive easily and forgiveness is not achieved easily. People here work very hard for the pleasure of Darkness and the respect of Light. Those who don't or who seek short cuts around the rules pay a mighty price for inciting my disapproval."

The resonance of his voice was terrible, he knew. The power of his tone was one of his greatest tools, sometimes a stunning weapon. He could tell it was working as she stared at him with open surprise and wonder. And now, for the kicker.

"Now realize this, *K'yindara*, because it is so dire that you understand me. Are you listening?" He only continued when he saw her nod. "Good, because I want you to seriously think about what it means should that scenario happen in reverse. Five hundred years, *K'yindara*, with no sexual congress of any kind with any other man if I tell you I don't wish to be with you. That means no sexual intercourse with anyone other than yourself for the rest of your natural life, because it is as much my right to say no for whatever reasons as it is yours."

"Men don't ever not want sex," she observed meanly.

He should have waited, he thought with hollow realization. This was better done after some familiarity had grown between them. Some faith and some trust. However, it was becoming clear to him that his private life was already food for gossip in his own house. What he had once thought was between himself and a woman he had trusted for two centuries, was now spread as far and wide as it wanted to be . . . and probably inaccurately and for all the wrong reasons. This undermining of his strength and his position, he realized now, was the reason why there were traitors in Sanctuary.

"*K'yindara*, listen to me," he said with a soft sort of warning he knew she would understand the seriousness of. He swallowed back all the residual dread and interfering flotsam of his mind. "I never had sexual relations with my previous handmaiden. There was never anything between us except for . . . the warmth and affection of a brother and his sister." He all but choked on the description he had stupidly and blindly believed until six weeks ago.

Gods, he didn't want to do this. He didn't want to have another handmaiden. Not yet. He was too damn raw still. It was unfair to her and doubly so to himself.

But *Drenna* would not be denied. His goddess had plagued him relentlessly with visions of his new religious wife, driving him to distraction and making it impossible for him to do what it was that needed to be done to ferret out the corruption in Sanctuary. When Darkness had begun to show him dire danger and death cut across the face of his young maiden, he'd had no choice but to begin wooing her. He had stepped into Dreamscape, found her, and invited her to be his. *K'yindara* wouldn't remember it, but she had agreed wholly and with an almost fierce enthusiasm.

"Wait. She didn't let you touch her for two centuries, and you were okay with that?" Again, he saw her cynical disbelief. But even though she wasn't the one with the power of truth, he was going to make a believer out of her.

"I would have been," he said, meeting her eyes without so much as blinking, "but it wasn't she who denied me, rather than it was me denying her."

This was the second time he had made her gape-mouthed speechless, and he had expected something like this. He had been less than precise with Karri when he had explained his reasons for his self-denial, feeling it was a private issue and choice, the one thing he shouldn't be required to share with anyone but himself and his goddess. It had led to disaster. This time, he was going to make it very clear so there were no surprises.

"Do not mistake me, *K'yindara*. I am a man with all the emotions and drives you might accuse me of, but I am also a being of higher reasoning and control. Lovemaking and sexual pleasures are quite beautiful and have a rich place in our lifestyles. There is no reason to shame such relations, or to fear them, when the right respect and admiration is involved. You would have learned all this had you been schooled. You would still be in school learning, come to think of it, at your tender age.

"But a long time ago, I made a personal choice not to bring the complications and extreme emotions of sexual relations into my relationship with my handmaiden. It was my belief that we are here to serve others more than ourselves. After hearing so many maidens and priests confessing to me in private of the troubles in their relationships with their religious partners, I had to ask myself how they managed to function clearly and selflessly through the night when they were obsessing over their home life. We are supposed to be different. Not a lot, but just enough above our followers to keep things clear in our minds and to focus on how to show them the best way through their lives. We are religious guides and mentors and fulfill dozens of crucial roles in this society. We haven't the luxury of splitting focus or energy into selfish pleasures like sex.

"If it truly could be just about the physical release, then it might have a place, but it is impossible for two people to share such intimacy and then deny all the understandable emotion that comes with it. It is simply better, to my mind, to never cross the line in the first place. This way, no one has expectations, disappointments, or is hurt in any way, and focus can remain where it should be; on the well-being of Sanctuary and those who come here and need us."

"And what about the natural needs of the body?" she asked him, her eyes narrowed in utter fascination.

"Masturbation," he replied frankly. "A fair enough substitute."

She nodded slowly, but he knew it wasn't an agreement so much as it was her way of absorbing the information. "I see," she said quietly. She stepped back, her mind obviously churning as she looked him over slowly. Actually, there was something discomforting in the way she assessed him. Magnus didn't know why exactly, but it was as though she were pulling him apart by pieces with just the power of her mind. Then she came forward again, reaching out her hand, but hesitating with her fingertips only an inch from touching his stomach.

"May I touch you?" she asked, cocking up a thinly arched brow, a small smile teasing the corner of her mouth.

Magnus was shocked by the rigid scream of denial that locked through his entire body just then. It was so powerful it all but took his breath away. He furiously shook the weakness off, savagely wrenching control of himself back in hand.

I am in control of this, he told himself tightly. *That faithless little liar will not have this victory over me! She will not own a single moment of triumph over me for what she has done.*

"Of course," he said, his voice even and calm.

She moved forward, her fingertips sliding over the smooth textured fabric of his shirt, the warmth of her touch quickly radiating beneath it and his next shirt.

Magnus knew the minute her palm came flush against him that he had just made a critical mistake.

Chapter Three

"A handmaiden," Daenaira said speculatively, "bathes her priest, I was told. She dresses him, undresses him, and tends his body and his wounds. She is a maid and a squire, seeing to all of his needs as a domestic wife and an assistant would, freeing him to fight for their beliefs and their people. My mother told me this. She said it sounded so romantic."

Dae smiled a little, taking a moment to feel the textures of his shirt, but more importantly to marvel over the absolute hardness of the rippled muscles beneath. He was very warm, almost hot, she could say. He radiated strong heat from even stronger muscles that processed energy and motion at peak efficiency. For male attributes, they were surprisingly appealing.

Magnus was wrong, though, when he assumed she had had no sexual education. Not formal, perhaps, but a bar rat got to see more than her share of bawdy behavior between waitresses, customers, and even her own mother. She had seen expert methods of flirtation and temptation, not to mention that last-minute flip of denial. What men liked to call a tease. What they *loved* to call a tease. They stomped and growled about it, but they always hung around for more.

It wasn't that she wanted to be that mean or anything, or even that she wanted to play the tease, because frankly she shouldn't tempt fate when this arrangement was actually beginning to appeal to her a bit more.

"I am very young," she noted as she moved a little closer to him, because she was enjoying his warmth and because the rich scent of him reminded her so much of a time when big, brawny men had been really nice to her. "Don't you think it's unfair to ask me to decide right now what sacrifices I am willing to make for the rest of my life? Especially sacrificing things I have never experienced? Aren't you concerned that I will always wonder what I'm missing? Aren't you concerned I won't abide by your rules and decisions or I will become tired of them?"

Dae couldn't have realized how close to the raw wound in Magnus's soul she was striking, but she found out instantly when he grabbed hold of her arms with sudden and barely leashed violence. He drew her up so hard and high against his body that she clacked against him like a loose marionette. Then everything settled and there was only the bruising force of his grip around her and the fast, hot rush of his breath against the right side of her face and neck.

"Oh, yes," he said softly, his voice so even that she could feel the rage broiling beneath it in each and every breath. "Believe me when I tell you, I have considered this quite a lot. In fact, I agree that you are young and uneducated in some of the ways of the world and that you are in no position to decide loyalties and faith when nothing in your experience seems to have generated either one in your heart. Light, I don't even know if you believe in our gods."

Daenaira felt the touch of his lips then, firm and warm and dry against the sensitive edge of her ear. It gave her a queer and powerful chill that coiled in a rapid spiral along the outer edges of her body.

"But," he continued tightly, "my beloved goddess of Darkness, in her infinite wisdom, has plagued me with visions of a girl with strange red hair and the face and form of a beautiful warrior. She didn't even wait until that . . ." He swallowed what he was going to say, and she felt the repressed fury shudder through him. "My previous handmaiden was five minutes from death the first time *Drenna* showed you to me. She wasted no time at all before driving me all but insane with the need for you. You were Chosen, *K'yindara*, and not by me. And *you* considered this fate for a week before you agreed to it. Knowing now what your alternative was, I can only imagine you thought very carefully about it if you considered saying no and risking yourself for a few more years in your relatives' house."

"You never asked me a thing!" she gasped.

"I did. I entered Dreamscape while you slept and I found you there. I made my proposal, and you turned me down quite quickly. You made me woo you, my little *K'yindara*. Every night I came and spoke with you, quelled your concerns and answered your questions. I spoke to your soul, sweet girl, and all but begged you to come to me. Anything. I would have done anything to ease these visions of you as they haunted me in ways I can't even begin to describe. I know you don't remember this, and *Drenna* designs it this way, so now I will have to woo you all over again here in Realscape where it will count just as much. But make no mistake, this was your choice and you have already made it. The price was paid and I doubt you will ever fully realize which of us bled the most for it."

There was pain. Oh, so very much pain in those last words that Daenaira physically felt it shredding through her. Yet his voice and tone never wavered, never changed. She sensed in that moment that, though their worlds were so vastly different, they were far more similar than it appeared.

"You asked me everything about this before?" she queried softly, unable to resist the urge she had to reach and touch his tension-hardened cheek. She drew back, all but kissing his lips when they slid past so close to hers. She made him look into her eyes and discovered the dark gold of his were filled with what he did not allow his voice to reflect, though she doubted he realized it.

"Not every last thing, but the essentials." He eased the grip of his hands a little as his anger came under control. "I asked for your unwavering loyalty in return for mine. I asked if you would give all of your faith to this religion and the gods it represents. I asked if you would help ease the path of a man with a life far more difficult than outsiders will ever appreciate, taking on many of those difficulties with just as much responsibility as I do. I asked everything of utmost importance to us both, and you blessed me with your agreement. Your soul is sure, even if your mind is not."

"And what about my body?" she couldn't help but counter, even though it wasn't all that important to her in her present state of mind. However, she had never narrowed her mind to possibilities. "Did you ask me if I was willing to sacrifice the needs of my body? And I do not condemn you by saying this, because I am one of those outsiders who has no idea how difficult a path you travel. However, I am smart enough to realize that people are the most trying creatures on earth, and we drain energy from one another in wasteful useless ways, and that would make those who need that energy from you pay a price. So, you see? I can comprehend your reasons, whether I agree with them or not . . . and I don't know either way as yet. But did you ask my soul if I was willing to ignore the needs of a woman for five hundred years?"

Daenaira heard and saw him swallow, and she knew his answer.

He had been too afraid to ask.

"I'm sorry," he said hoarsely, his voice finally reflecting his emotion. "I should have. I filed it under loyalty and faith, though, and thought I could leave it at that. But I should have known better. Gods . . . and after everything that . . . I should have known."

"All right, then," she said gently, soothing a thumb over

his lips and using her touch to comfort him as she had not done since her mother had died. "Let us say this much then, M'jan Magnus. Let's say that you have expressed your desires and intentions to me, but at this moment it is merely a suggestion and not a dictate. Believe me," she added quickly when she felt his jaw lock, "at the moment I have no interest in sexual congress or anything remotely close to it. I clearly will have enough to do as I learn how to be what I agreed to be.

"But it is wrong for you to hand down a dictate to me for the rest of my days as if you were god Herself. You are a man of power and I respect that, but you are not Darkness or Light, you are flesh and bone. Your rights to deny me are only yours on a moment-to-moment basis, and mine to deny you are the same. Just like everybody else. Out of respect, however, I will try to control myself."

The last she said with amusement dancing in her eyes and twitching at her lips. When Magnus saw it, he pushed her away with a click of his tongue for her teasing, but she saw his lips jerk with a smile in spite of himself.

"Gods, I can see you are going to test me to my limits," he shot at her, trying to come off sharp but not fooling her in the least.

"I will consider it a part of my daily duties," she said cheekily.

"Come here," he said, grabbing her elbow and dragging her back to his room. "Let's get those damnable cuffs off your feet. Not to insult, but you are in desperate need of a bath and some decent clothing."

Trace stared at his foster father as though he had completely lost his mind. It was one of those rare instances where the royal vizier couldn't think of a single diplomatic thing to say. So, because this was his father, Trace went with his knee-jerk response.

"Are you fucking kidding me?"

"*Ajai* Trace," Magnus warned him, even though they were in the privacy of his office. Respect was an issue that transcended soundproofing.

"I am sorry, M'jan, but you just cut ten feet off of my guts."

"Well, now you know how I felt when you told me you had gotten Ashla pregnant out of wedlock," Magnus returned dryly, shuffling aside some papers on his desk but not really seeing what they were. He had dreaded this conversation with his son exactly because of this reaction.

For Trace, the remark about his wife was a low blow, albeit an accurate one. Shadowdweller tradition placed a great deal of shame on those who were thoughtless and sexually careless enough to create a child while having no plans to provide a sound home environment in which to raise it. But to be fair, in his case, there had been extremely extenuating circumstances.

"M'jan, that is hardly fair," he complained. "I didn't even know she was real! And I was in the throes of Shadowscape euphoria at the time!"

"Don't argue with me, Trace, or I might have to remember that you broke the rules and had *sex* in the women's dormitories knowing full well it was prohibited. You grew up here. You were practically born knowing it was against temple law. And don't you still owe me penance for that?"

"So, tell me why you decided to get a new handmaiden." Trace altered the conversation quickly, his face flushed under his dark skin. "After what Karri did, I'm not sure I like the idea of a woman so close to you. Touching your food, responsible for your health and your battle gear?"

"It isn't as though I have a choice in these matters," Magnus returned. He looked up and met his son's darkly troubled gaze. "I am following *Drenna*'s wishes in this."

"Are you sure? Are you sure it's not *M'gnone* fucking with you?"

"Trace!" Magnus barked. "Do not speak His name aloud! Gods, what is wrong with you?"

"Nothing." Trace shrugged. Then, with sarcasm, "I guess after watching the last faithless whore you called a handmaiden poison you, my wife, and my unborn child nearly to death, I kind of have a few trust issues, okay?"

Magnus sat back with a long sigh. "Tell me about it," he muttered. The priest couldn't help but remember, as he always did, how Karri had had the gall to poison him and then in the next breath attempt to seduce him while waiting for it to take effect. A small fact of the day his son was not privy to. But the emotional and physical enhancer she had chased her poison with, combined with decades of his hard-won discipline, had worked against her in the end.

But to this very day he couldn't see what his son had seen those moments before Trace's blade had cut her throat. For two hundred years he had lived almost every single day at the side of a sweet-natured healer with the face and freckles of an innocent young girl. When he tried to conjure the vindictive and unfaithful harpy who had shouted private, personal information to his son, the Chancellors, and all their company, he simply couldn't create what he needed.

"On the other hand," he said slowly to his son, "I could use an ally here. She is not what you might expect, and I don't think anyone else will easily figure her out. Also, I cannot condemn her for another woman's crimes. But being new to the temple, and to Sanctuary, she may be just the resource I need to find out once and for all who is behind the sedition I feel slithering through my house."

Trace watched his father scowl blackly, the thunderous look of anger almost painful to see. Magnus had been betrayed in the worst ways. Trace knew his father's faith had been shaken to its very core, and he hated to see him this way. Despite his ruthlessness when hunting down Sinners, his father was a forgiving man who loved nothing more than to guide others to better lives through advice, penance, or teaching. Mostly teaching. Trace might have wondered why Magnus had aspired to such a high administrative position when it was clear he wanted to mold the youth of their species more than anything, except he knew his father had a driving need to control those gifts from a level where he would make the most powerful impact. It wasn't about making himself happy.

It had always been about the care of others over the care of himself. Until recently, he had followed his faith and allowed the woman assigned to him to care for him wherever needed. How hard it must be for him, to be filled with such doubt now. Was he questioning everything he stood for, as he stood there and watched pieces of it decaying out from under him? Trace hoped not. He prayed his father saw quite clearly that the body was sound, that it was only the virus that needed to be destroyed before any more damage could be done.

He wished he could do more to help, but Sanctuary was no longer his home, and he had heavy responsibilities awaiting him elsewhere. He had a family being created; a government to guide as it, too, fought the disease of corruption; and very dear friends who were in just as much turmoil as his father was, which brought him to the original purpose of his visit.

"I heard Tristan came to see you," he said casually, although he knew his father would never buy the uninterested act. "He is not the religious one between the twins."

"He is not devout as Chancellor Malaya is, no," Magnus agreed. "That doesn't mean he does not have faith."

"Yes, but . . ." Trace frowned, knowing how infantile he was going to sound no matter how he put this. Magnus was his father, after all, and he knew him far too well. "You wouldn't care to tell me what he felt you could provide for him that I, his vizier, could not, would you?"

Hmm. Jealousy? From his son? Magnus was almost amused at the petulance edging Trace's tone, except he knew the vizier was a supremely confident man who had suffered many difficult trials as he had helped the current regime reach its place of security. Taking that into consideration along with the strange visit from Chancellor Tristan earlier that day, he began to get a sense of the troubles in the upper government that had nothing to do with politics and everything to do with people just being people.

"Now, you know that anything Tristan says to me in temple remains in confidence."

"*Drenna*! M'jan, I can't accept that!"

Trace lurched to his feet and began to pace, not realizing and clearly not caring when the painstakingly crafted wooden scabbard of his new katana smacked hard against the chair he had abandoned. On principle Magnus should have laid into him for that, but he forgave him when he saw how agitated he really was. His son's well-being would always be more important to him than the gifts he had given him.

"You know you have to, otherwise you wouldn't be so angry. And you knew what I was going to say." Magnus rose to his feet and rounded his desk, stopping to lean back against it as he watched Trace pace. "So it begs the question, 'Why did you come here'?"

His son frowned, stopping still and running a hand through his short black hair. He had never liked to wear it in the long tradition as so many men did. The quirk made Magnus smile softly.

"Is it Tristan's behavior that is really bothering you? Or perhaps you are finding your new life as a husband and father-to-be more stressful than expected?"

"Hey, Ashla is an angel," he snapped defensively, pointing rudely at his father, "and don't you suggest otherwise."

"I wasn't. I was asking about how you were handling it, not how she was contributing to it."

"Oh."

But Magnus suspected therein lay the problem. Something that his son confirmed only after a minute of silence.

"M'jan, she is tying me into knots," he confessed in a

rushed whisper, as if it was wrong for him to even think it. "She is constantly sick from the baby, and you know how thin she was to begin with, and I feel like I'm watching her get the life sucked out of her all over again. I feel like . . ." Trace swallowed. "You're right to lecture me for being an ir-responsible ass. She is too frail to be pregnant. It should have waited. For more than one reason. She has the confidence of a whipped puppy half the time, and she cries, completely convinced she is not going to be good enough to be a mother. She is terrified she won't be healthy enough to carry to term or that because she is a half-breed of human and Shadow-dweller, something will be wrong with the baby. She thinks because her mother was such a twisted nightmare, *she* won't know the right way to love the baby." Trace looked up with incredible angst and fear in his dark eyes, taking his father's breath away.

Gods, his son loved this woman.

For the priest, it was the most amazing transformation he had ever seen in his life. This alone was what had helped him to maintain his faith in the twisting mess that the world had become so recently. But watching his son transform from a victim of torture who couldn't bear the touch of a woman, to a man in love who couldn't live without the woman who had stolen his heart, was enough to prove that all things hap-pened for a reason. Even the deception of a handmaiden whose acts of treachery had forced Trace to see and admit to the feelings he had developed for a pale, blond half-breed girl who needed him just as badly.

"Son, she is breeding. You cannot attach too much ratio-nality to feelings that are being exacerbated by hormonal fluxes. Not that you shouldn't find them genuine, but they will seem so much sharper to her than they realistically should. As to her health . . ."

That was a separate issue. All of the healers in Shadow-dweller society were—like all the teachers—priests and handmaidens. Without knowing who had been tainted by the foulness permeating his house, neither Magnus nor Trace could find it in himself to trust anyone with the care of a woman and child of great importance to a priest who had clearly been marked for a fall.

Which made him incredibly glad that his new hand-maiden was clearly a scrapper. He had been terrified of making an innocent girl vulnerable to the vipers hidden around them both, and he had resisted it as long as possible, but as he had told her, in the end he'd had no choice in the matter. Now he was struggling with how much to tell her to keep her safe, and how much *not* to tell her to keep her safe. He had already gotten the sense that she was people savvy enough to watch herself very carefully, and she wasn't going to trust anyone lightly . . .

But he wanted her to trust him. And more importantly, he wanted to be able to trust her. *Drenna*, he wanted that more than anything. It was bad enough that his existing relationships were crumbling down around him because of his shattered ability to trust. He needed to reclaim himself. He needed desperately to nullify Karri's collateral damage.

Most of all, he needed to find the miserable *bituth amec* who had twisted Karri away from him in the first place.

Magnus could only hope that, in the end, he wouldn't discover that he was looking for himself. Karri had blamed him with her last breath for turning her against him, citing rejection and loneliness and who knew what else because she had grown tired of her celibate life. Honestly, he couldn't blame her at all for the needs of her carnal self. He was no more immune to them than she had been. The difference was, he had given precedence to his work and the followers he guided and it had all seemed worthwhile to him. Karri had not found that same satisfaction of the spirit, and instead of being honest with him about it and giving him a chance to resolve the issue, she had pretended as if nothing at all were bothering her or hurting her.

She had lost faith in him.

Then she had turned on him.

"Ashla is herself a healer, Trace. You have to trust her body to care for itself the same way it cared for you and for me when we were ill. The sickness will hopefully pass soon, and then you and I and the entire royal household will no doubt stuff her with good things until she is as fat and round as *K'yan* Julie was when you were young."

The reference made his son chuckle in memory of one of his favorite handmaidens. It served to remind them both that there really were very good women in Sanctuary, and they shouldn't condemn them all for the acts of one. But caution was regretfully necessary now. Two attempts on Trace's life, one on his own, and Karri's aborted attempt to kill Chancellor Malaya had seen to that. That was to say nothing of damage like what Ashla had gone through. The little half-breed healer took on the properties of the illnesses she healed before her body purged them, and her delicate constitution had made that a dicey trick on more than one occasion. She was now prohibited from doing any healing until the baby came.

Magnus smiled softly, catching his son's curiosity.

"My granddaughter," he said in answer to the unspoken query. "She will be my first grandchild, and I am eager to begin training her for religious duty."

He was teasing, and it was obvious, so Trace chuckled.

"I think she will be more inclined to politics," he informed his father.

"Hmm. I suppose we will have to wait and see."

"I suppose so."

Trace was no fool. He knew the sound of a gauntlet hitting the floor when he heard it.

Chapter Four

Daenaira inspected herself in the floor-length mirror very carefully.

For the fifth time.

"Light, you're a vain bitch," she muttered to herself.

In actuality it was more about never having put on a new, tailored sari before. When you wore a rag, it didn't really matter what it looked like. However, she had been given a brand new midnight blue sari, the uniform of a handmaiden. It was made of a beautiful and fine velvet that gleamed against every curve of her body before draping over her shoulder. The long-sleeved blouse she wore with it ended just beneath her breasts, hugging her snugly every inch of the way. The low scoop of the neckline wasn't exactly shy about cleavage either, especially considering she had a pretty generous amount to work with.

The underskirt holding the pleats of the sari was gossamer soft, brushing against her legs like delicate air and making her wince whenever it caught against the rough calluses of her knees. She would have to see if she could find a cream to help ease and soften the rough places on her body. She was highly aware of their ugliness, and the other handmaidens she had peeked out at now and then were all so soft and beautiful and feminine. Their hair shone, where hers was dull and stripped from the harsh soap she had been forced to use. To hide it, she had tightly plaited the mess and curled it into a cobra knot on the top of her head. Those other women had no flaws or bruising that she could see, and even those who forwent slippers to go barefoot had the prettiest and smoothest feet Dae had ever seen. They also wore black kohl to outline their dark, lovely eyes. She hadn't tried to use eyeliner since she'd gotten into her mother's at age ten and had made quite a mess of herself.

On the vanity there was a pretty new pot of the stuff and an application brush as well, but she was afraid she wouldn't do it right and would look foolish. Twice as foolish, she thought grimly as she touched the scarring and burns at her throat. She had a feeling they would always be there, for the rest of her days, always reminding her of exactly where she had come from. She had seen some of the women wearing jewelry, so she would probably be able to cover it up with something one day. But ornamentation cost money, and she didn't think handmaidens got paid for their work. They were paid in the things they needed, and those needs were provided quite lavishly. Every single touch in her rooms and her small new wardrobe was finely done and generous, but not in the least vulgar. The only actual gold and precious elements she had seen so far had been artistically inlaid into the pommels and scabbards of the weapons collection of her priest.

Her priest.

And what a priest!

The great and venerable M'jan Magnus, spiritual leader of all Shadowdwellers and, most especially, the twin Chancellors who now ruled over them. The mighty and terrible Magnus of whom she'd heard frightening tales from her spot on the bar rail. Tales of unrepentant Sinners and a 'Dweller priest, deadly and devoted, hunting them down and gutting them. Warriors of all clans had feared the wrath of Magnus. Others had marveled over his skill when they had seen him in actual battle. She remembered hearing such amazingly varied accounts of him; it was as though he were a myth, not a true being.

Well, he was real enough. She had felt the reality of him on every level available to her at the time. He was more volatile in temperament than she would have imagined for one so wise and experienced. She also knew better than to poke a stick at a cranky bear, so she would try and tread carefully until she figured things out a little.

On the whole, she had to look at this whole thing as a decided improvement. Warm room, new clothes, no chains and no zapping. She still wasn't certain it wasn't just a prettier form of slavery, but she believed what he had said to her about Dreamscape, and she had been comforted by the way he had apologized to her and relented about his heavy-handed dictates. It wasn't the topic she took issue with, she just didn't want him thinking he could make unilateral decisions and she would step in line like some—well, a slave. Dae was well aware that she only had as much power in this place as that man allowed her to have. However, the trick would be in the way she made him want to manage her. This could quickly degrade into anger and fear and some vicious fights if either of them wasn't careful with the other. She could sense quite easily he didn't trust her any more than she trusted him. For the moment, though, they had both decided to trust each other enough to give this thing a test run.

Magnus cleared his throat and nearly made her jump out of her skin. She turned with a gasp to look at him. How in Light was he able to sneak up on her like that? Better yet, was he willing to teach it to her? All 'Dwellers had remarkable hearing, as well as a bevy of other keen senses. To fool them was an amazing trick, one she absolutely had to learn for herself.

"You look very nice," he complimented her evenly. "The blouse seems to fit."

"It's a bit snug," she corrected wryly, smoothing a self-conscious hand over her breasts, making certain the sari draped to hide the lush swell of her cleavage.

"It's supposed to be snug. A woman's body is one of the most beautiful things we have on this planet. Do you know what the sari represents in our culture?" When she silently shook her head, Magnus continued. "Traditionally, it was to do the two most important things every woman should receive. The underclothing is sheer and snug, flattering the shape and displaying lovely charms that deserve to be shown proudly. The sari is meant to protect those charms, while at the same time symbolizing that every woman should always be draped in comfort, protection, and a fine cloak of queenly grace."

Magnus slipped around behind her and looked into the mirror with her. He met her eyes even as he reached around her to smooth the sari back into its natural fall, instead of hiding her. It brought the heat of his big body cradled up against her back, brushing her as he moved and somehow making her very aware of his fingertips traveling across her breast as he followed the drape of the sari to her shoulder. In a way, he was almost embracing her, with his arm crossing over her like that. Daenaira felt suddenly trapped by all of that strength and ominous power, her skin rippling with chills and heat in turn as she broke from him and turned around, bumping back into the cold wall mirror as she crossed her arms over her bare midriff under the sari.

Magnus looked at her, his golden eyes looking puzzled for a moment. Then understanding seemed to dawn as she heard him swear softly under his breath.

"I'm sorry. I promised I wouldn't do that and I keep breaking that promise. I hope you can forgive me if I tell you . . ."

No. He couldn't tell her about the familiarity of his visions of her. Visions were just possibilities; he knew that even though he had never had them before six weeks ago. It was as though Karri poisoning him had unlocked some kind of shuttered door within him, and now everything was rushing to show itself to him. *She* was rushing to show herself to him. But Chancellor Malaya was a true precognitive, and he had seen her struggle, from an up-close perspective, with comprehension of the things she saw in her mind over the years. They could be tricky, taunting things, visions. They were always truth, but it was often imagery of truth and other unreadable or unreliable representations.

Of course, his visions had been stark and clear.

Raw.

Magnus swallowed the sensation of nerve-rushing heat that the admission chained through his body. He reminded himself that, since sexual needs had been the issue that had boiled away the Bond between him and Karri, dissolving their sanctified trust, it was probably *Drenna*'s way of warning him to keep very aware with this new maiden. That being the case, he forced himself to focus on the fragile trust he was trying to create with her.

"No one will be allowed to touch you if you do not want them to, but you will see we are a warm and affectionate group here. The women are kind and friendly and will want to hug you in greeting. The men will want to welcome you with hand-clasping. I tell you this so you understand my forgetfulness, but also because I will need to know how you wish me to handle it for you. I can request that you not be touched."

"No. Please. It will just make me stand out like . . . like some sideshow. I can tolerate it. Don't . . . I don't want anyone to know what bothers me."

Advantage. She meant that she didn't want anyone she met to have an edge over her. Magnus was sorry she had to react in such a way to the world around her, but at the same time, in light of his troubles, her suspicion and caution would help protect her.

"Tomorrow I will start to make your sai," he informed her. "But I was wondering what your preference of holster was going to be." Sai were an unusual choice for a woman, their bulk making them obvious and tediously heavy on occasion. They also could get in the way of a woman's daily activities. Since handmaidens in Sanctuary only wore saris or *k'jeet*, both of which were dresses, thigh holsters were awkward and unattractive.

"Really? My choice?" She licked her lips, clearly anxious to respond even though she was surprised that he was going to arm her. But Magnus wanted her to be able to defend herself in any moment.

"Yes. Your sai, your holster, your choice."

He could appreciate that she hadn't had much in the way of choices in her life. He also appreciated the slyness of her smile.

"Calves. But . . . one for boots and one set for without. If . . . if that's okay."

It was clever and devious, he thought with amusement. With the long fall of her sari, as long as she was careful, no one would even know she was wearing them. They would be completely out of her way, also, and impossible to disarm from her. Not both at once. And Magnus didn't doubt for a second that she was aware of every single one of those details.

"I will make both," he agreed, watching her smile snake in wicked satisfaction. The sly thing. That little grin of hers was going to get her into trouble. "But only if you tell me where you learned to use them."

It was like throwing a gate across her face. Total lockdown. She went rigid and her crisp eyes narrowed on him. She didn't like ultimatums. She liked even less having to barter personal information for something he knew she wanted very badly. She hated him for using it against her.

"Keep it. I never asked for it in the first place," she snapped. "I never asked for any of this. Not in my waking hours," she shot out, cutting off that avenue of argument.

Dae was furious. She pushed past him and stripped the sari from over her shoulder. She destroyed painstakingly created pleats and unwound it completely from her underskirt, and once she had the yardage in hand she couldn't seem to control the urge to throw it in his face.

"Priest or man, you're still a bastard!" She shucked off the blouse and threw that at him, too. "Here! Why bother with little tactics like too-tight blouses? I'll walk around like this and you can show me off just like all the other pretty little cows I see herding through the hallways!"

Magnus drew the velvet, still warm from her body, away from his face and saw her standing there, feet braced hard in righteous anger, fists clenched by her sides, and her body, naked from the waist up, on proud display. From the waist down the close-to-sheer underskirt pretty much completed the picture of her entire figure.

Holy Light.

She was something else. Bruised and battered, thin under her ribs, too slim at the waist, but . . . skin the color of a light touch of milk in coffee, so even and beautiful as it flowed over her very generous breasts. Her nipples were large and dark, a luscious maroon that accented the perfect teardrop shape of each breast. Below that was the span of a flat, taut belly that had seen a great deal of work tucked into its shape. Just above the low-riding skirt was the slightly darkened indentation of her navel.

The urge to tongue her in that spot rode onto him like a storm out of a clear blue sky.

His gaze shot up to hers and he hoped to Darkness the fiery desire of that thought wasn't in his eyes right then. Not that he didn't expect to be attracted to women or to have sexual cravings, because he was still a man, after all, but not toward her when she might see and be further insulted.

She's the one who stripped to the skin, his libido reminded him dryly. *What does she think is going to happen?*

"We have time to settle this," he said, really quite impressed with himself for his flawless tone of voice. "The sai will take a week to make. Instead of throwing tantrums, we might discuss this." He held out her clothes to her. "Please dress yourself."

Her response was rude, crude, and, he was certain, anatomically impossible. He wondered how furious she'd be the day he asked her to tell him where she'd learned language like that.

She marched up to him, shoving the clothing out of his grip and onto the floor. Her face was flushed with her anger, her dark eyes like amber on fire.

"Don't you dare talk to me in that condescending, holier-than-thou tone like I'm some kind of recalcitrant child pitching a fit! I am no child! And you will damn well stop trying to train me like a puppy with rewards and treats if I'm a good girl and withholding if I am bad! If that's the way this relationship is going, I am walking out of this gilded cage and never coming back. I don't care what you dreamed with me or what price you paid. I'd rather be a slave in my aunt's house than a well-heeled lapdog for you!"

Then she swung at him. She almost caught him, too. Would have served him right for letting himself be distracted by the way her furious body language jolted through her amazing breasts. *Gods, you'd think you'd never seen a naked woman before!* he tried to sternly lecture himself. Just the same, he caught her wrist tightly in hand, saving himself a bruise, and jerked the little spitfire forward and off balance. She crashed into him, all softness and warmth everywhere, and Magnus instantly recognized his error. She was too close. Much too close. Now that she had bathed and groomed herself, she had an incredible scent that rode on her body warmth like a dolphin skimming waves. He was eye to eye with her, nose to nose with that fury as she glared up at him, but all he could think about was the aroma wafting up from all of that bare skin. Sweet. Soft. Yes, it was like sweet whipped cream. Light and delicious and decadent.

"*Drenna*, you smell good."

Oh, Light and damnation. Had he just said that aloud?

Obviously he had. The shock on her face was probably only half as amusing as his, and his throat was completely paralyzed as he tried to figure out how to counter such an incredibly stupid blunder. He'd be lucky to walk out of that room without severely bruised balls.

"Excuse me?" she said numbly, her free arm curling protectively across her chest.

Magnus had lived a long time and advised a great many people on how to repair all kinds of situations, but he was at a complete loss right then. He reacted, breaking away from her and walking around her toward the bath at a rapid clip. He should have gone for the hall, but he didn't doubt for a second that she would follow him just as she was. She wasn't the type who made threats she wasn't prepared to follow through with. He was passing the water when she caught up to him, grabbed his arm with both hands, and forced him to turn toward her.

"We haven't settled this!" she hissed at him. "Don't you dare walk away in the middle of an argument."

"What are you going to do if I do?" he snapped irritably. "I'm done. We'll talk when you are rational and *clothed*."

"Oh! Fuck you!"

That mouth. Quite the weapon, just as he had suspected. And just distracting enough for her to throw all of her kinetic force into a huge shove that sent him staggering back off balance.

Magnus hit the bath with the most satisfying splash Daenaira had ever heard. Uniform, weapons; the whole kit and caboodle. She probably shouldn't have jumped and cheered. She should have been running really fast. Instead she waited for him to surface, hands on her hips and a smug smile on her lips.

"That will teach you to brush me off, you big jerk. And for making me swear at a priest!"

She held her chin up and marched back to her room. She found her blouse on the floor and tugged it on quickly. This time, there was no way he could be silent as he approached her. For one, he was streaming water. For another, he was rip-roaring mad, and there was no mistaking it in his step. Just as he reached for her, she figured they were going to kill each other. They were both so dominant they would end up tearing each other apart to make a point.

But quite abruptly he seemed to stop behind her. After a moment or two of listening to him drip on the floor, she turned and looked over her shoulder at him. He was soaked, of course, and his jaw was clenched as tight as his fists. She tried not to look too superior as she lifted a questioning brow.

"Can I touch you?"

The request rasped out of him on a hard breath, a combination of his repressed anger and . . . she had no idea what else. She'd never heard anything like it before. Surprise and curiosity warred with common sense and, more importantly, the understanding that despite his roaring temper he was struggling to keep his promise to her. Struggling and succeeding. Daenaira had very little experience with how to respond to someone respecting her wishes. Considering the indignant dunking she'd just given him, she couldn't help the desire to relent—and to see just what he was going to do.

"Yes," she said, obviously surprising him. It passed quickly, however, and she turned forward as he stepped up tightly against her back. Oh, he was vibrating with anger. She could feel it all through her body. When his hand touched her waist and slid around to cover her bare stomach, she couldn't help but jolt at the wetness and heat, and the dread of what he was going to do next.

"It's time you started learning your duties and the rules to go with them," he said in a low and dangerous tone.

"Rules. I see. You mean when I can and cannot have a will of my own."

"I mean respect for the religious role you are playing, as

well as for mine. If you have no interest in that, then you *should* leave. I will find somewhere for you to go and live in peace, and that will be the end of it."

"That better not be an empty promise," she said sharply. "I'm obviously not the right person for you. I don't care what *Drenna* thinks or what you think."

"You are more right for me than you know," he corrected her, the soft promise in his voice as it whispered lightly over her ear giving her all-new kinds of chills. Was there such a thing as hot chills? There had to be, because they were scudding over every inch of her skin, making all kinds of things pucker in response. "I don't want a lapdog, little spitfire. I had one, and she turned on me and went for my throat."

Dae gasped and spun around in his hands, making her realize they were both on her waist, but she didn't even care about that. She instinctively laid her hands on the wet fabric lying over his strong chest.

"I want a companion, *K'yindara*, who is going to fight tooth and nail to make me realize what she wants and needs. I want a partner who will beat the shit out of anyone who tries to screw with her head. I want—" He stopped and she saw him struggling to crush the emotions trying to overrun him. Unable to help herself, she reached up and smoothed her fingers over his mouth again, strangely unable to bear the strain she saw drawing at it so painfully.

"What do you want?" she asked him, whisper soft, creating a cloud of intimacy around them with her gestures of kindness. Dae knew he understood she was not a kind person. Not that she liked to show, at least.

Magnus raised a hand to her face, his thumb tracking over her lower lip slowly as he cupped her jaw in his palm. Here, he thought, was temptation in its glory. Its finest moment. Even though she showed the discoloration from the guard striking her, she had symmetry to her features that drew attention to her sleekly beautiful eyes, their sultry tilt such a flirtation. And the perfect foil was her mouth with its curvy, succulent lips.

"I want to trust you," he admitted, though it was a hard, harsh thing to do. "And I am afraid I won't be able to."

"Because of the bitch that bit you?"

That made him smile for some reason. He supposed it was the way she stripped the bullshit away from everything and laid it all out the way it was. He could get used to that. Although he wasn't sure about the rest of Sanctuary.

"Yes," he agreed.

"Well, just keep in mind, I'm a whole new kind of bitch, okay? And I won't bite unless one of two things happens."

"I'm listening."

"First, you don't ever try to cut my balls off just so you can be top dog over me. I won't do it to you if you don't do it to me. We'll figure out some way of doing this on equal footing. Okay?"

"I can live with that. Give me room for some minor screwups?"

"Very minor," she warned.

"Deal. And don't ever give me a reason not to trust you, *K'yindara*. I know I don't feel it yet, but I'm trying, and Darkness help you if you ever betray me for any reason. You don't know the meaning of the word 'penance' until you cross me."

"Deal." She gave him a succinct nod.

"And what's the second thing that would make you bite, *K'yindara*?"

She grinned.

"If you ask me to, of course."

"Of course," Magnus sighed. He stepped back and looked down at her body. "Are you going to get dressed now?"

"Are you?" she countered, impishly eyeing the damage she'd done.

"Yes, brat." He pushed her away and started for the door.

"Daenaira," she corrected. "Or Dae. Brat is so passé."

The information stopped him in his tracks and he looked back at her with an inscrutable look on his face.

"Fine," he said, continuing into the bath before calling back to her, "and if the wood of my scabbards warps, Daenaira, I'm taking each one across your backside."

Dae snorted softly at that, not believing it for a minute.

She was so tense he could have snapped her in two.

Magnus watched Daenaira out of the corner of his eye because she hadn't moved from the spot exactly one pace behind him and a little to the right. She had followed him into the dining hall and looked like she wanted to bolt ever since. Well, to him she did. To anyone else she looked quite placid. But placid on Daenaira was just wrong. He had the damp hair to prove it.

When she had dunked him, he had wanted to wring her neck so badly his palms had itched. He'd been ready to blow up, to do everything she was probably expecting him to do, no doubt proving to her that people were the same no matter who and no matter what. Then he had realized that he was supposed to be better than all of that. He was supposed to be gaining her trust. Instead, he was doing exactly like she said, trying to train her like a child that needed to behave. No chains, no electrocution, same intent.

Gods, had he felt like an ass.

Now he had her swimming in the deep end of Sanctuary society when he should have taken it easy on her this first night and dined alone with her in his rooms. He was really racking up points for being a thoughtless idiot today. The idea made him frown. He was supposed to be better than this. It was too late now, though. She had to be introduced to everyone now that some of them had seen her. Besides, he wanted her to have the freedom to walk around Sanctuary unquestioned as soon as possible. She shouldn't feel confined to her rooms.

Dae stood very still, her eyes on the crowded room as her heart raced at the sheer volume of people. She hadn't anticipated this. Such a wide array of such beautiful men wearing the violet slacks and tunic of priests, and all those well-heeled women at their elbows in midnight blue. She felt like an imposter. A pretender.

"Well, Magnus, who is this?" one of the handsome men asked, smiling down at her.

She instantly disliked him. Disingenuous and perfect, his smile rang false.

"M'jan Shiloh, this is *K'yan* Daenaira, my new hand-maiden."

"*Drenna* has blessed you," Shiloh said expansively, reaching to seize her hand. She jerked both hands behind herself and stepped closer to Magnus's back, hating herself for the reaction. "Shy little thing, isn't she?"

"It's her first night. I remember being overwhelmed myself," Magnus said easily. "Dae, this is *K'yan* Nicoya. She is M'jan Shiloh's handmaiden."

Now Nicoya was familiar. Just the surety and superiority of her smile told Dae exactly who she was. All she was missing was the nine-tailed cat. Tall, majestic, and beautiful, she was definitely the queen bitch in charge. Daenaira stayed right where she was, very carefully guarding her tongue and other impulses. She could make enemies just as well later as now. Meanwhile, she let Nicoya think she was as delta as they came.

Things were not looking very promising so far.

"M'jan Cort and *K'yan* Tiana," Magnus continued.

Dae never lost track of a single name or face. Nor did she greet anyone differently than the rest, despite how easily she felt she could read most of them. In the end, there were a few she liked, a few she did not, and surprisingly a few she couldn't get a bead on. One such was the priest named Sagan. He had no handmaiden, and from what she gathered he hadn't had one for some time, and it was a point of interest to everyone else but the tall, silent man. He had clearly heard it all before and didn't give a damn what anyone else thought. His idea of greeting her was a cool nod before continuing on his way. She couldn't decide if he was being rude or if, for the first time, someone had gotten the picture that she wasn't in the mood to be slathered with social graces.

She didn't understand the handmaiden named Greta at all. That the veteran handmaiden was hostile toward her was clear. She didn't even hide it from Magnus, which was probably pretty ballsy. Dae could actually respect that. However, she didn't care for being judged without having even done anything yet. She liked to earn her contempt the old-fashioned way . . . by pissing people off.

K'yan Hera was going to be interesting. She was the first woman Dae had ever met of such an advanced age that she actually had developed silver streaks in her black hair and crow's feet by the corners of her eyes. Dae wondered how old exactly one had to be before they started showing it like that. Had this woman been a handmaiden for every single one of those years? There had to be some kind of retirement plan, didn't there? But besides her agedness, the human equivalent of nearing fifty as Dae understood it, she had a keen smile and a sparkle in her eyes that gave Daenaira the feeling she had been sized up to perfection at first glance and, thankfully, given a measure of approval. All without a single word spoken or a hand shaken.

One she liked, though, was M'jan Brendan. She quickly realized that he was the closest thing Magnus had to a best friend in this place. The two men came together and for the first time, she felt Magnus's body relax. He became easy and friendlier. Brendan teased her for hiding.

"Magnus, where's your katana?" Brendan asked as they were eating at the same table later that evening, lifting a brow in clear surprise to find Magnus's entire weapons belt missing.

"Being cleaned," he said without missing a beat.

Daenaira choked on her wine as she tried to swallow a laugh at the same time. Brendan caught the undercurrent but for the life of him couldn't figure it out. He sprawled back in his seat, relaxed and casual as he eyed the newest handmaiden.

"You surprise me, Magnus. I've never seen a priest take another handmaiden so fast. It's been a year since I lost Nan to Crush, and I still can't find a replacement."

"Perhaps you shouldn't be replacing her. You should be finding a new companion."

Brendan instantly sat up with surprise and a laugh. "I'll be damned. She can talk."

"Only when I have something important to say," she noted.

Brendan looked to Magnus, who gave him a single-shouldered shrug.

"I see," Brendan countered, "and you know this after a single evening of being a handmaiden?"

"No." She paused a beat, just long enough for him to get cocky. "I'm not a handmaiden until I take my vows. I just know this because I am a sensitive woman with a brain. Excuse me."

She stood up and left the table, keeping her smile hidden until she was out of the dining hall. Once she was out of sight, she breathed a sigh of relief to be hidden from so many staring, contemplating gazes. Dae had paid careful attention to the route they had taken to the dining hall, and she moved quickly to backtrack. She didn't know where the more public bathrooms were, so her only choices were to go back into that organized chaos and ask someone for help or to just go back to her room.

It was probably silly for her to practice avoidance. After all, she had grown up in a full and rowdy crowd far more dangerous than this one. It had just been a few years since she had been with so many people.

She was on the stairwell when suddenly there was a flash of brilliant and burning light. She screamed, terrified as any

'Dweller would be, as she was scalded and blinded. The burn was sharp and quick and then gone. A strobe of some kind. Her heart was pounding as she stumbled back down to the last landing, trying to keep her footing and hear what was happening around her. How far was she from the hall? With all those people in it, if she screamed for him, would Magnus hear her? Their senses were keen, but this was stone, earth and sheets of marble in her way.

She heard a step behind her almost too late. She threw her back to the wall as a fist blew past her, glancing off her already bruised cheek, which pissed her off mightily. Dae heard cloth as the punch overshot, and she reacted, in an automatic lock of her muscle and bone, trapping the arm to her body. Now she was completely oriented to her attacker, although not knowing their height would throw her off for a moment. She wasn't certain, but she thought it was a woman. A beefy woman or a lean man, she was too blind to tell. She went for the gut, the closest and surest target. She launched herself upward as she yanked down on the arm she held. Her knee hit badly for both of them. She bit back a curse and took satisfaction in the stagger and groan of her opponent.

Right up until she was grabbed from behind, her head nearly wrenched off her neck. Now this was a man, she knew, the sheer strength of him yanking her up off her feet and a wall of muscle against her back. Then she was thrown down onto the floor.

"Keep watch!" he growled, purposely roughing up his voice, she knew. She struggled to figure out where his legs were, desperate to orient herself to his body as his hand closed around her windpipe. He said nothing else, and didn't have to. She felt him shove at her skirts, the damn dress making his plans so easy it infuriated her. She kicked out, clawed out, but made no purchase. He was sighted, pinning her, and too quick.

Tired of fighting her flailing legs, he rolled her over as he bared her backside to the cool stairwell air.

Not while I'm conscious, she thought viciously.

Turning her had forced him to relinquish his grasp on her throat, and she could breathe. She sucked in air and tried to think. She felt his weight then, heavy and oppressive, and hot flesh pressing to her below the waist.

Thanks, asshole, that's all I wanted.

A target.

She shot her hand back, grabbed a handful of whatever she could, and twisted mercilessly. His scream was absolute nirvana. When she didn't let go, digging her nails in to boot, his partner jumped in and kicked her in the head.

Stunned, she rolled on the floor until she suddenly dropped off the landing and down the next set of stairs. She all but threw herself into the tumble, not even stopping to get a breath when she hit the next landing. She stumbled for the door, shoving through it and onto the dining hall floor.

"Magnus!"

Brendan was gaping, he knew, as the not-so-shy girl exited the room.

"Boy, she's got you pegged," Magnus remarked, pausing in his meal to grin at his friend.

"Yeah, huh? I think I'm jealous."

"No, you're not," Magnus returned calmly, although Brendan knew there was nothing calm about it. It was a warning, plain and simple. It made Brendan frown. The Magnus he knew would never have been that insecure. It infuriated him, thinking of how screwed up everything had gotten with Karri. Poison! The idea of a man like Magnus being left to die that way! It was unconscionable. The man was a warrior and should die as a warrior, not at the deceitful hand of the one woman he had trusted the most.

"Probably not," he agreed. "I like them a little more on the loyal and bubble-headed side. Like Nan was."

"Nan was a fantastic lady. Darkness keep her safe."

"I know. And I miss her like hell." Brendan shed the emotions that came with the thought by smiling. "Especially around bath time."

"Bren." Magnus chuckled.

"Well, she had a way with a sponge," he said unrepentantly.

"Keep it up, I'll have you doing penance for besmirching the dead."

Brendan wisely changed tack, although he went for the throat when he did. "How do you feel about Daenaira?"

Magnus knew Brendan was just about the only one who would have dared ask the question. He supposed it needed asking, though. "I'll let you know when I know her for longer than five seconds."

"You don't even have a feel for her yet? Where'd she come from? She's not a student here. I would remember, err, her attributes."

"Bad edit, my friend," Magnus warned him. "A little respect, please."

"You're right. Sorry. But, uh, I was talking about her hair color, my friend," Brendan said with amusement.

Magnus looked up in surprise. Brendan had a huge grin on his face, enjoying having his trap walked into so neatly. Magnus had no choice but to smile a bit sheepishly. "Yeah. She's got quite the, uh . . ."

"Hair color," Brendan added helpfully.

Both men chuckled.

"Magnus!"

Brendan watched his friend freeze for three of the longest heartbeats on record, and then they were both on their feet and running. Magnus touched his hip as he ran, but there was no weapon there. Brendan grabbed for his backup, a Lithe dagger, and slapped it into the other priest's palm. They both tore down the hall toward the main stairwell, hoping to *Drenna* that she called out again because everything split off from there. Then Magnus came up short.

"No. She doesn't know this way. She wouldn't wander."

He doubled back, cursing himself for not thinking straight. It was only another corridor to the back stairs, but it seemed like miles as his heart raced with dread and worse.

When he saw her crawling over the floor, he felt the world drop out from under him. He dropped to his knees as he skidded to a halt beside her, the dagger clattering to the floor as he gathered her up tightly to himself.

"Where?" he rasped, unable to catch his breath as she clung as hard to him as he did to her.

"The stairs," she said.

Brendan was off in a flash, running through the doors behind them.

"Gods, let me look at you," he demanded, dropping his hold a few inches so he could see her. She was burned. Her face was bright red, her hands and chest as well. "What in Light did they do to you?"

"A light. A strobe. Gods, it burned! I can't see." She swallowed and coughed, and he wanted to hold her tighter but feared hurting her where she was scorched. "He tried to . . . shit. Shit, shit, shit."

She was going to cry like some big stupid baby. Dae did not cry. She fought. She won or she lost, but she never cried.

"Tell me you fought really, really dirty," he commanded of her.

"Like mud in a pig's sty," she said with a shaking laugh that helped thwart the urge to cry. "I think I have penis under my nails."

Magnus laughed, a hard fall of sound as he hugged her tight again despite his concerns. "See, that's what I wanted. A fighter."

"Okay, but please can we keep it to once a day? That was a bit of overkill."

"Yes, baby, it was. I'm so sorry. I can't seem to keep any promises for you today. I said no one would touch you."

"Well, I touched harder. That counts for something."

"Yeah, it sure does."

Magnus looked up when Brendan came back through the doors and shook his head.

"Aw, fuck. I can't believe he got up!" she grumbled when she realized Brendan had returned empty-handed. "I thought I had him good."

"You blooded him well enough," Brendan said with a grin.

"Great. Now we just have to get everyone to drop their drawers and we'll have our man," she said dryly.

"Okay, let's get you back to our rooms," Magnus said softly, rising to his feet with her.

"She should go to a healer."

"No!" It was a single, terrible word, but it spoke volumes about Magnus's shattered trust. Brendan wasn't inclined to push him again.

"I found this. This guy had a damn death wish, using something this strong." Brendan showed Magnus a battery-operated lamp with a focused beam of light before he shattered the bulb against a wall. "Where the hell does someone get something like this down here?"

Magnus and Brendan looked at each other.

"Hydroponics," they said together.

"Yeah, that stands for 'the place with the lights,'" Dae sighed.

"It's a highly secure area. Very few people have access to it. This could narrow our search immensely," Magnus told her.

"Great. Magnus?"

"Yes, *K'yindara*?"

"Can I have the heavy sai now?"

Chapter Five

It was two days before she left their rooms again.

If she felt like a sideshow before, the sensation was only doubled now. Her only recourse was to ignore everyone and do what she had set out to do. Her goal for that first day was mapping. She had an uncanny sense of direction, so it wouldn't take long for her to learn the entire layout of Sanctuary. She was armed this time, not with the sai, but with wrist daggers—small knives in sheaths hidden under her sleeves. It had required a looser blouse, which she had found amusing. Magnus, however, had lost all of his sense of humor. She could understand. He wasn't used to this sort of thing like she was.

Dae could rebound pretty quickly, though, as long as she could think of a way of retaliating. Her method of the day was to make herself familiar with every turn, step, and cubby she would have to regularly travel.

Of course, the downside to this was that she was bound to run into just about everyone she did or did not want to run into. The first encounter happened in the courtyard near a fascinating onyx fountain that depicted many of the faces of

Drenna and Darkness. There was a similar one of white marble in front of Sanctuary that displayed all of the images of *M'gnone* and Light. Her favorite by far was the one in the temple itself that ran like a tributary along an entire wall, cut from the natural stone of the earth and into the artist's splendid imagination of what Dreamscape was to him. There was an image of a stunning warrior, standing tall with wind whipping through the curls of his hair and a long sword in one hand, while the other reached to draw power from the sky. She wasn't certain if it was meant to, but the carving of the face with its strong and masculine lines reminded her a great deal of Magnus.

It was Nicoya who cornered her by the fountain. M'jan Shiloh's handmaiden walked with her hands folded neatly together in front of herself, but rather than the impression of faith and serenity one might expect, it had Daenaira thinking she did it because it made her arms press to the sides of her breasts, plumping and pronouncing them above the neckline of her very snug blouse.

"Well, if it isn't our new shy mouse," she greeted, a sly smile making it hard to read whether that was a sarcastic remark or not. Dae decided to be neutral for a moment or two. Or at least until she inevitably pissed her off. She could smell impending trouble on the entire situation.

"Good night to you, *K'yan* Nicoya."

"Good night. How are you feeling, dear? I heard what happened. Imagine, such a thing in these very halls. It seems as though Sanctuary is falling apart. First that whole mess with Karri—well, you do know about Magnus's previous handmaiden, don't you?"

Not in specific, but she figured she knew enough just from that one remark Magnus had made. Nicoya's inference only solidified it.

"I heard a little about it, yes," she replied honestly, her subtle instinct to imitate the way Nicoya was holding her arms bringing her hands closer to the concealed weapons she carried.

"Such a tragic and terrible happening," Nicoya confided in a whisper as she leaned forward slightly. "So treacherous. It makes you wonder what it was about M'jan Magnus that would drive a woman to attempted murder."

Murder! Karri had tried to kill Magnus? She had thought betrayal or something serious, but to have the gall to murder her own priest? And such a priest! To know that if you failed, you would face the wrath of the most renowned penance priest in all of their history? Nicoya was right. It begged the question why.

"Well, I suppose if anyone will find out, it will be me," Dae observed carefully. "Frankly, I did not ask to be here and I did not wish to be here. But there is food, shelter, and more freedom than my previous position, so I can cope while I find out more details."

"You didn't . . . ? Really?" Nicoya seemed very interested in that as she hid a smile behind affected concern. "Poor thing. Most of us are so eager to come to Sanctuary. We never consider those who are Chosen without wishing to be."

"Does that happen often?"

"I suppose once is one time too often," the other maiden said philosophically. Dae couldn't help but think that this was a very good point. But after two nights of Magnus's concerned attendance on her as she had healed in her bed, the weight of his unexpressed guilt for her attack had told her much about him. He had spoken of demanding trust and loyalty, but it was clear that he was just as willing to dedicate his interest to her as she was supposed to dedicate hers to him. There was a measure of equality to that, despite the seeming subservience of a handmaiden's position. "And then for him to fail to protect you! I must say, it did not instill confidence in those here who were already beginning to question him. Not that *I* think that way. Magnus will always be

Magnus. Shiloh is his most dedicated advocate, and I follow wherever my priest leads me." She touched a spread hand over her heart and bowed slightly. It was a beautiful sentiment affected just as beautifully.

"Magnus must feel great relief knowing that. In fact, I will have to tell him as much."

"Oh no," she demurred. "I would hope he already knows. Now, about you, dearest. Are you coping well enough? There are so many rumors, it's hard to know the truth. Were you . . ." She made a moue of sympathy. "Of course you don't have to talk about it if it troubles you, but were you tainted by this beast who attacked you? Were you raped?"

The audacity of asking such a question really surprised Daenaira, though it probably shouldn't have. Nicoya liked to hurt others. It was clear as crystal in her jasper black eyes. What better way to undermine and wound an already wounded victim than to quickly remind her of her rape and to refer to it as a "taint," as if she were now ruined forever by the act.

"I would rather not talk about that," Dae said quietly, lowering her face and eyes. She didn't know why she was continuing this farce of submissiveness, but as always she went with her instincts.

"It's okay, dearest." Nicoya went to pat her hands and Dae jolted back away from her.

Damn it. That was no affectation! She just refused to be touched without permission anymore. She didn't excuse herself for the reaction either, as Magnus had done in the dining hall. Dae had a right to her personal space and she was going to keep it!

"Well, I understand," Nicoya clucked sympathetically. "I have a class starting soon, so I really must get going, but please feel free to confide in me anytime you need someone to talk to."

"I will. Thank you." *Not likely.*

Nicoya left looking far too satisfied with herself.

The next encounter of Daenaira's night was in the laundry

rooms, ironically enough. The large machines were kept running by a handful of maidens and servants who managed constantly flowing and enormous piles of garments and sheets in beautiful dark violets and midnight blues. However, it was the unexpected brilliance of goldenrod, scarlet, and lavender that had attracted her into the busy place. She hadn't seen these colors anywhere before in Sanctuary. She was still looking around, of course, but such brilliance was not common to their culture. They wore dark colors to help them blend into shadow at a moment's notice. They only wore jewelry when in the depths of the city, lest its gleam give them away, which was significant since gold and precious gems and metals like it were a much-treasured fashion for the men and even the women.

She followed the colorful sheeting into the folding room, where she hoped to touch it for herself if she offered to help with the task. She found Greta there and knew instantly that wasn't going to happen. Greta narrowed cold, mean eyes on her immediately, the murky gray color chilling in its viciousness.

"Why are you here?" she demanded. "Come to rub my nose in it?"

"In what?" Dae asked, raising a brow as she glanced wistfully at the lavender silk Greta yanked out of the pile for folding.

"Oh, please. Your shy act doesn't fool me. I heard how nasty you were when they brought you into his rooms. Both of those guards spent two nights in penance thanks to you and your lies. I can't believe no one questions the convenience of you being 'nearly raped' twice in the same day. What bullshit."

"Excuse me? I hardly think being attacked was my fault."

"I think you probably asked for it and then tried to cover your tracks. I'm sure Magnus is already regretting choosing a little whore like you for his handmaiden. I must say you worked quickly."

Daenaira had been called so many names in her lifetime that she didn't even blink at the inference. "Did I?" she asked.

"I don't know how you did it!" Greta burst out suddenly, slamming down the fabric in a wrinkling mess. "Ever since M'jan Figano died, leaving me free, I knew in my soul that Magnus and I were destined to be paired together. But with Karri in the way, I thought I was out of my mind. Then suddenly she was dead and I just knew! I knew if I was patient enough, Magnus would come to me and choose me to be his next! I've seen him looking at me, you know. He envied Figano. He didn't fuck Karri once in all those years, and he won't touch you either," she spat nastily. "But he wanted me. Oh, yes. I know he wanted me."

The dark-haired girl was flushed with her conviction as she leaned into Dae's face and sneered. "He took me once. In Temple. He broke all of his vows and all of his rules, bent me over in the rectory and fucked me within an inch of my life. He covered my eyes and kept behind me, thinking I wouldn't know, but he wears a distinctive scent and everyone knows the marks of his weapons! I found one of his shurikens at my feet afterward with his emblem etched into it, and that's my proof. But I knew even before that. I knew because a woman knows the feel of the cock of the man she dreams of." Her look turned dreamy. "All of that savage power hidden under so much civility. He fucked me and fucked me. He came twice inside me before he was finally satisfied." Greta's eyes shot back to Daenaira and turned venomous. "But instead of choosing me when he has the chance, he chooses you! I can smell the lowest of classes on you. You're filth and don't deserve to touch him! I should be the one dressing and undressing him, giving him ritual baths after battle, sating his body of his carnal needs!"

Daenaira smiled just a little, always a dangerous thing.

"I imagine if that were true, you'd be on your knees right now doing just that. However, it was me he chose. It was *my* bed he was in last night." Okay, so maybe he had been sitting on it bathing her burned face, but this nasty cow didn't need to know that. "And he seems to like all my low-class talents."

"You're a liar!" Greta screeched. "He wouldn't!"

"Look, obviously someone pulled one over on you, you stupid cow. They put on Magnus's cologne and got a free fuck off you. If he'd wanted you, M'jan Magnus would have taken you and you know it. But here I am." She spread her hands and arms out. "And that's why you're pissed off. Because you know you got reamed against the rules and you're going to have to cope with it. And since that isn't my problem, I'm going to find someone far less gullible and pathetic to talk to. See ya."

"You bitch!"

Dae had turned her back on Greta on purpose, guessing the silly twit would try to fight only if she thought she had the advantage. Greta lunged for her and Dae simply stopped, pivoted, and struck the heel of her palm into the momentum of Greta's bullish charge, snapping her right in her nose. She hit her so hard that Greta's feet flew out from under her and sent her smacking to the floor on her back with a cough. Blood immediately drooled from her nose as Dae tsked and leaned over her prone, groaning adversary.

"You call me a bitch like it's a bad thing," she noted conversationally. "From my perspective, I just don't see it. In this case, I think it's good to be the bitch. Don't you? Especially if being the bitch means I'm not the dumb-ass bleeding on the floor. Now please, can we avoid having this conversation again in the future?" Daenaira straightened up and then, as an afterthought to her new position in life, she added, "Oh. Also? I forgive you for being a stupid cow," she said benevolently.

She reached out to stroke her fingers over the lavender silk and then continued on her tour.

Malaya smelled trouble.

The exquisitely lovely Chancellor sat down and crossed her legs beneath her full-flowing skirt, the gauze legs of her *paj* rubbing almost sensuously together as she did so and making her shift in subconscious response to the stimulation. Malaya was a physical creature from tip to toe, and one could even say she was quite carnal; however, she was conservative and circumspect and held herself under very strict control.

Unlike her sex-maniac twin brother, Tristan.

She took out her energy in things like dance, her job as co-ruler, fight training, and more. Tristan had been more or less the same until a few months ago. His behavior had since turned into the definition of a fast and loose playboy, with a different female in his bed every day (although they did sometimes repeat later in the week), and making quite the ruckus of it to every Shadowdweller with natural-born hearing in the palace. On the one hand, she thought with a sly smile, she was quite proud of the randy bastard for his prowess. Those women screamed for mercy and, by the sound of it, Tristan had quite an impressive recovery time. The rumors flying about that particular talent were almost enough to offset the comments about how cavalier he was being with his responsibilities as a ruler.

Malaya knew him better. He took his leadership quite seriously. Always had. He had been with her through war and strife every step of the way, helping her use their bloodline claim to an ancient throne to revive the monarchy that their people had so desperately needed. Tristan had single-handedly engineered the construction on this Shadowdweller city safe underground in the Alaskan mountains. It had been his idea since inception to move the Senate and Sanctuary under one "roof," so to speak, and then one by one to draw the supporting clans in to reclaim their status as a Nightwalker power. When the clans had finally been dissolved completely, everyone had been welcome into the city, and now it was the center of their culture and lives. It deceived the eyes of humans, and it protected every single 'Dweller who lived there. Fed, clothed, kept warm, and simply provided all needs. Education. Religion. Political voice.

These were not the accomplishments of a mere playboy drunk on the sex his position could get him. But people forgot these details so quickly, and Tristan had done nothing to rectify the problem.

It was almost as if he wanted to self-destruct.

The trouble she could feel coming.

Malaya looked at her vizier, Rika, who was a slim and fragile woman many years older and wiser then Malaya herself, although she often looked like the younger of the two with her unusual delicacy. Their race bred tall, Amazonian women, strong and vibrant and usually loaded with curves. Malaya was all of those things, right down to the curves, although her active lifestyle kept her from gaining too many of them.

But Rika was an exception. At least, she was now. Though she was of average height, illness had ravaged away everything except her enduring beauty. The disease was called Crush, and it was aptly named for what it did to both its victims and those who loved them before it was finally through with them. Rika's had progressed to blindness just recently, and it only seemed to be gaining momentum. Still, despite that deficiency, Rika cast her eyes in Malaya's direction and rolled them comically as the orgasmic cries of her twin's latest happy sufferer could be heard echoing down the hallway.

"He's in rare form tonight," she mused wryly.

Indeed, he was. Which, in truth, wasn't a good thing. Tristan retired earlier and with a vengeance when his mind was heavily weighted. It was as if her brother feared he would snap if he didn't purge his demon thoughts through the release of his sexual self. She had listened to his athletics, although she was hardly able to avoid listening to them, and had already noted that despite his partner's joy, he had yet to find release of any kind. This after over an hour already.

Malaya slid her gaze over to Guin, her bodyguard and deeply entrusted attendant. The big, braw male warrior had been by her side for fifty years, which meant he had also known Tristan for that long. He was well aware of her worry over her brother, and as he stood there at a silent, monolithic attention, he was frowning.

"You're a man." She spoke suddenly, startling his attention to her.

"Yeah," he said slowly, his brow curling in amused puzzlement. "I can pretty much show proof of that every time I wake up."

"Oh my. Too much information." Rika chuckled.

Malaya smiled. "I think it's safe to say Tristan has him beat in the 'too much information' category for life," she noted. But she went back to Guin. "What do you think would drive a man to such distraction?"

Guin hesitated, as if he were stepping around a field of land mines.

"No. Be honest," she encouraged him. "I don't keep you here for your ability to blow smoke up my backside."

"Good, because he sucks at it," Rika said with a giggle.

Malaya had to laugh. It was good to see her vizier in such good spirits. It was a good week for the ailing Rika. A not-so-good week for Tristan. Therefore, a vacillating week for his twin sister.

The bodyguard thought on it for a moment. "Well, I can't presume anything because your brother and I don't think the same way about very many things. We agree on the important topics, though. Like keeping you safe. But I might venture to say it's a woman. Not these he keeps spending himself on, but another one. Maybe one he doesn't feel he should touch? A woman he thinks is too good for him."

Malaya thought about it, but it didn't ring very true. Her brother was confident almost to a fault. If he wanted a woman for his own, he would go and take her. She shook her head. "I find that difficult to imagine. As Chancellor, no woman is out of his reach . . . except perhaps a handmaiden. But I highly doubt . . ." She hesitated, then shook her head again. "No. He doesn't waste his energy on useless infatuations. That cannot be it."

Guin gave her a dark and narrowed look, a muscle jumping in his square jaw as if her remarks had ticked him off, though she couldn't see why. "Why do you ask my opinion if you are not going to take it seriously?" he demanded testily.

"I did take it seriously. Then I analyzed it and dismissed it. Give me a new opinion."

"I think you should consider that topic you mentioned where you and Tristan are in agreement, Guin," Rika suggested.

Guin raised a brow and thought about that. "True. One thing guaranteed to upset your brother as much as it would upset me is *you*." Guin nodded his heavy, saturnine head toward Malaya.

"Me!"

"Yes. You. You and your safety. Your life in threat. Your health, emotions, or well-being in danger of being harmed in any way. This threat of a traitorous vein in the Senate and in Sanctuary—"

"But this started before we knew of that! Long before!"

"Gods, woman!" Guin exploded, marching up to her, his leather armor creaking over the sound of snug denim and rustling weapons. He reached out for the hair at the back of her head and gently gripped and pulled until she was looking all the way up at him. "Ask him! Tell him you have had enough of this and demand he tell you, just as you would me! Tell him his tireless cock is driving us all out of our minds because I promise you, if I have to listen to this for six more months, I am going to do something rash about it for myself! Not everyone here has the freedom to indulge in the needs and desires listening to this night after night that presses upon them, Malaya."

Guin suddenly seemed to realize what he was saying to

her, a tremor cutting through his big body that she could feel through the hand in her hair. He swallowed hard and cleared his throat, looking at his booted feet in discomfort for a moment.

"Guin," she said softly. "I hadn't even thought . . . If you need time for yourself, you should take it. This suite is your home just as it is mine, and you know you are free to entertain a guest if you—"

"Bituth amec!" The guard exploded in furious rage, and Malaya stared at him in astonishment. "I don't fucking want to entertain a guest!" he roared, snapping back away from her and pacing in quick, angry steps. "If I want sex, *K'yat-sume*, I know how and where to go to get it and how to arrange to be away from you to go about it! This is not my point! Fuck! Rika, what in Light is my point?" he demanded with total frustration as he ran a hand through his hair.

"I think he means your brother is driving the entire palace crazy in one form or another, and it is high time you confronted him about it and forced him to tell you what is happening before we all go quite insane," Rika supplied.

"That's exactly what I mean!" Guin huffed sharply, a hand slapping down hard on a thick thigh. "I am sick of watching you worry yourself over him when he's in there having a balls-happy time."

"Guin, really," Rika scolded, biting her lips to keep from chuckling.

"I'm just being honest," he said harshly. "Trust me, he isn't going to come to the resolution he is looking for while he's . . . he's"—Guin growled in frustration when it went against his nature to edit his coarse way of expressing himself—"while he's dick deep in pussy night after night!"

Malaya covered her mouth, pressing back a snicker, but he noticed anyway.

"This isn't funny," he warned her.

"Oh, Guin," she tried to soothe him around a giggle. "I know. And you're right." She stood up in a smooth gliding movement and walked up to him. She slid her arms around his ribs and hugged herself to his rigid body until, as always, he relaxed in her grasp and reached to hug her back with an arm around her that squashed her tightly to him. Malaya didn't see that his fists never opened or that he turned his nose against her hair to breathe in her scent as his eyes closed for a brief moment.

"You love to test me," he accused her, his deep voice rumbling beneath the ear that lay against his chest.

"For once, that was not my intention," she assured him.

Guin sighed and shook his head. He fell silent under her affection, just long enough for the sounds of her brother's activity to dominate the room again. This time Malaya sighed, tipping her head back to look up into the turbulent granite of her bodyguard's eyes.

"I think at this point I am afraid to know what drives him so."

"You mean besides his—"

"Guin." She giggled, cutting him off and making the brute grin down at her. "I'm serious. I've never seen him like this. And it isn't as though I haven't been pestering him for months about it."

"Stop being sisterly about it, *K'yatsume*. Be a queen. Kick his ass. Before I do," he added gruffly. Guin disengaged her arms, stepping out of her sphere and walking away. He reached out and popped a finger on the tip of Rika's nose affectionately as he passed.

"Where are you going?" Malaya asked.

"Out of earshot for ten minutes. I'll send someone in. Ihram, probably, because I think Kill is off duty. Start thinking about knocking that sibling of yours around."

"Oh, I am," she assured him.

Guin exited the room and, after sending Ihram in to watch over the women, he walked down the long corridor of the royals' private wing. He paused, leaning back against a wall for a moment and finding himself surrounded by the nearer moans of Tristan's efforts of the moment. He closed his eyes and actually thought to pray to *Drenna* for the strength to bear this until Malaya got her twin under control. He didn't think he could take much more of listening to rabid sexual antics every night while Malaya insisted on torturing him with sweet hugs of affection and the jasmine scent she washed through her hair. Her total ignorance was all that saved him, but it wouldn't last for long if he ended up getting a painfully obvious erection within notice of her as he had just almost done.

Well, the erection had definitely happened, but he had moved away in time, allowing his clothing and his exit to hide what he could not.

Fuck.

Something had to give.

Since he had no intention of pursuing a woman ten times his worth and who clearly looked on him like a big oafish brother, it meant the environment had to return to normal or . . .

Or he would have to leave.

The idea of leaving her, of entrusting her constantly endangered life to the care of anyone else but himself made him sick to his stomach. It infuriated him to find himself so weak and affected. He had no right to risk getting her killed just because he couldn't keep control over a ridiculous . . .

Infatuation.

That's all it was. He had never been so devoted to a single person before, never had the honor of being the companion of someone so pure of heart and intention that it dazzled his jaded eyes. It had been like that from the very first night he had met her, and it hadn't wavered once. It was all just a stupid fantasy; one that a big, undereducated ex-mercenary like him had no cause to indulge in, yet he did it just the same. Malaya shouldn't have to pay any price for the fact that he had a libido and an imagination that liked to crave perfect, exquisite things far, far beyond his reach. And even if he ever did get his hands on that perfection, how in Light would he know how to treat it?

It was best to maintain the status quo, of course. She would remain infinitely untouchable; not only to himself, but to anyone who wished harm upon her. He trusted no one else to care for her. Not even the one he had left her with. Not even her brother.

Guin frowned at the thought of Malaya's twin, his sharp hearing knowing quite well by now the sound of the man finally reaching the point of climax. *Thank the gods!* He had been dead serious before. If Malaya didn't resolve this soon, he was going to approach the damn fool himself. Guin hated to see Malaya hurting, which, despite all her laughter and giggles, was exactly what she was doing. It wounded her deeply that her beloved twin would not come to her and entrust her with his troubles. In her room at daytime, beyond the door he slept in front of to guard her, he sometimes heard her give in to pained tears of worry and angst so deep it tore through him without mercy.

If he hadn't known how much it would hurt her to lose her brother, he would have killed the selfish bastard months ago.

Something had to give.

Daenaira was on the second floor of Sanctuary, in a large hallway, finding things pretty quiet because it was during classes and she was in the educational section of the building. She came up on a large glass dome set in the middle of the floor for seemingly no reason. It was surrounded by a low rail and there were book rests at regular spaces. She was trying to figure out who would read a book while standing and facing a big hunk of glass when she looked down through the dome leading to the room below.

"Holy Light," she whispered.

There, many feet below her but more than easy to see, was a large bed. In the middle of the bed was a couple. They were completely naked and . . .

She jolted back, her face flaming as she quickly looked around. They were having sex! Right where everyone could see! Then some other things began to register and she peeked back through the glass.

She was looking down on a classroom!

There were about twenty-five people sitting all around the center bed on various chaises and sofas, and they were all watching the couple. Some were even taking notes. Daenaira pressed a cool hand to her burning cheek as she looked down at the center attraction again. The woman was a plump and pretty girl with very dark skin and shoulder-length black curls that hung in dozens of corkscrews. She was on her knees, but not her elbows, while the male penetrated her from behind. The male had a lean, whipcord strong physique and short brown hair that hung over his eyes a bit. Neither one of them was moving, as if they were frozen in time. His penis was only half inside his partner's body and he was actually breathing quite steadily, by the rise and fall of his chest, and exhibiting a strong impression of control.

"Who can tell me what is important for our male to keep in mind in this position?"

Holy Light! She'd know that voice anywhere! Sure enough, the lecturer stepped away from the far wall where he had gone unseen by her until that moment and he moved to approach the tableau in the bed. The closer he got, the more his voice carried up to her. Not that it needed any help. It resonated right through her.

"And, no, Henry, I will not accept 'oh, yes, baby!' as an answer."

The class erupted in laughter, including the models, and Dae snorted out a soft laugh.

Just like that, Magnus's head shot up and his sharp golden eyes looked straight at her. Her first ridiculous instinct was to duck, like some kid caught doing something wrong, but it would be stupid to move. First of all, he'd already seen her. Second, she wasn't a kid. Dae watched him as he hesitated significantly, and then she finally got up the cheek to give him a little wave.

He looked away.

But she saw a twitch of a smile stroke his lips just before.

"Jalia?" he addressed a young woman to his right.

"Depth?" she asked more than answered.

"True. Depending on the male, of course, the instinctive urge for deeper penetration should be tempered if there is a size issue. The cervix is easier to strike and bruise for many women in this position." He cleared his throat and looked up at Dae again. "Kiren?" he said without looking at the student.

"Stimulation. A woman isn't as easily brought to orgasm because of the way he moves across her pleasure spots. Or rather, doesn't move across them."

"Not naturally, no," Magnus agreed. "But this is easily rectified by bringing her up onto her hands, perhaps, and canting his stroke at a steeper angle."

The models moved as he spoke, demonstrating what he meant, and Dae heard the woman keen in a soft, lustful moan after several steady strokes by her partner.

"Oh my," Daenaira breathed softly.

When Magnus looked up this time, she gave a little jump. Damn it, she had to keep her mouth shut. The man had incredible hearing.

Magnus's lecture was completely shot the minute he had heard that first unmistakable laugh, and he had no idea why. *Drenna*, he'd taught just about the whole damn city how to have sex. What did it matter if Daenaira was watching him do it?

But when she whispered that breathy little "oh my" in response to what she was seeing, she completely blew out his focus. He felt his very blood jolt in his veins, and suddenly all he could remember was seeing her in a full, glorious temper, naked from the waist up and showing off her outstanding breasts.

"M'jan?"

Magnus snapped his attention to the student calling him. "Yes, Avel?"

"I know you say there's never an absolute right and an absolute wrong, but he isn't touching her anywhere except by penetration. Isn't that a little . . . I don't know . . . selfish?"

"I don't hear her complaining," Henry noted with amusement, making his classmates snicker.

"Shut up, Henry," Avel shot out petulantly. She was an unusually sensitive girl and hard to draw out sometimes. Magnus would have to speak to Henry after the lecture about keeping the smart remarks limited to just his teacher. He didn't want anyone's curiosity curtailed for the sake of a class clown's easy laugh.

"Perhaps. He needs to listen to her. He needs to judge what she might need. And she needs to ask for it if he's being thickheaded." Magnus refused to look up again and turned to his models. "Killian could reach around to stimulate her clitoris or touch her breasts. Likewise, Dae—uh, Diana could reach to . . ."

Thank *Drenna* Diana's actions were self-explanatory, because he couldn't seem to spit out the rest. Gods, had he really just done that? More importantly, had Daenaira caught it up where she was?

Magnus looked up, unable to help himself. Sure enough, there it was, that sly little smile of hers and the most incredibly speculative look he'd ever been on the receiving end of. Meanwhile, Killian was working magic on his enthusiastic partner and her moans of pleasure were filling the space between them as their gazes locked and held.

"Magnus!"

Magnus jumped, though he quickly told himself it wasn't from guilt. When he saw M'jan Daniel hurrying through the doors, he knew something was very wrong.

"Killian, feel free to finish," he said quickly, hurrying toward the other priest. "What is it?"

"Brendan sent me to fetch you. He said he found someone you were looking for and that he was hunting him in Shadowscape."

Daenaira's attacker. Brendan had been quietly seeking answers in hydroponics and had apparently flushed out the culprit. But Brendan wasn't a penance priest. He was capable, but not up for a pitched battle if the enemy was well trained. Like the assassins that had tracked and hunted Trace a few months ago. Those sorts of professional killers were nothing Brendan could match himself to.

There were only five penance priests: Magnus, Shiloh, Cort, Ventan, and Sagan.

Then Magnus had the horrible thought that it might be one of those highly placed males that Brendan had ferreted out. If that were the case, he was as good as dead. Magnus darted into the corridor and took a breath. Deep in the darkness, he began to zone out everything around him, focusing on the energy inside him that would help him to Fade. Fade was the dissolving of a Shadowdweller's physical existence in one dimension so they could arrive in another. There was a long moment of shuddering suspension and a metallic taste across his palate, and then he was in Shadowscape. An exact replica of Realscape, Shadowscape was a completely lightless dimension both inside and out of the underground 'Dweller city. It was just a step out of phase with the real world as they knew it, but it was enough to keep out anyone who wasn't in Fade.

He moved forward, reaching to unsnap the hard leather pouches holding his shurikens. They wouldn't fall out even in a full aerobic battle, unlike the bolos, so he wasn't worried about making them a moment more accessible.

"Okay, M'jan," he muttered to himself, "let's work some magic."

As convoluted and inconstant as Dreamscape was, he had

an unlimited number of tricks and resources available to help him hunt and battle. Shadowscape was based in all of the same physical laws as Realscape, except those pertaining to light. The only magic here was what he brought with him.

He ran out of Sanctuary, following his instincts. He could already sense the enemy would lead Brendan away from his most familiar ground. It was likely he would even take him aboveground and hope he could force the less experienced fighter into a spontaneous Unfade. It was close to daylight in Realscape. If he was caught out in the open far enough from the city . . .

"Brendan, remind me to kill you when I'm done saving your hide."

The hardest thing for a penance priest to learn was to listen to instinct more than he listened to logic and the whispers of his own mind. Very few men could do this. Most kept looking for the trick, the track or the telltale sign. These would drown out the primal hunting instincts all of them had been born with since the inception of the earth. It wasn't about scent or sensation. It was beyond that.

Magnus burst out into the frigid Alaskan winter, cursing at the blinding snowstorm he found himself in. He hadn't stopped to prepare any more than Brendan had, and no doubt they were all caught out in the cold. Even with a Shadowdweller's constitution, there was no surviving freezing, wet temperatures like this for long.

Luckily, he was hit with a throwing dagger right then.

It struck him in the right rear thigh, making him stagger. But he already had shurikens in each hand, and after a moment to orient to a straight dagger throw, he sent them singing through the thick snowfall. As soon as they were gone, he drew his katana.

"Brendan?" he shouted, moving quickly to change his locus. Sure enough, another dagger sliced the air where he had been. Whoever this was, they had an excellent ear. Although not good enough to realize he had moved. He wished he could see the dagger better and perhaps identify it, but he didn't dare pull it out in case it had hit a major artery.

"Well, well, M'jan Magnus. Nice of you to join the party."

Magnus rolled his eyes. Not very original. Cocksure *and* stupid.

"Yes, I heard someone wanted to get their penance on," he returned blandly. He moved low, the next dagger whipping above his head as he slid a shuriken free. The snow was deep, making it hard to maneuver, and Magnus had to watch where he directed his prey. If his enemy found his blood trail, it would put Magnus on the defensive, and Magnus was definitely leaving a blood trail.

"Hey, that is one sweet piece of ass you brought home, Magnus. I don't care what the rumors say; you clearly know a nice pair of—oof!"

That was a definite hit, Magnus thought with a smile sly enough to do Dae proud. Prick bastard. He hoped to Light the shuriken had caught him somewhere tender.

His enemy laughed, albeit a bit breathlessly.

"Temper, temper, M'jan."

He damn well knew that voice, Magnus thought. When he found out who it was, there would be Light to pay.

"Wouldn't want to tell me where Brendan is, would you?"

Magnus silently moved closer. He wanted within blade distance of this miserable Sinner.

"Nope. Figure he'll freeze or bleed to death by the time you find him."

That remark left Magnus little choice. He needed to get close enough to touch his enemy and compel the truth before he killed him. If Brendan was out there in this freezing mess . . .

Distraction.

He realized it in time to parry a deadly blade swinging at his kidney. He shoved his opponent back and got a look at him.

"Daniel!"

"Help, help, Magnus!" The priest mocked him in a high-pitched voice. "Brendan, your lover, needs you!" Daniel taunted him by swinging Brendan's blade for him to see. "Do you find it ironic, teaching all that heterosexual sex when it's not your thing? I mean, you had that little Karri and didn't take a single poke at her for two centuries? Not even a little suck-off or hand job? Which was really dumb, honestly, because I hear she was really great on her knees."

Something wasn't right.

How had he followed a trail if Daniel had been following behind him the whole time?

The answer came from behind as a vicious saw-star buzzed out of the snowfall, curving and striking him in his weapons belt, slicing the hardened leather half through and then sinking into his hip. Magnus went down, unable to help it, but as he did he snared the bolos from their pouch and flung them at Daniel. One ball whipped around and snagged the blade he held and the other lashed around the traitor's throat. Daniel gagged in shock and Magnus lurched back onto his feet, lunging for him and grabbing hold of him as he ran him through back to front, the wicked sharp end of his katana bursting free of Daniel's belly.

"Where's Brendan?"

Daniel could only tell him the truth.

"Hydroponics!"

Hydroponics.

Drenna, it was almost daylight! The light cycle started at dawn!

But Magnus had another enemy to take care of, and he was badly wounded. He drew free of his victim's body, listening carefully. Daniel hadn't had a shuriken wound. That meant he'd hit the other attacker before. This had all been a setup. Brendan had flushed them out, all right, but they'd taken care of him right off. They knew Magnus was the real threat, so they had constructed this clever ruse, using his own abilities against him. He should have known better. Brendan wouldn't have sent a go-between. But Magnus had been distracted . . .

Proving his point about sexual distraction between priest and maiden entirely.

Magnus wasn't known for giving up on a fight, which, he realized, was why he had to do exactly that. His opponent was using his own nature against him, manipulating him to keep him occupied until dawn. Magnus could track this Sinner down again later, but Brendan needed help right now.

He was about to Unfade and run back through Realscape when he heard a gagging grunt in front of him. Blinded by snowfall, he listened carefully and heard the distinct sound of a body falling into deep snow. He heard a long sigh.

"*Now* can I use the heavy sai?"

Cort. She had killed Cort. Cort had been one of the most vicious hunters among them, not known for his ability to show mercy. But Daenaira had snuck up behind him as he had focused on Magnus and run the aforementioned heavy sai right through his spine at the shoulder junction. Using a sai as a stabbing weapon was hard enough, but to pick such a spot! However, Magnus knew she had done it because she had realized she had to kill or completely incapacitate with her first hit. Cort was too tall for her to reach the brain stem comfortably, and a heart shot might have missed. This way the shoulder blades had been her guide and Cort had been a quadriplegic before he'd hit the ground. No threat there any longer.

He didn't take the time to feel what he was going to feel about any of it, because he had run for hydroponics. Thankfully, Brendan was not badly wounded and they reached him before the light event began. Bren had no qualms about going to a healer, but Magnus refused. Leaving his friend at the infirmary, he left a trail of blood all through Sanctuary as he stormed back to their rooms with Daenaira walking behind him in deceptive obedience. The instant the door closed them off from the rest of Sanctuary, he rounded on her in cold fury.

"Are you out of your mind?" he roared at her. "You do *not* follow me to battle until I say you are ready to do so! Not one instant sooner!" He was vibrating with rage as he made like he was going to grab her and shake her, but as livid as he was, he remembered not to touch her. Especially in violence.

Dae didn't say a word, which surprised and confused him. She just stood there absently toying with the remaining sai, spinning it in her fingertips. Then she tossed the weapon on her bed and reached for his hand. Catching hold, she pulled him into the bathroom.

"Don't you have anything to say?" he demanded of her.

"Get undressed."

Magnus blinked. Then he watched dumbly as she reached to unfasten his weapons belt. She freed it, easing it away from the saw-star embedded in his hip, and then she dropped it onto the cushioned bench behind him. She reached for his regular belt next, deftly making short work of it before sliding the leather free. She quickly moved on to his priest's tunic, but he was too tall while he was standing, so he did it for her. She reached for his pants and he closed his hand around hers.

"What are you doing?" he asked at last.

"My job. You're wounded. These need stitching and you need to bathe. That all falls under 'handmaiden.' "

"You don't have to do this. I haven't even had a chance to teach you . . ."

"What? I know how to stitch and I can give a bath. What's to teach? It's not like it's sex technique."

Damn her, her blatant tease made him smile in spite of being mad enough to spit nails. He let go of her slowly and she undid his slacks as efficiently as if she undressed men all the time. Very carefully, she followed the fabric to his hip and eased the cloth over the remaining jut of the metal. The embedded star was shaped like the circular saw it had won its name from in both appearance and sound when it was thrown. It looked deep and painful, not to mention that he was streaming blood from the wound.

She stepped behind him and slid her hands down over the muscular curve of his backside and on to his thigh, inspecting the nasty little throwing dagger that penetrated the thick muscle. She reached for the wrist blade up her left sleeve, the wickedly sharp steel slipping into the hole in his slacks and cutting them sharp and fast toward his waist. Once she had enough freedom to keep from accidentally dislodging the blade in his leg, she returned to his waist and, after replacing her knife, she slowly dipped her fingertips below his waist-line against his skin, drawing down his pants and underwear until she could ease past the dagger.

Daenaira was working with a smooth efficiency, as if she did this all the time, but it was really her bravado and her determination to repay him for his efforts in her defense that made it seem so. The wounds were terrible and disturbing, yes, but it was also strangely disturbing to run her fingers down over hard, heated muscle under smooth dark skin. She tried to shake off the impression as she worked the laces of his boots free and helped him step out of the rest of his clothes.

On her knees on the floor, Dae slowly looked up over the tall, magnificently sculpted body before her. Taut dark skin, dusted in curling black hairs, displayed just how beautifully physical he was. From the gold and amethyst armband locked tight around bulging biceps, to the half-sun and half-moon tattoo in the low curve of his back, and on to the steady brace of his feet, there wasn't a single ounce of lazy flesh to be found. A roadwork of veins ran beneath his skin, over and around each distinctive muscle, leading up to the pulse she could see in his throat even from where she was kneeling.

Dae slowly got to her feet and walked around in front of him. Magnus was already searching for her eyes, studying her as if to read her mind. She didn't give him the opportunity, not knowing how transparent her admiration of his gorgeous physique was and not wanting him to get the wrong idea. After all, she was allowed to appreciate a beautiful male form. She had not seen many of them—well, not of late. And certainly not naked. When she had admired the soldiers in the bar at age twelve, it had been hero worship at its finest. She hadn't known what "sexy" was.

She realized she did now.

Dae walked out of the room quickly and invaded his weapons supplies. She found a pair of pliers and thread and a needle. He would fight infection and heal on his own quickly enough, but stitching would halt the flow of blood and help facilitate the healing process.

She came back and caught up his hand, moving him closer to the padded bench. Then she sat down and, laying her hands on his hips, she turned him toward her until she was facing down the evil saw-star. Dae ignored all of the blood, though it didn't bother her much, but what she found herself most distracted by was finding herself practically eye level with his penis and the nest of black curling hair it rested against. She had seen naked men before, and penises in various sizes or states of excitement, the most recent being Killian, the male model from his lecture. Because of this variety, she thought she was competent enough to judge just how incredibly big Magnus was.

And she was fairly certain he wasn't in the least bit excited.

Grabbing the pliers, she snared the exposed edge of the saw-star and looked up at him briefly.

"Hold on."

He took her literally, his hand falling onto her shoulder even as she felt him brace for the inevitable. Locking her free hand on his hip for counterforce, she yanked on the star with all of her strength, turning at the same time counter to the curve of the blades so they would slide out more than tear out of the bone.

Magnus made a savage sound inside his chest, staggering under the agony and the force of her pull. He clamped down on her shoulder unthinkingly, but she figured it was nothing in comparison to what she was doing to him. It took two more pulls before the nasty thing ripped free, spraying them both in his blood.

Magnus's legs gave out, but she anticipated it a second beforehand and was there against his body and supporting him as she helped him to his knees.

"Gods and fucking Light," he gasped, his hand catching hard against the floor as he bent forward.

"It's okay. It's out now. The worst is over," she said soothingly, hating the torturous pain ravaging his darkly handsome features. They both knew it was half a lie because she had to stitch him yet before he lost any more blood. Her new sari was absorbing most of it at the moment as she leaned into his side on her knees. "You should lie down on your side," she urged him.

He was in no space for arguing. Magnus was barely even coherent as pain and nausea raged through him with a vengeance. The next minutes passed in a haze for him, but finally he began to regain himself, the touch of Dae's hand in his hair helping to rouse him out of his pained stupor.

"It's over," she whispered softly into his ear. "Both wounds are done."

Magnus had no idea how long she had tended to him, but he had begun to feel well enough to sit himself up, albeit using her soft shape to lean on.

"M'jan, we have to get rid of this blood. I don't know about you, but it's starting to get pretty icky for me."

He exhaled a soft laugh and nodded. Getting his uninjured leg under himself, as well as his sturdy little handmaiden, Magnus was able to approach the stairs into the bath.

He took the first step down, blood clouding into the water before disappearing.

"Wait," she said, urging him to sit on the edge of the bath after two more steps. Then she drew back and stripped away the fall of her sari. She was standing calves deep in the water, so her skirts were already wet, but that hardly hampered her as she shed her velvet blouse and the underskirt next.

Magnus watched her turn to lay her clothing on the near ledge, her lush body a curving line of mocha skin that was completely nude . . . save for the weapons still strapped to her wrists. There was something primal and erotic about that, seeing soft, sexual femininity and sculpted, tempered steel strapped in leather. Perhaps it was the weapons smith in him that made it seem that way. She unwrapped the sheaths from her arms and set them aside, and then she dipped her blood-stained hands in the hot water and washed them clean. She looked up at him and smiled, reaching to brush back her red-black hair where it had escaped the cobra knot she kept it in. Magnus moved forward into the water, letting his natural buoyancy help him balance as he came closer to her and took her hand, drawing her down into the deeper part of the pool. Then he reached up for her hair, disengaging the pins and clips until the thick mass was untwisting through his fingers.

"I don't know if you noticed," he said quietly, "but hand-maidens always wear their hair loose in Sanctuary."

"Why? Priests don't."

His lips twitched at that. "You are right about that. I only meant to say it is tradition." He drew the thick mass of sleek crimped waves down over her shoulders and breasts. "Consider it part of your uniform. Besides, you have unique and stunning hair."

"Stunning?" she echoed. She snorted out her characteristic giggle. "I think you're suffering from severe blood loss."

"Hmm. And I think you don't know how to accept a compliment."

Daenaira backed away from his touch, walking through

the water slowly to reach the alcove of shelves nearby that held all of his bathing accoutrements. She picked up a firmly bristled skin brush and a bar of soap that smelled rich and masculine, and rubbed one against the other as she moved back toward him.

"I'm not exactly used to them," she pointed out.

"No, I don't suppose you would be," he agreed, watching the way the water flowed past her hips as she moved. Through the clear liquid he could see the triangle of tight curls protecting her sex from his curious eyes. He wondered if they also had that deep tinge of red to them. "I think we'll have to start changing that."

"I don't need compliments," she said with a shrug as she came right up to him, close enough that she had to tilt her head back to meet his eyes again. "I just need to be safe, clothed, fed, and free."

"Nothing more?" he asked as she handed him the soap to hold for her and touched the brush to the skin of his chest.

"Nothing I can think of at the moment."

"What about companionship?"

She didn't respond right away, instead focusing on the swirling strokes of the brush she was using. She was moving slowly and thoroughly, sometimes very lightly, other times a bit harder. Magnus felt his skin waking up beneath the stimulation, the feeling brisk and invigorating. She covered his chest and arms, cleaning his hands and fingers of any blood. She worked her way along his sides and stomach, and Magnus felt the dipping stroke of the brush straight through his gut and racing down his legs.

"I haven't needed it. Survived without it. But . . ." She smiled winsomely, the expression taking his breath away as it turned her instantly beautiful before his eyes. Not that she wasn't beautiful to begin with, because she was, but in that moment it was like seeing precious sculpted art; eyes carved by a lover's hand, a mouth shaped to reflect his lust for it, and the turning curve of her cheek begging for the stroke of a reverent touch. "But I might learn to like it," she finished, looking up at him.

Magnus lowered his eyes, covering under the action of turning his back to her so she could continue her task. Whether she saw the evasive tactic for what it was, he did not know. He assumed not, because she didn't even hesitate to reach for his shoulders and continue bathing him. Close to a ledge, Magnus reached out both hands and braced himself against it. His legs were steady, but the rushing of his blood and the spinning tilt to his senses made him require support.

He took in a long, slow breath as quietly and evenly as he could manage, trying to calm his hurrying heart. He was a man, after all, he reminded himself. He was going to feel desire. It could hardly be avoided so long as he was in his sexual prime. As she ran her brush down his spine and her free hand absently curved forward over his hip, her fingertips tickling against sensitive skin and hairs, his internal logic double-timed.

It was normal to feel excitement, especially after the adrenaline rush of battle. Soon he would crash and he wouldn't even be able to stay awake. It was all physiological, acts of predictable biology. The trouble was that the actual act of sex couldn't stop at mere biology. It was too intimate, and with intimacy came difficulties. Distractions . . .

Her wet, warm body leaned against his back, the slippery weight of her breasts sliding prominently against him, including starkly tipped nipples that were reacting, no doubt, from the temperature clash between the water and the cooler air. It was one temptation too many for Magnus's control to manage, and he began to develop a rapid, heavy erection in response. He gritted his teeth, closing his eyes and trying to get a hold of himself. He didn't think she would understand. It would send her a mixed, confused message and she was too inexperienced and uneducated to know how the male mind and body functioned in this way.

You're a teacher, for Drenna's sake! he hissed to himself. *Find a way to explain yourself!*

"Daenaira," he ground out between tight teeth. "Do you understand about an adrenaline rush?"

She laughed, obviously finding it an odd turn in topic. She skimmed her industrious brush down past his tattoo, over his ass, being just as thorough as she could as she shaped around his uninjured hip and cheek and thigh. The sensations she created were so incredibly good, and so damn close to pleasure, that he began to ache with the steady throb running the length of his cock.

"Yes, of course I do. It's a natural high. It can give you power and strength when you need it. I feel it when I fight."

"So do I," he informed her roughly as her brushing glided around to the front of his pelvis. She barely missed running her knuckles up against his cock, but then continued down his thigh as far as she could reach. "It has other effects to. It can . . . uh . . ."

Dae suddenly moved forward, leaning her entire body around as she reached for the bar of soap he had abandoned to the ledge. She ducked under his arm when she couldn't quite reach and stood in front of him with her back to him. The luscious curve of her backside swished only a few tempting inches away from his turgid sex, and Magnus was overwhelmed with the urge to latch on to her hips and drag her back against him. Instead, he dug his nails into the marble ledge.

Then she turned around and his time for explanation ran to a fast halt. The brush hit the water with a splash, a little thunk following a moment later as it hit bottom. Her amber eyes dashed up to his and she could see, he knew, every bit of the way he was struggling for control of himself.

And then she looked straight back down again and stared at him with open admiration that just about set his balls on fire.

"Oh my," she whispered.

Just like she had done when she had found herself aroused by the couple modeling for his class. *Of course* she had been aroused. She was young and healthy and starved of exposure to such things. Plus, it was only natural. There was always some element of excitement in the voyeurism of a classroom experience.

"I'm . . ." He couldn't make himself apologize, no matter how much he wanted to. He made a sound of frustration. "Adrenaline," he said rather lamely.

"Oh," she said softly, still staring at him. "That's . . . uh . . . quite a rush," she noted.

The cheeky observation made him want to laugh and groan all at once. He forced himself to breathe, to smile as if it was no big deal, and then reached to brush a damp hair off her cheek.

"Men can't hide things like women can," he said tightly. "And we aren't all that hard to please as a sex. We tend to be very visual. And you, *K'yindara*, tend to be very visually stimulating."

"Thank you," she said, looking slightly stunned by the backhanded compliment. "You're very visually stimulating, too." She punctuated her obvious sincerity by slowly licking her lips. Magnus's heart tried to bolt out of his chest when he saw the provocative and subconscious invitation. "I have to touch you."

Magnus went deadly still, even holding his breath as it burned his chest in demand.

"I mean, to finish bathing you," she amended. She reached out a tentative hand, her fingertip coming to within a breath of the head of his erection where it broke the surface of the water. "Is that all right?"

No! Absolutely not!

"Of course," he said, forcing himself to shrug. "We're going to be doing this a lot, Dae, and this is bound to happen from time to time."

Holy Light, he'd actually managed to sound casual. Casual was good. They had to be casual. Relaxed. Get past the awkward steps and settle into a matter-of-fact routine.

"Okay."

Oh gods . . .

But she pulled away at the last second and laughed. "I need a sponge. Not certain you'd like a brush in more sensitive places." She ducked below the surface, sending water ebbing against him as her hair floated toward him in a wild cloud. Just when he could imagine himself wrapped up in the dark and beautiful strands, she surfaced with the brush in her hand. She set it on the ledge, clearly intending to get back to it, and ducked back out from between his braced arms.

This is a bad idea, M'jan, he warned himself.

No. He could handle this. It would be a minute or two of sheer torture, and then she would move on. Any Shadowdweller male worth his heritage could bear up under a two-minute tease. All he had to do was treat it like any lesson. A handmaiden's lesson. *Just teach her how to be thorough and efficient. Be clinical.*

Daenaira popped back under his arm, waving a sea sponge in triumph. Then she swept up her soap. It was obvious to him that she was all business. That should help, he told himself. It had to help. His testicles were starting to ache. There was no describing the pulses of heat that rushed down his shaft as he watched her lather up her sponge between deft hands.

She didn't affect shyness, whether she felt it or not. She just tossed aside the soap and reached to take him in hand. Efficient, casual, and even clinical.

Until the thickly lathered combination of her sponge and her free hand stroked him from tip to root and back again.

"Are many men this thick around?" she inquired, awe obvious in her voice and eyes as she studied every motion of her hands almost as closely as he did.

"It varies," he managed to say, though he hardly came off sounding neutral.

"Should I be careful? Usually I'm going for pain when I catch hold of a penis," she noted. "Not sure if I know how to be nice."

"You're fine."

Bullshit. Her touch was ecstasy. Gods, he needed her to be a little quicker. *Yes, faster. Much faster.*

Dae slowed her touch, her soapy fingers inspecting him in deliberate increments. "How amazing, how different we are. Men and women, I mean. This doesn't hurt you?"

Not like you mean. "No," he breathed.

She slid her sponge in a thorough path past the base of his cock while holding him snug in her opposite hand. She swirled soap and water around his taut testicles, the massage all but bringing him to his knees. Fire burned suddenly up his tense thighs and through his gut. The preliminary urge to climax was on him before he could even recognize it. He reacted violently and unexpectedly, grabbing hold of her wrists and jerking them out of the water and to a safe distance into the air.

"Go," he gritted out, struggling to keep control as he ground his teeth down to nubs.

"But . . . did I do something—?"

"*Go!* Leave me!"

He saw her temper flash, a knee-jerk response to her embarrassment. *Damn me to Light, I'm doing the very thing I try to prevent by the classes I teach. Causing shame. Fear. Resentment.*

"Dae, please," he begged her then, the honesty in his torn voice the only thing he could give her.

It quelled her temper a bit, but she still rushed from the bath in obvious upset. She stormed into her bedroom, no doubt wishing she had a door to slam on him.

But Magnus couldn't focus on her as he stumbled for the steps. He couldn't drag himself beyond the top step and fell back gasping for breath as his blood sang with unbearable heat and need. He took himself in hand, trying to squeeze a calm into his urgency, but it was no use. He was stroking in hard, almost savage pulls within seconds, groaning low in his throat as he lay back across the floor and abandoned himself to the inevitable. His climax came roaring through him with a vengeance. His hand clutched his cock in quick jerks as he burst apart, semen jetting in harsh, hard spurts high into the air. He growled in low, pained release, fighting the urge to shout out and risk gaining Dae's attention. He didn't want her to know how damn weak he was. What a hypocrite he felt like. He had sent her away, but it had all been her.

And she hadn't even been trying. She hadn't even realized.

Magnus collapsed into relaxation even as he still felt spasms working through him. He gasped to catch his breath, only then realizing his hip was on fire with pain, the ripping tension of orgasm tearing at Dae's careful stitches. He opened his eyes to look at himself, covered in his own ejaculate and bleeding again.

His attention jerked to the right when he heard the softest sound of movement, and his whole body and mind froze as he stared into wide amber eyes. His heart began to race again as he tried to know what she was thinking. But before he could move or speak, she had disappeared back into her room.

Chapter Six

Oh, boy.

This could be very, very bad.

Or it could be very, very interesting.

Daenaira was still dripping as she paced a small path next to her bed, her arms folded and a lip between her teeth.

Having realized suddenly that she had trotted off obediently, like that proverbial lapdog, Dae had instantly turned back to the bath with a fury, ready to cut stripes up and down his ungrateful, annoying, self-superior hide. She had stopped cold when she had seen him lying sprawled over the tiled floor with his thick, straining cock in his furious hand. It hadn't taken but a few seconds for him to start seizing with his climax, and she had watched with awe and a swift, fiery burn along the nerves beneath her skin as he had shot out an abandoned release that had rained back down onto his body in a wild, wicked pattern of chaos.

She had stood and stared at him in total disbelief. It was the second time in a single day that she had felt an overwhelming rush of sexual arousal. Not bad, she thought, for someone who had never felt it before. Zero to a hundred in two seconds.

What was even more interesting, however, was finding out how much incredible bullshit the head priest of Sanctuary was really full of. Damn him anyway, using her naïveté against her like that! Gods, what an idiot he must think she was! She had fallen for all that "no sex" crap, trying her best to be as neutral as he had said he'd wanted her to be. And it hadn't been easy! Just because she had no practical experience didn't mean she didn't feel things! When she had turned around and found him so amazingly erect, she couldn't help her reaction . . . although she had damn well tried. She had never been so up close and personal before—not voluntarily—and he had made her think it was okay for her to express her curiosity. She had thought that to him, it was just like another class.

Dae's face burned as she realized he had basically just used her to get himself off. A feeling that was confirmed when he suddenly looked at her with guilt stamped clearly in his golden eyes. Well, at least he had the conscience to feel bad about it—although he probably wouldn't have if he hadn't been caught! Gods, and to think she had defended his honor with that nasty little cow Greta! What if it really had been him she'd bent over for that day in the rectory?

She had walked away, her throat tight with disappointment and confusion. She didn't understand. She had believed him. She didn't believe anyone, but she had believed he was going to be different from all of those others.

Well, he was different. Instead of force, he used rules, traditions, circumstances, and her damn stupidity to get what he wanted! Or he snuck around behind a girl's back. Literally!

Then her mind flashed back to the image of his body running stiff with the throes of his orgasm. She'd seen illicit moments of a man's climax as a child, but while it had always looked somewhat painful to her young eyes the way they would groan and thrash and buck, there was also the unmistakable sensation that the man was lost in a moment of pure bliss and release. But seeing Magnus so rigid and agonized, it was almost as if he had been fighting it every step of the way. And for that matter, why make her leave? So she didn't realize what he was up to, or so she didn't realize what she had made him feel?

Daenaira's anger and outrage suddenly ground to a full halt as every moment of the bath replayed in her mind. He had worked so hard to downplay the state of his body. The sound of grinding teeth arrived late to her memory. She had been so fascinated by the shape and feel of his flesh that she had ignored the stressful sound. A sound of restraint. Had he wanted to resist, or just hold back long enough to get rid of her?

Please.

He had all but begged her to obey him, needing her to leave but trying to circumvent her confused anger.

Because he didn't want her to know he desired her so strongly. Light, she realized, he didn't even want himself to know it! He found her pleasing to his eyes, he'd said. Was that all? Was there much more to it than he was letting on? Maybe his denial was more about tricking himself than it was about tricking her.

The thought of being responsible for that kind of reaction in a man as powerful as Magnus just took away her ability to breathe. Still wet and naked, she sat down on the edge of her bed in numb thought, her body humming uncomfortably all of a sudden. She thought about the couple from the classroom and how hard it had been to stop watching them in order to follow her instincts and pursue Magnus. Thank *Drenna* that she had. She might be the worst handmaiden of all time, but she would be damned if her priest was going to get killed inside of a week.

Come to think of it, she was pretty mad at him about all of this. Something really scary was going on in Sanctuary, and he hadn't even seen fit to warn her about it! He wasn't about to convince her that, out of the blue, two trusted priests decide to assault and attempt to rape a handmaiden for no reason and then turn on Magnus!

Magnus's handmaiden.

Oh, great! *Now* she got it! She was Magnus's new toy, and his enemies were trying to undermine him by going after her! Actually, it was a bit of a relief. She had thought for a minute there that she had offended someone before she'd even intended to and brought trouble to Magnus.

Turns out it was the other way around.

Daenaira surged to her feet and marched into the bath. Except for the blood on the floor and the discarded weapons and clothes, there was no sign of Magnus. So she continued straight into his rooms. She saw him sitting on the edge of his bed, just as she had been doing only a few moments ago, wet and naked and mulling over heavy thoughts.

"Do you want to explain a few things to me," she demanded of him, "or are you determined to keep me clueless and stupid?"

Magnus scowled at the accusation and moved to gain his feet, but she jumped forward and pushed him back down.

"Stay there! Gods, you still haven't stopped bleeding! Just . . . sit! Sit and tell me what I need to know! Stop protecting me or whatever it is you think you are doing and just be honest with me! I know you look at me and you see a child of only twenty winters, but you have to believe me when I say I have aged well beyond that in my spirit and in my heart. Give my mind a chance to catch up. My body, too, for that matter. Talk to me before I hit you!"

She knew her frustration was getting the best of her, and she was starting to sound like the whiny child she was trying to convince him that she wasn't, and it just made it all worse. Dae stood close to him, standing between his knees and cupping his face between her hands and making him meet her determined eyes.

"I need you to be honest with me."

Daenaira wasn't expecting to feel his hands shooting up to lock around her biceps. He grabbed her and pivoted, slamming her down onto his bed. She let out a surprised cry and then backed it with a gasp when he followed after her, looming over her and caging her beneath his warrior's body. Her vision filled with the image of flexing, bulging muscles, and then it was wiped away when his mouth suddenly swooped to catch hers.

But shocked as she was, she knew instantly that he was giving her exactly what she had asked for.

Honesty.

She froze, her heart suddenly stopping.

Magnus felt her do so and immediately pulled back. To his surprise, though, her hands shot to his shoulders and held him to her. The mixed signals confused him for a moment, but then he saw the awkward doubt on her face and he quickly understood.

He shifted just a bit, keeping contact with her, but at the most neutral points he could manage with them both being naked. Then he cradled her pretty cheek against his hand and tilted her chin up gently, readying her for his kiss.

"It's okay, *K'yindara*," he said to her softly and soothingly. "Give me your mouth."

"I don't know how," she gasped, her eyes wide with distress. "You know everything anyone has ever done, ever, and I don't even know how to be kissed."

"Everyone has to start somewhere, *K'yindara*. Let's start you off right here." He dipped for her mouth, touching lightly and drawing away. "Relax. Soften your lips. There. Match me, now. Copy my pressure. Yes."

Magnus was convinced he had completely lost all grasp of reality. Was he really thinking he was going to pit three hundred years of sexual education, and two hundred of those years in abstinence, against a girl who couldn't even kiss?

Scratch that, he thought a moment later as her mouth went

truly soft against his when she stopped imitating and switched into instinct. She could kiss. The sudden wave of intent and emotional desire that shimmered through her was a physical change he felt all the way to his bones. And he hadn't even taken a real taste of her yet.

Magnus didn't rush her. He didn't rush himself. He had never grown tired of watching a student blossom and grow, no matter what the topic, but experience couldn't have prepared him for the stark contrast of innocence and canny wisdom that she used to find her way. He drew back, amazed to find that such simple kisses could so arouse him.

"Open your mouth, sweetheart," he whispered as he brushed a kiss over the bridge of her nose and then each cheek.

"I don't like it," she panted in precipitous anxiety, shaking her head. Clearly, she was remembering some sloppy attempt to force a kiss on her.

"*Jei li*, this isn't going to be like that. Give me just two kisses, and if you still don't like it, I will stop."

She was breathing so rapidly, clinging to him so hard. She would be damned before she'd admit to being afraid; he knew that much, but he wouldn't allow her to dismiss anything out of hand just because some pig had groped and blundered with her.

His thumb touched her chin, and he smiled when her lips parted hesitantly. The tension in her jaw was ridiculous, but he wasn't concerned. If he had learned anything in this past hour, it was that she had every instinct she needed to drive a man to distraction, whether she realized it or not. Magnus lowered his head, kissing her in gently increasing increments, but then flicked his tongue against her lips in slow, tiny strokes. She watched him, eyes wide open and unsure, her sharp little mind analyzing when she would call it quits. She was so occupied on that point that she wasn't expecting to feel his fingertips running down the underside of her arm and then down along her side. She gasped softly, opening her mouth wider. Magnus took full advantage.

Daenaira suddenly found herself flooded with the taste and feel of Magnus's tongue. He sought her, stroking softly and slowly again and again until she was quite certain they had gone past more than two kisses. Then again, she was surprised to realize she liked the way it felt to have him filling her mouth in this way. As she relaxed, she thought to mimic him, and to her delight she heard him groan low and soft when her tongue slipped into his mouth and tasted him curiously. His flavor was something so unique, strong and subtle all at once, but it seemed to spin her away from the defined world and make it more acute all at the same time.

"There we go," he encouraged her hotly, his own desire filling the spaces between them so she would feed off of it. "*Drenna*, but you taste good," he said in a rush of heated breath and undisguised want. "I'm so sorry about before, *jei li*. Light and damnation, I'm sorry for this, too. I shouldn't be making love to you." But even as he said what she should take as an insult, he was starting to devour her sweet mouth, filling his hands with fistfuls of her darkly damp hair.

When his mouth trailed down her throat, she gasped out for breath and sank her fingers into his loosened hair. She clenched her fingers hard at the roots, quickly gaining his attention, his golden gaze jolting up to meet her amber one.

"Then don't. Stop now. Let me up."

Magnus went stiller and stiller with each cold dictate she slapped into him, and felt as though ice was spearing through his chest. As he stared down at her, he could see she was glacial with fury, but she was also breathtakingly beautiful. Resisting his weight and no longer soft and pliant beneath him, she looked as if she were ready to kick his ass all over creation.

"Daenaira . . ." he said hesitantly.

"And don't you ever start something with me again unless you are damn sure you are going to commit to it. I'm not some toy you can play with halfheartedly! Get off me!"

Magnus obeyed her command with slow reluctance, moving carefully off her. "I meant no insult to you, Daenaira. I only meant—this is going against every ingrained habit I have! You don't understand how hard and how long I have worked to make Sanctuary what it is! Two hundred years of sacrifice had to have had something to do with that! I can't believe it didn't."

Dae pushed out from under him, getting to her feet angrily. " 'What it is?' You want to know what your precious Sanctuary is?" she growled in threat.

Just like that, deadly danger fell like a cloak over him and he surged to his feet and loomed over her. Through tightly clenched teeth he said, "Don't. You. Dare."

"It's a den of killers and rapists," she hissed, daring and more as she stood toe to toe with him. "*Drenna* only knows what lies in the hearts of some of those treacherous bitches you introduced me to the other night!"

"Shut your mouth!" It was nothing short of an explosion, punctuated by the way he snared her around her throat and all but slammed her back down on the bed. "Three days you are here and you think you can judge? You give no faith, no commitment to me, and you damn well don't listen to half the things I say, and you have the nerve to judge my haven? My world!"

"Your haven tried to kill you an hour ago," she reminded him on the softest rasp of a whisper, her hands locking instinctively around the wrist that constricted around her. Yet he did not hurt her and did not restrict her breathing despite his unmitigated fury. "You give no faith, no commitment, and you *damn well* don't listen to any of the things I say," she rounded back at him. "You demand from me what you won't give! You knew there was danger here, and you lied to me and told me I was safe! You gave me no chance to defend myself, and when those bastards were out there killing you, you gave me no chance to defend you!"

"I don't need defending and I don't need you or your disrespect! *Drenna* forced you down my throat, plagued me until

I could barely function." He let go, and furious gold eyes raked down over her bare skin before his hand plowed down over her breastbone and the center of her body. She tried to maintain her grasp on him, but he easily ignored her resistance until the bend of her wrists forced her to let go. Daenaira tried not to react to the feel of his roughly callused palm as it scraped her every nerve to full attention. "Do you know what the worst of it was?" he demanded, his features a mask of lust and dark anger. "The smell of you." He lowered his nose to her, the tip just barely grazing her skin as his hand continued relentlessly down her belly. "My goddess inundated me with the sweet, sultry scent of you." His eyes closed and she watched with a pounding heart as he took in a deep breath, drawing her scent into him, his expression changing to one of unmitigated need and pleasure. "The sweet cream aroma I can practically taste," he said, the register of his voice hitting rock bottom. "It makes me *want* to taste you. Until I can't think of anything else."

Just then his traveling fingers sank into the black tangle of curls guarding her sex. Daenaira had become so mesmerized by the massive clash of desires and emotions running over him that she hadn't even considered where he would end up. There was a poetic tragedy to the struggle she could see him fighting within himself, but she couldn't let him continue to mess with her already dizzy head any more than he already had. Panting for breath as his stroking fingers sought to continue farther, tickling against her cleft as they burrowed for her heat, she clutched for his shoulders with her nails bared.

"Magnus, stop! You can't keep doing this to me!"

"Why not?" he snapped sharply, his fiery gaze burning up at hers. "You keep doing it to me! *M'gnone*, look at what you do to me!" He shifted against her and she felt the hottest touch of flesh. He was hard and thick with his arousal, that alone stunning and impressive, but the true impact was how he burned against her hip. And once he made contact with her, he couldn't seem to control his need to move in restless pressure against her. He bored his gaze into hers, the lacing of pain in his eyes the only thing that kept her from lashing out in desperate defense. "I know it isn't your fault," he said quickly, a tempest of conflict slashing over his face. "Gods, it's wrong in so many ways to make this about blaming you. I'm not blaming you. I swear to you, I'm not."

His desperation made the sudden slide of hard fingertips against her most intimate flesh come as a blinding shock. Callus-rough and yet so gentle, he slid his finger between the folds of her sex, and the sensation made her hips jerk as though he had struck a match and thrown it against her. Catching fire, her skin exploded in sheets of billowing heat that climbed up through her until her whole body was flushed with it.

"M-Magnus . . ." she choked out, her nails digging into him as uncertainty and fear made her chest ache.

"All I want," he whispered as his mouth lowered to drift in sensuous rubs against her solar plexus, "is a taste, little spitfire. I want to know if you taste as sweet and soft as you smell." His tongue flicked out against her skin, the touch of it like delightful acid as he repeated it for fuller contact. Then he kissed away the moisture he had left behind as he moved farther down her belly.

Dae was numb and overloaded by turns, her brain quickly muddled by too much information and so much sexual awareness it was like lying on the tips of needles. His words of desire and need combined with every virgin caress she experienced to dizzy her until all she could do was breathe in a series of soft, hitching rasps. She shook her head and closed her eyes, trying to break from the strange sexual spell she was swept up in, but it was impossible when he was lazily stroking his fingertip everywhere except just where she needed it most. Wherever that was.

"Magnus, please," she begged him frantically, her fingers finally releasing his skin to catch into his thick hair. "Don't."

She actually felt the bastard smile against her skin, and it made her want to rip his hair out. In a minute. Just one minute . . .

Daenaira felt liquid warmth easing from her body to wet his passing fingertips, and she blushed hotly in embarrassed confusion.

"Yes, baby, that's what I want," he groaned as he felt the viscous proof of her arousal. "There's my treat."

He shifted over her, parting her tense thighs firmly until he could see the beckoning plum of dark, wet tissues. Just looking at her made Magnus realize how agonizingly hard he was for her. *Drenna*, he'd just climaxed not fifteen minutes ago and already he felt like it had been forever. As he anticipated his little sweet feast, it only became more intense. A wild urge to connect with her beat through him like a massive drum. Not just plunge into her, but *connect*. Link himself to her. Join. *Yes*. Join. He needed to join his very spirit to hers, via the moist little sheath waiting so innocently for him. Just the thought brought him to the edge of climax, his cock dripping in anticipation of it. Never had he reacted so strongly to a woman. It was embarrassingly out of control, almost juvenile to a man of his age and skill.

Magnus had avoided her budded clitoris on purpose, wanting the first touch to be the one that had all but driven him mad inside his ruthless visions. The touch of his tongue. The smell of her arousal was overwhelming, that heady, sweet lure that made his head spin and the feminine purity of musk that used every pheromonal trick in the book to snare him. He looked up her body to see her liquid amber eyes.

"Don't," she whispered almost soundlessly.

Her fear struck at him so hard it left a stinging flavor of distaste across his tongue. Stunned to realize she was in such a different space than he was, Magnus went still. He shook his head, trying desperately to shed the spell possessing him so mindlessly, but with the scent of her pervading him it was a losing battle.

"I won't hurt you," he said hoarsely.

"How can I believe that?" she asked as her hands shook within his hair. "How can I believe anything you say when you never tell me the truth?"

"I never lied to you!"

"You never tell me the truth," she echoed numbly. "I only get to feel it in sharp stabbing moments when you use sex against me."

"Against you?" Magnus surged up her body, his hands beside her shoulders caging her as he braced himself over her. "I'm not using sex against you! This isn't a battle, *jei li*! These are not tactics!"

"Don't you call me that! Don't you dare call me that. Nothing you have done has given you the right to call me *jei li*! You use me and make me feel things . . . You confuse me and hurt me and you think I am just going to give in to you and let you master my existence any way you please. Well, I won't! I am not your goddamn slave!"

Magnus jerked back away from her as if from a punch. He lurched off the bed, grabbing hold of her arm and dragging her to her feet as well. He shoved her toward the door joining their rooms so hard that she stumbled.

"Go then!" he spat at her. "Do not lie here and take my unkind abuses any longer, little girl. Run away and hide like the child you are."

Daenaira felt the sting of the insult lashing viciously across her back.

Just like the nine-tailed cat.

With her chest aching and eyes burning with emotions she refused to feel, never mind show to him, she moved to leave.

"Dae . . ."

She couldn't help herself. She had to stop when she heard the plain hurt and confusion in his voice. Her chin held high, she turned to look at him over her shoulder. She chilled herself to the vulnerability in his eyes, however. She wouldn't be tricked by it again.

"You think you are so superior to my aunt and my uncle," she said hoarsely, knowing she was doing what she had always done best. Going violently for his balls. "But you're so much worse. At least they were honest. At least they never fucked with my head by pretending to be anything other than the monsters they were."

Daenaira turned her back on him and left.

Daenaira left Sanctuary.

Not for good. Not that she knew of yet. She just needed to leave the cloistered environment and find space to breathe different air. She didn't go very far before she saw someone she realized she recognized. He wore the uniform of a royal guard, but she had no idea how she would know someone like that. The idea that she couldn't remember his face both mystified and irritated her.

He was chatting casually with another man as she watched him from a distance and tried to figure out where she knew him from. He had an easy smile, warm and friendly eyes, and a straight tousle of dark brown hair that was cut much shorter than most men around him; the only exception was the man he was talking to, whose jet locks were trimmed tightly to the back of his neck, though it was a little longer where it fell in feathered layers against his temples.

She looked back at the guard whose lean athleticism tickled her memory as he leaned back against a stone outcropping. He was an animated talker, his whole body moving as he related a tale to his amused audience. Finally, curiosity got the best of her and she boldly walked up to both men. The story stopped cold when the guard caught sight of her approaching him, and he glanced at his companion before letting a wolfish smile cross his features.

"Excuse me, but don't I know you from somewhere?" she asked directly.

"Uh, I don't know, honey. Do you?"

"I think so. I was just trying to place you."

He shrugged. "Probably around the palace or something. I think if we'd met, I would remember you." He slowly let his eyes roam over her figure in the *k'jeet* she was wearing quite openly in public. Women only wore such things in the privacy of their homes. They were provocative, the way they were held to the body with only two ties beneath the breasts and one in between. That was to say nothing of the fact that, even though the material was a deep scarlet, it was quite sheer. Also, tradition dictated that no undergarments were worn when a woman wore a *k'jeet*. She was as good as naked as far as he was concerned, and his smile grew. He was used to women coming on to him in all manner of ways, but he had to admit this was pretty bold, especially considering whom he was standing with.

"I've never been to the palace," she said with a shake of her head that made her unusual hair shimmer with color. The funny thing was, she looked very serious as she made a show of racking her brain.

Daenaira was entirely serious, of course. She had worn the *k'jeet* because it was the only thing she owned besides her now-ruined sari. Since walking around butt-naked was the only alternative, this was the least provocative choice.

"What's your name?" she asked him, hoping it would help.

"Killian," he responded with amusement. She really was quite a little actress, the guard thought.

"Oh." Then he watched her color pale right before she flushed and her eyes grew large. "Oh! Oh, okay. Thank you. I'm sorry I interrupted," she said hastily, retreating from the men quickly.

Killian looked at Trace and blinked.

"What in burning Light was *that*?" he demanded.

Trace held up his hands. "Don't look at me, friend. I just stand here basking in the glory of your manly charms." The vizier chuckled when Killian scowled at him.

"Tell me she wasn't just trying to pick me up," he demanded

of his friend. "She was, right? I mean, who in Darkness doesn't know who I am? That's almost as bad as asking who Tristan is!"

"I'm sure there are people who don't know you. You aren't as memorable as most," Trace dug at him.

"Keep it up, smart-ass. I'll tell your wife you've been making up excuses to avoid her."

Trace didn't find that funny in the least. So, in retaliation, he decided to do something he never did.

He gave out bad advice.

"Well, if you're so convinced of her intentions, you better go after her. She's probably waiting for you to follow her. You know how women like to be chased."

"Yeah." Killian licked his lips as he stared after the shapely figure moving quickly away from him. "Damn, I swear there's something in the water lately. I just left Diana a little while ago." He grinned at Trace. "We did a class. She completely gets off on being watched. She kept having these silent little orgasms every time someone asked a question. Do you have any idea how that tests a man's sanity? I had to keep completely still sometimes and she would be milking me relentlessly. *M'gnone,* it was Light. I was so damn glad when Magnus was called away unexpectedly." Killian looked back to his new feminine target. "Say hi to Ashla for me, okay?"

Trace nodded. After listening to Killian's rather lustful description of Diana, Trace was more concerned with finding his wife and saying a hearty hi for himself. But first, he very much needed to witness the crash and burn of his cocksure friend.

Daenaira was so embarrassed she could hardly see straight. *He was the model from the class!* The minute she had heard the name, she had gotten a perfect recollection of whipcord strength in taut nude skin and an impressive erection that had made his partner moan quite loudly. She had had more than enough sex lessons for one day, thanks, she thought with heat as she pressed chilled fingertips to her cheek. She should have realized! The only others she had met were priests and handmaidens!

A few minutes later, she heard a hurried step coming up behind her just before he grabbed her arm and drew her to a stop.

"Hey, baby, where are you rushing off to?"

She turned at the inviting rumble of the male voice, a frown darkening her features when she saw Killian.

"Please remove your hand," she said coldly, glancing down at his offensive touch. After everything that kept happening, she wasn't about to let anyone touch her without her permission. Not anymore, damn it.

He released her, smiling with obvious charm as he moved a couple of steps around her and touched her shoulder with the back of his knuckles in a long, slow caress.

"Were you going to tell me how you know me?" Killian asked her, his dark eyes full of his amusement.

"If I had intended to, I would have. However, I did not. I thought the walking away part would have made that clear. Silly me." Dae struck the palm of her opposite hand hard against the inside of his wrist, harshly knocking his touch from her body. She stepped back to brace her balance, her knees flexing automatically.

Killian gaped at her as she took a defensive stance. Then he laughed. He couldn't help it. She was too cute. All sexy curves, youth, and an overblown attitude. Trying to be aggressive toward the head of city security! All this while dressed in her nightie! And she didn't like him laughing at her, if he read those narrowing eyes right.

"Come on. Don't be like that. Where do you know me from?" he asked playfully. "I'm not letting you pass until you tell me."

"You think you're going to stop me?" She snorted so cuttingly he had the urge to wince. "Trust me, you shouldn't test that theory."

"Okay, let me get this straight. You are standing there

copping an attitude with a top-level security officer and threatening him while—and this is the part I love—in a dress the consistency of tissue paper?" He leaned forward with a cocky little grin. "I could reach up and pull that thing off you, leaving you butt naked in front of the entire city, and then you'd be begging me for my protection, hiding behind me and clinging to me like a vine."

Daenaira looked down at the dress in question and then back at the guard. She reached down for the skirt at her hip, grabbed the fabric, and tore a hole in it.

"Hmm. Pretty flimsy," she agreed, her amber eyes flashing as she tore the skirt completely down to the hem, snapping it in two and leaving herself with a ragged slit up the entire length of her leg. She turned her hip outward toward him, making a show of inspecting the damage that draped the smooth length of her very long limb. Killian's eyes dropped like metal to a powerful magnet. The guard completely missed what Trace could see from behind them. She settled her weight back on her opposite foot, her strength coiling fast and tight, and the vizier winced in sympathy for his friend even before she moved.

Dae whipped her leg up and snapped her shin hard against the arrogant jerk's cheek, not bothering to pull the strike in the least. The guard went spinning down to the ground hard and fast, laid out in a single shot as he had stood unprepared for her attack and the strength behind it.

"Holy Light," Trace swore. Too late the vizier realized some of Killian's coworkers had been watching his antics, and the instant the girl attacked, they lunged for her. It was their job, after all, to stop aggressions, fights, and anyone who attacked anyone policing the city. Trace realized how ugly this could get and quickly rushed forward. Not fast enough by far as she punched one guard in his teeth and in the same back movement elbowed another in his eye. She'd stunned three good fighters in three seconds, and he stumbled when she ruthlessly caught the next one between his legs with such brutal force he could see the man's feet lift off the ground.

Trace was still recovering his balance when he saw his father appear out of nowhere, grabbing the hellion by the arm and barely jerking back in time to let her fist blow past his cheek. Then, as if they were dancing, he spun the woman around by her arm in a full pivot, just about 360 degrees, her torn dress spinning tightly against her legs. It was an attempt to throw her off balance and to disorient her, but she recovered with remarkable alacrity, turning on his father with such a rush of savagery that, for the first time, Trace doubted his father's ability to meet her without injury even though she was, as yet, unarmed!

"Dae!" Magnus shouted the word in her face, plucking her out of the air as she rushed him. He forced her to look at him and shook her as he yelled at her again. "Dae! Stop!"

And, she did. Like an animated toy suddenly reaching the end of its pulled string, she stopped and blinked at the priest as if she were waking up from a nap. Trace ran up on them, still gripping his katana anxiously. The world reeled a little farther on its axis for him when he saw his father drag the little savage up against himself and caught steady hold of her lips against his own.

Daenaira had seen nothing but red from the instant she'd struck Killian. Everything else had blurred and spun into a cloud of rage and fury until familiar hands had caught her and a hard voice whipped her to attention. Then he was kissing her gently, like he had no right to do after he had treated her so badly. But the beautiful red anger melted away from her and left her hollow and alone to face the pure tenderness of his kiss. She tried to call it back, swinging a fist into his shoulder and punching him hard, but he only pulled her closer and made her melt like softened butter against him. She hit him with her other fist, although there was no power to it as weakness washed through her until she could barely stand on her own. Her chest burned with pain and betrayal, with lies and abuse, with the weakness of emotions she had never needed before and damn well didn't want now.

Magnus lifted from her trembling mouth just far enough to whisper, "I'm sorry. I'm so sorry."

Trace was trying to absorb the shockingly incongruous picture of his father the *priest* kissing a woman off the street as if he were her lover. His father would never break temple law! There was only one woman with whom he could be intimate. Religious law demanded it. As he represented the goddess, the handmaiden represented the god. Only these two divine forces could be a match to one another. His Darkness to her Light, his serenity to her fire. He was safe and steady, a constant and natural state, and she was wild and unpredictable and disruptive. She was . . .

"Holy Light," Trace whispered.

She was his handmaiden.

Trace stared at the inconceivable image for a long, unflinching minute. This little dervish of fury was his father's new handmaiden? This was the woman he was sleeping so close to every night? This woman was the creature Magnus was going to try to trust in the wake of the disaster with Karri?

Even more shocking, if there was such a thing, he was actually being intimate with her? Karri had turned on Magnus, striking him down with a hissing vengeance, because his father had not shown her any passion in all of their time together. She had confessed to that just before dying, slapping Magnus's private existence out in the open for all to see. Was his father doing this now so that he didn't find himself with another viper at his breast? It wasn't like his father to change who he was and what his convictions were out of fear. No. He would be the last to ever do such a thing.

Trace was at a loss. The one thing that was perfectly clear to him, however, was that he absolutely didn't like this woman near his father. He'd already come too close to losing the man who had raised him, the only man he loved more than he loved his monarch, and he was infinitely loyal to Tristan both heart and soul.

Daenaira was going to cry. Damn him! It *wasn't* okay! He couldn't just kiss her and make her melt and think that was going to make everything all better! She was too exhausted and too upset to deal with any of this right now. She never cried and she wasn't going to start now!

"No, honey, don't," he coaxed softly as he brushed tender fingers across her face so sweetly it made her ache inside. "Don't leave me. I know. I know I'm destroying everything, doing it all wrong, but please . . . don't go from me."

"Why? You don't need me, remember?" she flung back at him, gritting her teeth when his eyes flickered with an almost imperceptible flinch. "You don't want me. I was forced down your throat."

"*Drenna,* stop!" Magnus wrenched out, forcing her to stop by covering her mouth with his own. He couldn't stand to hear the cruel things he had said to her, even though he knew he deserved the pain of it and more. Penance. He deserved the harshest penance for what he had wrought today. "Hate me, if you will, but do not leave. Make me repent to you, sweet *K'yindara.* Make me earn back what I want to deserve. It doesn't have to be anything more than your friendship in the end if that's all you want to give, but I'm begging you not to leave me without giving me the chance to fix this mess I've made."

The one thing that made her hesitate, besides the incredible desperation she felt radiating off him, was that she knew in her soul how intensely private a man Magnus was. But he hadn't dragged her off to Sanctuary and asked her behind closed doors to forgive him. He was humbling himself in public to her, even though her actions had drawn a curious crowd.

She bit her lip with heavy doubt. She didn't trust him. He would be so sweet, and then suddenly he would be hurtful and cruel. How stupid would she have to be to think that would change? Was she some kind of glutton for punishment just to be thinking about it?

"Let go of me." She said it on a whisper, but it was cool and clear as she was looking into his golden gaze. "And this time you never, ever touch me without my permission, or I will break your fingers."

In silent agreement, Magnus released her, letting her step free. He looked up to see the crowd around them and found himself staring dead into his son's troubled eyes. Breaking the contact quickly, Magnus turned to reach a helping hand toward Killian, who was stunned and more than a little embarrassed as he staggered to his feet.

"What the *fuck* was that?" he demanded furiously. He made as if to approach Daenaira, but Magnus's hard, immovable hand in the center of his chest stopped him cold.

"I believe *K'yan* Daenaira was merely expressing her feelings about being touched by strangers," Magnus said pointedly.

"K'yan?" Killian paled under his racial coloring, his eyes darting from the sexy little spitfire standing half naked in public, and back to the priest. This meant that Killian had unwittingly put his hands on a holy woman. He had also taunted and flirted with her with no show of respect for her position in the eyes of the gods. "Magnus, she never said a word! I had no idea. I would never do that!" Then the guard swallowed hard as he realized something else, his brain a bit slower after being kicked around inside his head. "She's yours?"

Bad enough to disrespect a handmaiden; worse to disrespect the handmaiden of the most powerful man in the temple. Whichever way it was looked at, it was a punishable offense. It didn't matter whether she had identified herself or not. Even the plainest woman should be able to walk the street without feeling threatened or accosted. Killian had stepped over the line and he knew it.

There would be penance to pay.

Trace flinched at the embarrassment and horror of Killian's predicament, acknowledging his part in the whole mess and feeling damn guilty about it. He had expected Killian would be assertive, maybe get snubbed or, at worst, smacked across his face before his target stormed off in a huff, but he had never expected this.

"Magnus, this is just a really bad misunderstanding." He spoke up, feeling terrible for goading his friend.

"Yes," the priest said with flat cool. "One that got physical. Would your friend care to repeat what he said that made Daenaira feel she had to hit him?"

Killian flushed with a dreadful guilt, his gaze jolting to Dae's and clearly begging her not to repeat it in the open. It soundly confirmed what Magnus had already known with utter confidence; he knew Dae wouldn't ever hurt someone without good cause. She had been the target of too much senseless violence to randomly dispense it herself. Magnus had no doubt Killian had deserved what he got. The trouble had come when Daenaira hadn't been able to stop. She hadn't been able to halt her actions, step back, raise her hands, and explain her measures reasonably to the other guards.

Daenaira, Magnus realized, had the fighting instincts of a berserker. For her, once battle began, it didn't stop until she no longer felt threatened. This, Magnus understood, was the heart of her third power. Every Shadowdweller could blend in with and skip across connecting shadows, and every 'Dweller could Fade, but sometimes a Shadowdweller was born with an uncanny third power. An example was his ability to compel truth from others. Or his son's impressive ability to skip shadows that weren't even connected; a line-of-sight teleportation between patches of darkness.

Every priest and handmaiden had a third power. Those who were born with a third power often became one or the other. When they didn't choose religion or get chosen by it, they tended to become very powerful people in their world. Magnus had wondered what her power would be, and he hadn't had the chance to ask her if she even knew what it was. If this wrathful power of combat could be tempered, he thought, it would mean *Drenna* had sent him an amazing gift. A woman and a weapon, both of which would be invaluable at his side as he executed his tasks as a penance priest. The trick, though, was figuring out how to control her. How, as a weapons smith, could he shape her into something as beautiful and deadly as he knew she could be? How could he counter the cold rage that was inside a woman who trusted no one and believed in nothing?

Magnus closed his eyes briefly as the painful understanding struck him. *Drenna* had not sent her to him because he had needed her; She had sent her because Daenaira had needed him. Darkness had entrusted this raw and unique creature to him so he could use the kindness, patience, and wisdom he was renowned for to help her. But, still bitter and damaged from Karri, he had failed to serve her as he had been expected to.

Daenaira took pity on Killian, although she didn't express it as such. She sharply turned away from the gathering and strode back toward Sanctuary.

"I think we're done here. Killian," Magnus said distinctly, "I will see you tomorrow an hour past daybreak."

There was no need to say anything more. Everyone knew what that tone and that appointment meant. To his credit, Killian took comfort in knowing he could compensate for his mistakes. He touched his hand to his heart and gave Magnus a respectful bow.

Chapter Seven

Seven nights.

He hadn't touched her in seven nights.

Magnus paced the privacy of his office with stiff steps, his usual smooth ease of movement nowhere to be found as tension racked his body so tightly he was astounded his bones didn't snap. He had stripped off his weapons belt and thrown it over the back of a chair, his beloved katana hanging almost sadly in a sheath it wasn't meant to be in. The wood of the previous one had warped, as he had expected, and he wasn't about to put his fine blade in an imperfect sheath. However, the new one was plain and serviceable, not fully suited to the magnificence of the katana. Every time he looked at the thing, he wanted to seek out its now-warped companion and set it to the impertinent backside of the woman who had destroyed it, just as he had promised he would.

At least it would be an excuse to touch her.

Magnus groaned as he came up on his desk. He set his fists on the marble surface and leaned his weight on locked arms, hanging his head in an attempt to stretch out the knot that seemed permanently wrapped around his neck and tied into place between his shoulders.

He was obsessed.

Like the fabled fox staring with pathetic longing at the unattainable grapes, he was craving the impossible. The fact of it was he had fouled up so badly that there was no compensating for it. There was no penance. He had never thought he would ever be capable of something like that, but he had been. Worse, he feared it went to a depth that also included Karri. He couldn't have been wrong about that sweet, adoring nature for two whole centuries. She had borne his rejections and her loneliness one too many times, and someone had taken advantage of that. So soft-spoken and accommodating, Karri had never thought to rail at him as she had become angry and, eventually, felt betrayed by his coldness toward her when she had so clearly needed more. She had been ripe for the plucking, a crafty thief taking the opportunity to steal away her loyalties by inciting her anger and keeping her wounded pride sliced wide open and bleeding.

And Magnus had done nothing to stand in the way of it. He had remained ignorant up until the instant he had collapsed from the poison coursing through his veins. Her aborted seduction that day, he believed now, had been her last attempt at salvaging what she had already thrown into the fire. But as much as he had cared for her, it had always been as a brother to a kid sister. He could have blamed it on the differences in their ages and the fact that she had become his handmaiden when his son had been the exact same age as she was, but the truth was there simply had not been that kind of chemistry.

Now he had chemistry in spades.

Damn it to Light.

The only time Daenaira let him come close to her was during fight training. Gods, the girl was crazy about fight training. He'd finally found a way to make her happy, and she was eating up every single minute of it ever since he had insisted she start. But she took the classes and battled her partners and, although he taught her how to stand and how to move, she wouldn't allow him to touch her. Gods! She even let Killian touch her! She had grown to like the guard she now affectionately referred to as a horse's ass, somehow making him laugh in agreement every time; this in spite of the severity of the penance Magnus had made him pay for his insolence. The priest had asked Daenaira to clarify what had set her off, for the sake of measuring Killian's punishment. When she had quietly and dispassionately told him that Killian had threatened to strip her in public, Magnus had quickly excused himself.

Then, rather than seeking Killian out and killing him in twenty different ways, he had promptly challenged Sagan to a practice session.

Sagan was uninterested in any power that didn't come from his own body or the physical skills of another, which was why Magnus found him more trustworthy than most. Unlike Shiloh, who was constantly jockeying for Magnus's position or the placement of heir to that position, Sagan wanted only to bring justice to Sinners and penance to those in need of it. Otherwise, he wanted to work his body and skills to the wall, and would tear through a chain of sparring partners every single day in the process. When Magnus had approached him, his smile had been positively feral with his acceptance of the challenge.

They had made a regular appointment of it every day since.

Sagan was probably aware that Magnus was purging demons. He was perhaps even aware that he was purging one redheaded demon in specific. However, to his credit, he never once brought up a personal question about it. That was something else he liked about the other priest. Sagan disliked people nosing into his business, especially as pertained to his lack of a handmaiden, so he never gave anyone cause to go tit for tat with him on personal matters. He kept the door firmly shut, minding his own business. It was exactly what Magnus needed.

Well, not *exactly*.

Exactly what he needed was to take a little spitfire in hand and prove to her it was worth her while to give him another chance.

However, he didn't see himself being very successful at that if he couldn't even manage to keep himself sane after only a week of getting a very cold shoulder from her. How in Light was this ever going to work? Her role with him was supposed to help ease his existence, not tangle it up into knots! And how was she going to carry out half her duties if she was determined not to come near him? Gods, how was he going to even train her for them?

But the clever minx was already a step ahead of him, it seemed. She had ferreted out two handmaidens to spend her time with when she wasn't in classes. Hera was one of them. Like the queenly goddess she was named after, Hera had the experience and wisdom to guide Dae in every way possible. She also had a certain cunning to her that, quite frankly, Daenaira had plenty of already. She hardly needed further lessons in that curriculum.

Dae's second choice had been a bit more enigmatic. She had chosen to befriend the recently shamed and outcast Tiana, M'jan Cort's handmaiden. The shocking defection of Cort's loyalties against Magnus had thrown suspicion on his handmaiden, and forgiveness had been in short supply in the temple. Even Magnus confessed he was wary when Dae spent time alone with the seemingly unfortunate girl Cort had left behind. She had always seemed sweet and unassuming, but then again, so had Karri. What if she was really a part of the bigger picture of deception? Magnus wanted to think the disease of corruption had been eradicated along with Cort and Daniel, but he knew bone deep that this was not the case.

So for the most part, Daenaira had begun to settle in quite nicely.

Everywhere else.

Magnus, however, was still quite firmly in the doghouse. And he had started to dream again.

Visions. Half of them confusing images of fear and violence, a sense of horrible loss that woke him in a cold sweat. The other half of them soaked with lust and need, the scent of sweet cream, and the heat of wet divinity clutching around his fingers, his tongue, and his cock. When he woke from these dreams he was shaking, but he was anything but cold. His body would be screaming in an agony of demand. He had quickly learned not to take relief by his own hand because it only seemed to make matters worse. If he did that, he would fall asleep and it would begin all over again. If he suffered through it, he would remain awake, but he could eventually calm himself and distract himself with the work of daily living.

Yet she slept peacefully for, no doubt, the first time in years. Knowing that, he could not bring himself to begrudge her well-deserved rest. He had even begun to accept *Drenna*'s messages as a comeuppance equally well deserved. He had apparently been in need of some humility, because he seemed to be getting it in large doses of late. No doubt it was in answer to his having allowed the house of the gods to swing so far out into the land of corrupt behavior.

He wanted to fix this mess. The temple. All of Sanctuary. And most of all, he wanted to fix things between himself and Daenaira. He wished he could say it was purely lust and physical need that drove this desire, something a great deal of frantic and passionate lovemaking could sate and satisfy, but despite all of the torturous dreams in his sleep, it was her pain and accusatory anger toward him that was destroying him. Knowing he had thrown away her offer to relearn trust together was a wound on his conscience and his soul.

Magnus's thoughts were interrupted by a tapping at his door. He straightened, taking a deep breath and trying to find a relaxed stance.

"Come."

He knew the minute he saw his son enter the room that things were not about to get any better, so he sighed.

"Trace," he warned.

Trace had darkened his doorstep every single night for the past week, making his feelings about Daenaira repetitively known. He didn't trust her. He dreaded her having free access to Magnus's throat as he slept. He felt she was damaged and unstable. Magnus had bordered on reminding him that both he and his new bride had both matched those descriptors until recently. Trace had suffered nearly a year of torture at the hands of a vicious and deadly woman named Acadian, after he had been taken prisoner during the wars. It had taken all of the years since for him to finally fully recover, the last step only taking place when he had met Ashla. Ashla herself was plagued with memories of a twisted parent who had raised her to believe she was a devil, when in fact she had been the product of her human mother's illicit affair with a Shadowdweller male. It had taken Trace's kindred spirit to help guide her to a new life with the other half of her heritage. Together they had taken broken pieces and glued them into a whole.

Trace was, unfortunately, still very prejudiced toward women. He had difficulty trusting them, and Karri's deceptions had not helped matters. After seeing Daenaira's viciousness in a fight, and still shaken by Magnus's poisoning, Trace had become determined to convince his father to shed the danger she represented.

"Trace, go home. Go home to your wife and your king, both of whom need your advice far more than I do," he said wearily. Magnus sat down behind his desk as dismissively as possible.

"M'jan, I need you to come to the palace."

Magnus looked up at his son quickly, the tension he heard in his voice raising every kind of alarm.

"What is it?"

"I wish I could tell you. Tristan calls for you but will not tell me why. Malaya is beside herself with worry for her brother. She knows it is not like him to turn to his religion to solve his troubles. Yet Tristan has demanded you come to him. He will not exit his rooms, nor will he let anyone else but Xenia attend him."

Magnus was already on his feet, snaring his katana as he passed. "I have to fetch Dae."

Trace stopped short from following him out. "Her? What for?"

Magnus turned slowly back to his son, his eyes narrowing to warn Trace that his disrespectful tone was treading on dangerous ground. "Tristan calls for his priest. She is my handmaiden. Where I go, she goes. Having been raised in Sanctuary, you know this."

Of course he did. They both were well aware of that. Magnus was only reiterating it to give his son opportunity to rectify his manner.

"Yes, M'jan," he said quietly, respectful, albeit not pleased about it.

Content, Magnus turned back to the corridor and hurried to find his handmaiden. She had been practicing in the training hall, but she should be in her religious instruction class at present. Magnus turned into the education section of the building and found Hera's lecture hall. He walked into the room, stopping short in surprise when the room was empty, save for Hera herself.

"Greetings, M'jan. How may I help you?"

"I'm sorry, *K'yan*, I thought you were holding class now. I was looking for Daenaira."

K'yan Hera stood up behind her desk very slowly, meeting his gaze as she straightened her spine. Magnus felt the bottom drop out of his stomach as instinct told him he wasn't going to like what he was about to hear.

"I do not have a class at this time, M'jan. Dae has been taking private instruction from me for her religious studies at a different time."

"I see," he said carefully.

She had lied to him. Every day she had attended practice

and then, she had said, religious instruction. It had never once occurred to him to second-guess her, and since he was not in charge of the class scheduling, he hadn't realized there was no class.

"Thank you, *K'yan*."

Magnus turned to go, but at the last moment he caught sight of Hera clasping one hand nervously in the other. The woman was steady as a rock. A tell like that was not like her. Magnus turned back.

"Something you would like to share, *K'yan*?" He offered her an opportunity.

She sighed. "Please, don't be angry, M'jan Magnus. Dae-naira meant no harm."

"*K'yan*, my patience and my time are growing short," he warned her.

"She is . . . on the first floor in the relations lecture."

"She's . . . *where*?"

Magnus didn't need a repeat; he was just so shocked and furious that he couldn't contain his reaction. *The relations lecture*. The early-hours version of *his* sexual intercourse lecture! Except Brendan was the instructor for that session.

Magnus was in the hallway in an explosive instant.

"Trace, go to Tristan and tell him I will be there within the hour," he instructed sharply. Whatever happened next, he didn't need his foster child looking on in cold disapproval.

Trace was well aware he was being dismissed, and he wasn't happy about it, but he figured that he was superfluous at this point. Apparently, Daenaira was busy digging her own hole and didn't need any help from him.

Magnus ran down to the second floor and spied the glass dome leading down into the main lecture hall. There were two students standing there watching the lecture below. He strode up to the rail and looked down, wanting to get a look at the layout so he knew right where to retrieve her. The way his temper was brewing, he didn't want to be in that room any longer than he had to be. He didn't need any witnesses to his anger.

What he saw brought a swift and murderous end to that intention.

"Bituth amec!" he spat, startling both students.

Daenaira was lying on the thrice-damned bed!

Her sari had been removed, leaving her in her velvet blouse and the thin underskirt. She was sprawled over the bed on her belly, her cheek resting on her folded hands and her unbound hair streaming down her shoulders and back. She had her eyes closed and was smiling like a contented cat. Magnus felt his heart seizing as he raced to fill in the blanks as to what would cause the appearance of the sly smile he hadn't seen so much as a glimpse of in seven damn days. He gripped the railing, the wood creaking under the strain of his growing wrath.

"Okay then. We have our willing participant." Brendan's voice carried up to him. Magnus watched as the younger man moved up to the bed and slowly began to survey and circle his prey. His *willing* prey. "Men," he continued, "are inherently visual creatures. It's pretty much a constant across the races. We can become aroused by just the sight of a beautiful woman lying in our beds, waiting."

Brendan grinned when Dae lifted her head to stick her tongue out at him. The rest of the class snickered at the teasing interplay. The priest moved to kneel on the bed with one knee, indicating the woman before him.

"Women are different creatures entirely. They are more cerebral and, by far, more tactile."

If he touches her, I'm going to fucking kill him.

Magnus became aware he was being watched and he jerked his head to meet the stares of the students. "Get to class!" he snarled at them.

"But, M'jan, we don't have—"

"I suggest you find one!"

Without further argument, they beat a very hasty retreat, allowing Magnus to look back into the room below. He should be running. He should rip the doors off that room and tear her off that bed—or better yet, he should make her scream in pleasure for the next three lectures! If she wanted to play the role of a sexual model, he'd be damn happy to oblige her!

"Now, I look at Daenaira and I can see what I like, and just like that"—Brendan snapped his fingers—"we have achieved foreplay for a man." It was said tongue-in-cheek, and the class laughed. Magnus, however, was not amused. "But guys, we have to rewind. Our ladies do not warm up so quickly. So what I recommend is that you very slowly consider each of those visual things you enjoy, and brainstorm on how to turn it into what I like to call a tactile tactical advantage. And please, for the time being, let's eliminate our obvious favorites: the right, the left, and the in-between." Brendan flirted with death as he made gestured references to each of her breasts and her sex. "Let's start with the reason I picked Dae, since she has such a gorgeous asset."

Now Magnus ran.

Brendan withdrew the wooden hairbrush from his pocket and absently ran the boar's hair bristles across his palm.

"We tend to forget what a sexual organ hair can be. Well, technically the organ is skin. The scalp is loaded with nerve endings and has an incredibly high concentration of blood vessels. Of course, if our Dae was a Lycanthrope female, hair brushing could conceivably be the equivalent of tonguing her across her clitoris, because their hair has both live blood vessels and nerves in each strand. She won't be quite that sensitive, but you have to imagine that she is. With every stroke of the brush, you have to liken it to a very intimate massage. If I do this right, my partner will come out of this feeling both relaxed and stimulated, not to mention thinking I am quite the considerate lover." Brendan reached out to touch the vibrant red hair that was waiting for him.

"Brendan."

A single word, his very own name, had never sounded so dreadful to the young priest before. He went perfectly still, only his eyes flicking up to look at Magnus. The penance priest stood on the main runner into the classroom, his feet braced hard apart, his expression a perfect, flat calm, and his breath coming quick as the click of the closing door finally announced his arrival. His hands hung loose and open at his sides.

But even if Brendan had been a far denser man, there was no mistaking the dark gold flames of possession and rage within his hard eyes.

Brendan slowly drew back even as he felt Daenaira lift her head to look at Magnus. He knew she wasn't any less observant than he was, so when she put her cheek back down on her hands and waited patiently for him to continue, Bren knew she was purposely baiting the senior priest. Feeling like an animal caught in the crossfire of a war, Brendan hesitated.

"M'jan Magnus," he said at last, quickly clearing the altered pitch from his throat. "I was borrowing your handmaiden for my lesson in tactile perception." He eased off the bed and held out his hand with the brush in it like a man surrendering a weapon. "She has such uniquely beautiful hair, as you know."

Magnus was silent as the grave.

"But perhaps now that you're here," Brendan said quickly, "you can take over the demonstration while I continue my lecture."

Brendan saw Dae's head snap up, and at the exact same moment he saw a very predatory smile draw over his mentor's lips.

Permission to touch.

She had given it to Brendan, and Brendan had just passed it to Magnus. For a blood-rushing instant of triumph, Magnus could have kissed his young friend. He just hoped that the gods and Tristan would understand being made to wait for a few extra minutes. This was an opportunity he simply could not pass up. Dae couldn't back out of playing model without airing their grievances in front of students, and he knew she would not disrespect him like that.

"I would be happy to," he said, trying not to sound as eager as he was. He came forward to take the brush from Brendan, looking down into simmering eyes of amber. He was cheating and he knew it. What was more, *she* knew it. Trapped on the spot, and hoping she was unwilling to deny him publicly, he tried to give her the opportunity to speak her permission just the same. "Provided Dae doesn't mind."

She gave her permission silently, laying her cheek back down and simply turning her gaze to one of the far walls, passing on the opportunity to deny him. He took the brush and leaned very close to Brendan before asking, "Did you explain the rules to her before you invited her up?"

Brendan looked a bit startled. As Magnus had suspected, Brendan had seen no reason to explain rules that everyone entering his lecture was supposed to already know. He hadn't questioned a handmaiden's casual appearance in his classroom, nor had he considered a grown woman wouldn't already have all of her preliminary education.

The rule of the room was simple. If you sensually touched the major erogenous zones on yourself or your partner, you were required to continue your display for the benefit of the students until you were through. Autoeroticism included. It wasn't unheard of at all for a priest and handmaiden to model for a lecture together or alone.

A simple touch could have landed his Dae in something she was not ready for. Light, he didn't even know if she engaged in masturbatory play in private. She could have ended up learning with a classroom of strangers looking on.

And *Brendan* would have been the one teaching her.

The thought made him glare at Bren with unconcealed temper and the burn of uncontrollable jealousy. Even though it hadn't happened, the idea of how naïve she had been and of how a male might have taken advantage of that, drove him out of his mind. No one, he thought fiercely, was going to teach her a damn thing except for *him*. That she was even in this classroom at all made him crazy, though he didn't understand entirely why. She had a right to learn whatever she wanted to learn.

But she will learn it from me!

Magnus moved up to the bed, looking down on the comfortable sprawl of her amazing curves. The gossamer float of her skirt around her knees as she idly kicked up her feet radiated the innocence of her sexuality. However, it also broadcast her natural, latent sensuality. Her issues with touch notwithstanding, she had a body that was craving attention. He could see it in the curve of her exposed spine, the lift and sway of her cocked hip, and the way she waited patiently with her eyes closed.

Suddenly, he didn't want to do this.

Not in public. Not in front of anyone else. He wanted her with him behind closed doors where he could enjoy her without an audience, without rules and without restriction.

As Magnus reached down to unlace his boots, he felt the pressure of his situation closing against him from all sides. There were the eyes of the expectant class that he didn't want, the indifference of the woman who didn't want him, and the demand of a monarch who needed him. There was his friend who now had to conduct his lecture knowing he had to be very careful not to offend him, and there were the needs of Sanctuary itself, simply waiting for him to return to all that it required from him. All he was missing now was a Sinner demanding repentant justice, and that was usually just a matter of time.

He didn't realize he had sighed until Daenaira looked up at him. He dropped his second boot, then slipped off his weapons and laid them aside. "Are you comfortable this way?" he asked her. "Perhaps you might like to sit up so the entire class can see you?" *No. No. No.*

She decided, again without speaking, and slowly sat up. Her free hair draped and slid over her neck and shoulders as she changed position, long dark tendrils spilling down over her breasts. Sitting cross-legged in the center of the bed, she smoothed her skirt down over her knees. Magnus kneeled and slid into place at her back. Setting the brush down for the moment, and wondering why he suddenly couldn't take in enough oxygen, he slowly reached past her shoulders to gather up her hair in his hands. He couldn't help himself, his fingertips stroking the powder-soft skin of her throat and neck as he swept all of her hair back beyond her shoulders. Magnus felt the almost imperceptible shiver that tremored through her, and he leaned forward slightly to hide his smile against her hair, also taking advantage to inhale the scent of sweet strawberry shampoo and the luscious natural cream beneath it.

Anything he said to her would be heard by the class, so he kept it simple. "Put your hands on your knees, *K'yindara,* and do not move them. This is very important, as we do not wish to require ourselves to exhibit anything more than hair-brushing technique. Correct?"

Only because he was so close to her did he realize her body had frozen in shock and, quickly on the heels of that, fear. He was glad for it because it meant she had understood him, or at least gotten the gist of it. He gently touched a kiss of reassurance to the side of her neck and then reached to slide his fingers into her hair at her temples, filtering them through along every rooted strand he could contact.

"Who can tell me which organ is being stimulated on Daenaira at the moment?"

Light, I am definitely going to kill Brendan.

"Skin," came the confident answer.

"And?" Bren prompted.

Magnus tuned out the voices as he focused on the task at hand. It wasn't hard to do, the sensation of her body-warmed tresses proving to be more than riveting. He continued to finger-comb her hair until he could hear soft, breathy sighs coming from her and the rigidity in her spine eased. He didn't even want to pick up the brush. He knew they were both content with just the use of his fingers. But it was a lesson, and not everyone would like things just like he and Dae did. So, he lifted the brush and began to play with her hair in long, soothing strokes. He went excruciatingly slow at times, and a bit faster at others. He turned her hair in his hands as he worked, and then released it to unwind in a whisper of softness. Then Magnus bent her head forward and brushed her hair backward against its natural fall, exposing the nape of her neck and hiding her face behind the curtain of blackened red.

Seeing the delicate hairs at the nape of her neck and the smooth cappuccino color of her skin was far too tempting, just as the pale band of scarring around the base of her throat was a stark reminder of where she had come from. Magnus barely even knew when he had stopped fighting his craving to have her, and as he stroked the back of her neck with his slow-moving fingertips, he tried to understand why. This distraction and loss of focus from the importance of his work was exactly what he had been afraid of. If he had any sense, he would repair their relationship, build a friendship with her, and adamantly refuse himself anything further.

But it was rapidly becoming clear to him that keeping away from her was, in and of itself, the distraction. Denial only made the desire worse. He had no proof, of course, that satiating himself on her would work any better, but he couldn't simply experiment with her and then decide. If he opened this door and walked through, it would be forever shut behind him. No going back. Not unless she demanded it.

Right then, however, the only thing she was demanding was his attention. She had unwittingly relaxed back against him, her spine tucked snugly up the center of his body as she became like liquid. Without even realizing he was giving in to the impulse, Magnus bent forward and brushed a kiss up along the slope where her shoulder joined to her neck. For a moment she went taut, her closed lashes lifting as she tilted her chin to look at him.

Daenaira quieted again, that liquid quality pervading her once more and her head drifting to sweep back against his shoulder where she remained resting with sultry blinking eyes that spun a knot of raw need in his belly. Not for the lust that fired his soul, but for that empty place that had craved the warmth and acceptance of her permission to touch and to hold her like this.

"Magnus?"

The priest looked away from the beautiful peacefulness and hypnotic sensuality on Dae's face and glared at Brendan.

"M'jan, the class is finished."

Dae responded to that with quick attention.

She blinked and looked around the room. Most of the seats were empty now, but there was a sluggish sort of milling about by the students who were trying to affect exiting while still watching the compelling sexual energy between herself and Magnus. She realized just how receptive she had been to him. After a week of sending a very clear message to him that she wouldn't easily be swayed by his kindnesses and undeniable charms, she had completely abandoned herself to him. And for what? The way he wielded a hairbrush?

Embarrassed and angry with herself, Dae quickly moved away from him and off the bed. She walked over to the chaise where she had left her sari and hastily began to dress herself. How had he found her there? Damn it, she didn't want him to know she was coming to sex classes! The arrogant ass would think it was for him! It wasn't. She just hated her ignorance. Now faced with the opportunity to school herself as she had never done before, she wanted to destroy all of her ignorance, or at least eliminate her stupidity about topics even an adolescent should know. Religion. Language. Politics. Sex.

She didn't look back at Magnus as she heard him dressing as well, but by the time she had draped her sari over her shoulder, she could feel him coming up behind her. All she knew was that he had better not touch her again now that they were out of that bed and the demonstration that had come with it. He stopped very close to her, close enough that she could feel him all along her skin at the back of her body in radiating waves of intense heat. The easy desire to lean back into him again was instant and overwhelming, the sensual warmth of him so strongly compelling.

"We are needed at the royal household," he said quietly, his tone gruff and low, like a whispered promise he didn't speak. *Later*, it vowed.

"We?" she asked, rubbing the side of her neck where he had kissed her earlier as a wash of sparkling sensation shimmered over it. "What would you possibly need me for?"

"We shall discover that as each situation develops, Daenaira. You are my handmaiden and my partner. I will almost always need you by my side."

"Yes. Of course," she said, the flatness of her agreement an obvious reminder of his remarks to the contrary that still stung her memory. She shrugged and moved forward. It was apparent the man had no idea what he wanted or needed from one minute to the next, and she wasn't going to wear herself out vacillating right along with him.

Dae just wanted to be good at something. Not until she had come here had she had even the remotest possibility of that; or so she had thought. It turned out she had been good at fighting all along. All of the viciousness and temper channeled into her speed and instinct of movement was the raw material she could now pour into advanced training. Her bar rail lessons on weapons and emulating a warrior had discovered the prodigy within her, and the last eight years had been lessons in pit fighting. Now she was learning in a way that would combine all of that and more and, admittedly, she was learning from a genius in the art form.

She had known penance priests like Magnus were all but

undefeatable, but knowing and seeing were two separate things. In the training hall he was a thing of deadly and brilliant beauty. He never went all out while in class, but even as he slowly walked his students through every movement, explaining the why and the where of it, it was mesmerizing to watch the fluid control he had at his command. He could fly while his students were barely learning to crawl, and it showed. But it was his patience that had really impressed her in the end. Not just with his students, but with her.

He went out of his way to carefully respect her dictate to keep his distance. He never lost his temper with her, no matter how much she snubbed him or ignored him, so long as she never disrespected him in front of others, which she would never do. He deserved her anger, not her scathing disrespect. Not when the damage it could do would touch far deeper beyond just him.

Dae was nervous as they emerged from Sanctuary for the first time since she'd gotten in that fight with Killian and his men. The memory made her smile now because, after learning what a rascal Killian was, she knew it had served him right. He'd been showing off having sex with one woman, and within an hour had been sniffing after another. Casual sex was one thing, but that was just so wrong somehow. Well, to her it was. She realized that there were large groups of their society that lived completely unreserved sex lives. There were very simple rules. No one gets pregnant and no one gets hurt—hurt encompassing sex without permission to sex by deception. All were considered dishonorable and, like all other rules, when these were broken, they came with a price of penance to pay.

She realized Magnus looked on her treatment of him as a penance he had to pay for his confusing and hurtful behavior, and that if he was just patient enough, he could reach the end of his punishment and life would go on for the better. But he was forgetting that punishment was not the goal of penance, something she found ironic, actually. Penance was meant to be a deterrent for future repetition of the flawed behavior.

She did not have much faith that he understood just how and why what he had done was so wrong. For someone so wise, he was having a hard time seeing the big picture. He had intended to fit her into his life, a silhouette trimmed to perfect dimensions before being placed over the picture of his last handmaiden. Life and people just never worked that way. People and relationships were inconvenient. That's just the way it was. Sectioning himself off to minimize that inconvenience just proved how out of touch with that Magnus really was. He didn't want to get messy? Well, life was messy. She was messy. And she wasn't in the mood to be shaped into a tidier version of herself. She would grow and she would change naturally, but not unnaturally.

Fuck him if he didn't like it. He could just stay all tidy by himself. He could try to trim the fat to make Sanctuary perfect, thinking he could just snip off a few threads and that would fix the tear running through it, but it wasn't going to work that way. Not that she believed he didn't know how to work hard to achieve a goal, but simply that he was still struggling with denial of how bad things really were because he was much too close and too personally invested.

Dae felt bad for him when she realized that. The pressure he was under had to be incredible. She knew he wasn't the type to confide in others easily, and probably less so now in the face of finding traitors in the ranks, so she worried at what kind of weight must be lying oppressively over him. She had even felt guilty when, during religious instruction, Hera had explained so soundly why the dynamic of priest and handmaiden was crucial when it came to the handmaiden relieving her priest of as many mortal worries as possible. Without her, Magnus had no one to help relieve his burdens. Especially because he was at the top of the food chain here. One sign of weakness and there were others like that slimy Shiloh snapping at his heels for his position.

She had never been to the palace before, so Daenaira was a bit overwhelmed at their arrival as its large, shadowy beauty loomed up all around her. It was opulent and artistic, cool and beautiful. The urge to drop behind him was thwarted by Magnus when he slowed his step to match hers, keeping her by his side. He didn't look at her or comment, but she knew he was aware of her sudden intimidation. His silent actions, however, made it clear that she would get to be as equal to him as she had demanded, whether she liked it or not.

Magnus knew his way and had absolute freedom to pass the intense security she saw everywhere. She, however, was not looked on without heavy suspicion. The legacy, she realized, of his previous handmaiden.

Magnus entered Tristan's rooms without hesitation, knowing the monarch was waiting for him. He realized immediately that the exterior sitting room was empty, leaving the bedroom and bath for choice. He listened for a moment, then walked to the bedroom and tapped at the door.

"Yes, Magnus," Tristan bid him impatiently.

The priest entered, and just the thickness of the air in the room told him a couple of key things. First, Tristan's tension was at an all-time high. Second, the Chancellor had spent quite a few hours trying to purge himself of that tension in his usual way, in the body of a willing female.

Magnus swept his eyes over the room, pausing on Xenia, the Chancellor's impenetrable bodyguard, who stood leaning back against a wall looking deceptively bored, her arms crossed over her armored breasts. Then he found Tristan in his bed, thankfully alone at the moment, but clearly naked beneath the careless cover of a single sheet.

A cover that disappeared a minute later as Tristan got to his feet and walked across the room to the bathroom.

"I called for you an hour ago, Magnus," he said irritably as he passed his newly arrived guests along his route.

"Certainly enough time to dress yourself, *M'itisume*," Magnus returned tightly as he glanced at Daenaira. She was standing steadily and outwardly unaffected. She would never show the fact that she was not used to the utterly uninhibited way of living the royals were used to. They lived with twenty-four-hour guards and servants who had long ago eradicated a sense of modesty or privacy from them.

"Hmm?" Tristan reappeared, the point lost on him in an instant as his thoughts crowded it out as unimportant. "I do not often call for you, M'jan, I realize, but rarely would you make my sister wait so long."

"Then consider this the rare occasion, *M'itisume*. I had a pressing issue to handle before I could attend you."

This time Magnus heard Dae react. With a soft indrawn breath, she realized he had put off the leader of their society just so he could brush her hair. To her credit, she recovered quickly from her surprise and redrew her expression of neutrality.

Tristan sighed, rubbing at the back of his neck as he reached for his robe.

"Of course. Forgive, M'jan. I know whatever it was must have been important to you."

"Yes," he replied carefully. "It was very important to me." He cleared his throat for segue. "*M'itisume*, I do not believe you have met *K'yan* Daenaira as yet. She is my handmaiden."

Not new handmaiden, just handmaiden. The lack of distinction was, to Dae, in and of itself a distinction. It was the first time he had not tacked "new" in front of the description, and for some reason it pleased her a great deal. Meanwhile Tristan turned with surprise as he closed his robe, noticing her for the first time, apparently.

"No, I have not. Greetings, *K'yan*."

"M'itisume," she greeted him with a heart-touched bow of respect. And that was about the end of her abilities in royal protocol! She hoped to *Drenna* she wasn't asked to do anything else other than stand there!

"Killian told me you had joined with a new handmaiden, Magnus. She is every bit as lovely as she has to be to get *Ajai*

Killian in so much trouble. Women, you see," he directed to
Dae, "are my head guard's favorite pastime."

"Unlike yourself, of course, *M'itisume*," she responded
with a sly smile. And the instant she said it she recalled who
she was talking to and her eyes shot to Magnus in despair.

But Tristan laughed out loud, his bodyguard chuckling in
the background. "Damn me, I must do something about my
reputation," he noted with amusement, his jet eyes glistening
with humor. "I like her, Magnus. No shy little miss, this one.
Honest. Speaks her mind. We could use more of that around
here."

"Speaking of," Magnus said, "was there something on
your mind, Tristan?"

"Yes," he sighed, striking a hand back through the sleek
black curls of his shoulder-length hair, "back to business,
right?" He frowned, the expression creasing his handsome face
so deeply that, for the first time, Daenaira became aware of
the scar flawing his left temple near his brow. "M'jan, I believe my worst fears are about to come to pass."

"Worst?" Magnus quantified, a raised brow marking his
opinion of the monarch's drama.

"Well, damn near bad as!" he exploded in sudden temper.
"You and I both know they are just doing this to destroy this
house! Enacting some archaic law over us! And me, knowing about it since I was warned at the end of the last Senate
session, and I still haven't grown the spine to tell her! Every
time we walk in the Senate I am terrified that this will be the
night. It's getting to the point where I—I can't make myself
walk outside of this room. I know it is childish and cowardly,
but she will not go without me, and they will not bring it up
without us both being there."

"*M'itisume*, allow me to tell her. We have discussed this
before. I am as close to your sister as you are, in the sense of
her reliance on me. But you know she needs to hear this
from one of us before she hears it in the Senate, because
once they drop this demand on her, she will ask us both if we

knew anything about it. Your behavior alone will make the answer obvious. She will feel betrayed when she realizes we left her out of our confidence. She will have to face enough as it is without that added weight."

"M'jan, they are going to force her to marry, and there is nothing either of us can do about it. Malaya is a woman who respects tradition and they know that. They are *using* that! They think to force a husband on her, tearing us apart and dividing our strength. Tell me this doesn't reek of these traitors we seek! If they have the power to get a majority vote in the Senate, then you and I both know this means the corruption has reached a depth we may never recover from."

"I know nothing of the kind," Magnus retorted evenly. "*M'itisume*, just because a small group is clever enough to talk a flock of traditionalists into agreeing does not mean all is lost. If anything, it will reflect the fact that there are still some tender egos left behind after the thrashing your sister and you gave them in the war. This is a power play. They want to see if you will cede to them on matters of tradition. This is where Trace will be best to advise you, or Rika, but you and your sister can discuss how far you are willing to let them take this."

"I am not letting them sell my sister like some kind of a regal prostitute for the sake of their campaign to ruin our standing! I am not going to ask her to marry for convenience. If she had wanted to join and breed babies, rather than focus on the needs of this society, than she goddamn well would have done it!"

"*M'itisume*," Dae scolded him softly.

"Your pardon, *K'yan* Daenaira," Tristan said irritably but with sincerity.

Dae was unaware of how she had just shocked Magnus into total silence. Daenaira correcting someone's use of language? It was all he could do not to burst into laughter. Somehow, he managed to control his countenance. However, the struggle left a silence she felt compelled to fill.

"If I may say so," she said politely, although Magnus could see she had begun to fold a repetitive crease into the fabric of her sari, a habit she had developed that signaled when her temper was roused. "*K'yatsume* Malaya is as powerful and as important as *M'itisume* is. Yet, because she is female, she is being held to an archaic chauvinism while your unmarried state is being ignored. They should either mind their business when it comes to your personal lives, or they should demand joinings of you both."

"Gods! Now *that* would be my worst fears come to pass!" Tristan choked, staring at Magnus as he pointed at the handmaiden. "Isn't there something inherently contradictory about a handmaiden feminist?" he demanded.

"One would think," Magnus observed, the effort to keep his expression even completely foiled by the amusement in his golden eyes. "However, Dae has a unique way of asserting her desires for equality into the traditions of her role."

"Hmm." Magnus could see Tristan's mind dipping swiftly toward the licentious. "I could see the advantages in equality when it came to certain traditions," he mused.

"So can I," Dae shot back, giving the ruler a cheeky wink that all but knocked Magnus back on his ass. *Drenna*, he absolutely was *not* going to blush! Not at his age and not because of a girl with two seconds of sexual experience!

Gods, he couldn't wait to get her back to Sanctuary.

"This should be your action," he said succinctly to the Chancellor. "You must tell your sister or have me tell her. Then you must tell Trace. Trace, Rika, and Malaya can join you as you sink your minds into how you will respond to this when and if it does come."

Tristan sighed and sat down on the edge of his bed.

"I know. You said as much last time."

"I don't understand your hesitation, Tristan. Nor is it like you to shy from your duties or your troubles. Might I also add that you're driving my son mad every time you choose to speak with me rather than confide in him?" Magnus knew why this was, though. Tristan was trying to make an inside ally of him, knowing Magnus would be the first one his deeply religious sister would call on to help counsel her past her shock and any fallout of emotion she might have toward Tristan for keeping this from her for so long.

"He is afraid she will agree to it."

Magnus saw Tristan jolt tellingly and knew Daenaira had hit it on the head when the royal narrowed a glare on her and said defensively, "I am not afraid of anything."

"Then you would be the first," she observed dryly. "We all have fears. *M'itisume* knows his sister is a woman of tradition and respect, and you fear she will decide to take a husband who will find a place between your close relationship." Dae stepped a little closer, though not much; just enough to hide her face from her male counterpart. "You are afraid of the change. Afraid she might forget you as she turns to the interests of a new family. Everyone knows how extraordinarily close you are to *K'yatsume*, how deeply you love her. My mother owned a tavern when I was young, and the soldiers I met there raised me on the stories of the war. I would hear about how like a ballet, a pas de deux, it was to watch you in battle together. It inspired and amazed battle-hardened men who would tell a starry-eyed girl that it was because you had such perfect love for each other. It was the loyalty, devotion, and love they themselves followed. And yes, you are worried that it will disrupt your power and position, but I think for the first time you are more afraid it will disrupt that perfect love.

"So you are taking this time of hesitation to push her away first. Women. Amusement. Alcohol. Petulance. Behaviors she will frown on and, coincidentally, will force her to focus her attention onto you. But you're foolish if you think she won't see through you soon enough, and when she does she is going to be livid. No woman likes to have her emotions toyed with, or to be treated like she is too stupid to be informed fully about things that directly affect her life. Most of all, your lack of trust and faith in her is going to be devastating to her. It devastates me," she said, laying her hand on her heart with passionate hurt, "because I am still at heart the little girl in that tavern who loves to believe in the brother and sister who are like one because they have perfect love in one another. But it isn't even close to perfect if you can't trust it to stand on its own merit. Not if you have to try and control it and play games to try and shape it to your will. This doesn't save it, it destroys it. And it certainly does not protect or save you."

Daenaira wound down from her impassioned scolding of their king, and then, as if suddenly realizing where she was and who she was with, she lowered her eyes and stepped back awkwardly.

"Excuse me, please," she murmured softly, raising a hand to shield her expression as she hurried out the door.

Magnus stared after her for a long, frowning moment, his instinct to follow her almost overwhelming him. But he forced himself to turn back to Tristan, who didn't look any happier than Magnus felt.

"Shit," he groaned. "That was my mistake all along. I should have asked a woman!"

"Yep." Xenia finally spoke up, pushing away from the wall and walking toward the door as well. "Trouble with men is they spend so much time misusing our true potential that they just end up causing themselves twice the work and twice the grief in the long run. But lucky for you, we enjoy forgiving you for being a little dense. It reminds us we're the superior sex and that you'd be lost boys without us."

"Spoken like a true Amazon," Tristan shot after her as she exited the bedroom. *"Aiya,"* he sighed, "now she's going to be smug for a week. Do you have any idea what it's like having a smug woman around who can kick the shit out of you if you're not careful?"

"Umm." It was Magnus's turn to slyly smile. "I think I can conceive of that, yes."

Chapter Eight

"Thank you for your help, Daenaira. You made a significant impact on Tristan's situation."

"Did I?" she asked, sounding a bit distracted as she walked back to Sanctuary beside him without looking at him. "I'm glad if it helped. Has he decided what to do?"

"Yes. He will tell her himself within the next twenty-four hours, which no doubt means we will be making this walk again very soon. Malaya depends on us greatly for guidance and religious clarity."

"I know. You've been to see her almost every day this week. But you did not take me then," she noted.

Magnus couldn't decide if she was feeling slighted by that fact. She was being very unreadable at the moment. He didn't understand what was bothering her. She should be proud of the progress she had achieved while helping a follower. Especially a follower of such significance to their society.

"Malaya and I have always taken a private audience together. She prefers it that way. You are welcome to come, but you will only be left to wait alone while we converse."

"I didn't say I wanted to be your happy little joiner," she

said sharply. "Obviously you realized my time was better spent in Sanctuary. That's all you had to say."

Magnus stopped short, holding out a hand to stay her since he didn't want to touch her. "Would you please tell me what was so wrong with what I just said that you had to be so nasty?"

She huffed a laugh and rolled her eyes. "It figures you'd have no clue."

"Apparently not! That is why I am asking. If I am ever to get back into your good graces, I need to figure out the things I am doing that so offend you!"

"Okay then," she shot out, her hands dropping onto her waist, "how about that you just treated me like a child again?"

"I did no such thing!"

She threw up her hands in exasperation and marched into Sanctuary. Magnus stepped quickly after her and stopped her sharply by stepping into her path.

"Magnus!" she warned.

"How? How did I treat you like a child?"

She cocked her head, tapping her foot in temper for a moment. "Try this." She pitched her voice softly and bent as if speaking to an imaginary child. "Aww, honey. I'm sorry, but you can't come with Mommy. Mommy has to do grown-up things. If I take you with me, you'll just be bored." She stood up straight and cocked a brow at him.

Light and damnation.

"I didn't mean it like that," he said with a frown.

"Then you need to learn to say what you do mean, because at this rate we're in big trouble."

She walked around him and continued on her way.

For ten seconds. Then he was there again, this time crowding her a bit. "All right then, since we're airing grievances. What in cold burning Light were you doing in Brendan's relations lecture?"

"That is self-explanatory."

"Why would you take the class from someone else knowing I teach the same thing later in the night?" He didn't want to sound petulant, but he supposed he did. He looked around, but the corridor was fairly empty.

"Again, self-explanatory. I didn't want to take instruction from a man who pisses me off so damn much!"

"You lied to me!" he accused with a hiss. "You said you were with Hera. Do you have any idea the trouble you could have caused yourself by going into that room without proper preparation?"

"So I didn't know a few rules. Big freaking deal." She sniffed, the brush off making his blood boil.

"Oh, it is a very big deal, *K'yindara*," he promised her, leaning in close to engage her ear at a whisper but not touching her. "The way you were practically purring in my lap, it would have been so simple to reach around you and fill my hands with these luscious breasts of yours, and I guarantee you that you wouldn't have reacted badly to it at all. And the very instant you moaned softly or your nipples contracted to beg for my attention, we would have been committed to performing in that bed, class or no class, for the educational benefit of all who wanted to watch."

"Without my permission?"

"Permission is implied at that point, *K'yindara*. You agreed to come to the bed, you agreed to engage in foreplay, and you would have agreed to the eroticism of the touch of my hands. In that bed, you are an exhibitionist. You choose what to exhibit. Brendan had no idea you were so raw and uninformed. There are rules here, *K'yindara*, that are distinctive to Sanctuary, and rules distinctive to specific rooms of Sanctuary. Before you run around behind my back doing things half-cocked, I suggest you discuss it with me first so I can keep you from walking into things accidentally! This is why you should be training with me instead of those who do not understand where you've come from!"

"Well, until you showed up, I didn't have to worry because handmaidens can only sleep with their priests!" she snapped irritably, refusing to admit he might be right.

"Or *themselves*!"

Daenaira drew in a soft sound of surprise. Her face flared with color and heat as she searched his tempestuous golden eyes to judge his legitimacy. "That's not possible," she whispered fiercely. "I'm a *girl*." She looked nervously up and down the corridor as she scrubbed at one of her blushing cheeks.

Gods, she was raw. Worse, she was naïve and refused to admit it to anyone, including herself. He wanted to correct her misconception, one he was used to hearing from prepubescent girls, but he needed a moment to cool his temper. He eased away from her, stretched out that incredibly tight knot that seemed to have taken up permanent residence in his neck, and studied her for a long minute.

"We need to have this conversation somewhere else. You can choose. Our rooms. A private tutoring room. Or my office."

Definitely not their rooms, Dae knew. Being alone with him in their rooms and talking about sex was not her idea of safe tactics. His office was totally his territory. She knew better than to meet her opponent on his territory.

"A private tutoring room," she responded, her chin up as she tried to prove to him she wasn't afraid of him or the topic at hand. The truth was, she wasn't exactly sure about any of it. She was shaken to hear about all of these weird rules. "Why would someone make up a rule like that?" she grumbled at him as he led the way.

"It is meant to attract a certain kind of person, Dae. When we first opened these halls during the war, it was difficult to find models for classes. People were leery of each other, scuffling about trickling clan issues, disliking the idea of Sanctuary having been moved from the lowlands to here. That rule titillated those who were exhibitionists. It became a flirtation for others. It's a form of foreplay all on its own. People are tempted to test themselves. There are three lecture halls here, and all share the same rules. We almost never lack for models, with or without class being officially scheduled. We have a servant who has only one job, and that is to change the bedding in these rooms as frequently as it is used. Even if it is just what you and I did."

He was walking past the lecture halls in question as he spoke, but then stopped and crossed the hall to one of the doors on the opposite side of the corridor. These were the only doors in Sanctuary with locks on them that weren't residential rooms. She had never seen inside them and watched warily as he took a key from his pocket and opened the door. He gestured, and she preceded him into the dark space. He had already shut and locked the door, throwing an inside bolt as well, by the time she saw the bed.

"Oh no! No, you don't. Let me out of here."

She about-faced and found him standing in front of the door, leaning back against it and studying her carefully.

"What did you think happened during the private tutoring labs for the course you are currently taking? Or didn't you realize they are a requirement here in Sanctuary? Another rule."

Well, he didn't have to sound so damn superior about it, even if he was right. "Private . . . but, umm . . . the students aren't allowed to have sex . . . I thought."

"Unsupervised sex. Not until they are responsible enough to keep from getting pregnant or hurting themselves or others, physically or emotionally. A teacher judges what they are ready for. A teacher introduces them to themselves."

"But we're the teachers. And we can't . . ."

"Students invite willing partners when it's time for that, after discussing it with their tutor first, of course. The choice has to be the right one."

"Well, *you* aren't the right one," she groused.

"Well, unfortunately, I am all you've got, *K'yindara*. Or did you want Brendan to tutor you privately?"

He tossed off the question almost carelessly, but Daenaira could hear and feel the danger reeking out of him. She took a cautious step back.

"I didn't think . . ." she stammered hesitantly.

"No. You didn't think. But we've rectified that now. You wanted tutoring in sex, and now you have a tutor. Let's get started. Unless you'd rather continue in the penance chamber."

"The penance chamber!"

"Of course, Dae. Avoiding course requirements is, after all, a punishable offense."

"You're a prick," she spat, backing up when he began to move toward her. It quickly began to feel like he was stalking her, and her heart began to race with her anxiety. She didn't like feeling like prey. She didn't like feeling her hands sweat as if she were afraid of him or something.

"I think you've made that much clear to me before," he acknowledged.

"You promised you wouldn't touch me without my permission!" she cried out as they quickly ran out of room. She retreated all the way to the alcove that held the roomy bed so prettily made up in violet silks that, ironically, matched his uniform.

"And I won't. I believe our topic for today is masturbation."

She snorted out a sarcastic laugh.

"No, thanks. Already seen you do that. Not my idea of something I need to relearn."

Magnus sat down and casually crossed his legs, making her realize there were chairs across from the alcove and bed.

"I meant for you. Although I have to say I am surprised you haven't figured that out. What has Brendan been teaching all week?"

"Well, you saw," she replied uneasily. "Tactile foreplay. Yesterday it was foot rubbing. The day before was this whole thing with a feather. It was odd."

He was silent for a moment. "Tell me you didn't volunteer for any of those demonstrations," he demanded quietly.

"No. The hair was the first. What do you care if someone rubs my feet? They're just feet."

"That question is exactly why we do intensive touching courses before we allow students into the relations lecture. It's also why we have private sessions like this. Get on the bed."

"How about . . . umm, no." She went to walk around him and went for the door. She threw the bolt and tried to open it, but it wouldn't budge. She looked down at the knob after the first few tries and saw a key lock.

"It's a double lock. Locks from both sides. You need a key to get in and to get out. It keeps students from doing exactly what you are trying to do."

"Get away from a maniac?" she snapped.

"Run away in fear without discussing it or facing that fear. Throw the bolt again, please. I wouldn't want someone walking in on you."

"I could scream, you know," Dae said.

"And you would ruin my reputation as a trustworthy teacher and priest for the rest of my life. Please be certain your fear is worth that," Magnus said calmly.

Daenaira hated to be trapped and she was furious with him for this, but he was right. She couldn't do that to him.

"Give me the key," she said, holding out her hand as she stepped up to him.

"Lock the door, Dae. You aren't going to win this."

"Give me the thrice-damned key!"

"Take it from me and you can go. But," he added when she moved forward, "you have to figure out how to do it without touching me, because if you do, I get to touch you in defense of myself. Once you cross that line, Dae, all bets are off. I will use every tactic at my disposal to keep you in this room, and trust me when I say I have a great many of them. Now, throw the bolt and get on the bed."

What choice did she have? She had run out of ideas and arguments. Magnus was so . . . quiet. His calm was twice as intimidating as his anger, while at the same time it conveyed the impression of a dispassionate instructor. She didn't know if she trusted that. She certainly didn't trust him. Just the same, she threw the bolt as requested and returned to the bed to sit down with a huffy flounce reflecting how peeved she was with him.

Magnus smiled softly. Had she had any experience, she could have charmed that key off him in dozens of ways, but it didn't occur to her that she had that power. Once she did realize it, he was in a lot of trouble. She had used what she had seen somewhere else against Killian, a flash of her sexuality and the knowledge of men that she had learned, he was assuming, at that bar her mother had owned that he had just heard about. It had literally allowed her to drop-kick a man who was all but impossible to defeat in a battle of strength and skill. Killian would have made an excellent penance priest, if not for his appetite for women.

"Take off your sari, *K'yindara*."

"I'm not getting naked in front of you."

"I said the sari, honey. You can keep the rest."

"Oh." She reached up and slowly pulled the sari from her shoulder. She toyed with the velvet cloth of it before she started to pull the pleats from the underskirt just as slowly.

"I have all the rest of the night, baby," he all but purred to her as he leaned forward and put his elbows on his knees. "And Alaskan nights in winter are so very long."

Daenaira shot him a look that wished it could kill him. She whipped off the sari and threw it into his lap. Then she thought better of it, went to retrieve it, and pushed him back in the chair by his shoulders. Looping one end of the sari around the arm of the chair, she caught his wrist and quickly tied it down. When Magnus cocked a brow in query she said, "I'm not going to go for the key. I just don't trust you."

"What makes you think I would trust you after you lied to me before?"

"I didn't lie. I said religious instruction. Technically, all the instruction here is religious. It's all taught by priests and handmaidens."

"That is splitting hairs," he said.

She shrugged. "Anyway, you and I both know you are strong enough to rip the arms off this chair. Just give me this."

Magnus dropped his free hand onto the opposite arm of the chair. Dae strung her sari across and tied him tightly. She bit her lip nervously as she backed away from him and stopped against the bed when she hit it with the backs of her legs. Her hands were suddenly cold and she rubbed them together to warm them even though she knew it was a terrible tell. She couldn't help herself. She was actually surprised he was being so compliant about being bound. He didn't seem the type to tolerate it. Even though she was right and he could break free if he wanted to, it would take time and effort that a man of his sense of control would dislike. Vulnerability for even a second was still vulnerability.

"Get on the bed, *K'yindara*," he said softly.

Magnus very artfully walked himself into summer daylight.

That was what the end result of this lesson would be, after all. He acknowledged that. The sheer insanity he was going to work upon himself filled him with reluctance. But what choice did he have? To turn her loose on another instructor? Brendan? Shiloh? Gods, no. Never. *Never*. If he refused to let anyone else instruct her, then that meant he had to swallow the beautiful agony of teaching her himself. She deserved the knowledge she craved, and she deserved to feel trust with her instructor. He would prove that she could trust him if it was the last thing he ever did.

He absently twisted a wrist against her significantly tight bindings as he watched her obey his last command and sit on the bed. She tucked her legs under herself and smoothed her skirt over them so only her feet and ankles could be seen.

"Are you wearing panties?" he asked.

She opened her mouth to retort, probably to say it wasn't his business, but she realized it was a silly argument given the situation. She nervously brushed back the heavy fall of her well-brushed hair and licked her lips slowly.

"Yes," she said. "Should I . . . uh . . . ?"

"No. I was asking for instructive purposes. Are you comfortable sitting like that? You may shift at any time, by the way. I actually encourage it. I want you, ideally, to feel what your body wants and to flow with it instantly. If I tell you to stop, I want you to stop just as instantly. Okay, *K'yindara*?"

"Do I have a choice?"

"I could do it for you," he reminded her, grinning when he got a nasty look for his troubles. "You see, there's always choices."

"Yeah. Unless you're chained to a wall," she responded wryly.

The remark bled the humor right out of him, making him realize just how difficult it must be for her to be in a locked room like this. There was suddenly much more impact to her need to bind him, and he felt a little sick from the powerful depth of her mistrust of him. It made what he was doing right then very wrong. He was the wrong person, from her perspective, to be teaching her. A private sexual instructor should be one of the priests or handmaidens a student trusted most. But selfishly, he couldn't bring himself to guide her elsewhere. Not even to Hera.

She was for him.

The gods had sent her to him, and she was for him.

"Lie back. Relax."

She responded, reaching to spread her hair back behind

her. She lay in profile to him, streams of gorgeous hair and swells of generous curves accented by her clothing.

"Start by touching your own body, *K'yindara*. Your face. Your throat. Your shoulders and arms. Bypass your breasts for the moment and touch your belly, your thighs."

Magnus swallowed his growing tension as, after a long hesitation of looking at him distrustfully, she started to obey.

"Do you recall your lesson earlier? Men are very enamored by the images of a woman in their bed. Watching you touch yourself is something that will be deeply arousing. However, it needs to be deeply arousing to you first. When you are alone. When you learn this, you will be able to use it as a tool for relaxation or release when sex is inconvenient or impossible. It is also an excellent tool for seduction."

"Just . . . touching myself?" She drew slow fingertips over the flat of her belly.

"You'll see," he promised. He was already seeing. She had no idea how sexy she looked to him, so serious and distrustful, yet touching herself so naturally. He let her continue quietly for a few minutes. "How do you feel?"

"I—a little silly. It feels a little like taking a bath, only without the water."

"Someday, if I can gain your permission, I will bathe you as you did me, and I will show you exactly why I had the reaction that I did."

Dae remembered that reaction, and he could see her entire body flush hotly with the memory. For the first time, her breathing altered pace.

"Sexual memory and fantasy are often integral to the pleasures of masturbation," he told her. "Close your eyes and draw up images and moments where you felt aroused. Delete anything negative, filter it away, imagine it the way it could have been if everything had been perfect for you." Magnus watched her lips part and saw heat simmer across her breasts just as her nipples became pronounced beneath her blouse.

He would have sold his soul right then to be a telepath; to know what she was thinking. He sat forward, just as far as was comfortable within his bindings, but still a few inches closer.

He watched as she relaxed and focused on what she was thinking and feeling, his hands gripping tightly to the arms of his chair as she unwittingly drew closer and closer to her breasts and the areas inside of her thighs.

"You create the sensation of your lover's hands on your body. He isn't there in the bed with you, but you can create him using your mind and your hands."

Or you can damn well get up and untie him, Magnus thought hotly as he watched her natural sensuality awaken with a vengeance. Her body shifted and slid in a luscious undulation of awareness, and she hiked the slender fabric of her skirt high on her thighs.

Gods, she had beautiful skin. Her legs were so long and well shaped, bringing attention to her round hips and, he knew, delectable ass.

"Put a hand under your blouse, *K'yindara*. Feel how soft and warm you are between your breasts. Begin to shape yourself."

She looked at him then, a little questioning.

"I know. I didn't take the time to touch you like that when I should have, but if I had it to do over again, I would feel your shape and weight in both of my hands, learn where you are sensitive; but I wouldn't touch your nipples just yet. I'd want to tease you a bit first, make sure I had every nerve beneath your skin paying full attention."

Magnus was already starting to feel the pressure of his building erection when she sighed and moaned in a single breath. The instant she did that, his entire body flashed volcano hot, molten and raw, and he hardened with a vengeance.

"*Drenna*, you are so tempting, *K'yindara*," he uttered. "A saint would sin to have you."

Dae looked at him, taking in the straining tension of the way he sat and the covetousness he couldn't hide in his eyes. The little minx smiled slyly, so very pleased with herself for getting to him. What was more, she took pleasure in it that heated her already hot little body.

"Take off your blouse, Daenaira," he ordered her, hearing the roughness in his voice and not even caring how obvious it was. "Let me see your beautiful breasts. Let me see those dark and lovely nipples you're going to be playing with very soon."

She looked at him again as she took the bottom of her shirt between her fingers. When she slowly inched the velvet up, he realized she was gauging his reaction with intense interest, her tongue appearing in the corner of her lips as she did so.

"Do you have a question, Dae?" he asked, making sure she could see everything she wanted to in the covetous burn of his gaze.

"This excites you even though you aren't being touched?"

"Yes. Very much so. Does that bother you?"

She seemed to think about it. He knew his reactions excited her. It was obvious. However, he also knew she wouldn't be willing to admit that too easily.

Daenaira sat up, simultaneously drawing off her blouse. She not only bared her breasts, but she sent her hair flying around her in a cloud of darkest red. The silken network of strands feathered against her shoulders and breasts and ribs, and Magnus felt the gorgeous agony of wanting something so very badly, but knowing he couldn't have it. He hadn't earned it. He didn't even deserve it.

"Dae, you're so beautiful," he exhaled quickly. "Please tell me I've told you that."

"You have." She smiled at him and he felt gifted for it. He had missed her friendly cheekiness and honest smiles.

"Good. Now pull back your hair, honey. I really want to watch you do this. I know this isn't about me, but I need you to know exactly how powerful you are as a woman. I would love to see you learn it and, though it might just kill me, I want to be victim to it."

Daenaira felt every single word he spoke go through her as if someone were dumping buckets of molten metal over her. She drew back her hair as requested, watching the tension crawling through him as she exposed herself to him. He was gripping the chair so tightly she heard the wood creaking softly on occasion. The way he was losing control of his calm fascinated her. It reminded her of when she had caught him in the bath in the throes of an orgasm he couldn't stop, looking like he'd been hit by a train even as he gasped in pleasure. This was the power he was speaking of, and the understanding made her flow with a liquid burn that damped her panties.

Liking the sensation, and curious about his intensity, she decided to try hooking her fingers into her skirt, releasing the tie at her waist and slowly working it down over her hips. She instinctively turned around, remembering Killian's approach to his partner from behind and guessing it was something men enjoyed. She bent at her waist as the skirt glided past her backside and revealed the thong she wore. The whole time, she watched his body and his face, seeing if she was successful in her guesses and instincts.

She was.

"Gods, Dae," he rasped softly as his eyes devoured her body. "Where in Light did you get those?"

She knew he meant the pretty little panties with their simple midnight blue cotton and satin piping in gold. They accented her hips, led his eyes along barely covered places, and were a young woman's fashion.

"Tiana, actually. She loves these and buys them in large numbers for the women when she is migrating. Apparently she has a store she likes that they pass every year."

"I see. I hadn't realized our women wore these."

She smiled a bit wickedly. "We like to be mysterious like that. At least that is what Brendan says."

Magnus's gaze snapped to hers, brilliant heat flaring in his golden eyes. "You were discussing your lingerie with Brendan?"

"No. M'jan Brendan was teaching about how men enjoy being teased and tempted. To be kept guessing. He said that women are naturally mysterious to you, but that we are also quite good at creating mystery, too."

"That you are," he agreed tautly. "You are a mystery I would take enormous pleasure in unraveling."

It was a dark and heated promise, the sheer burn of his eyes scalding her skin. Suddenly she could picture herself unraveling quite completely at his command. She left her skirt in a puddle on the floor and turned to show herself to him as she ran her hands over her skin once more. Now she was truly beginning to appreciate what he was trying to show her. Her whole body was alive and aware, zinging with stimulation and effervescent warmth. She wondered if it felt the same for him, or if he was restricted because he couldn't touch himself.

"Are you thinking you would like to touch me?" she asked him curiously. "Is that why you're so tense? Because you can't? Or because you can't touch yourself?"

"I don't want to touch myself," he ground out, his expression dark and savage, "I want you to touch me. What I want more than that, though, is to have my hands all over that sweet skin of yours. *Drenna*, do you know I can smell you from here? I know you're wet and excited. It's driving me crazy."

"Really?" She sat on the bed and slowly reclined in profile again, her whole body teasing him mercilessly even as she narrowed sultry eyes on him. "Would you prefer we stop the lesson?" She drifted her fingertips over the rise of her breasts, fascinated by the way his attention became fully riveted to what she was doing. Every instant, every movement, she was learning more, gaining power. She began to wonder just how far she could push Magnus before he broke and crossed from observer to participant. She never even questioned what would happen after that. She just wanted to do it.

"I'm fine," he said, looking and sounding anything but.

Magnus knew he was being played, but that was all right with him. He would do just about anything to watch her sexuality continue to blossom with this amazing speed. She was a natural, and she was the perfect blend of cunning and innocence so that she figured things out quickly and instinctively, but hesitated every so often as she marveled at something new or doubted what she wanted for a moment.

Now she was teasing him as she teased herself with the very tips of her fingers on her chest and breasts. She slid her hands up her throat and against her lips, and he knew the very instant she resisted the instinct to take a finger into her mouth.

He felt blood throbbing through him as if powered by thousands of pistons. His heart was raging for speed. Most of all, his cock was being throttled within the confines of his clothes, begging not only for freedom, but for Daenaira.

Dae finally brushed over her nipples, and she seemed a bit startled. She hadn't been expecting it to feel so strongly sensitive, nor so arousing, he was betting. She was so focused on teasing him that she had forgotten she was also teasing herself.

"If you think that feels good, you should try the scrape of your nails, *K'yindara*. Or even better, take a nipple between your fingers and lightly pinch yourself. If it were me, though, I would have my mouth on you. I'd suck you until you were drenched with wet and moaning for me."

Daenaira gasped as the pull of her fingers seemed to suddenly become the pull of his mouth to her mind. Her eyes shot to his, wide with surprise and pleasure.

"You see, *K'yindara*? This temptation works both ways."

Dae realized how true that was. Suddenly she craved what he had just promised, craved to know what it would feel like to have his mouth drawing at her breast. Her eyes roamed over him and she remembered the heat of his mouth and tongue. She remembered the teasing flirtation of his fingers on her sex.

"Magnus?" she said, her breathless confusion so beautiful on her flushing features.

"Come untie me, Dae. Untie me and I will do it. I will do everything," he promised hotly. Yes, he could easily have fought his Bonds and won, but what he was really asking for was permission.

She shook her head, closing her eyes as her body squirmed. Magnus rode the buck of wild frustration, shaking it off.

"Then slip your fingers into those damp little panties of yours, baby, and tell me how wet and hot you feel. Just tell me that."

Without even missing a beat, she did exactly as he asked, her fingertips skimming low on her belly and disappearing beneath the band of her underwear. Watching her touch herself, seeing the slow progression of her fingers beneath that midnight blue fabric, just about unmanned him.

"Bituth amec," he gasped, unable to catch his breath to save his life as he watched the change come over her face and body. She writhed gently, frustration and confusion warring with her rushing pulse and the washes of heat she experienced. *"Tell me,"* he demanded fiercely.

"I . . ." She exhaled a soft sound of aching need. "I feel hot. It's like . . . warm syrup." She looked at him, distress and desire battling each other in the depths of her wide eyes. "I don't understand."

"When you get sexually excited, your body prepares itself for the penetration by your mate. It will ease the way, relieve friction, and, I promise you, drive me out of my fucking mind. *Untie me, Dae.*"

She withdrew. She turned her head away from him as she pulled her hand back, breathing hard and trying to stop the uncomfortable demand of her body that she couldn't figure out how to satisfy, yet was afraid of at the same time. For someone who had known so little pleasure in life, it must be overwhelming to her.

"Gods," Magnus groaned, leaning back and shifting uncomfortably himself. She heard him and looked at him, her eyes roaming his body with slow intensity. She looked like she wanted to nip and nibble at him for a few hours. And he would never deny her. When she sat up and then rose to her feet, he lurched forward toward her approach. "Untie me, Dae."

She shook her head again, her hair swishing everywhere at her vehemence. Just the same, he watched as she knelt down between his feet. He became suddenly nervous, a feeling he wasn't used to. She reached for the ties of his boots and quickly worked to slide them off his feet.

"What are you doing?" he asked, swallowing hard when she rested her hands on his thighs for a moment.

"Making you more comfortable."

She reached for his belt and he almost ripped himself out of the chair right then, making her startle.

"Don't!"

She blinked in confusion. "Why not?"

"I-If you touch me, Dae, I . . ."

"You won't like it?"

"Drenna," he hissed. "More like I will like it so much I will embarrass myself. Please . . . just untie me."

"No. Can I touch you or not?"

How could he deny her when she was kneeling so beautifully naked between his feet like some kind of concubine? How could he say no when he was screaming with need to feel her any way he could?

Magnus gave her a sharp nod, tightened his grasp on his chair, and braced himself for hell.

She slid open his belt with a touch so light he could hardly feel it. But that didn't matter in the next second when she pushed up his tunic and deftly unfastened his pants. She rose up, bending over him so close he could smell the sweetness of her skin and hair.

"Lift up," she instructed as her hands slid into his slacks and against his skin. He did as instructed, and she smoothed the fabric away from his body, freeing his suffocating erection and stripping him from the waist down. She laid his clothes aside and returned to her kneeling position before him. By now he was gouging his nails into the wood of the chair's arms. When she reached out to touch his bare thighs, he thought he was going to lose his mind.

"Dae. I swear to Darkness, you better untie me. I won't let you do this to me again!"

"Do what? I'm just touching you."

"Daenaira, you've seen what you have the power to do to me just by touching me. The next time I come for you, baby, I am damn well going to be inside you at the time. Do you understand me?"

"I'm probably not ready for that," she noted almost clinically. But there was nothing clinical in the feel of her fingertips brushing along the underside of his engorged penis. "This is so amazing," she marveled. "You are as hot as I am, only not wet. Except right here." She rubbed her fingertips over the weeping tip of his cock and he threw his head back as the racing agony of lightning-sharp pleasure scorched through his body.

"Fuck! Dae!" he gasped for breath as she closed her hand around him. "Don't. Gods, I am begging you."

"But I like this. I like seeing you react this way. You should feel what it does to me." She smiled as she thought about how he had said he craved the taste of her. It made her think of how to show him what she was talking about. She stood up on her knees and reached to slide her fingers between her legs. She couldn't help the shudder and moan that came over her as sensation spiked into her heated systems. She flicked a gaze of pure aroused passion at him as she withdrew her touch and reached to rub a wet fingertip over his lips briefly before dropping her hand into his lap and encircling him with the sample of her drenched state that coated her palm.

All Magnus could do was strain against his bonds as he

licked the taste of her onto a famished tongue and surged into the slick noose of her hand when she slid it wetly up and down his throbbing shaft.

"Darkness and Light," he choked out, agonized tears pricking harshly across his eyes as he began to tremble under her stroke. "Un-fucking-tie me, Daenaira! Gods! Stop! You don't understand!"

Two hundred years. It was too long. Too long between feeling like this. From famine to feast in sixty seconds, and he couldn't bear it. He was going to shame himself with his lack of control. She was too damn intense and so perfect! It wasn't fair. He had wanted this to be about her. Her discovery. Her power. Her pleasure. She had turned it around on him and she wouldn't listen.

Desperate, he wrenched against his bonds, hearing the satisfying crack of wood. Daenaira just looked up at him through her lashes, that little smile of hers flirting over her lips. It was a challenge. Could he free himself before she had her way? To tilt the odds in her favor, she imitated the stroke she had seen him use on himself in the bath.

When he got free, Magnus thought wildly, he was going to kill her. One orgasm at a time! She was going to pay for what she was doing. He pushed out against the arms of the chair and wood creaked ominously. But the strain of his efforts only thrust him into her clever hand, and he knew he was in big trouble. Huge trouble.

"Dae, I swear to *Drenna* and *M'gnone*, if you make me come like this, I will keep you locked in this room with me for two whole nights paying you back for it."

"Uh-huh," she acknowledged with an uncaring shrug. She was too focused and having too fascinated a time at his expense.

Dae could almost hear the last of his control snap. He threw back his head and began to surge up into her strokes, his whole body lifting to thrust through her fingers. He groaned savagely, his cock oozing heavily from the tip and making everything slippery and quick. She felt him, so thick and straining in her grasp, and she could tell he was close to climax by the raging of his breath and the animalistic sounds grinding out of him.

"I swear," he gasped, "you're mine after this. You're mine!"

"Yes," she agreed softly. "I know."

It was like igniting gunpowder, the way he suddenly seized when she said that. If he hadn't been so close already, the mere sound of her capitulation would have driven him over anyway. Just knowing she was finally going to give herself to him was enough to send him screaming into release.

Magnus felt his whole body surrender at once, breath, heart, and ejaculation exploding out of him in a burst of wild, fitful spasms. She was so delighted with her supremacy over him that she forgot to guard herself from the hard spurts of liquid release coming from him. Hot ejaculate dashed across her chest, and she actually laughed at the new and rather sticky sensation. The sight of it made the orgasm all that much more extreme for Magnus and he gritted his teeth together as his balls strained to paint her as much as possible.

Drained at last, he collapsed back in the chair.

"Stop," he begged her hoarsely when she continued to stroke him gently. "It's too intense."

"Okay," she said almost soothingly. She let go of him and sat back on her heels, reaching to swipe a finger through the sticky substance on her chest. "This is so . . . so . . ."

"Messy?" he supplied a bit breathlessly.

She giggled. "Well, yes. There is that. But I was thinking more about the scent of you. It's thick and . . . I think I like it."

"Good," he sighed. "Because in a few minutes, I'm going to start marking you with it until everyone will be able to know you're mine."

"You already started," she noted with a laugh.

He lifted his head and narrowed a look on her. "This was your way. Now I'm going to do it my way. First, though, you better untie me. Then you can use one of the cloths in that warmer to clean off." He nodded to the little black box about the size of a small refrigerator. She ignored the command to untie him and went straight for the box. The wet, hot cloth was perfect for the task, and it felt wonderful besides.

Magnus was done being bound and ignored. With a single vicious wrenching, he ripped one of the arms free of the chair. He had his wrist free of the sari binding him in a heartbeat and was out of his seat in another.

It was time to settle the score.

Chapter Nine

Tristan was so angry with himself that he could hardly see straight.

He was the co-ruler of an entire species. He was a king, a prince born to a noble house and raised in a noble tradition. He had started a war to end all the petty bullshit bickering that was keeping his people living a backwater existence while other Nightwalker races flourished beyond them and looked down on them like they were the embarrassing black sheep of the Nightwalker family. He was loved and paid loyal homage by his twin sister, who trusted him and had an undying faith in him to be so much better than he probably was. He had killed for her, run for her, lived for her, and almost died for her.

And now he was failing her.

Miserably.

He had never been so afraid in all of his life, and he was ashamed for himself because of it. To make matters worse, his behavior these past months had made his sister frantic with worry and concern for him. She knew he wasn't himself. She knew something was disturbing him. As if she didn't have enough stressing her right now? Rika, her best friend and advisor, had gone blind, the disease that ravaged her body destroying her optic nerves and promising to destroy much more than that before it was through. They were a breed of fast self-healers, but there were diseases like Crush and Jilk that were impossible for them to fight and had no cures. And why would they have cures? They were 'Dweller diseases, affecting 'Dwellers only. The only way such things could be analyzed and perhaps cured by conventional technology would require things like blood samples that would not only expose them for the supernatural creatures they were, but would expose that blood to things like microscope lights, which would burn it up into ashes instantly.

So now his sister was facing the imminent death of her beloved Rika, stressing with fear for a brother who was acting too unlike himself, and now, he had to tell her the government she ruled was going to try and force her into a loveless joining with . . . gods knew who.

He had wanted better for her. He had thought that when the clans were dissolved, the archaic way of marrying sons and daughters off to each other as a way of obtaining truces would no longer be a fate she would have to face; that she would finally have the freedom of the below-classes to marry purely for her emotional needs.

But no. The prick bastards in the Senate had uncovered an archaic tradition, using the twins' own tactics of reviving the monarchy against them. Tristan knew it was no coincidence this had happened just as they were uncovering traitorous Senators and unexpected deception in Sanctuary. If Baylor, a Senator, had not tried to recruit Trace against Tristan, they would never have known. But when Tristan's vizier had explosively denied the bribe, Trace had almost lost his life to Baylor's dagger in his ribs. They would still be in ignorance had it not been for Ashla and her miraculous ability to heal, which had saved Trace's life.

Now Trace had the worries of a new wife and coming

child, added to his regular duties and concerns in their political world, and this was why he had turned to Magnus. That and Tristan knew his sister trusted the priest and her faith beyond anyone else but himself.

And he had ruined that. Dread, cold and terrible, told him that. Perhaps if it had been only a month—maybe even two. But that had to be stretching it as it was. She could have forgiven him that much. But how would she ever forgive him for half a year? How could she forgive him for not telling her before Senate session had restarted? Magnus was right. He should have warned her. Prepared her.

But Magnus's sassy little handmaiden had been right, too.

Tristan was afraid of losing her to another life. To a new family. Children. A husband she might love. He had been so damn selfish it was unconscionable.

"Coward," he hissed to himself.

He had killed men with his bare hands. Fought off everything from sickness to fire and lived to tell the tales to any doe-eyed woman who cared to listen to his pompous arrogance, but he was a coward where it counted.

Tristan looked at the double wooden doors in front of him, the carvings so beautifully wrought and depicting a warrior princess standing in triumph over her enemies with her twin brother by her side. The doors to his chambers were duplicates of the design, only their positions were reversed. In both, the doors latched closed right where their hands and fingers were woven and interlaced together, signifying the Bond between them that had never been broken no matter how hard others had tried to come between them through the long years.

He glanced toward Xenia, who stood, as usual, silently contemplating her charge. She was the most brutal and efficient killer he had ever known, except perhaps for Guin, her counterpart who guarded his sister's life. Though she was a woman and it was highly irregular for him to choose an intimate guard of the opposite sex, he had insisted. Her quietude was one of the reasons why. Oh, she obviously had her opinions, but she kept them to herself for the most part unless they were meant to save his hide. Occasionally, though, she would make offhand remarks when she wanted to and always managed to make him feel stupid and moronic in the process. He had needed to be kept that humble, he supposed. Plus, he had promised Malaya he would choose the best to protect himself, and he had.

"What are you looking at?" he demanded of her irritably.

"I don't think you actually want me to answer that, *M'itisume*," she observed.

He sighed. "Yes. Probably not."

"I wish you had said something about this earlier. I think I know when it was you were warned about this and who it was that warned you, but you waved me back so I didn't hear the details."

"He wouldn't have talked with you standing there glaring at him like you do."

She brushed it off with a click of her tongue. "I don't glare. I study. I had to make certain I could kill him in under three seconds if I needed to. That is my job."

"Right," he said dryly. "I'm astounded as to why that would put people off."

"Now, now, no need to get sarcastic, *M'itisume*." She smiled smugly. "It's not going to make this any easier."

No. It wasn't.

And nothing could make it any harder either.

Tristan moved to the door.

Daenaira felt Magnus come up against her back within seconds, sweeping a steely arm around her and pinning her to the wall of his body. She dropped the washing cloth into the discard bin and reached to latch on to his wrists as his hands plastered to her skin. His hunger for the feel of her had been obvious for days, but now with free rein it was like unleashing a beast. The very first thing he did was to run his hands up over the breasts he had said that he'd so sorely neglected and desperately wanted.

She filled his palms and fingers heavily, the deep breath she took enhancing her shape and size for him. He held her tightly a moment, then slowly began to shape the lush fullness of her until she was squirming back against him and releasing little mewls of frustration. Her nipples sat between his fingers, but he did nothing to stimulate them despite the way she tried to seek him out.

"You didn't think it was going to be that easy, did you?" he asked in a deep purr against her neck. Magnus stepped back, grabbed hold of her arm, and swung her fully around to face him. "Let's see what we can do to keep you busy while I catch my breath a bit, hmm?"

Daenaira found herself soaring back onto the bed with a bounce, her hair flying all around her face. She pushed it free of her eyes in time to see him stripping off his tunic and filling her vision with darkly muscled masculine beauty. All he wore now was the biceps band of his office and the sexy dusted furring of black male body hair. He was so beautiful, and she wished she'd taken advantage of him more when he'd been tied up. She wanted to touch him all over his gorgeous body, but she had a feeling he wasn't going to let her.

He knelt onto the bed between her raised knees, his hands sliding onto them and up the insides of her thighs. He parted her legs wide so he could see her little panties better. When he reached out to touch the small triangle of fabric shielding her, she felt a shiver of stimulation wriggling through her as he lightly brushed his fingertips over her. Then he hooked on to them and swiftly skimmed them off her, snapping them away from her ankles and discarding them onto the pile of clothing.

"There now. Here's how the gods intended you, *K'yindara.*"

He studied her body with open intimacy, his fingertips absently tickling her near the inside of her left knee as he took his time. Dae laughed a little nervously as she tried to figure out what was so intriguing to him. Oh, she knew she was attractive to him, and was even figuring out which parts of her body were an undeniable lure to his eyes and senses, but she still couldn't always conceive of why.

"What is your schedule like for the next two nights, Daenaira?" he asked her.

"Busy," she breathed in anticipation.

That made him laugh. "True. Very busy. Are you nervous, honey?"

She scoffed at him, which meant she was, but wasn't about to admit it if she could help it. Magnus bent forward and kissed the inside of her knee. He very carefully kept a lid on all of the urges the musky scent of her sent stampeding through his brain, and just lightly touched his fingertips along her legs.

"Let's finish this lesson now, shall we?" He settled back onto his heels. Kneeling between her legs and then taking her calves in his hands, he gently relaxed her legs in a drape over his thighs. She must have realized the view the position afforded him, because she squirmed in an attempt to shield herself, but he held fast to her so she couldn't move from how he had positioned her.

"Magnus," she complained with hesitant discomfort.

"Let's return to touching, *K'yindara*. I want to see your hands all over your skin, sweetheart. Whatever feels good."

"You feel good," she noted in invitation.

"Oh, you'll feel me soon enough," he promised her, enjoying the immediate flush of response it provoked over her skin. "But this is something every woman should know. It will feel good for you, honey, and watching you will feel damn good for me, too."

Truth be told, he would love to give her her first orgasm. However, he knew it would be better for her like this. Let her learn the path first, and then he could take her back down it again and again with increasing intensity.

"Let's go back to those delightful breasts of yours,

K'yindara. Touch yourself. That's it. Your skin is so beautiful. The color of your nipples is so vibrant to me, like berries
on a vine, and I am dying to taste them."

Dae cupped herself, and with an arching of her back to sit
up, she offered him what he wanted. He knew she was curious about the sensation he promised, and he was craving her
reaction. He leaned forward and touched warm lips to her
skin along the rise of her breast. Instead of doing what she
wanted, though, he moved up to her shoulder and neck. Sucking gently against her pulse for a moment, he then drifted
over her jaw and found her mouth. He wouldn't commit to
the kiss, though, drawing back every time she tried to insist.

"Bossy little thing," he accused her, reaching to push her
back on the bed and sitting on his heels once more. She
groaned in her frustration. "Touch yourself. You don't need
me to feel good. You copped out once already by turning this
around on me. Well, it won't happen again. Why won't you
let yourself feel your own touch, sweetheart?"

"I just know it will feel better when you do the same thing."

"Yeah. It will," he agreed, licking at his parched lips. "But
we have two nights to compare. And the sooner you do this,
the sooner it's my turn."

That seemed to work. Really well, in fact. Magnus watched
as she drove suddenly eager hands all over her skin.

"Pinch and pull at your nipples, *K'yindara*. See how it feels.
Yes, you like that, don't you?" Her surprised breaths inward
and then soft moans to follow were quickly reviving his ap-
petites, so to speak. He began to grow hard again in quick increments, especially when he guided her hands down to her
pouty sex with its wet, waiting lips. "Slide your fingers into
your pussy, *K'yindara*. No. Don't. Don't be afraid of that feeling," he countered when she grew upset and restless again
and tried to withdraw. He caught her hand under his and sin-
gled out her center finger. He used it to guide her up to her fatly
flushed clitoris.

"You feel that? That little gem is your clit. It's a nexus of nerves that, when we stimulate you right, will make you come nice and hard for us. It's just like stroking my cock, baby. It'll make you explode."

"Will I be . . . uh . . . messy? Like you?" She flushed, feeling stupid for the question, but he smiled.

"Gods, I hope so. Wet, hot, and messy."

Daenaira felt her whole body flash with intense heat just listening to his anticipation. She dropped her gaze along his body as he slowly showed her how to slip her touch in circles against herself. He was glistening with perspiration all along his skin, every contour and muscle standing out in stark relief. She saw his penis was heavy and stiff with renewed excitement, and it altered the entire landscape of her arousal, charging it up to a new level of expectancy. She realized what would be happening soon between them, and little vignettes of the sexual scenes she'd glimpsed in her life began to stutter through her mind as a strange sensation of spiraling pleasure etched through her—and then faded.

He let go of her fingers, watching her continue and feeling the picture of her autoeroticism burn him from head to toe. Magnus should have encouraged her to dip her fingers inside herself, but he couldn't bring himself to do it. That, he thought fiercely, was *his* threshold. It was his to take. She could finish her lesson just like she was. Feeling her legs clutching restlessly around his thighs and watching her hips lift toward the stroke of her own touch assured him of it.

"Don't stop. That's it. Just let it take you, honey. Yes. Gods, you're gorgeous. Show me how you come, Dae." She was primed, her free hand restless on her skin and breasts now and her eyes closed as she immersed herself in her own touch and the encouragement of his voice. "And as soon as you do, then *I'm* going to show you how you come. I'm going to show you a whole different way. I'm going to feel you a whole new way. Dozens of new ways." Each promise brought her breath faster and harsher, and she shook her head in resistance again. He ignored the gesture because she didn't draw away from herself. She was just very close and she didn't know what to make of what she was feeling. She was so dripping wet he could see it and hear it as she touched. She had begun to moan softly, whispering his name and short words of denial.

"No," she cried out softly.

"Yes, Daenaira. Just let it go." Gods, she was killing him. Something had to break really soon or he wasn't going to be able to keep still much longer. After so many decades of denial, he couldn't believe how easy it was for him to fall back into this rush of need and craving. He couldn't believe how hard it was to maintain even the slightest control. But he was beginning to think it had far more to do with the woman than it had to do with the deprivation. He had seen hundreds of women in hundreds of classes rise to crest and orgasm, and he had been mostly unaffected. Brushing her hair had been the most exciting classroom experience that he could remember. Watching her go liquid like this again, it felt so good it hurt.

He felt her body shaking in quick trembles against his, and he whispered soft commands to her to keep her on track. She was gasping, her body bowing, and she was incredible. The mixture of stark sensual pleasure and unadulterated anxiety was a stamp on his memory forever. She shuddered, contracted into herself, and burst like fireworks. Magnus could tell instantly that it was a raw ride over the edge for her, her whole body far too worked up for its own good. He reached to quickly replace her touch against her spasming little clit when she jerked her hand away. He put pressure against her, easing the sharpness of the twisting tide for her. Her thighs clutched against his forearm and she cried out.

Daenaira did not feel the relief she had been expecting. Not in the least. Her heart was pounding and her muscles trembled as the too-keen pleasure spit through her in ragged seizures. Just when she thought she would scream, he eased away from her clitoris and left the little spot twitching and throbbing, hard and alone.

As she tried to catch a breath, she felt confused by what she had felt, but at the same time it had felt rather like he had looked that day in the bath—in pleasure and in agony, both against his desires.

"Easy, *K'yindara*," he said softly as he moved up over her trembling body to her mouth. "I know how that must have felt. It's like that sometimes when there's been such a drought of sensation that strong."

"Like for you that day I saw you."

"Yes. Exactly like that. It kind of turns you inside out."

"Kind of?" She laughed at the understatement.

But then she saw his smile as it spread slow and wicked over his features. "Yes, baby. I'm about to show you something a bit more specific."

"Oh, no, really, I think I'm done," she breathed, pushing her hands against his shoulders.

He laughed at that. "Done? We haven't even started." Magnus feinted for her mouth but she turned her head and laughed uneasily.

"Magnus, I'm serious. I don't want to feel like that again."

"You won't," he promised.

However, her belief in that promise would require something she wasn't sure about. It required she trust him. Oh, she didn't doubt he knew what he was doing. After all, Hera had told her there was hardly an adult in the city he hadn't taught sex to in one form or another. Considering what a sexual breed their people were, well, that said something.

So she didn't know why she was hesitating all of a sudden. Even as she pressed her hands against him in resistance, she wanted to feel him under her palms. Before she realized the impulse, she was curving hungry fingers up around the thick muscles of his shoulders. Gods, he was packed with power, and she could feel it vibrating through every inch of his hot flesh.

"I'm not ready for this," she confessed awkwardly.

"You're just afraid, Dae. It's perfectly natural, especially the way you've had to fight to keep control of your body over these years. What you are supposed to feel is a total abandonment of control. Resisting that is what makes it almost like pain for people like us who try to fight what should be coming naturally. You and I don't like to give up control. But for you, I think I would give up that and a whole lot more. That's something I've never felt before. Light, I've never felt half the emotions I feel because of you before."

"You mean pissed off beyond coherent thought?" she asked with a giggle as he bent to kiss her in the hollow at the base of her throat.

"That's one, yes," he sighed, finding her pulse and licking against it. "Also, possessive. Violently possessive. I wanted to rip Brendan apart today when he was reaching to touch you. Light, even watching him get on that bed with you just about made me lose it completely."

"Really?" Daenaira had no idea why something like that would make her smile, but she did, hiding it against the softness of his hair. The black curls were woven back into a plait at the base of his neck, small simple gold rings having been slipped onto the design at intervals. He didn't wear ornamentation like that often, she realized, but she rather liked it. It was masculine in its way, and sexy.

"And stupid," he sighed, drawing back to look down into her eyes, his hand coming up to touch knuckles over the arch of her brow. "I haven't made so many mistakes with one individual in all of my life." At least he didn't think he had. He suspected Karri might have been a close second. The thought made him frown.

"Why do you think you have?" She stroked him around his ear. "Am I really that difficult? I mean, I just don't seem to work right with anyone. Not even the best priest in all of Sanctuary."

"You are perfect for working with me," he countered quietly, "and don't let my idiotic confusion make you think otherwise. I'm getting this straight now. Not flawlessly, not yet, but I'm beginning to understand that there's a bigger plan to you and me than I was willing to commit to. Luckily, my goddess sent me a spitfire who could set me straight."

She gave him her signature smile, unable to help the slide of her hand straight down his chest and belly until her hand wrapped around his thickened member.

"Quite straight at that," she observed.

"Cheeky little bitch," he growled at her before snagging her in a kiss.

Dae instantly recalled how beautiful his mouth felt against hers, her breath sighing into his lips as he dipped for her taste. But the light flicker of a tease was all it took to blow oxygen onto the banked ashes of the passion they shared. He made a rich sound of need low in his throat and speared his tongue in hot search of her flavor.

Daenaira felt renewed heat rushing beneath her skin, infusing her tissues more deeply and vibrantly with every hungry tangling of his tongue with hers. Whatever his intentions had been, even as inexperienced as she was, she could feel them rapidly deteriorating as the fire in his kisses grew wilder and fiercer. She was breathless and dizzy by the time he began to touch her face with his fingertips. Dae could feel him pulsing hard between her fingers, her limp, distracted touch around him turned incidental as he assaulted her inexperienced senses with kisses that couldn't possibly be normal. She was learning how to catch up with him at first, and then how to keep up, but it wasn't long before even his aggression and passion couldn't suit them enough and she had to invest her own.

She let go of him, only to wrap herself tightly around his

broad shoulders, lifting herself off the bed to press her chest against him because she was starving for more contact.

"Drenna!" he gasped when he could finally pry himself away for air. "You're a siren. You've bewitched me from the start. *Aiya!* I'm desperate for you," he cried into her mouth as he took her again, his fingers streaking roughly through her hair.

"Magnus," she moaned restlessly, her legs climbing his body. "Touch. I need . . ."

"Yes, honey," he agreed, his large, rough hands leaving her hair to streak down over her face and throat. He gripped her silken shoulders, sliding his arms behind her back and thrusting her breasts upward as he pulled from her mouth and lowered his head to rub his lips down the skin of her breastbone. Her sugary cream scent pervaded his senses thickly because of how long she had been aroused already, the state intensifying the heady aroma especially between and beneath her breasts as he kissed and licked the salty sweetness of her perspiring skin.

When he caught her nipple abruptly between the ginger bite of his teeth, she jerked herself concave to the sensation, but had nowhere to go with his powerful arms at her back. A moment later, she no longer had any desire to pull away. He nipped and drew at the pointed tip until she had both hands dug deep into his hair and she could hear her own cries echoing into the room.

"Hush," he soothed her, licking a slow caress to ease the pleasurable sting of his teeth. "Save that sexy voice of yours, sweet Dae. You're going to need it later."

She laughed breathlessly, knowing by his tone that he was teasing her. She could feel the racing of his heart against her belly and the hot drip of his cock against her bottom. He was just as aroused as she was, if not more, and he thought to act superior as he wove his hot magic against her skin. Well, it wasn't as though she hadn't seen a few things for herself and hadn't been paying very close attention. She clearly needed to pull her wits about her long enough to remind him of that.

Now that Daenaira had that in her focus, she was a little bit better able to concentrate in spite of his teeth returning to rub and nibble wickedly at her again. Though she'd never known the sensation, his taut tugging made her crave the full seal of his mouth. She wanted to feel him suck at her strongly, the way she knew he wanted to. He was just enjoying his torturous play and her wild reactions so much that his superiority was getting in the way of their mutual want. He shifted to the opposite breast and she bucked beneath him. Dae had to wait for her brain to clear of the explosive cloud of pleasure it sent hazing over her before she could concentrate on a little payback.

She wriggled a hand free of his hair, only then realizing just how deeply she had entwined her fingers into the plait, and waiting for a moment when he wasn't watching her face she quickly ran her tongue up the inside of her palm. Dae had to pause a second when the combined flavor of both of their bodies danced over her taste buds, swallowing a groan and the delicious essence they made together. Then she watched him very carefully, a wicked smile already teasing her lips as she wriggled her hand between their bodies and reached to wrap him in her wet fingers.

This time it was Magnus's turn to surge sharply upward into her, the oath that slipped out of him coarse and guttural.

"M'jan," she taunted, tsking her tongue softly against his ear, "such language."

Magnus's golden gaze seared against hers, a world of decadent promises lurching from them in time to the thrust of his thick erection through her slick grasp. Together they worked him into a near frenzy, the swelling hardness of him seeming to grow in leaps and bounds. Then he swept himself out of her grasp with a wet pop of sound and seized her wrists in his hands, pinning them far above her head and catching her in a single locked grasp in order to free the hand he then burned sharply down her body. Her breast was targeted by his mouth and finally, *oh gods, finally*, she felt the savage draw of his lips sucking her nipple into contact with the flickering taunt of his tongue. His fingertip dipped briefly into her navel, then raked a winding path through tight little curls until he was swimming in slick and ready heat.

He touched that nexus of nerves he had shown her, and Daenaira gasped as the draw of his mouth sent out a stab of need that sang straight to that contact. Magnus released the rigid nipple he held prisoner, blowing softly on her in his own wake, smiling when she squirmed madly, trying to make him reclaim his kiss against her.

"Now what kind of lover would I be if I only focused on the right, the left, and the in-between?" he asked gruffly, teasing her with Brendan's blithe references from his class. When her eyes went wide in surprise, he chuckled.

"How long were you standing there anyway?" she asked him breathily.

"I saw that part from the rotunda ceiling." He lifted away from her and his gaze glided hungrily over her damp, glowing skin. Passion became her, he thought heatedly. He'd never seen a woman so stunning in all of his long years. "This view is much more appealing," he added. He drew his fingers from her slick folds, watching as he rubbed the liquid mark of her onto his thumb and taking a moment to remember the too-brief taste he'd had of her. Looking up into brightly fevered amber, he brought his thumb to his mouth and licked her essence from himself.

"M'jan. *J'esa vela duwea,*" she begged him restlessly.

"Oh, but teasing you is the best part," he countered with an arrogant smile.

"I know the feeling," she retorted, reminding him quite soundly that she was way ahead of the game when it came to teasing him beyond his tolerances.

"Little minx," he hissed softly, his eyes flashing a promise of sweet vengeance just before he bent to trail his mouth over her skin again.

Magnus was overwhelmed with the erotic taste of her on his tongue. What he wanted was to bury himself tongue first "in-between" for a good long time, but she had challenged him and he couldn't let it pass. He did return his fingers, although now he avoided her clit and used a ghostly, fluttering touch that taunted but refused to satisfy. Meanwhile, he covered her body as far as he could reach with kisses, licks, and those little nips she liked so much, all the while keeping her pinned down by her wrists and the wrap of his legs around hers. He wasn't satisfied until she was alternately cursing him and moaning softly, her skin wet with his saliva and her perspiration. Then he swiftly rolled her over, trapped her again, and began once more. This time he walked his touch down the line of her spine, following it all the way to the tip of her tailbone and on to her perineum before finding her vaginal rim and teasing her mercilessly with light flickering touches and pressing just the pad of a thickly callused fingertip into her.

"Bituth amec!" she gasped raggedly as his teeth nibbled along the line of her shoulder. "Magnus!"

"What is it, *jei*—?" He caught himself at the last minute, cursing silently against her skin. The last thing he wanted was to say or do anything that would anger her. The anger she was expressing at the moment was passionate frustration. It was all that was allowed. He didn't know who had made the terminology of affection such a negative thing for her, but he would cut their tongues in half for the offense if he ever got hold of them.

"I can't bear this," she sobbed.

"Yes, you can," he countered, glad she was too distraught with her need to have noticed his faux pas. "Pretty Daenaira. You're made of much tougher stuff than this. Tell me, *K'yin-dara*, what you would have me do? I'm curious. When I finally thrust inside you, Dae, what position is it you've dreamed of? Where have your fantasies taken you? And I know you've had them. I've kept my promise never to touch you, but I watched you during the daylight hours while you slept so restlessly in your bed."

She gasped at that, trying to wrench around to see him.

"I sleep unclothed!"

"I know." He chuckled. "Intriguing habit you picked up about four days ago. I'm interested as to why."

"Maybe it's because I knew you were there and I hope I tortured your perverted ass to death!" She was so furious he could see her skin flushing down her back. He smiled as he felt the heat radiating against his face.

"Oh, is that why you called my name then? Torturing me from Dreamscape?"

"Yes, you arrogant bastard!"

"You sound mad, honey. Perhaps we should stop and talk about this."

Magnus withdrew his touch, then his kiss, and began to lift his body from hers.

"No! Wait, I—"

Magnus waited. She growled in frustration into the bedding.

"If you tell me the truth," he coaxed in a whisper, "I will turn you over, spread these fine thighs, and show you what a man's tongue against your clit can feel like."

Dae whimpered softly at the sexually charged promise. She didn't even understand why she found the idea so thrilling, other than realizing that everything he had done to her so far had felt a thousand times better than anything she'd ever known in her lifetime. Better than she had even dreamed those nights she had called for him unwittingly in her sleep. In her waking hours she had been righteously infuriated with him, but in her sleep her body had remembered and craved him. Her waking sexuality had not borne the distance from him well at all. She'd been flooded with visions of them together that she could hardly comprehend the vividness of. How had she dreamed so clearly of things she'd never known?

"I dreamed of you," she confessed weakly, her body running hot as she anticipated the reward he'd promised with every word she spoke. "I dreamed of you coming inside me as hard as when I saw you in the bath. I . . ." She swallowed. "I could feel you, like Killian and Diana, entering me from behind while I reached to have you slide through my fingers every time you withdrew."

"Gods!" Magnus choked out suddenly, his powerful hands flipping her so fast her hair tangled over her face, forcing her to shove it out of her way. Only then did she realize her hands were free, but it didn't matter the next instant as her thighs were drawn open in his strong hands and she felt his breath cascading over her hot core.

The most Diana had done to Killian was fondle his balls on his in stroke, Magnus recalled all too clearly. The dream she described, the *vision* she described, had been one of his making. Or so he had thought. If he'd had any doubts about whether he should be indulging in this craving he had for her, they would have been instantly eradicated. *Drenna* had destined her for him. She had done all in Her power to bring them to this point, even in spite of how close he had come to destroying Her careful plans.

However, he had left those doubts at the door long, long ago. In his soul he had already known this was where he was meant to be. Everything, even Karri's betrayal, had been designed to bring him to this woman's embrace.

"How did I ever think I could turn you away, *K'yindara*?" he murmured softly as his lips ghosted a kiss against her. "What did I do to earn you or your forgiveness?"

Daenaira figured it was a rhetorical question because the swipe of his tongue against her was designed to rob her of speech. She reached for him, her fingers clutching into his hair, the feel of warm golden rings clacking against her nails. Tears leapt into her eyes as one flick turned into a longer stroke and then a longer, slower stroke after that. He groaned against her, the vibration of sound shimmering up through the center of her body until she shivered with sensation. His fingers slid along her labia, parting her lips wide until she felt exposed and vulnerable, the perfect victim for his next sensual attack. When his lips drew against her clit she almost leapt out of her own skin.

Then he was suddenly wrapping both arms around her thighs, hauling her bottom off the bed as he threw her legs over his shoulders and buried his face against her. The next few minutes were a blur of unadulterated bliss for Daenaira, her sight hazing into blackness as her entire world became focused inward and the sensations of his mouth and tongue dancing against her. The only time he left her clit was for forays to the rim of her vagina. Then he thrust his tongue deep into her sheath and her entire universe exploded into color and the screams of a woman in ultimate pleasure. Her body bucked and writhed, her throat locked in the cries she realized were originating from her own vocal cords.

This was the release she had been looking for before. For days. For years. This time there were no agonizing drawbacks, no painful wrenches of remaining need. She flew while the rest of the world crawled, and it was beautiful.

When Magnus surged up her body to kiss her, she was crying, tears dripping into her hair as her sounds of joy turned into sobs bordering on panic.

"Shh," he soothed her, kissing her mouth softly as he brushed at her tears. "It's okay, honey. Just breathe, baby."

She tried her best, but it was hard to do when she could smell and taste herself on him with every kiss and it began a whole new ache inside of her. She was hollow and needing, and she knew he had what it would take to fill her and satisfy her. The fear, however, was that it went deeper than just the physical demands of her awakening body. But Dae forced herself to push that and the rest of her racing thoughts far away. She focused on the powerful male she held clutched between her legs, and with an aggressive thrust of her tongue she took over the kiss of sentimentality and shoved it back into the realm of desire and raw sexuality.

As successful as she was, though, it took only the first sensation of hard, heavy male arousal along the valley of her sex to bring one very singular thought of terror racing to the front of her mind. Her hands had fallen to his shoulders and, unwittingly, the burrowing of her nails in his flesh gave her away.

"K'yindara," he called softly to her, making her realize she had screwed her eyes shut tight and that she was still weeping in spite of herself. "Talk, sweetheart. Tell me."

She shook her head, licking her lips nervously and refusing to open her eyes. He went carefully still, and she exhaled, breathing, she noticed, for the first time in ages.

"Daenaira, talk to me."

Her wet lashes parted, casting his handsome features into a crystalline kaleidoscope of color. She shook her head again, unable to stop the denial even as she said, "I don't want to know. I'm not ready to know. I don't . . . I can't . . ."

Magnus should have been completely mystified; after all, she wasn't really making sense. However, all it took was one look into her swimming amber eyes and he knew.

He just knew.

She didn't want to know, beyond all doubt, whether she had been taken against her will during her captivity.

"Listen to me, Dae," he said, making sure she looked deeply into his eyes as he spoke, "it never happened. Look at me," he said sharply when she closed her eyes. She obeyed him, surprise widening her pupils. "Do you know what my third power is?" She shook her head. "I can compel the truth. Whether you realize it or not, you know the truth of what did or did not happen to you. Now I can compel you to witness this as the truth, or you can trust me and believe me when I say *it never happened.*"

"How can you say that? How can you talk about something you and I both know you don't know for sure?"

The truth was, he did know. He had already compelled the truth from someone else. He had wanted to tell her, but there had been no way to broach such a sensitive topic when she was so angry with him. Magnus knew that, as she studied him, it was only a matter of time before she understood for herself, so he had to figure out the best way to handle this. He was convinced, however, that bringing up the names of the Sinners who had done her such awful injustice was not the way. They did not belong in this moment between them, and so he would find another way.

"Stay with me," he encouraged her softly, making her focus on his eyes as he slid himself into place at the entrance to her body. "Shh, just trust me," he soothed her when she tensed. "Believe me, *K'yindara*. Just believe. This is the moment of permission. Nothing before this ever took place because you were strong enough to decide your own fate. No beatings, no extreme devices were ever stronger than you were." He bent to kiss her gently, unintentionally starting her tears again with his tenderness. "Tell me I can touch you, Daenaira. Give me permission to touch you. Let me be the very first. Trust me to be the very first."

Dae swallowed, wanting to shake her head again—and yet wanting to believe him with all of her heart.

"Say it, *jei li*," he whispered, the endearment the only thing he could use at that instant. "Give me permission to touch you."

Tears falling so quickly they tore his heart in two, she nodded.

"Touch me, Magnus," she rasped on a broken sob. "Please, touch me."

"Okay," he breathed against her lips as he kissed her slowly. "Okay, *jei li*. This might hurt a little, you know that, right? Just the first time."

She shook her head, but he wasn't sure if it was because she didn't know or because she really didn't believe him after all. She was so courageous in that moment, though, it hurt his soul to look at her.

Magnus shifted forward, the shallow push merely an introduction to his girth which, he knew, was substantial for an untried girl. In his favor was the unbelievable slickness of her prepared body. He should have introduced his fingers into her first, but instinct told him she wouldn't be able to bear waiting without panicking now that she was focused on placing her faith with nothing but his word to reassure her.

"It is believed that when a handmaiden comes to her priest a virgin, it increases the chance of a Bonding. You know what this is?"

"When a priest and maiden c-can develop a telepathic Bond," she supplied, her unsteady voice squeezing his heart.

"Relax, honey, just a little. You're really tight," he said, trying not to close his eyes from the overwhelming sensation so he could keep her anchored. "You're right. *K'yan* Hera taught you that?"

Magnus eased forward and the tight ring of her entrance popped over the head of his cock, fitting hot and so damn snug it took his breath away.

Daenaira gasped, the first sting of pain lancing up through her, and her eyes shot wide open. Incongruous to the pain, she let out a shocked laugh. *It hurt.*

"It hurts!"

Magnus would be really surprised if it wasn't the first time a woman had ever been so wildly delighted to feel the pain of losing her virginity.

"Want me to slow down?" he asked, trying not to chuckle.

"That would mean going in reverse," she noted dryly.

Now he laughed, at least until she gasped because it shifted him inside her about another half an inch.

"Hera?" he prompted again, rubbing a tender thumb over the rise of her flushed cheek. This would have gone so much easier on her if they'd been lost in the pleasure of the moment, but that wouldn't be possible this time.

"Sort of," she exhaled. "She was telling me about M'jan Kincaid."

"Ah. Waxing nostalgic, was she?" Magnus watched her smile and then wiped the expression away by easing nearly out of her and then forward again.

"Magnus . . ."

Now her fear was returning, shifting focus as her pain increased.

"She was Bonded to him. Kincaid loved her in a way priests are not supposed to love anyone but our gods." Magnus knew he was going to have to move them to a different pace, and he leaned to catch her mouth against his in order to capture the cry he knew would come.

Magnus thrust as deep as he dared in one strong move and Daenaira sucked in a wild gasp of pain, her hands going from grip to push as she suddenly tried to shove him away from her.

"No! No, stop! *Sua vec'a!*" she cried.

Magnus reached to grab her wrists, pinning them to the bed and using her wrenching attempt to escape him to sink into her the rest of the way.

"*Jei li!* It's done! Stop. Stop!" He let go of her, bracing for the strike he knew was going to come. He figured it was fair play, after all.

"Don't you call me that, you lousy bastard!" she sobbed, tears spilling from her lashes. "I told you not to call me that!"

To his surprise she didn't hit him. She just lay limply against the bedding, crying until she just about broke his heart with it.

"I'm sorry, *K'yindara,*" he soothed her softly, bending to kiss her tears away. "I didn't want to hurt you. It was the only way. It will be better now."

"It's already better," she sniffled, reaching to stroke his temple. "I'm a virgin," she explained at his perplexed look.

"Uh . . ." Magnus laughed and glanced down between their tightly joined bodies.

"Shut up, you know what I meant."

"All right, so long as that's clear." He chuckled.

"I must seem pretty silly to you." She giggled.

"No, baby. Not at all. You seem . . ."

Tight. Gorgeously, beautifully, really damn *tight*.

Dae saw the expression that crossed his face and she watched with fascination as he shuddered and took a deep breath.

"Magnus?"

"Just . . . one second, Dae. I need a second."

Now that the worst of the sharp pain had passed, and with the relief of realizing Magnus had been correct about the sanctity of her body being intact, Daenaira's attention began to return to the same exact place Magnus's was coming back to.

"Mmm," she hummed. "I think you're beginning to feel nice."

"Well, that's good," he said a bit breathlessly. "Because I think I'm going to have to move very soon. *Drenna*, you feel amazing, Dae. And it's been a very long time since I've done this. If you hadn't made me come earlier, I would have probably climaxed already. Gods, did I mention you feel fantastic?"

"Yes." She laughed. She didn't realize she jarred him when she did that, but she discovered it quickly. Magnus groaned deeply, his forehead thumping against her breastbone.

"Right. You said something about feeling better?"

"Yes, baby," she purred teasingly.

"I get the feeling you're mocking me," he growled.

"Because I am."

"Mmm. Okay then. Let's try this."

He looked up, his golden eyes flashing wickedly at her before he dipped to the left and snagged her nipple between his teeth. Magnus reveled in her cry, nipping and flicking her until she was chaining out soft, mewling sounds of pleasure. Gods knew it was going to be a test in his endurance from that instant on, because every time he touched her she tensed up or shivered, the feeling shuddering through him cock first. He reached for her where their bodies were joined, his thick fingertips plucking at her clitoris, then soothing it with stimulating swirls. Before long, she was bathing him in fresh wet heat, her legs clinging tighter to his hips and her brutally tight channel loving him in strangling hugs of muscular contraction.

Oh yes, he absolutely had to move now. If she came around him too soon, he was going to completely lose it.

Daenaira had lost all sense of time and focus, her whole world swimming under the mastery of Magnus's torturous touches. She slid her hands down the flexing strength of his back, dipping into that place where his tattoo so beautifully accented his waist and the flare of his backside. She traced smooth skin over hard muscle, grabbing hold of his ass just as he drew away from her almost to the point of leaving her body completely. She felt a twinge of soreness ricocheting through her, but she didn't as much as flinch, knowing it would make him hesitate and stop all of the magic he was creating. She admitted to herself that she was afraid of the return stroke, but at the same time she knew there would be a point when it wouldn't hurt any longer. After all, so many people couldn't be wrong. The man who had taught so many people to love sex couldn't be wrong.

Sure enough, as he slid slowly into place inside her again, Dae completely forgot it was supposed to hurt. This was because of the unexpected wash of joy that hurried over her as the hand toying with her button of nerves and the mouth at her breast combined to send overwhelming messages of pleasure to all of her brain cells all at once.

After a couple more testing thrusts, Magnus lost all sense of reserve and purposeful finesse. His mouth came up to Dae's so he could devour her with soul-wrenching kisses and his hand gripped her hip and thigh as he got his knees under them both. He found a rhythm of quick, easy surges into her that rapidly deteriorated into something far more urgent and deeply primal.

"*K'yindara*, gods, how you feel. It's like Light, how you burn me!"

Dae felt the powerful flex and rush of his body within hers and also the scorch of the heat he was talking about. But it wasn't her that caused it, and she would swear to that to *M'gnone*. He was breathing in a rush into her mouth, his big chest rubbing tauntingly over her breasts until she wanted to scream from the stimulation. His cock was thick and like a rod of pure fire inside her. So hard that she felt full to bursting, yet he still drew himself under rein, just barely. A last thread was all that needed to snap, and Dae knew she would discover the brute that hunted sin so mercilessly. The defender of realms and faith would be unleashed if she could just figure out . . .

Why her vision from those long days of sleep returned to her just then she would never know. They weren't even having sex in the same position. But she reached between their bodies and wrapped her fingers around his wet erection as he slid free of her and then returned with a push that now took him past two tight clutches. Fingers. Virgin pussy. Lush wet heat that smoldered.

"Ah, Dae!" he ground out. "Gods, baby, you shouldn't have fucking done that!"

Yes, she thought slyly, *I should have*. Especially the way he ignited into feverish, near-violent thrusts. After barely sixty seconds of her torture he was catching her hands, holding her down, and slamming his hips into hers with a wild, savage canting need. Dae's whole body rushed with those wicked hot chills only he could create, and her nipples went rigid as her clit throbbed out a countercadence.

"Magnus?" she gasped, her whole body short-circuiting and feeling as though it were falling away from her.

"Hang on, honey. Just remember I'm here and . . . *Drenna*! Baby, I'm going to come really soon, and I want you with me, you hear? Just let it happen. Just feel it."

Oh, she was feeling it all right. It was the pounding pulse of his cock burrowing madly for her core, and she could swear he grew fatter and fuller inside her by the second. Then, out of nowhere, her whole body seemed to unravel all at once, everything turning weak and then tense and then sharply raw with sensation just before she detonated in orgasm so brilliant she swore she saw sunlight flash beneath her closed lids. She soared, crying out his name over and over.

Magnus lurched forward as she clamped down on him like a vise, his system locking with a level of ecstasy he could never have imagined. The force of his climax alone took his breath, but the pleasure returned it and drove him to cry out for her.

"Yes! Gods, Dae! *Dae!* You're mine, Dae!"

Daenaira dug her nails in for purchase as she writhed beneath him and bucked to take his savage release. He frothed inside her body in burning waves of ejaculation, and a whole new surge of culmination ran amok through her body. She keened for him, seizing and grunting out moans of sexual oblivion.

Magnus was shaking head to toe as he remained braced over her. They were both gasping for breath, and Daenaira slowly pulled her nails free of his flesh and soothed the stung areas with gentle strokes of her fingertips in apology.

"I don't deserve you," Magnus uttered in spite of himself, knowing it was a moot point because he wasn't about to let her go. "*Drenna* blessed me and I don't know why. Darkness knows I've screwed up everything I've touched lately."

"Well, you've touched me and screwed me, yet I'm still smiling," she pointed out with a snicker.

"That you are," he noted, smiling very softly, though he didn't laugh. "I'm sorry for what I said. That day, I—"

Dae stopped him with the touch of her fingers against his mouth.

"I am rather an expert on saying things I don't mean when I'm afraid," she pointed out. "It just took me a while to realize you weren't being cruel, just chicken-shit."

"Yes, I suppose I was," he said, narrowing his eyes on her as he moved forward to cover her with his weight, caging her between his elbows. "I didn't recognize it either. I haven't felt fear in quite some time."

"I can't blame you, though. Between Karri and the way people are betraying what you are trying to have here, I think you have a right to feel insecure."

"What I feel is anger. No," he corrected, "deeper than that. It's a holy fury, Daenaira. But I am going to ferret out this mess if it is the last thing I do."

"I know you will. And I will do everything I can to help you."

That made him frown. Easing himself away from her, he sat up on the edge of the bed and rubbed at the tension in his neck that had been so blissfully relieved for a moment there, but was now returning with a vengeance.

"I would rather you just try to avoid trouble, Dae."

She laughed incredulously at that. "You're kidding, right? You plunged me into trouble the minute you brought me here and told everyone I was yours! And thank you, by the way, for the warning. You shouldn't have told me I was safe here when you knew I wasn't."

Magnus knew her condemnation was well deserved. But he had to defend himself. "I didn't think they would go after an innocent girl. Certainly not within hours of her arrival. I was trying to gain your trust and I didn't want you to flatly refuse to stay with me." He sighed. "It was selfish, I know. I'm sorry for that. I didn't want to bring you here. I ignored my visions as long as I could tolerate them. Oh, don't get me wrong, I wanted you more than anything, even in spite of Karri, but I didn't want to bring you into a den of danger knowing I had already been targeted once. However, *Drenna* saw to it that my life became total chaos until I capitulated and accepted you. I could only find peace by obeying."

"Some peace." She laughed. "I am not a relaxing individual. So, uh . . ." Dae licked her lips nervously. "What were these visions about?"

"Sex and violence." Magnus smiled wanly when she startled at the bald honesty of his reply. "In my dreams I was either making love with you frantically or watching you, me, and all of Sanctuary be destroyed by violence. I can't be more specific because the visions themselves are unspecific. Worst part is, they've begun again. I dream what you dream, *K'yindara*. That vision of making love to you from behind—it's uncanny you would describe exactly what I myself have seen. Now I have to ask you if you dream everything that I dream. Do you see violence as well?"

She nodded slowly, staring at him. "I thought it was just flashbacks. Nightmares. Even though I saw you and Sanctuary, I just thought . . ." She paused. "Does this mean those things *can* happen or that they *will* happen?"

"Visions are possibilities. Actions are the only thing able to determine our futures."

"Oh." She fell quiet, but then that sly little smile appeared as she looked him over with a slow and steady hunger. "What actions do I have to take in order to get you to do that thing where you throw me up against the wall?"

Chapter Ten

"No! Don't touch me!"

Malaya sharply shrugged off her twin and walked away from him, shivering at the unnaturalness of the act itself as much as from her unmitigated outrage.

"Laya," Tristan begged softly.

"Don't you 'Laya' me! *Six months!* Six months you have known this!" She rounded on him, her entire body shaking with the fury seething in her whiskey brown eyes. "Leave me. Leave these rooms, Tristan, before I say something I do not mean and will come to regret. *Drenna* damn you, you go!"

Tristan swallowed hard. Malaya never swore using the names of their gods. It wasn't a good sign, and the surety of his misery was heavy and terrible. He turned and walked toward the exit as requested.

"Is this what it's all been about?" she demanded sharply before he could even touch the knob of the door. "All of your insensitivity? The cavalier attitude? The nonstop sexual orgy?"

"Yes," he said simply, not bothering to turn around.

"I was worried about you!" she accused him. "Worried sick, you selfish bastard! Not to mention I feel like I have been running this species on my own for the past few months! We're surrounded by enemies, our friends are being targeted for death and you . . . you're . . . you're . . ." She turned to Guin harshly. "How did you put it, exactly?"

"Dick deep in pussy," Guin supplied softly for her.

Tristan narrowed a deadly look on the bodyguard, but Guin just shrugged one big shoulder and gave him a little smile. The smile, however, was cold and quite deadly. The Chancellor was given the uncomfortable feeling that Guin would have given away a critical body part for the opportunity to have a go at him, whether it earned him a date with an executioner or not. *Just how many people have I pissed off?* he wondered.

"I don't think you want to hear me make excuses, so I won't," he replied softly. "I'll just remind you that, in my own idiotic way, I wanted to protect you. I kept thinking I could figure this out; come up with a solution, and make it a nonissue. I thought that, when the danger was past, I could tell you and we'd laugh it all off. But . . ." Tristan swallowed noisily. "I don't want you to marry because you have to. I want you to marry because you are in love. I want you to be happy. Even more than that, though, I want you here. With me. Just as it's always been. You and me against the world; undefeated, untainted, unbroken." He looked at her with angst in his eyes, knowing she would see his fears. "I guess you're right. That does make me selfish. But I always have been when it comes to loving my sister. It's childish, I know, but I don't want anyone to share what you give me."

Tristan shut up with a snap of his teeth. He knew how bad all of this sounded. He knew how unforgivably spoiled he was. None of this was supposed to be about him. His sister was being hurt and made a victim of circumstance, and all he kept thinking about was how it would affect *him*. He didn't blame her for her fury. Gods knew he was furious with himself.

"Tristan, you share what I give you with an entire species! What do you think motivates me to put up with all that is asked of me? Without devotion and love and loyalty, you cannot do what we do. And sacrifice, Tristan," she said sadly, her disappointment in him so sharp he could taste it. It made him wince. "We make sacrifices for the ones we love. Even if that means I will have to marry, I will do it to keep my people safe and happy. And if it meant letting *you* go to get joined, I would do that, too, no matter how much it would break my heart to put others between us. But, Tristan, we can't claim a perfect love if we are never willing to put it to the test, or are never willing to share it out."

"I know. *K'yan* Daenaira said something very similar. It made me realize what an ass I was being." He turned back to her cautiously. He knew better than to make any quick presumptions when his sister was this angry. "Magnus convinced me it was important we be prepared for this when it happens. I think we need to figure out how to protect you. Fast. We are the absolute power in the end, Laya. We can force them, but they can't force us, remember? I want you to stand against this. Demand your rights as a free, modern ruler and woman. No one will blame you for that."

"That isn't true and you know it," she snapped. "We are a society of tradition. I cannot thumb my nose at that and neither can you. Especially in the political climate where treachery against us foments! And I am not talking to you about this right now. You have had months to consider all of this and I have had barely fifteen minutes! Get out, Tristan. Go find some woman to play with and leave me to think."

Malaya turned her back on her brother and marched into her bedroom. She knew, even before Guin slammed the door behind them in reflection of her anger, that she was hurting her twin purposely, but she was angry and now she needed the right to be angry. She paced her bedroom sharply, ignoring the sound of her brother's departure, biting on a nail in her upheaval.

"Bituth amec," she heard Guin utter gutturally.

She paused to look at him, seeing the giant leaning back

against the door, his thick arms folded with barely leashed strength across his chest. The rigidity of his muscles and the darkly dangerous look in his granite eyes were more than enough to tell her how incensed he was. Just what in Light did he have to be so mad about, she thought irritably. He wasn't the one with an ass for a brother who had completely screwed up!

She was just mad enough to say that out loud. Malaya watched with some fascination as his fists curled tight, and she could hear the grinding pop of his teeth clenching brutally together.

"Don't you worry about me," he said tightly through his teeth. "You just figure out how you're going to get around this edict when it comes."

"You know, I really would like to know when I gave the impression to the men in my life that I needed them to tell me what to do!" she spat. "What makes you think I want to 'get around' it?"

That seemed to take the wind out of him for a moment, and Malaya could swear she saw momentary panic filter into his eyes.

Panic?

Guin?

But even though the impression of expression disappeared, she could still see how hard he was breathing, and there was so much tension in his big body she was surprised he didn't combust before her very eyes.

"You would whore for a powerless Senate just for some archaic rule about unwed female rulers?" he demanded, a muscle jumping furiously in his jaw.

"I whore for no one," she hissed at him. "What I do, I do for the good of my species!"

"Your species gets along fine without you being married!" he barked.

"Yes, but for how long? How long before my flouting of tradition filters down into the actions of all of our women and men? What if students decide to ignore their education? Hmm? Why not? After all, if the Chancellor can defy tradition, so can they! What of all those potential Sinners who stay on the good side of the law just because they know they can't get away with defying the way things have always been? Do I set them loose on Shadow and Dreamscape? Or maybe all handmaidens will think they can kill their priests just because they are limited to a traditional role and don't want to accept his right to say no to conjugal relations just as it is her right to do so!"

"*Drenna*, that is not the same issue and you know it!" he roared, surging away from the door and marching up to her.

"You think not?" she demanded, facing off with him fearlessly despite his significant size advantage over her. "Corruption is given permission by a single act, *Ajai* Guin." She lifted a single finger up between them. "One drop of water can cause ripples for miles! With murderers in the halls of the Senate and Sanctuary, you think I actually have the freedom to thumb my nose at any demand they make of me and think it will not give my enemy fuel for their fire? They want me to say no. They want me to say *yes*. They know that either way they win and this regime is weakened. Nothing you or my foolish brother says or does will change that!"

"You are not getting joined to a stranger!" the bodyguard exploded in outrage, his hands jolting out to grab her arms, shocking her with the power he used to shake her in his fury. "If I have to murder every one of those treacherous fucks in their beds and face down every priest in Sanctuary because of it, I swear to you I will not allow it!"

"*You* won't allow it?" she cried incredulously. "Who are you to allow or disallow anything of me? You're nobody to this regime! You are Our protector and Our friend, Guin, but you have no power here! You certainly have no right to treat me like you have any say in my fate. What in Light has gotten into you?" Malaya squirmed in his grasp, trying to free herself of the bruising power of his beefy hands. "Let me go!"

"Let you go?" he echoed. *"Let you go?"* He laughed, a

hollow agony to the sound that made her go very still. "I've been trying to let you go for fifty goddamn years, *K'yatsume*. If I managed to achieve it now, it would be a thrice-damned miracle. But I swear to you, Malaya, that if you let them do this—if you let them force you into the arms of an undeserving stranger, I *will* let you go. I will walk away from here and this house will never hear a breath about me again. And while I know that is of little consequence to my *friend*"— the term was positively snide—"and even less of consequence to my queen, it's all I have to threaten you with and save myself with. I won't stand by and watch you do this." His voice lowered to a rasp as he drew her so close she could feel his warm breath against her temple. "I won't sit and suffer so you can marry someone you do not want and do not love. You speak of sacrifice so easily, but you do not understand how hard it is for those who do not have the goodness of the soul that you do. Well, this is a sacrifice I am unwilling to make. Here I will not compromise."

Guin suddenly shoved her away from himself, making her stumble. She recovered and stared at him as if he had truly lost his mind. And then he did the most shocking thing of all.

"K'yatsume," he said, standing at a stiff form of attention. "In fifty years I have never taken time for myself. I respectfully request to be relieved of duty for a week."

"Request denied," she shot at him sharply. "Guin, what in Light is going on here?"

He laughed, shaking his head. "You won't free me? When I have never asked you for anything before?"

"I don't trust you not to do something stupid! You didn't answer my question."

"All I want," he said tightly, "is some time away."

"You want to hunt traitors and get your fool neck separated from your idiot head!"

"No," he said, shaking his head heavily, the single small golden loop through his left ear flickering brightly. "I won't do that."

"Then why leave?"

"Because I won't sit here and watch every minute of you coming to the wrong decision!" he bellowed sharply. "Gods! You always accuse me of lacking faith, but I swear that you try me like a saint! Let me go or I will leave without your permission!"

"Then do not bother returning, *Ajai* Guin!"

"Do you really think that will stop me?" Guin stepped forward again, fists tight as he crowded up against her. Feeling the overwhelming heat of his body and the power he held so tightly reined in, Malaya couldn't fight the urge to step back. Before she realized it, she was backed up into the tile of the far wall. She didn't understand why she was intimidated all of a sudden. This was Guin, for Darkness' sake! He had dedicated his life to seeing no harm came to her. He had bullied her in the past, but she'd always given as good as she'd gotten. The thing was, he had never threatened to leave before, and she had no idea what to make of his behavior. "Let me make something very clear to you, *K'yatsume*," he all but purred as he lowered his mouth against her ear. "You are standing an inch away from a man who is rapidly realizing he has absolutely nothing to lose. Don't. Push. Me."

Malaya couldn't seem to help the flash of temper that raced through her. What in Light was wrong with the men in her life? She depended on their predictability, but now two of them were acting completely insane! So she didn't curb the impulse she had to reach out and *push* him. Not that he budged very much at all, but he narrowed his eyes on her as he realized she was purposely baiting him. Granite eyes darkened as he raked them down over her, from the tip of her widow's peak to the bare toes peeping out from under her *k'jurta*. Then, to her shock and surprise, Guin reached out and hooked a finger into the loose neckline of her blouse, pulling downward until her breast was exposed right to the line above her nipple. Her rapid breath brought her dangerously close to exposure to him, which shouldn't have even mattered after all the years he had been with her and spent seeing her nude during the course of her daily life.

"You push, I push," he promised her, the low threat giving her amazing chills down the corridor of her spine.

"Guin, cut it out," she snapped, smacking his hand away.

Or trying to. Guin never moved unless he wanted to move.

The bodyguard re-hooked his finger into her blouse and included her bra this time, pulling both away from her skin. She looked at him in shock, watching as he held her gaze and purposely pursed his lips before leaning a bit closer and blowing warmly against her exposed nipple. She stiffened in response, in more ways than one, and her breath clogged in her throat with her surprise.

"Let me go, or else, *K'yatsume*, I will stay very, very, *very* close to you instead." His fingertip, rough with the calluses of his warrior's trade, slipped into her bra and rubbed over the pointed tip of her nipple very lightly. "So close," he promised, "that I will be as good as inside you. Then again, I may not stop at 'as good as.' "

"Guin, stop," Malaya breathed, stunned at his behavior and at the way her voice shook. Frissons of heated arousal began to spark inside her, and she blushed hotly at the very idea of being turned on by one of her best friends. Guin had never made a pass at her in fifty years!

Well, there had been that one time . . .

But that had been a moment of emotional stress and his usual bullying. This time it was well beyond bullying, though! Technically, putting hands on a royal without invitation was an act of aggression that her bodyguard was allowed to kill for.

Except what happened when it was the bodyguard himself doing the aggressive touching?

"Make your choice. Close or far. One week of either is all the same to me. Both will relax me, both will afford me the release I need. It's up to you."

"Fine!" she hissed, smacking him away more definitively

this time. "Go! Get yourself laid, killed, or whatever it is you want to do! But don't you ever touch me like that again!" Malaya shoved at him, squeezing out from between him and the wall and storming out of the room.

"Not even if you beg me to?" he called to her back, chuckling when she slammed the door on him.

Guin sighed, his fabricated humor evaporating as soon as he was closed off from her. Clearly, he had developed a taste for torture. He ran a hand down the front of his fly, trying to adjust himself in the wake of feeling her and smelling her respond so readily to his touch. He had taken a huge risk, offering her an alternative choice like that. What would he have done in the wildly unlikely instance that she had accepted his challenge? If he thought he had trouble getting clear of her now, he could just imagine what it would be like once he had learned of her sexual body.

Because there was one thing Guin was absolutely sure of.

He was an addict. He had never taken the drug, but he was an addict just the same. He would trade his life away, do anything, sell out anyone—sell his soul to *M'gnone*, if that was what it took, just to dive into the bliss of that drug forever.

But forever was the only option once he started, and he knew that. Just as he knew starting wasn't an option in the first place.

Never had been, never would be.

Magnus lifted his head from the bed of Dae's hair beneath his whisker-coarse cheek, cocking his attention to the energy passing in the hall outside. With a sigh, he reached out and gently shook Dae awake.

"What is it?" she asked without opening her eyes, rolling over into the warmth of his body. She snuggled close and it made him smile.

"They're looking for me," he said softly.

"You're kidding, right? What part of me screaming 'Oh, Magnus! Yes, Magnus, yes!' did they not hear, exactly?"

"Soundproofing, *K'yindara*. These are private rooms. People need to feel free to express themselves."

"Oh." She chuckled. "Well, I certainly took that to heart."

"That you did," he agreed, bending to kiss her temple. "No one knows that but us, however, and I like it that way."

"Then how do you know you're needed?"

"It's a sense. The way people are moving through the halls. I can see them in infrared. They don't realize we came back, so it wouldn't occur to them to check for us in here. After all, why would I have my handmaiden in a private tutoring room when I have two perfectly good beds to choose from in our quarters?"

"That shows you how foolish it is to assume."

Daenaira sat up away from him, robbing him of the enjoyment of her warmth, and began to dress herself. He didn't see how he had any choice but to follow suit. They would find him eventually. They always did. And he didn't want anyone using Daenaira as fodder for gossip.

"I'll leave first. I need a bath anyway. Unless you think you will need me at the palace?"

"So you think it's Malaya looking for me?"

"Of course." She shrugged a bare shoulder, attracting his full attention to the ripe sway of her breast. "You said yourself that she would be calling on us once Tristan got up the nerve to speak with her. Tristan doesn't strike me as the sort to procrastinate."

Magnus laughed at that, a little incredulous as he shrugged into his tunic. "How can you say that after he spent six months doing exactly that?"

"No. He didn't. He might like to say that he was, but he was actually executing a plan. Like I said. He was trying to cut himself off first. Now that he has a new plan, he'll do that as quickly as possible. Sometimes procrastination is an action, not inaction."

Magnus knew this, of course, but it surprised him that she had this kind of insight into the psychological condition of the mind. She'd been locked away for eight years—where had all of this knowledge of people come from? There was still a great deal about her that he didn't know.

He still didn't have his boots on by the time she was draped in her sari and bending to give him a quick, chaste kiss on his lips. Finding that unacceptable, he buried a hand in her hair and jerked her down into his lap, bending her back over his arm as he kissed her with enough depth to make her boneless and compliant within his grasp all over again. Not that he was going to take her again. The second time had already been rather selfish of him, putting her untried body at risk of soreness and aches he would rather she avoid even if she would heal quickly. But once she'd reminded him of that fabulous vision he'd—*they'd*—had of taking her hard against a wall, he'd been unable to stop himself.

Magnus whisked her up off his lap and back onto her feet, propelling her to the door with a smack on her luscious fanny. She rubbed the offended area a bit too slowly and suggestively as she threw a heated look at him over her shoulder before leaving. The priest swallowed hard, realizing that with a woman as bold as Dae was, opening the door of her sexuality was going to be like letting loose the proverbial tiger. She was beautiful and savage in her own right, full of danger and surprises. He had a feeling he was in for the ride of his life.

Daenaira left for their rooms with a smile on her lips and a twinge of awkwardness in her step. When Magnus had first entered her the second time, it had hurt a bit, but nothing like the first time. Just the same, she was happy and relieved when she slid into the hot waters of their bath. She had grown to enjoy the spoiling pleasure of luxuries like the bath. Sometimes she would feel momentary fear about that, because she knew life was unpredictable, and what she had been given could just as easily be taken away, but she had to trust Magnus to protect their way of life, if nothing else. Of course, if his enemies had their way . . .

Cold, hard dread filled her belly. Daenaira simply couldn't seem to make herself think cavalierly about Magnus's possible death. It was stupid, really, because especially given the environment of threat, it could very well happen, and she had to be prepared for that. She had to wonder what would happen to her. *K'yan* Hera had never been chosen by another priest and was living a life of contented solitude amongst her peers. She had been for the forty years since Kincaid's death. Sanctuary had even offered to generously retire her at any time when Kincaid had died. Apparently, they had realized that a Bonded handmaiden would never be able to give herself to someone else—this was how powerful the connection was—and they had offered to let her live peacefully as she desired.

But Dae wasn't Bonded, and she wasn't likely to be if it hadn't happened by now. The thought made her smile and shiver all at once. The shiver was a bit of a chill at the thought of being handed over to a priest who might very well have had a hand in Magnus's death. The sheer morbidity and echoes of her old life that were in that thought made her frown, not to mention the understanding that she did not trust anyone in Sanctuary. The smile was the better part of her thoughts. It was a memory of the past few hours and how hard Magnus had worked to see her through the lessons of sexual awakening she had needed and, admittedly, wanted. She couldn't imagine being so intimate with anyone other than Magnus. For all their difficulties, some of which were still as unresolved as they had been before, there was something powerful and undeniable between them physically. Before Magnus, she had never imagined being voluntarily willing to give her body to a man. Now she looked forward to his return with eager signs of arousal flashing through her.

Dae got out of the bath quickly after that. What she needed was to keep occupied. She should return to her classes for the night as if nothing had changed. Besides, she had to admit she was growing fond of the private instruction time she had with *K'yan* Hera. Not just because she liked the woman, but the topic of their religion had become a fascinating subject for Daenaira. Especially when explained in Hera's devoted voice and with her obvious eagerness for the topic at hand. Dae was coming to appreciate the nuances of the role priests and handmaidens played as physical representatives of the gods they worshipped.

She plaited her hair because it was wet, dressed in a clean sari, and headed out into the common areas again. She was just entering the main atrium when she ran into Tiana.

"Dae! Good night to you," her newest friend greeted her.

"Good night, Tiana. How are you today?" Dae felt bad for *K'yan* Tiana. The girl had done nothing wrong, but by association she was being treated as the pariah that Cort should have been treated as. Dae found it unfair that an innocent woman should suffer for the acts of a treacherous man. The only thing Tiana was guilty of, as far as Daenaira could see, was trusting the wrong male and being ignorant of his secret life.

"I am fine," Tiana lied. The handmaiden was quite sensitive to the way she was being treated. As Dae understood it, because she had been the maiden of a penance priest, she had enjoyed a certain level of prestige while Cort had been alive. Now she was quite removed from any of the influence she had enjoyed.

Despite the claims that all handmaidens and all priests were equal to their peers in place and power, it was clear there was a pecking order to be found, and the more powerful one partner was in either the male or the female order, the more powerful the other became by association. Magnus was, of course, top of the chain within the ranks of the males, with Shiloh a frightening second, but Karri had been second to Hera on the ladder in spite of that. Clearly age and wisdom had its place, but the Bonding was a trump card amongst the women. It was the ultimate achievement for a handmaiden, and therefore the ultimate determiner of position. Being young and new, Daenaira had no position at all, really, until she took her vow officially and developed a stronger relationship with her priest. The battle for position didn't really concern her though. She had enough to worry about just managing things between Magnus and herself.

"Will you walk with me?" Dae asked her friend. Tiana nodded happily.

Tiana was chatty for a few minutes, almost nervously so, making Dae smile at her. She stopped her in a secluded alcove, drawing her close.

"You're buzzing like a bee," she scolded her softly. "Tell me what is on your mind."

"Nothing. Really." Tiana laughed softly. "I guess I'm just glad to have someone to talk to. Things like this . . . you learn who your real friends are." The pretty little brunette frowned. "I thought some of these women were the best of friends, people I could trust with just about anything. But the way they treat me—when it wasn't even me who did anything wrong!" Tiana's lower lip trembled and tears swam in her eyes before she turned her face away to hide them. "Cort was such a mean bastard," she confessed. "Cold to the core. But I did what I was supposed to do and I didn't complain. No matter how roughly he would use me sometimes. He barely kept within my tolerances and I could feel sometimes how he wanted to go beyond . . ."

Tiana swallowed and looked back at her new friend. "I wasn't surprised it was him. When I heard about the attempt to rape you, I swear I felt ice freeze my soul. He was so close to that edge, and you could just taste it on him. But I swear to you, if I had been sure—if I had really known—I would have said so. If I had known him and Daniel and others were plotting, *I would have said so*. But I didn't. I was so stupid and naïve." She dashed away her tears and sniffled as her lip trembled all the harder with her repressed misery. Daenaira's heart went out to her.

"Why didn't you ever go to Magnus about how he was treating you? He would have listened to you."

"I don't know. Cort always made like he owned me, that all of this was his by his right as a priest." She indicated the length of her body. "And it wasn't always bad. He had this kindness sometimes. Humor. I figured he just liked rough sex. He was entitled to his preferences, after all."

"So were you. You could have said no," Dae said darkly.

"I tried that once," she confessed on a low voice, as if Cort were still alive to wreak vengeance on her for telling tales out of the bedroom. "He punished me for it. I never tried again."

"Tiana!" Daenaira was horrified. "Did he torture you?"

Tiana flushed a dark red under her bronzed skin-tone. "Not like you mean. Um . . ." She licked her lips with her discomfort. "I . . . rather liked most of it, actually. I guess that makes me foolish."

"No. It doesn't. I won't pretend to understand, either. I never had sexual instruction until Magnus began to teach me, so I'm a little raw still." Daenaira couldn't help but smile when she thought back to their time in the tutoring room.

Tiana studied her and a grin twitched over her lips. "Would you like to see something? But you can't tell Magnus. If M'jan Magnus knew I knew about this, or that I told you about this, he'd pop a major vessel and drop dead. Then Shiloh would take over and all Light would break loose on the 'scapes."

"Tiana," Dae scolded with a little laugh. She didn't like the idea of keeping purposefully directed secrets from Magnus, but considering all that was happening, she couldn't ignore any opportunities to get a deeper look below the surface of Sanctuary and the people running it. Maybe she could find a way to help Magnus in the long run. "What will you show me?"

Silently, Tiana hurried her into the corridors. They went

back toward the educational and residential wings, and traveled past the tutoring rooms and lecture halls. She led her into a small door after making sure no one was around. It all seemed so covert that Daenaira developed a chill.

When she realized they had been shut into a small storage closet, she laughed with a nervous sort of relief. She didn't care for small rooms, but it was empty of anything but sheets and other supplies for tending the teaching halls.

That relief lasted all of a minute.

Then Tiana moved to a shelf, inserted her hand into a small crevasse, and with incredible ease was able to move one of the heavy shelves out, taking a good portion of the wall with it. She gestured Daenaira forward, but now a steady sense of warning and dread was beginning to fill Dae's soul. Secret entrances to secret places in Sanctuary? Had Tiana implied Magnus knew about this?

Of course he had to know about it. Didn't he? He and Tristan had designed every detail of Sanctuary, *K'yan* Hera had told her. Cautiously, watching her senses for any danger, Dae moved to follow the other woman. Had she been wrong about Tiana all of this time? Was she being led into some sort of a trap by Cort's handmaiden? Was it foolhardy to simply keep following her?

Maybe, she thought wryly, but she had to continue. She could end up learning something valuable to Magnus if she did. Besides, she had proven to herself that even chained to a wall, it was impossible to get the better of her. If she just kept believing that and remembering everything she had been learning, she could do this and return to Magnus in one piece.

Tiana closed the entrance tightly behind them, and Dae quickly tried to find the release on the new side of the wall. However, she was unsuccessful by the time Tiana took her hand and started leading her through thin jagged tunnels cut straight from the hardness of the mountain rock. Keeping hold of her sense of direction, Dae realized they were doubling back. Tiana stopped and gestured to the right. There was a little alcove there and, from floor to ceiling at about the height of a man of Magnus's stature, there was a wall of glass. Daenaira moved up to it and peered through to the other side. It seemed strange her sense of direction should be off, because the only thing that should be on the other side of the glass was . . .

The tutoring room she and Magnus had spent the evening in.

All of the blood drained from her face and upper body, and Daenaira had to brace her hands against the walls on either side of herself to keep from slumping to her knees in total mortification. She could see inside the room. Every last corner. It had been cleaned, the bed made, all sign of their assignation completely removed, but anyone who had stood in this place could have seen every single detail of the encounter. The wall she stood at was the one that ran alongside the bed and the chairs where Magnus had sat watching and instructing her.

Oh gods! Had Magnus known about this? The glass was certainly *not* visible from the other side! On the opposite side, it was dark silvered tile. In fact, she knew how cold that tile was because this was the very wall Magnus had taken her against in such a greedy, passionate emulation of their shared visions.

Had he known all along that anyone who knew of these passages could be watching us?

No! She couldn't believe he would betray her trust in such a way! Not only that, but he had allowed himself to be made vulnerable to her where others might have witnessed it, and she knew he would not have dared to bare himself to his peers like that. *Would he?* After all, did she really know him that well at all?

Yes! *Yes*, a fierce inner voice cried out to her. He had been just as raw, broken down, and exposed as she had been, and she knew in her heart that he would only have allowed himself to be so if he had believed himself to be in complete privacy. Magnus was not a man to spread his weaknesses out before others. He had been nearly violent in his resistance as she had taken him across his own tolerances for restraint, but she knew he could have stopped her had he truly wanted to. Instead, he had given himself over to her, humbling himself to the depth of his need for her. He would never have done that if he'd even thought for an instant there was the remotest possibility someone could be watching all of it unfold. And she had to believe he would never have betrayed her trust of the sanctity of that room.

No. Magnus did not know this was here. He believed too much in the benefits of his teachings. Such a deception would have destructive ramifications for decades of students whose first awkward moments, thought to be experienced in private with trusted instructors, had been devastatingly exposed instead. They would all feel the way she was feeling now. Sickened. Shocked. Shamed. These were the very things Magnus sought to defeat by providing sexual education to his students; no way in Light would he condone a secret that could destroy that.

"What is so fascinating?" Tiana asked with a giggle. She squeezed in beside her and frowned. "There's no one in there. Come on, I think I hear someone in the next room."

Hear? So much for soundproofing, Dae thought numbly as she forced herself to follow the other woman. Again, another small alcove and more glass. This time there were people in the room, and Daenaira's face burned hot as she realized she was doing the very thing she prayed no one had done to her.

"This is so wrong," she whispered shakily.

"I know. Cort is the one who first showed this to me. He's a pig, isn't he?"

Dae blinked, trying to comprehend what Tiana was saying, but then she realized she knew the student and the priest in the tableau before her. Henry. The clown from Magnus's relations lecture. He was in private session with Shiloh. That would have been fine, she supposed, except the priest was stripped naked and his huge member was thrusting out toward the boy in full arousal. For all his slimy personality, Shiloh was a magnificent specimen of manhood. The thickness and weight of his impressive cock notwithstanding, he was also tall and broad in the shoulders. Handsome and charming even when he wasn't trying to be, he oozed ambition and aggression. Even completely naked he struck her as dangerous and deadly.

He was covered in a thick pelt of body hair, giving him an almost savage air as he commanded Henry onto the bed with him.

"Come on, boy," Shiloh coaxed the nervous young student. "You can only say you don't like it after you try it. Homoerotic experiences can be a thrilling part of our sex lives."

Shiloh's tone was reminiscent of Magnus's as he had measured himself into the role of an instructor, except it was clear that M'jan Shiloh was using that tone to achieve something for his own gratification. Whatever the priest's plans, it was against temple law for him to use anyone other than *K'yan* Nicoya for sexual gratification. It was against Sanctuary rules for instructors to cross sexual lines, with their students especially! Those chairs across from the bed were there for a reason. To create distance. Not to mention trust. What she and Magnus had done was different because they were meant to fulfill those roles for one another. Though he had been her instructor, they had both been all too aware that it could cross into more the moment they both gave permission. At that point, it no longer would be contrary to any of Sanctuary and temple edicts.

But this . . .

This was an aged and experienced instructor taking advantage of a fearful, raw child in an environment meant to create trust and security, not seclusion from all help. Shiloh was destroying the sanctity of his position. How many students had he done this to?

"M'jan," Henry protested weakly with a swallow of nervousness making his voice skip. "I thought you weren't allowed . . . I mean, *K'yan* Nicoya . . ."

"Oh, if we're both in agreement to bring another into our bed, then that is different," Nicoya spoke up, startling Daenaira into a soundless gasp. Nicoya had been leaned up against the wall next to the tile window! Dae hadn't even seen her. So this meant there were two against the one child! How old could Henry be? Sixteen? Surely not much more than that. All hormones, no practical experience. He hid his own fear and insecurity under those jokes he made in class, she knew. Now she could see why he was so insecure! Shiloh and Nicoya were messing with his head. Apparently they hadn't had their way with him yet. *Oh gods!* She had to stop them.

She watched Nicoya move fluidly away from the wall, walking like pure sex, completely nude, and approaching the boy. He was naked as well, but his fear had kept him relatively unexcited. Now his eyes fixated on Nicoya's gorgeous figure and generous breasts and his cock sprang to quick life.

"There we are," Nicoya purred, reaching down to stroke him in her hand with warm, loving caresses. Then she lowered to her knees and took the boy in her mouth.

Here, Dae realized, was the lure. Henry had a crush on Nicoya, or he was just incredibly hot for her; one or the other. She was now presenting him with the ultimate fantasy, but both Dae and Henry realized there would be a dreadful price to pay for it. They both looked at Shiloh's intimidating member as he took it in his hand and squeezed some kind of gel along the length of it.

"Oh no," Dae whispered, shaking her head. She'd seen a man prepare himself in such a way once before. A guest in her uncle's house had purposely left the door open for anyone to see his activity, probably for the added excitement, as he had done to his slave boy what she feared Shiloh wanted to do to Henry. The slave had had no recourse, and neither had Dae as she had been frozen in place, her paralyzed body forcing her to numbly watch. But in the case of the boy slave, it was clear there had been wild excitement on his part; even a great measure of invitation.

Henry wanted Nicoya.

He did not want Shiloh.

"I know. Shiloh is a pig," Tiana whispered grimly, biting on her lip nervously as she watched.

"You've seen him do this before? To others?"

"Cort used to bring me in here. He would gag me and make me watch while . . ." Tiana flushed. "He would fuck me within an inch of my life. He was a voyeur, I guess. Maybe I am, too. It was exciting even when I didn't want it to be. Like now."

"If it was scenes like this, it wasn't watching that got Cort off," Dae said darkly. "It was the victimization. Tiana, we can't let them do this to poor Henry."

"Well, we can't do anything! It's against rules to interrupt private tutoring. Besides, if Henry was really upset, he would be yelling or something, wouldn't he? He'd be trying to get away. That's what Cort used to say."

"Henry is being controlled by two trusted teachers, Tiana," she hissed. "He has been taught to obey and trust their wisdom, especially in matters of sex. They are using that for their own selfish ends. Luring him in—and how can he protest when Nicoya is giving him every boy's fantasy? Look at him! He's so excited by her he isn't comprehending what Shiloh's plans are. Has he even had a homosexual instructive course yet?"

"I . . . I don't know. He may have. He's just old enough to start making those choices . . ." She bit her lip. "You can't, Dae. No one is supposed to know about this. These windows. It would destroy Sanctuary if it got out that the children were watched."

"Watched by whom?" Dae shot back. "You think it was just you and Cort? That you were the only ones doing this? Someone showed this to Cort. Cort probably wasn't supposed to show it to you, Tiana. Either that or you were being primed for betrayal like Karri was." Dae's eyes narrowed on the distressed, guilty look of her friend. "But you've figured that out already, haven't you? I think that's why you're showing this to me. I think, in your heart, you really want me to tell Magnus about this and put an end to this."

"Dae, please," she breathed, her breathing panicked, "don't. I will get in so much trouble. Everyone will think they were right about me. I just . . . I just needed to tell someone. But I'm not ready to go to Magnus. I need time."

"Henry doesn't have time!"

Dae pointed into the room where the boy had closed his eyes, his jaw slack with pleasure and both hands buried in Nicoya's dark tresses. He was on the verge of orgasm already, but she feared that would change as she watched Shiloh stalk around behind him like a panther onto his prey.

"What do we do? Magnus isn't even here. Shiloh is a penance priest. He's a warrior. And there's no one else we can trust!"

Tiana was right. Suddenly she could appreciate the bind the other woman had found herself in. Forced to watch other degradations, she had become an unwitting accomplice. Once that had happened, she'd been terrified of the consequences. It was the thinking of a victim.

Daenaira was no victim.

"I think I know who we can count on for some help. He's the only priest in this place that Magnus trusts."

"Brendan? But Brendan can't fight Shiloh! If Shiloh gets caught like this, he will kill rather than face humiliation and penance!"

"No. Not Brendan. If he implicitly trusted Brendan, he wouldn't have been jealous of him. I'm talking about Sagan."

"Sagan! No one in their right mind would trust Sagan," she hissed.

"Tiana, what's your third power?"

"Uh . . ."

"Tiana! Hurry!"

"Telekinesis! But it isn't very strong! I'm lucky if I can lift a spoon!"

Daenaira quickly looked around the room through the window.

"There, on the shelf. The porcelain figure of *Drenna*. Make it fall. Don't lift it, just push it over. It should buy us time. I'm going to get Sagan. Promise me you'll do this. Stay and do this, Tiana. Don't let them hurt Henry. Cort isn't here holding you and gagging you anymore. You let this go and it's all on you this time. You hear me?"

Tiana nodded, her eyes spilling tears. Dae knew she would do what she was told. The girl had probably always done as she was told. It made Dae wonder just how long she and Cort had been together and just how long he had been dominating everything in her life.

But Tiana wasn't her main concern, and she ran back into the storage room. Hitting the corridor, she realized she knew nothing about Sagan or his schedule. She had no idea where she would find him. Then she thought about the one person she trusted most in Sanctuary, and knew she would be most likely to know. Running up to her classroom, she prayed the elder handmaiden was there.

She burst in on a class, no doubt looking wild and flushed by the way Hera reacted to her entrance.

"Your pardon," she gasped, "*K'yan* Hera, but would you know where I might find M'jan Sagan at this moment?"

"Most likely in the training halls. He teaches defense class at this time."

"Thank you," she shouted even as she ran out the door. The training halls were so distant! Frustrated with her sari, she stopped and scooped the back hem up and drew it up and forward between her legs and tucked it in at her waistband in front as she did when she was in fight training. It created makeshift pantaloons and freed her to run.

"Sagan!" she cried out, even though she wasn't even through the doors to the hall. She didn't care if everyone stared at her. All she cared about was the single pair of dark, deep sienna-colored eyes that belonged to the penance priest she sought. Clearly, her entrance was enough to provide clarity of need. He never hesitated, stepping over the student he had thrown to the ground just before her entrance. He hurried up to her and she was already running back down the corridor. He followed at her heels, his longer legs easily keeping pace with hers.

"What is it?" he demanded. "Is it Magnus?"

"No. It's much worse." She breathlessly explained the situation, and Sagan's features darkened into a storm of deadly, dangerous rage. He pulled a key from his pocket similar to the one Magnus had used earlier and had it at the ready as she led him to the door of the tutoring room. "Gods, I ran so slow!" she gasped, bending into the stitch in her side from her exertions through corridors, stairwells, and emotions.

"Are you armed?" Sagan demanded. Dae reached for the glave snapped to his weapons belt and jerked it free. She nodded sharply. "That's not for indoors," he hissed.

"Then I suggest you duck when I throw," she shot back. She flicked her wrist hard, the bladed weapon fluttering open like a butterfly blade before it caught on its grooved spine and held its shape tightly.

Sagan keyed the lock, and bracing all of his power into his legs, he crashed his shoulder against the bolt on the other side. It only took a second strike of his big body to make the wood splinter apart, but they both knew it was one strike too many. A man like Shiloh would move all too fast with a warning of even a second.

They burst into the room.

Chapter Eleven

Magnus watched his best religious student in all of his years as a teacher pace in frantic upset. He had taken a seat, feeling far too relaxed and mellowed to join her in her tension of the moment, sitting loosely in one of the large chairs in her parlor. His entire body felt alien and calm, making him realize just how tensely he had been living his daily life for quite some time. He smiled to himself when he thought about how his new relaxation technique could so easily become an addictive pastime.

"I don't understand him. He's never done anything like this before," Malaya said fretfully, her hands twisting within one another.

"Tristan was afraid he would—"

"Not Tristan!" she interrupted him sharply, the snapping tone so rare for her, especially toward her priest. "Guin!"

"Guin," Magnus echoed carefully. Gods, he had to pay better attention, he realized. She must have shifted topics while he had been daydreaming about Daenaira, and now he was lost. He glanced around and noticed for the first time that Killian and not Guin was standing watch over the Chancellor. "He's left you before," he hedged carefully.

"But not for a week! When has he ever left me for a week in fifty years?"

"A week?" Magnus realized he was beginning to sound like a parrot. "Guin asked for a week off? Away from you? Leaving you in the care of others?"

"You see! Listen to the way you're saying that. You know as well as I do that Light would have to strike him down before he'd abandon his post! And then what he did . . ."

Magnus could see the blush of heat that crept over every inch of her skin as she scrubbed a hand up over the curve of her shoulder.

"What did he do, *K'yatsume*?" he asked softly, tension returning to his body as he sat up onto the edge of his seat.

Malaya glanced over her shoulder at Killian, and then the door in the suite that had sealed a weary Rika away from them at his arrival. For Malaya to suddenly develop so keen a sense for privacy told him it was crucial he find out what had happened between her and Guin. Any disruptions to the natural order of their lives would only make it easier for enemies to pry them apart. The bond of Guin's loyalty to his mistress was one Magnus had deemed unbreakable. What had changed? First Tristan had damaged their relationship, and now Guin had abandoned her to the care of others? No wonder she was so heavily upset.

"I think I'm going to go check and see how Rika's feeling," Killian said suddenly, intuiting the reluctance to talk he inspired. Guin would not have cared. He'd have never entertained the idea of exiting the room. Then again, Killian realized Malaya was probably safer with Magnus than she was with him, despite his own formidable skills. So he didn't hesitate to leave her alone with him as he knocked for Rika, who bade him enter.

Malaya reached down for Magnus's hand and led him into her own bedroom, adding another door between them and the keen hearing of their friends. Magnus leaned back against the door, folding his arms over his chest and watching as she returned to her agitated pacing. The full material of her skirts swirled like a whirlpool with every sharp turn.

"What did he do, *K'yatsume*?" he repeated after a moment.

She responded with a nervous laugh and that rubbing of her hand over her upper chest, shoulder, and neck. It changed his theory about it being tension when she almost seemed to be caressing herself, rather than trying to massage away tight muscles.

"He . . . touched me and, um . . . I think he threatened me."

That she was confused and uncertain was quite obvious, and Magnus clung to that before letting a righteous temper run away with him. What she spoke of was among the worst of sins. Had she called him here to hunt? And of all people, Guin? There were very few Shadowdwellers capable of intimidating Magnus when he faced the idea of engaging them in a hunt, but Guin was by far at the top of the list. It was almost a tie between him and Sagan. Sagan might have made the art of war his entire existence, but Guin . . . Guin was a savage, cunning man who had that indefinable something that would always make him refuse to die even if his heart had been run clean through.

The purity of hate and evil could push a being well beyond his endurances and the physics of natural law, but what powered Guin so ruthlessly was something else entirely. Stubborn and relentless, primal and merciless, Guin was a man who would rather die than give up, and would rather die with his enemy in tow than alone. There was no compromise.

"*K'yatsume*," Magnus said with very soft care, "it is very important that you explain those remarks to me with the utmost of care and precision."

Malaya stopped pacing and looked up at him with a startled sort of surprise. Magnus took a measure of relief in that reaction. It was clear she wasn't expecting him to punish Guin, whatever his choice ended up being. She was, of course, too attached to Guin to see the matter clearly for herself, and the punishment of those who sinned was not within her purview. Unlike the law the Senate might try to impose on her, she had no control over temple law. She could choose to refuse the edict to marry because she was, after all, an absolute ruler. She could abolish the outmoded law with her brother's agreement and ride the tide of traditionalist disapproval. But she absolutely could not tell Magnus whom he should and should not hunt down for the penance of their sins.

She blinked and laughed, although it was a bit uneasily. "Really, M'jan, it's nothing like that. It was . . . well, it was . . ."

Damn! How in Light could Malaya explain what she didn't understand for herself? But she had to figure out how, because she had seen that cautious tension in her spiritual advisor before.

"I think he made a pass at me," she confessed, that hot wash of sensory memory flooding over her again. Her breast still smoldered with the fire his coarse flirtation over her nipple had started. Just the idea of Guin—*Guin*, of all people— arousing her! That he had even wanted to touch her in the first place . . . But he had only been bullying her as usual, that was all. It was just another one of those tactics he loved to use to throw her off-kilter. After fifty years, he was still able to mess with her mind completely. It was infuriating. "I'm sure he did it just to get under my skin, the rotten bastard," she muttered to her priest. "Do you know what he said? He said that if I didn't give him permission to leave, he was going to stay 'really, really close' to me. You weren't there, but it was clear what he was implying! Can you imagine? Guin actually threatened me with . . . with . . ."

"Sex," Magnus supplied, his frown deepening as he tried to figure out what in Light Guin had been thinking. "Malaya, why didn't he just ask you for a leave of absence without playing games?"

"Oh, well . . . uh . . . he did, actually," she said uneasily.

"And you refused him?" Magnus lifted a brow in surprise. "Guin has never once asked for time, and when he finally does—and I remind you how often you have told him he could do so—you refused him?"

"I thought he was going to go on a witch hunt! He asked me right after Tristan dropped that awful bomb on me. I wasn't thinking straight. And he always has this way of tying me up into knots of temper, the way he harps at me. He doesn't make sense sometimes. And he suffocates me! He's all pissed off about the Senate dictating my life, and I think that's because he resents anyone poaching on what he thinks is his territory. *Drenna* forbid anyone but Guin should have the right to tell me what to do!"

"Malaya, the point is you pushed him to assert himself. He always accedes to you when you are in the right. He deeply respects you. When you are wrong, that is when he fights you tooth and nail. Granted, it's his perception of right and wrong, but Guin does choose his battles carefully. I am not happy with him for putting unwelcome hands on you, however. That is absolutely unacceptable."

"Oh . . . well, Magnus, like you said, he was pushed to make his point." Though it had been a very bizarre ultimatum to hand down to her. Why, what if she'd said yes to his offer of . . . ?

Malaya felt her whole body shudder at the thought, pure unadulterated heat pluming through her every blood vessel like a fast-rising cloud of toxins.

She licked a quick tongue over her lower lip and met her confessor's gaze.

"And I don't think you could call it unwelcome," she said softly.

Magnus stood silently stunned for a moment, but quickly recovered, his expression as neutral as always.

"Like last time?" he asked her.

She nodded, exhaling as if she felt enormous relief for

admitting it to him. "Last time" had been a good many years ago. Over a decade. She had been just as confused and uncertain about Guin's intent then as she was now. Neither of them doubted his loyalty, nor did they doubt his dedication in seeing her happy and healthy. Sometimes, though, he behaved in such wild, irrational ways that it left them both a bit baffled.

But . . . now that Magnus had his relationship with Daenaira as a reflection, he considered that all of the hot temper and cold clinical extremes might be hiding something beyond the obvious. Regardless, though, it wasn't necessarily his place to spell these things out for the monarch.

"You know my advice already," he said gently to her. "Meditate. Pray to *Drenna* for clarity, Malaya. Let Her guide your mind. Try not to shut yourself off with prejudice, and make certain you consider all aspects." He paused, a small frown tugging at his lips. "Don't let fear write the course of your actions. I have done this myself, and I regret the pain it has caused."

"Fear? You?" she asked, incredulous.

"Yes, *K'yatsume*. When we have no trust, the vacant space that is left becomes filled with fear. Karri gutted me of my trust, and I glutted myself on the resulting dread. I am still in a war with faith and doubt even as we speak. But it is *my* war. The wrong of it came when it spilled out and hurt someone who didn't deserve it. Whatever decisions you come to, be certain it isn't fear guiding you. Despite his brute armor and monolithic strength, Guin can be hurt just the same as anyone else. Have a care."

"Magnus, you worry too much," she said lightly, though there was a hint of unease in her tone. "I couldn't hurt Guin. I need him far too much. I will find a way to please everyone the best I can, as always. The Senate, my brother, and Guin."

"You have forgotten someone, *K'yatsume*," he noted quietly.

"Drenna?" She laughed.

"No, love. Yourself. Don't forget yourself."

"Henry," Daenaira said softly.

The confused boy was sitting on the bed, knees curled to his chest and arms folded over his head. Naked as he was, there was a gangly, awkward appearance to his limbs, and he was, quite obviously, emotionally devastated. Sagan and Dae's entrance only made matters worse for him as he tried to turn himself away from the embarrassment of his exposure.

Daenaira wanted to move toward him, but Sagan held out a hand and stayed her. She realized then that the priest was right. Henry wouldn't want a woman to baby and mother him at such a terrible moment in his life, so she went back to the door and closed it to give them privacy.

The room was empty otherwise. Shiloh and Nicoya had made their escape, and Daenaira suspected they had used Shadowscape to get past them. Just the same, she kept careful watch around the small room. They could just as easily Unfade into the room as they had Faded out of it, and she didn't see Shiloh's weapons belt anywhere in sight. It meant he was well armed.

Sagan moved up to Henry and caught up the boy's clothing on the way.

"Henry?" he spoke softly, his deep voice focused and steady, not reflecting concern or sympathy so much as it portrayed the sense of understanding and solidarity. "Did they Fade?"

Of course Sagan knew this already. That wasn't the question he was asking as he handed the boy his clothes. Henry nodded, rushing into the tailored fabrics as quickly as he could, his face burning with his shame when he looked up at Dae. Sagan slowly looked the bed over, as well as the boy himself in spite of his speed of dress. His redwood-colored eyes hardened into the aged invulnerability of those magnificent trees, a grim set to his lips.

"Son, you know I have to ask you . . . to bear witness to any sins Nicoya and Shiloh have committed here today," Sagan informed him carefully. "It takes a strong man to righteously accuse those in power above him. I understand it is a great deal to ask."

Henry nodded, his knees drawn back to his chest now that he was dressed. Daenaira understood Sagan's approach to the boy, giving him an option that would help him to regain his sense of his manhood as he tried to cope with what his body had been subjected to.

"They said it wasn't a sin i-if they b-both agreed to it. I didn't mean to do anything wrong."

The sheer panic in his voice followed the way he looked at the penance priest in front of him. This, Dae realized, was how Shiloh and Nicoya had managed to victimize without ramifications. The fear of punishment, as with Tiana, kept them silent. But penance wasn't so terrible that it was worth this type of fear, and Henry should know that at his age. It was really Shiloh he feared. Gods, when Dae thought about it, she could imagine all too easily how a penance priest like Shiloh could abuse his power to dole out punishment in order to control his victims. Now Henry was fearful and distrustful of them all, and with terrible cause.

"Henry." She spoke up gently. "No permission, no sin. Remember that, okay? If you gave no permission, the sin is not yours. It is theirs alone."

"But . . . but I wanted . . . she was so beautiful." Henry looked at the wall, glaring at himself in the silvery reflective surface of the tiles. "I knew it was wrong. I fantasized about it so often."

"Fantasies are not sinful," Sagan reminded him. "They are normal and healthy. It is acts alone that must be judged. What did you permit, Henry?"

"She took me . . . i-in her mouth. It was . . ." He swallowed, flushing darkly. "I wanted that. I would never have done it if Shiloh hadn't said it was okay. I swear, I wouldn't have. But they're my teachers, and they said it was allowed!"

"I know, Henry," Sagan said with a nod. "And that is the sin that must be repaid. It was theirs alone, for taking advantage of you by misusing their positions in this school and by feeding you lies that led you to this pass. I am sorry you were hurt by that treachery. I promise you, though, they will pay for their sins."

"Especially Shiloh," the boy hissed suddenly. "Especially him! I didn't give him permission. I didn't!" Tears welled in the student's eyes and he scrubbed them away, frustrated when they came faster than he could erase them. "He waited until I wasn't paying attention. Let Nicoya distract me. Th-then he grabbed me from behind and forced me on the bed . . . and Nicoya helped hold me! I couldn't get them off me!" he ground out angrily. "Gods, it hurt! It was so much pain. B-but . . ."

Henry stopped, heavy sobs ripping from his chest now. Now, Dae knew, it was time for mothering. Sagan slid aside and made room for her when he realized the same thing. She went to the boy and wrapped warm arms around him, hushing him gently as she stroked his hair. Soon he turned into her softness and comfort, gripping her so hard she could barely breathe. He was a strong boy and he must have fought with everything in his body. She looked up at the intact statue of *Drenna*, and for a furious moment wanted to know why Tiana had failed to help buy precious time. One crash of porcelain and Henry would have seen Shiloh behind him. Perhaps in time to understand and make some kind of escape or protest.

But she knew it was an unlikely prospect just the same. Magnus had proved to her earlier how hard it was to escape a lesson in those rooms. She understood the principles, and they worked with those who were perfectly trustworthy, but Magnus had to realize that there was no trust in Sanctuary any longer. Not until he methodically removed the deception where it had taken root. If the top of the tree—like Nicoya and Shiloh and Cort—was rotten, you could bet it went down deep through the ranks all the way to the roots.

What Sanctuary needed was Magnus at his most powerful. It needed truth as only he could find it. He could no longer afford to believe in blind trust because of their shared faith and callings. Not when lives like Henry's were at stake. If not for Tiana guiding her to that hidden chamber, they could have killed the boy and made him disappear without a second thought.

"I didn't want it," Henry kept saying fiercely as he clung to her. "I didn't like it! I didn't!"

"No, Henry, you didn't," Sagan assured him, his fist clenching tightly in his anger as he repressed it for later. "Nicoya brought you to the edge, and what happened with Shiloh was a matter of physiology alone. Do not be ashamed for coming to climax. It's almost impossible for a male to maintain control when the prostate gland is stimulated in that way. Physiology, Henry. Nothing more."

Daenaira blinked quickly to hold back sympathetic tears. Thank the gods Sagan understood what had happened. Her sexual ignorance couldn't help poor Henry, and she felt stupid and inadequate for that. It made her more determined than ever to learn everything she could. Next time someone needed her, she wanted to know how to help them.

"K'yan," Sagan said quietly. "I will stay with Henry. I need you to go find Magnus."

Dae looked at Sagan in surprise. She understood instantly that he meant to give up the opportunity to hunt Shiloh and Nicoya to Magnus, in order to stay and comfort a boy in desperate need of a man's reassurances. It was a sacrifice she wouldn't have expected from a man who seemed to eat, sleep, and breathe the art of battle. It reminded her that Sagan was, after all, a priest as well as a dealer of penance. In that moment, she saw what Magnus must have seen in the quiet, stoic minister. She saw why he trusted the other male, even if it was only subconsciously.

Daenaira stood up and left Henry after giving him a reassuring squeeze of his hand. He looked like he had been burning in Light for an hour, but she had faith that Sagan would be able to help him. She left the room, and though she knew time was of the essence, she also knew Magnus would hunt his criminals down just as efficiently now as five minutes from now. She wanted to check on Tiana. She didn't understand why the handmaiden hadn't done something to help Henry. Had she simply stood there and watched the boy be violated? Dae quickly entered the hidden tunnel and worked her way cautiously, expecting the worst because she wanted to believe her friend was better than that. She came around to the room with Sagan and Henry in it, but Tiana was gone. She could see Sagan talking softly to Henry, the boy nodding with vehemence. He was clearly reiterating all of the things he had said to assure the boy that he was the victim and not the criminal in this situation.

She was so disappointed in Tiana that she surprised herself. Since when, she wondered, had she started expecting better things of people? After only ten days in Sanctuary, was she so quickly willing to forget what she knew of human nature? It made no sense. She knew better than this.

That was when she looked down and saw the brown stain on the stone by her feet. Daenaira cautiously kept her eyes on the tunnels as she knelt to touch the spot. It was still wet, and when she turned her finger over, the brown became redder and the scent of blood reached out to tickle her keen sense of smell.

"Oh gods," she whispered.

Had she left Tiana to be hurt, afraid, and alone? Where was she? Dae hadn't taken the time to explore the rest of the tunnels, having assumed it ran the entire length of the tutoring rooms, almost the entire corridor on both sides. She hurried into the as-yet unplumbed depths of the tunnel, drawing her wrist blade from the left sheath. The glave, collapsed and left hanging from her waistband like a pair of handcuffs, wouldn't work in such narrow confines. She needed something for close quarters. She wished to *Drenna* that she had those sai Magnus had promised her. She was good with the small dagger, but against a man like Shiloh it would take a precision hit to do any damage to him.

She eased carefully into each alcove, her stomach sickened as she interrupted privacy in some and met with empty rooms in others. Worse still, she found more brown droplets on the ground, the increase in amount and grouping mystifying and disturbing.

Then, as she rounded the bend to the other side of the corridor of rooms, the droplets suddenly became a foot-wide smeared path that led her eyes in a direct track to the slumped body of her unfortunate friend in the next alcove.

"Ti!" she cried softly, watching her back as she hurriedly knelt to check Tiana's pulse. To her horror, her fingers sank into the sliced-open flesh that was still dripping blood in spite of there no longer being any heartbeat to propel what remained inside her into the outside world. Tiana was dead, bled out like an animal in a slaughterhouse. *And for what?* Daenaira wanted to know with anger. What had she ever done to hurt anyone? Someone must have seen them enter the tunnels . . . or they had been there with them the entire time when they'd entered and they'd never realized it! Gods! Maybe if she hadn't left, she'd have been able to defend her friend. But clearly whoever it was had purposely waited until Tiana was most vulnerable. It also meant that with Shiloh and Nicoya occupied with Henry at the time, yet another suspect was on the loose. This didn't surprise her, though. It made no sense that Shiloh and his handmaiden would openly expose themselves if they had known they could be watched, unless it was part of the thrill for them. In fact, it made a great deal of sense that they might orchestrate Henry's manipulation for an audience.

That meant the watcher had been there when she and Tiana had arrived, hiding when they'd entered and then . . .

waiting. Daenaira felt sick all over again, as well as sensing how much danger she was now in. She wanted out of the enclosed tunnel more than anything, desperate to find Magnus and begin to search for vengeance for the victims of these cold, heartless betrayers of trust and faith. It enraged her to even think of it. She had lived a life without either one; and here, where trust and faith were supposed to be safe, cultivated, and enriched, they were being abused and destroyed.

Worse, she could already feel the pain this was going to cause one proud priest in particular, and it only incited her fury further.

Dae hurried away from the body of her friend and broke free of the tunnels, running to find her priest.

Magnus was stopped in the streets frequently as he moved through the city and back toward Sanctuary. He remained patient and dutiful to all who required something from him, but there was no denying the urgent need growing inside him at the thought of returning to Daenaira's soft and heated embrace. He could still smell her on himself, and he had to carefully avoid thinking about that lest he end up physically reacting to the memory of her while in public. Hunger was all well and good, and certainly to be expected in his case of famished lifestyle, but it couldn't interfere with his daily routines as a priest for the people who needed him.

Still, even *Drenna* had to cut him some slack. After all, She was the one who had designed this whole situation to be as powerful and humbling to him as it had been. Admittedly, he had needed it. He could already sense how it would affect his work in the future. His goddess had realized how out of touch he was with certain elements of the condition of relationships, and She had forced resolution on him. It was a penance he accepted happily.

He had to remind himself to slow down a little as his heart began to race in anticipation of potentially getting to see Dae before his scheduled lectures began. She had shed virgin blood for him only hours earlier. He had to have a care that he didn't hurt her in any way. At least, no more than he'd already been forced to do to get her past that point. He'd already shown a remarkable lack of control when it came to her, and he realized it wasn't just about sex and sexual deprivation. There were certain cravings that overcame him that had nothing to do with satiating his body—at least, not in that way. While he had craved the feel of holding her warm skin against his as they lay replete the second time around in the tutoring room, it had been satisfying a completely different kind of need. The need for contentment, the scent of himself on her body beneath his nose, the scent of her on his; all possessive and territorial urges, all very out of character for him.

And then there had been the inexplicable need to touch her constantly, as if to make quite certain she was real and not some figment of a sexually starved imagination. He had provoked her temper, just to see the flash of her eyes and to hear her acerbic retort, taking such pleasure in it that he had smiled and given himself away for baiting her. Her hard street philosophy complemented his sometimes overly idealistic one. She was grounding him. As things around him shook on increasingly rocky ground, he realized just how important that was going to be if he were going to regain control over his flailing house. The temple was *Drenna*'s and *M'gnone*'s, but Sanctuary was *his*. He would be thrice damned to Light before he would allow it to be torn apart without a vicious fight to regain its glory.

Magnus stopped still suddenly as a cavern breeze swept the frigid cold of the winter outside over him. More importantly, it brought him a gift of a scent of sweet cream and fresh strawberry shampoo.

And blood.

Magnus felt cold sink like lead into his soul as he jerkily swept his eyes over the passersby in the street. When he saw her hurrying toward him, he had a ridiculous urge to crumble to his knees with relief so he could pray his thanks to his gods for seeing her brought safely to him. However, the urge was swept away by another wash of dread when he saw the raw distress in her expression and the blood staining her sari and her hands.

"What?" he demanded, grabbing hold of her the instant they came together. "Are you harmed? Did someone hurt you?" She wasn't speaking fast enough, damn it!

"No! Tiana is dead. And Henry—oh, Magnus, I think Shiloh raped Henry. With Nicoya's help. I could tell you for certain if I wasn't so stupid about these things," she said with fierce frustration sparking hard tears in her eyes. "Sagan is with Henry, but the priest and handmaiden have escaped. I saw for myself what they were planning to do to him. I should have stayed and done something! Now Tiana is dead and Henry is devastated! I could have done something!"

Daenaira so rarely cried. She might feel the urge, but she had only ever done so once that he knew of, though she'd more than had cause on several occasions. So for her to spill tears where others could see her told him just how distraught and guilty she felt in that moment. He realized she was too upset to help him understand clearly what had happened, but she had made the important things known to him.

There were Sinners on the loose. Tiana was dead. One of *his* students had been violated.

It was the end of it all for him. The end of all further denial. The end of inaction and trying to play by the proper rules. It was the end of playing games of trust, and by the gods, it was the very end of his patience.

"Come with me, *K'yindara*. It is time we struck a match to your kindling."

Daenaira was puzzled by the reference as he took her elbow in his hand and tucked her tightly to his side. It felt protective and safe, feelings she wasn't used to at all, never mind finding them from an outside source. But she was too upset to lecture herself against depending on others to shield her from the harms of the world, and she simply allowed it to happen. It was likely he might fail her one day in some way, but she was willing to bet a little of her sanity that today would not be that day. As they walked quickly back to Sanctuary, she calmed down enough to explain in great detail everything that had happened since he had left her.

"Well, I think this gives a whole new perspective to phrases like 'I can't leave you alone for two seconds,' hmm?"

"I suppose so," she said, wrapping her arms around herself in a hug and drawing his attention to her blooded hands.

"Is that from Tiana?"

"Yes. Whoever did it, they were brutal. And they waited for me to leave."

"Thank the gods," he muttered. She gave him a sharp look but he was unapologetic. "I'm sorry. I know she was your friend, but it would have done no good if you had been there, Dae. Whoever this is, they are cunning and deadly, and given a choice I would not wish you alone face-to-face with them. If that makes me selfish, then so be it. I am tired of watching the people I care about get destroyed by this poison, and I am going to put a stop to it once and for all."

Daenaira could hear and feel how utterly furious he truly was, but it was in such contradiction to the softness of his fingers against the side of her face that she didn't know what to think in that moment. She remained quiet and uneasy. She didn't know exactly why, but considering all she'd been through in a single night, she was entitled to a little unease.

She also began to get the feeling that his familiar way of holding her wasn't necessarily something that was expected to be seen. People kept staring at them and then halting to whisper and sometimes shake their heads in obvious disapproval. Not that she ever gave a damn what people thought of her, but it disturbed her to think of what influence her presence could have on Magnus's reputation. It made her feel a little soiled and a little inadequate in his shadow, and the sensation made her throat ache. As his handmaiden, she was supposed to help and support him, make his job and his existence easier in the world so he could do the most good as often as possible. If she cast a poor light on him in some way, would it scald his effectiveness?

Daenaira would have shrugged out of his hold had they not reached Sanctuary just then. Once inside the building, Magnus took her hand and the lead, hurrying her forward and down the next levels until they entered the forge. Black fire burned hot at the many pits where metal smiths and blacksmiths were working their trades. There was one forge where black fire smoldered, the chemically treated combustibles used to make the lightless fire giving off black and clear flames that burned longer and stronger than human fire did. It did not, however, burn as hot, and so it made metalwork very difficult. It made tempering steel and the like into a careful art form consisting of perfect timing and flawless molds. She admired the jewelry makers for their patience, but it was weapons smiths like Magnus who truly earned her awe and her respect. Of course, she recognized that she was biased. Jewelry couldn't hold a candle to a beautifully crafted blade.

The forge he led her to was his own. No one but Magnus used it, and it was kept ready for use at all times unless he ordered it cold. Walking past so much burning heat, she was perspiring by the time they stopped. Magnus went to a small rack and drew back the tarp thrown over it.

Daenaira gasped so loudly, she could be heard over the roar of the other forges and the banging and sizzling of metal.

"Magnus!" she all but squealed.

Sai. Beautiful, unbelievable, breathtaking sai. Two pairs of them! She covered her mouth with both hands, moving only a step closer and bending to peer at the gorgeous metallic creations. It was instantly obvious the kind of time and effort that had gone into them. The most amazing detail. The smooth matte of utter blackness. These were no ordinary sai. The sai in his room were steel, the metal gleaming to a silvered shine. But these—these were pure black. Assassins' weapons, meant to keep a killer hidden in her natural habitat of the shadows without the flash of metal to give her away. The advantage was critical and thoughtful, and something she hadn't even considered for herself. In the seat of the pommels were onyx gems, the facets cut perfectly around the only bit of color he had allowed on the entire project. Etched in the stones, with pearlized midnight blue paint to fill it in, was her initial. Along the length of the long center prongs of all four sai, he had etched flames rushing from hilt to tip. *K'yindara*. Wildfire.

Unique to these sai, though, was the right-handed twist to the smaller prongs, which were also thicker than seemed right for the balance of the weapon. Daenaira felt his finger-tips touch her upper arm closest to him, rubbing her gently through her blouse.

"Pick one up," he encouraged her for what she did not realize was the third time. She was so shocked and so en-thralled it made him ridiculously pleased and proud. That he had made her so obviously happy seemed to mean every-thing to him in that moment. Magnus watched her reach out for a sai with shaking hands, and her reverence was painfully beautiful. She had tears in her eyes again, though he couldn't fathom why. She had known he was making them for her. Why was she so blown away by the gift, as if it were com-pletely unexpected?

"I didn't think you would really make them," she an-swered him as if she had heard his query. "I'm sorry, but I guess I thought . . ."

"You thought I was shining you on."

"Yes," she breathed. "Or that you wouldn't do it because I wouldn't . . . because I was being so cold to you."

Magnus tried not to be insulted by what she had truly meant by that. She had thought that he wouldn't keep his promise so long as she refused his advances physically or as a friend. But that was the life she knew from before, and he had to remember it was up to him to show her a new life. He was glad their fight had actually allowed him the extra time and energy he had needed to craft these for her. His frustration and even his temper had been a strong impetus to working them so quickly and going to the extreme of his skills in creating the lovely weapons. After all, they were going to be protecting her life. He couldn't afford to give her second best, and that was why he had refused to allow her to carry the heavier sai. Yes, she could handle the damn things frighteningly well, but they were not designed for a woman, and that made for executable flaws and weaknesses. He didn't want her depending on imperfect weapons.

He wanted her to depend on these. He knew they were as close to flawless as was possible. His added touches, too, would only solidify that. She still hadn't touched them, so he reached out to pick one up where it lay next to its sheath. He turned it nimbly so the hilt faced her fingers and touched it encouragingly into the seat of her palm. She closed her fingers around it and he smiled when her eyes went wide with surprise and delight. The weight, he knew, was perfect for her. He had paid close attention in their classes, even taking note of the way she tended to hold the sai at a quarter turn inward so the steel and her forearm aligned to make a more powerful brace against the strike of an opponent who was stronger and heavier than she was. The twist on the lower tines allowed for a better purchase when she hooked an enemy weapon. She used the trick often, and he had seen her snap two blades this week alone. Not his blades, of course, but nothing too shabby either.

He moved back and let the warrior in her take over. It always happened that way, like a possession, when fighter met weapon for the first time and made a perfect match. She whipped the long end around, pressing it to her forearm as her fingers wrapped snugly around the fork and hilt.

"The stone is black fire onyx," he informed softly as he walked around behind her. "Second in strength only to a diamond, *K'yindara*. You can use the butt of the weapon to hit anything and it won't shatter. I had it set by Caidywynn, our foremost jeweler in the city. There are no gaps, no air, nothing but the steel at its back, which makes it as good as a steel post, only prettier." He reached out to stroke a knuckle down the side of her face. "Call me a chauvinist, but you deserve pretty. Anyone who looks as beautiful as you do in battle deserves equal beauty in her weapons."

"Thank you," she whispered, reaching to take up a second sai. It was one from the other set, and he was not surprised she had noticed there was a difference between the pairs.

"These are balanced. Streamlined. So you can—"

"Throw them," she breathed. "Throwing sai!"

"Only women should use throwing sai. That is why they are rarely used as such. Only a woman can use steel this light with optimum efficacy in a battle. Throwing the heavier sai is clumsy and risky. You are basically giving up your only weapon, so it had best count for something. The throwing sai are in the boot sheaths. The standard ones are the leg sheaths. I also had another made for your back, for when the sari is not in your way."

Daenaira dropped the weapons on the table with a clang of metal, turned, and threw herself into his body. Her arms wrapped around his neck so tightly she almost choked him, and all Magnus could do was return the savage little hug with equal measure.

"Thank you," she whispered against his ear. Then again, even more fiercely so he would understand her perfectly, "Thank you, M'jan."

Magnus held her firmly, "Now, my spitfire, it's time you earned your keep." She stiffened in his embrace and he chuckled. "My *K'yindara*, always expecting the worst. What will I ask of you that you haven't already freely given me? I only mean that it's time you come into battle with me. Nicoya is a well-trained fighter, and Shiloh a penance priest. I cannot wisely face them both alone. You are just the edge I need to handle her while I seek him."

"Oh," she said sheepishly, "I'm sorry."

"No. Not at all. It will take time for you to understand what I do and do not want from you, Dae. Although," he said, lowering his voice and lips against her ear, "you should expect me to demand a more physical thank-you later. And in exchange, I would love to attend any . . . adrenaline rushes you have."

Daenaira laughed at the tease, pinching his arm smartly for his blithe reference to her naïveté. She turned and nipped her teeth at the line of his jaw, a free hand gliding down his rock-hard belly in a brief, promising tease.

"Come on," she invited softly, "Let's get to hunting. I owe that bitch for Henry in a big, big way. And if either of them so much as touched Tiana, I'm going to make them pay." As she spoke, her skin was flushed with temper and the ambient heat of the forge. She reached up to strip away her sari, shedding the outer wrap and throwing it into a discard bin nearby.

Magnus watched as she left herself in her blouse and underskirt. Her skin across her belly shone warm and golden, the sheerness of her skirt showing the full outline of her body. He watched her lift a foot, jerking up her skirt as she strapped the sheaths onto her bare calves one at a time. Watching her arm herself with the weapons he had made for her was somehow sensual and intimate all at once. At the same time, he struggled with a sudden knot of apprehension as he began to doubt the wisdom of bringing her with him. He was tempted to say she wasn't ready, but her third power made her naturally ready, and he hadn't been lying when he had told her he needed her to keep Nicoya busy.

Besides, there was no one else he trusted enough to depend on them keeping up their end of the battle without being afraid he'd have to watch his back at the same time. If Dae's suspicions about Tiana's killer were correct, there was a third killer in the mix. All he knew was that he had reached his threshold for what was happening in Sanctuary a long time ago, and now he was going to do something about it or die trying.

Even if it meant he had to sacrifice Daenaira along the way.

The thought was cold and dreadful, but he had to make himself face it, just as he faced the potential deaths of any of the penance priests he sent out to hunt down Sinners for the sake of their victims. In truth, he couldn't afford to lose her or any other good soul. He would need them all to rebuild Sanctuary into the institution he had intended it to be; that he believed it had once been. Also . . .

Also . . .

Magnus pushed away all of those extraneous thoughts, feeling a suffocating sensation closing in around him. He couldn't allow himself to fear. He couldn't let those visions of violence that had shared space with his passion for her to interfere with what he needed to do now. *Drenna* had shown one clearly, and the other in intelligible flashes and blurs. Just because their powerful passions had come to life, it didn't mean the images of death and danger he felt surrounding him since he had begun to dream of her were just as accurate. If he believed they were, he would only paralyze them both.

Daenaira looked up at him as she fingered the back sheath and debated taking the lighter set of sai with her as well. She would need practice before it was practical to bring them, so she thought it best to leave them behind. She did keep the glave hanging at her waistband, however. Dae went still when she saw quite clearly that Magnus was struggling with heavy thoughts, the darkness of his frown and the fierceness of his eyes giving her a liquid sensation of dread through the center of her belly.

"Don't," she begged him suddenly, barely knowing why as she moved forward to lean her warmth and weight along the length of his rigid body. "Don't doubt. Not me, not you."

"How can I not?" he asked on a soft rasp. "Everything I believed was just a delusion. I endangered everyone because I let myself get so wrapped up in politics and things outside of the purview of Sanctuary . . . and then when I saw the first signs of trouble here, I stuck my head in the sands of denial. And I don't doubt you," he added, reaching up to sweep a gentle touch beneath the amber of her eye. "You are the only thing I don't doubt. I even question *Drenna* for her wisdom in letting me lead her children into this mess, but I don't question you." He reached to cradle her face between both of his strong hands. "I fear for you, but I don't doubt you."

"I've survived much more difficult things than you, M'jan Magnus," she said softly to him, cuddling warmly against him as she nuzzled a kiss against his cheek where he was starting to grow rough from the shadow of his whiskers.

"I know, *K'yindara*. But I don't want to be one of those things you need to survive," he told her on an intimate whisper against her throat. "I tried my hand at that already, and I didn't like it. I'll not repeat the mistake, Dae."

"That's good to know," she said, her throat trying to work past the tightness suddenly stuck within it. She hadn't ever thought simple words could have such an impact on her, but his did. The words and the depth of sincerity she could feel behind them told her she would not be a fool to believe him this time. She had not had anyone care anything about what happened to her since her mother had died, and she had forgotten how powerful it could feel to trust that feeling and believe in it. She'd been alone so long—was it stupid of her to want to enjoy him so much? Was she just feeling this way because she was so naïve about so many things when it came to him? She'd never had sex before, and he had gently led her into that world of incredible bliss. She'd never been given a gift before, and here he had painstakingly created her beautiful sai in a way that told her he actually gave a damn about what happened to her. She'd never been asked to fight with someone instead of being expected to fight against them, and that, more than anything, affected her.

"Come, wildfire. It's time to hunt these pretenders down," he said, reluctantly moving from the enticing warmth of her. "I haven't had time to tell you much, so I will explain this and nothing else. I will offer repentance to all Sinners if it is in my power to do so, but do not hesitate to destroy them in their sin if your life is in the balance. Also, there is a good chance they are no longer in Shadowscape."

"Dreamscape?"

"Yes. And Shiloh at least is a master of that 'scape just as I am. Nicoya . . . I can only assume he has trained her just as fully, since she often fought with him on his quests to bring others to penance." He frowned, worrying again. "Remember, anything is possible in Dreamscape, Daenaira. It is the power of your belief that draws from the energy there. Unlike when you are asleep, though, when you Fade into Dreamscape, you have total control over your environment unless someone else manipulates it and you within it. Your will is strong. You have very few fears."

Dae could see he wasn't comforted by his own reasoning. On the one hand, he had faith in her strength, but he was trying to reconcile that with his shaken faith in those he had once thought just as confidently of. Suddenly, it was very important to her to prove to him he was right about her, if nothing else. He was a good and wise man, and the evils of others shouldn't be allowed to undermine him like this.

"Don't worry," she said with her usual sly cheek. "You haven't begun to see the shit my brain can come up with. Let's go."

Magnus smiled at that, letting her take his hand and lead him from the heat of the forge.

Chapter Twelve

Dreamscape.

Gods, he didn't want to be here. Or rather, he didn't want to have Daenaira here. It was too soon and she was too raw. He must have been mad to bring her. He could have left her with Henry and brought Sagan . . .

No.

He wasn't about to turn his back on her again. When he thought of Tiana and how very close Dae had come to meeting her fate, his stomach clenched into brutal knots. He needed her here where he could keep a close eye on her.

Magnus tried to breathe, tried to focus on his hunt for his prey. He had never been so unfocused preparing for a battle in all of his life. Daenaira, he realized, had become the very distraction he had always feared a woman could become to a man if he let her get too close to him. And yet, he would damn himself to Light before he would regret a single second of it. He wouldn't give his enemies that satisfaction. He had listened to her gloss over the discovery of the room they had shared, but he had felt the knowledge that they had potentially been watched during such private moments like a kick in the groin, and he knew it had to be even worse for a young woman with such little exposure to things like voyeurism. He dreaded what could happen to the trust and sanctity of Sanctuary once knowledge of these tunnels became known. Decades of youth would be violated. How in the name of the gods had these things been built? He had entertained the idea of something similar only once, briefly, when he and Tristan had designed Sanctuary's new halls together. It had occurred to him that there should be a checks-and-balances system so he could make certain none of the students were ever abused by their teachers, but he had dismissed it as an act of faithlessness in his peers.

Had Tristan gone ahead with the tunnels anyway and not told him? Perhaps designing it as a "just in case" scenario in the event that he changed his mind later on? Now it so happened that was exactly what he was doing. The tunnels would be locked, and only he would be allowed to enter and observe to make certain what had happened to Henry would never happen again. The question was whether he would make it general knowledge the check system existed, or if he would be more covert about it. Just how many people in Sanctuary knew they existed, anyway? And were those tunnels limited to just the tutoring rooms? He needed to consult with Tristan as soon as he got the opportunity.

"You're miles away," a soft, sensual voice whispered in his ear. Dae's remark brought him face-to-face with her amber eyes, the glow of them so brightly enhanced by Dreamscape. The mellifluousness of her voice had always cut sharply into his libido, but equally enriched by the magic of this 'scape, it distracted his entire body, pulling him to her like a divining rod toward water. He'd experienced a similar effect those times when he had visited her as she had slept, in order to gain her consent to join her life in Sanctuary. That all seemed so long ago now. So much had come and gone between them.

She was right. He was miles away, and it wasn't improving. He had to get his head in the game before they both ended up dead. He gave her a nod of acknowledgment and redoubled his attempts to focus. He needed to pick up Shiloh's trail before the other hunter picked up theirs.

He watched out of the corner of his eye, though, as Daenaira held a hand over her eyes and bravely dared to look toward the distant light. Sunlight. But darkness followed them as they walked the surreal landscapes around them. All light remained on the fringes of what was safe for their breed, moving always out of reach of them. Dreamscape was not, after all, meant to harm those who spent time there. There were nightmares, of course, but overall it was meant to be a place of rest, safety, and fantasy. Whether in Fade or in sleep, it wouldn't cause them harm unless someone else made the magic around them malevolent.

"Careful. It will still blind you temporarily, and you can't afford any hindrances."

"I know. I just never saw sunlight before. I've always been so afraid of going out in the fresh world. I grew up in the tavern in the Clan Gerranic caves not far from here, and my mother never let me go outside. Then eight years with my relatives."

"You're Clan Gerranic?" he asked, surprised.

"There are no clans," she returned smugly.

"Not anymore," he agreed with a chuckle. "Not officially. But no one will ever forget their clan. Rather like how American humans never forget their European ancestry. But Clan Gerranic is a bit notorious for growing the best assassins money can buy. It explains your third power. You speak of your mother, but never your father."

"Mmm. I don't believe she knew who he was." She shrugged at his arching eyebrow. "Someone lied to her about being on birth control. Like most of our women, she couldn't tolerate methods for herself, and it is so rare to find a male who won't take a simple herb. All you guys have to do is drink tea once every couple of weeks and it totally screws up your fertility. Women, however . . ."

"I am aware of that." He chuckled.

"Right. Sex education." She sighed. "Anyway, Mom had it tough. As a society we aren't kind to single parents. And to be frank, it's never the man who gets stuck with the living, breathing stigma to remind everyone they screwed up. All too often they've already hit the road by then. Or they did, before the city. Maybe it's different now that we are more insular and less clannish."

Magnus didn't respond. He was recalling how hard he had been on his son for getting Ashla pregnant out of joining. He had known it was a fluke. Trace was too responsible to have let it happen cavalierly, but none of the normal laws of their world had applied at the time of conception. However, they were hard on those who conceived accidentally because it was usually so easily prevented and there were few excuses in such a highly sexually educated society. They never blamed the child, of course, but he had never taken into consideration how the suffering of a stigmatized parent would translate onto the children.

"I suppose we have a very long way to go before we can consider ourselves on par with a Nightwalker society like the Demons."

"All Nightwalkers have their flaws. Mistrals are xenophobes. Vampires are cavalier in general, bordering on lawless if not for Prince Damien."

"More than you know. Things have changed for that race. Vampires recently discovered they can acquire the powers of other Nightwalkers by drinking their blood. It released a whole new breed of criminals we all have to fear. We've already lost a few 'Dwellers to them."

"I didn't know that," she said quietly, her expression grim. "I guess my mother was right to be afraid to let me go outside."

"Perhaps. But she did you an injustice by—" Magnus stopped short and turned to her in surprise. "Are you telling me that the first time you ever went out of doors was when you followed me and killed Cort?"

"Well, I suppose I was transported to the city somehow, so I guess I was outside then, but they made sure I was out cold. Can't have a secret slave if she starts screaming or something." She frowned. "I wish . . ."

"What do you wish?" he prompted her, still a bit floored at how courageous an act it must have been to step outside for the first time in twenty years just to face down a trained killer. She would never cease to amaze him.

"I wish we could slap a whole lot of penance on Winifred and Friedlow, is all. And they have friends. There are other slaves I saw. Oh gods! I never thought of them! In all this time! I should have—gods, I'm so damn selfish sometimes!"

"Hardly that," Magnus said sharply. "You were a little busy surviving and adjusting. And you were angry with me. Why would you trust someone who hurt you like I did with that kind of information? We'll fix it after we fix this for Henry," he reassured her, reaching to rub a hand across her back.

"Touching, Magnus. Touching."

Magnus and Daenaira both froze when they heard that voice echoing wryly around them. Magnus's hand went to rest on his katana's hilt.

"Draw that blade, M'jan, and your little tart will find herself missing an eye at the very least," Shiloh promised.

Shiloh was an expert at thrown blades. Magnus didn't doubt the promise for an instant, so he let go of the hilt and held his hand loosely at his side.

"And before you think about being clever," Shiloh continued, the echo of his voice in the 'scape keeping his locus a mystery, "you might recall how close your son came to dying after feeling the touch of one of my saw-stars a few months back."

Magnus gritted his teeth as the information filtered into

him. Trace had been attacked in Shadowscape by an un-known assassin, nearly dying from the encounter. Dae looked askance at him.

"He dips his blades. Poison," he responded softly.

"Racially engineered poison. Designed just for our breed to be as effective as possible. For which you can thank your former love slave—err, I mean handmaiden. That Karri, she certainly had a way with poisons. Oh, but you know that now, don't you?" Shiloh chuckled. "Say, tart. How's that fine boy doing? I must say I'm a bit irritated with you. I was quite close to finishing when you and Sagan came banging on the door. Watching the boy climax was a thing of beauty. I love a virgin, don't *you,* Magnus?"

There was no mistaking the implication, and Magnus pressed his fingers tighter against Daenaira when he felt a tremor hurry through her. He didn't look at her, though, being quite careful to continue scanning the horizon. He had learned long ago not to let Sinners bait him. However, he couldn't deny the rush of fury skimming the underside of his skin at the poten-tial confirmation that his and Dae's first sexual encounter had been observed. The remark was too general, though, and he wouldn't give it credence yet. Just the same, Shiloh would answer for the attempt on his son's life as well as for his nu-merous other crimes. He was beginning to realize, though, that the penance priest was more valuable to them alive and talking than dead and repentant. He could be the key Mag-nus needed to unlock the hidden corruption in his house.

"Trace remarked how you fell back like a green trainee when he wounded you in Shadowscape that day you fought him," Magnus countered. "I think you got cocky and you didn't expect my son to be as good as his father."

"If he were as good as his father," Shiloh retorted, "he wouldn't have gotten his bitch pregnant out of joining. But then, you were celibate enough for both of you, so I can see that as understandable."

"Tell me, Shiloh," Magnus said conversationally, purposely eradicating all use of M'jan, a title Shiloh had abdicated the instant he had betrayed trust, "how many children have you bullied into your bed, whoring out your handmaiden to pimp for you?"

"Just enough to satisfy, not enough to notice." Magnus could almost hear his cavalier shrug. "Besides, Nicoya loves to whore. My dirty girl gets off watching me make a boy come against his will. The thrill, you see, is in knowing Henry will question his sexual preferences for the rest of his life because of it."

"There is no shame in homosexuality. Henry will learn that." Magnus drew a soft touch along Daenaira's spine beneath her braid. She looked at him with the smallest shift of her eyes. He needed to remind her to keep an eye out for Nicoya, but he didn't know how to best signal her. Tension coiled tightly through his frame as he readied himself to act in a split instant. If any of Shiloh's blades broke either of their skins, it would be as good as a death sentence.

"Stop telling me what to do!" Magnus startled when Daenaira suddenly screamed at him, jerking away from him and railing at him angrily. "I'm not a fucking idiot!"

"Dae!" he hissed, his eyes on the streaming colors of an ever-changing horizon.

"No! You dragged me in here, got me into this mess. I'm not dying because of you! Frankly, you don't mean that much to me," she said snidely.

And then, with alacrity he hadn't realized she was capable of, she ripped out of her Dreamscape Fade.

Daenaira materialized in Shadowscape an instant after she withdrew from the second tier of her Fade, leaving Dreamscape. She whipped her sai out of their sheaths quickly, checking around herself for the as yet absent Nicoya. She smiled when she found herself out of doors, in the center of a field deep with snow and cold.

She wasn't happy to have left Magnus, but she had so strongly sensed his fear for her well-being that she'd had no choice but to eliminate herself from all of his equations. He would have spent all of his energy thinking he had to protect her instead of focusing on his enemy. Now she prayed that Nicoya had been watching, and that she would follow her here instead of helping to gang up on Magnus. If Nicoya didn't show herself soon, Dae would return to Dreamscape and try to approach the battle from a different angle.

"Now, that was very disloyal of you, *K'yan* Daenaira," a familiar voice purred from the tree line some distance away. The vast emptiness of the area made her voice echo, however, making it hard to pinpoint her other than to realize she was somewhere to the left.

"I don't owe that man any loyalty. I'm just here for the free food, warm bed, and the sex. Admittedly, that last one was an unexpected bonus."

"Yes, I heard you gave it up to him. I heard he was surprisingly randy for a man who had shown no interest in it for two centuries. Then again, what man wouldn't be randy after all that time?" Nicoya chuckled.

"Maybe Karri just wasn't one of those women who inspired men. Certainly not like you," she replied, "who has every pubescent boy in Sanctuary salivating for her."

"They are adorable, aren't they?" Nicoya appeared in the tree line, her charcoal slacks and T-shirt looking very relaxed and loose-fitting. Even so, Dae had to admit she could see why men found her so attractive. Not just because she was blessed in all the right places, but because she practically oozed her sexuality. She'd have to learn how to do that, Daenaira mused.

"I am curious about one thing," Dae said conversationally. "If all you do is fluff up those boys for Shiloh, where exactly is *your* relief? What's in it for you?"

"You think I do this for Shiloh?" She snickered at that.

"Typical. We Shadowdweller women take so much pride in our strength, and yet we continue to play these subservient roles to the men of this backward society. Handmaidens? Please. Try whores enslaved for the purpose of keeping these so-called men of the gods from straying. We bow and scrape and kowtow to them like slaves. Ritual baths." She snorted derisively. "More like cheap thrills. Oh, we can say no to sex, but that doesn't keep them from getting off on having us naked in the water with them, stroking them off. Isn't that right?"

Daenaira went carefully still, keeping her expression quite neutral. There was something about the snide assuredness of the query that made a chill walk down Dae's spine. Nicoya had said that as if she had witnessed the bath she had shared with Magnus. Was it just because the same thing happened to many of the women in Sanctuary, or had she actually seen it happen *in their bath*? Were there more tunnels than the ones she knew about? Ones that peered into the privacy of their chambers?

Sickened by the possibility but knowing she could not show it, she nodded as if she agreed with Nicoya's resentment. Anything to lure her in closer. But Daenaira had experienced true slavery. She knew all too well what the difference was between that and the life she had begun to live free of that. She believed that Magnus would never have forced her to become his handmaiden against her will. There had been a choice. They all had choices.

"Do you have a point?" Dae asked archly, twirling her sai nonchalantly in her fingers.

"The point is you don't have to cater to Magnus to have food in your belly and clothes on your body. You don't have to fuck him. And, if you play your cards right, you can turn the tables on him."

Dae chuckled. "Make Magnus submissive to me? Oh, like Shiloh is submissive to you?" she asked dryly.

"Exactly like that," Nicoya said with supreme confidence, her ruby-lipped smile flashing cold and white in the darkness.

Again, Dae stilled. Was Nicoya saying what she thought she was saying? "So you're going to stand there and tell me that you are dominant over one of the most brutal, power-hungry penance priests in all of Sanctuary? A penance priest who is considered second in command to Magnus?"

"And no one the wiser," the other handmaiden said smugly. "You see how perfect it is? He crawls on the floor for me, Daenaira. He comes on command for *me*, not the other way around. He takes those boys because it's what *I* want him to do. I want to watch him destroy the men they will become. I want to watch and see how many times they will submit to the humiliation of unwanted homosexual sex, just on the hopes that they will get rewards from me."

"But Shiloh said—"

"Do you always believe what a man tells you?" she snapped irritably. "Little fool. I thought you were made of tougher stuff than this. Cort couldn't move for hours after the way you tore into him in the stairwell, but it was all worth it to him because I bathed his wounds. And Daniel . . . well, Daniel was Shiloh's very first victim. He's been mine since he was just a boy. Three men, Daenaira, at my total beck and call. Kissing my feet." She gestured to her booted feet concealed under the chill snow. "I would watch them in the tunnels. And they knew I watched. Just like I watched you make Magnus lose total control earlier today . . . and that time in the bath. How do you think I discovered the tidbit that Magnus was giving no satisfaction to poor Karri? She would cater to him, flirt with him, do everything shy of begging or complaining to him. When I sent Cort to seduce her, she was so ripe to be fucked she let him do everything to her. Pain, humiliation, you name it, she let him do it. Anything, just to be touched. She was weak and an embarrassment to our sex."

"So why bother with her?" Dae asked, her body so tight

with anger that she had to force herself to continue her casual stance.

"Because I knew she could get to Magnus. It took time. She was such a—how did you put it? A lapdog? You know, faithful and loyal, so pantingly happy, looking at him in such adoration as if he could do no wrong?" Nicoya spat on the ground, obviously disgusted. "I enjoyed twisting her against that. I relished the day she poisoned Magnus on command. When I ordered her to assassinate whichever royal she could get closest to, I knew she would fail, but I needed a scapegoat. She'd outlived her usefulness. She was so pedantic. Of course, she fancied herself in love with Cort in the end."

"And what was the point of making Greta believe she'd been targeted by Magnus?" Dae asked, taking a shot in the dark.

Nicoya laughed throatily at that. "Oh, you know—sowing general seeds of discontent. Besides, Daniel wanted her. I knew she coveted Magnus obsessively, so I sent Daniel to her as a reward to him for his loyalty to me. You see, deception is the key here, Daenaira. Shiloh, even now, has made himself out to be this incredible threat; this intense penance priest supposedly on par with Magnus. You've been here what, now? A week? Almost two? In all of that time, have you ever seen him spar with anyone else here? He taunts Magnus about Trace, but he had nothing to do with that day the priest's foster son almost died." Nicoya started walking across the field, and Daenaira saw the black sojourn blade she swept almost carelessly around herself. "I lost a perfectly good assassin to Trace that day. One of my stable, you could say. It's amazing, you know, how often men who are powerfully dominant in their daily lives are so willing to submit to a strong, skilled woman at the first opportunity."

"And you are a strong, skilled woman?" Dae asked, stepping back carefully to slow Nicoya's progression toward her.

"Oh yes. You could be, too. I've seen you fight. You thirst for the blood of men. You have everything inside you to make them submit. Look at how easily you tamed the most powerful man in all of Sanctuary! And the gem of it is he doesn't even realize it! But I think *you* do."

Nicoya saw what she wanted to see, Dae thought grimly. Magnus had submitted to her to prove he had meant her no harm. But there was no denying her priest's stunning dominance as a man and how easily he had dissipated her anger once he'd had her closed away with him. But if she looked at their interactions from the outside, she could easily see how Nicoya would think she had control of Magnus. The truth was, however, there was a certain measure of equality to be found in the way the power of their relationship constantly shifted between them.

What concerned Daenaira, though, were Nicoya's implications that Shiloh wasn't the deadly penance priest everyone thought he was. If this was true, then where did the reputation come from?

"Are you telling me that, in truth, *you* are the real penance priest?" she asked, the inflection of amazement in her tone not at all fabricated.

"See! Clever girl," Nicoya praised, swinging her blackened blade in the air until it sang softly for a few moments. "I'm the one who poisons my blades. I am the one who came so close to killing Magnus's son."

"You're the one his son injured. I'm guessing he took you by surprise when he wounded you."

This took some of the air out of her and Dae saw her temper flare. "Until that day, no blade had ever touched me. Mark my words, he will pay for that. Why do you think I decided to kill his father so soon afterward? But now that his bitch is with child, I think I will wait a while and let him get all sentimental and attached to them both. Then I will skewer them on posts side by side outside of his door. See if *that* doesn't break him. Mother would be so pleased."

"Mother?" Dae repeated.

Nicoya waved that off, though. She came closer still. "I

can explain all of this another day. Right now, we have to talk about your future."

"My future?" Dae was beginning to sound and feel like an echo. She figured it was the safest thing to do until she figured out how Nicoya wanted her to react to all she was telling her. She had a pretty good idea where this was going, though, and she needed to think fast.

If what Nicoya was saying was true, she was in a great deal of danger and Magnus had no idea. He thought he was dealing with the true threat in Dreamscape. If Nicoya was not exaggerating or lying, it meant Daenaira had drawn the short straw instead.

"Oh come now, don't be modest. You know I mean for you to join us."

Dae laughed, unable to keep the incredulousness from her tone. "Pardon the analogy, but wouldn't that make for two roosters in one henhouse? You and I would kill each other eventually."

"Not so. Unlike men, dominant women can live together quite easily. Did you think I was alone in Sanctuary? You give me too much credit if you think I can orchestrate that business with Henry *and* kill that nosey little bitch Tiana at the same time."

The watcher in the tunnels they had unwittingly interrupted. But who could it be? There were so many women at Sanctuary, it could be any of them! Or, ironically, it could be a man pulling Nicoya's strings after all.

"How many of you?"

"Yeah. Unlike a man, I'm not stupid enough to tell you that until after I figure out where you are going to lay your bets and loyalty. If I hadn't seen the way you manipulated Magnus into panting after you like Karri used to pant after him, I would have already killed you. But it's clear to me you enjoy your power over him. How artfully you played him earlier. He even let you *tie him up*! The great and mighty M'jan Magnus! Bound like a slave to his mistress! It was beautiful. And the way you refused to free him, jerking him off and coldly walking away to enjoy your superiority. Absolutely brilliant."

"Thank you," Dae said with careful neutrality, amazed at how well she succeeded at masking her furious temper. Every single moment of their assignation had been watched by this demented harpy and twisted into something ugly and mean! Granted, Dae had thrilled in her power of the moment when she had pleasured Magnus, but the key word was "pleasure." It would have meant nothing to her if Magnus had felt no pleasure. And as far as her refusal to untie him, that had been all about fear. She had been afraid to free him and take the next step. The capitulation and tenderness that had followed had been quite acquiescent on Daenaira's part, but Nicoya had put that down to manipulation tactics.

Again, she saw what she wanted to see.

And therein lay her only advantage. Because if Nicoya was truly at the par of a penance priest, she was too deadly a threat for Dae. She'd be the first to admit there was a big difference between fighting Friedlow or even Killian versus someone the same caliber as Magnus.

"I'm curious as to what the benefits would be to me, though. As you said, I already have the most powerful man in Sanctuary wrapped around my fingers." She curled her fingers suggestively around the hilt of the sai and grinned. "Or should I say I have my fingers wrapped around him?"

Nicoya chuckled, her blade still swaying as she came within sword's length of Dae. Daenaira was very aware that the other handmaiden never let the blade touch the snow. Either she was as anal as Magnus was about blade care, or she was avoiding diluting any poison that might be on it.

It occurred to her that someone had to have trained Nicoya to fight. Probably Shiloh at first, and then Cort once she'd grown beyond Shiloh. Then she had propped up her priest as a way to get in under Magnus . . . but really she had covered her bases by owning Cort as well, or so it appeared. All she'd had to do was wait for the right time to strike Magnus down and maneuver herself into a position no female in history had ever attained. And since the Chancellors had no purview in Sanctuary or the Temple, she would have been an absolute ruler in her own little world. It was a deadly clever plan.

But who else was a part of it? Was Nicoya really *this* clever? Dae didn't know her well enough to be certain there wasn't someone else even deeper beyond the obviously twisted and damaged mind of this woman.

"I like you," Nicoya said happily. "I know others have their doubts about you; they think you're a wild card or, at the very least, a maniac, but I like you."

"So if you like me, what's with the blade?" Daenaira flipped her sai, banging the prong of the weapon against the last four inches of the blacked blade, metal sliding against metal before she pulled back. Nicoya's eyes widened, but when Daenaira backed off casually and began to toy with her sai again almost as if she were bored, Nicoya laughed again.

"Can't blame me for being cautious. Magnus has this way of rubbing off goodness onto everyone. It's very difficult to sway people closest to him away from him. Honestly, when my friends in the Senate thought it would be amusing to lure Trace away from Magnus's teachings and the Chancellors, I knew they were wasting their time. He's cut right from his father's ass, for all they aren't true blood."

"I do believe he hates my guts," Dae mused, having been well aware of Trace's animosity from the moment they'd met after her encounter with Killian.

"Of course he does, dearest. Have you met his bitch? Simpering little submissive thing. *Drenna*, she turns my stomach. If that's the way he likes them, then women like you and I must make his prick shrivel up tight in fear. And you do know how attached they are to their pricks."

"All right then, say I buy into this whole scheme of yours. Isn't it over now? I mean, Sagan knows. Magnus knows. It's all unraveling."

"Ah. Well, what are two bodies in the grand scheme? Here's the beauty of it. I can take on Sagan and win, but only if you take out Magnus if Shiloh fails to do so. And I must admit that I doubt he'll succeed. But he could get lucky, in which case, you won't have to bother. However, when he fails, there is only one resource I have left that can keep him off my back and get close enough under his guard to get to him, and that's *you*."

"Seems a waste," Dae lamented softly. "He's rather . . ." She smiled slyly. Genuinely. "Gifted."

"Now, dearest," she scolded lightheartedly. "There's good cock to be found all around you. You only need to look."

Dae arched a brow.

"Brendan," Nicoya offered with a grin. "That man is hung like a prize thoroughbred. Sagan . . . but he's going to die," she recalled with a momentary frown. "You're right, it is a shame. But there's a nut you can't crack anyway. Sagan is rigidly into the whole temple monogamy. Although a few more months without a handmaiden, and a stud like him will find it very hard to resist the right woman. He was made for sex. He just channels it all into his fighting and practice at the moment. Knowing how good he is in the lists, you can imagine how well it would be to redirect his energies to where they belong."

"And the boys, of course?" Dae asked.

"Mmm. Buckets of them. Ripe for the plucking. They are bursting to experience a woman. Quite literally." She giggled. "But as I said, the fun is in the training. We could potentially train a Sanctuary full of future priests completely submissive to the handmaidens."

"Okay," she said carefully, drawing in a breath.

"Okay?" Nicoya prompted cautiously.

"Boys do not interest me, but Brendan does. A few others. I find I am not a one-man woman. And Brendan, I've already noticed, could be so easily controlled by the right female."

"You think so?" Nicoya asked with amusement. "And that would be you?"

"That would be a goal worth risking my ass for, among others. Freedom. True freedom." She took a deep breath. "That is what I really crave. I've been a slave to men for long enough."

"Excellent!" Nicoya stopped pacing through the snow and turned a darkly sinister smile on Dae. "But I'm going to need a reason to trust you before I take your word for it."

Now here, she knew, was the danger. Nicoya would not be easily swayed, and the price she would demand would be very high.

"I'm waiting," she offered.

"I want you to kill Brendan," she said with a shrug.

Dae raised a brow. "Brendan?" she echoed.

"Yes. You just admitted you want him. He has value to you. Lure him to Shadowscape and kill him while I watch and I will know you mean to do as you are told. There would be no going back for you after murdering a priest. Magnus would then only be a further chain in the link. Consider it a rite of passage."

"Just like that? Has he offended you in some way, or was this an arbitrary choice because I mentioned his name?"

"He is Magnus's best friend in all of Sanctuary. And as I said, you want him. There is nothing arbitrary about it." Dae watched as she closed her eyes briefly, turning attention into herself. After a moment she said, "Good. He is in Realscape in his rooms, which will guarantee he is alone." She smiled and explained. "My third power. I can locate any specific person I think of across 'scapes. It's how Shiloh and I can find those we hunt. It's how we found you and Magnus just now."

"Very handy," Dae said, suitably impressed. "Then let's go find him. Realscape, Shadowscape . . . If he's alone, what does it matter where I do this?" She began to walk through the snow, glad for the movement because her legs were nearly frozen from the knees down. Their breed could tolerate cold very well, but she needed to see about getting some boots! The banal thought made her laugh on a soft breath. What she really needed to do was to figure out how to kill Brendan without hurting him. She had to admit, she had not expected Nicoya to take time out to *recruit* her. But she had to try and stretch this as far as she could if there was any hope of glimpsing who else might be behind this. That Nicoya had mentioned the Senate had unnerved Dae. Just how far did this go? Where was all this plotting really going to stop? She had heard Tristan's implications of traitors and such, but at the time she had thought it was mostly dramatic upset. Now she was forced to take him quite literally.

But she couldn't worry about the Senate. She would leave that to the Chancellors. Her focus needed to remain on Magnus and Sanctuary. Despite Nicoya's derision, she knew that Shiloh would not be an easy mark for Magnus. If Magnus was wounded or wearied by the time he faced Nicoya . . .

Daenaira tried not to think she was a coward for not challenging Nicoya here and now and getting it done with. She had to be smart about this. She couldn't afford to get herself in trouble this time. Lives like Henry's were at stake in so many more ways than just the mortal.

They were in the city shelter again rather quickly, and Nicoya showed the way to Brendan's rooms. She kept a keen eye on Dae and never gave her the advantage to attack under her guard. Daenaira kept hoping something would show itself to her advantage, but it never did. Her mind worked overtime to figure out how to pull this off. She was beginning to fear it might come down to deciding between Brendan's life and the lives of so many others. Did she have the strength, *the right*, to make a choice like that?

But she kept seeing and feeling Henry's ravaged features and destroyed confidence and she knew she had to do whatever it took to protect the children of the future from Nicoya and her mystery companions. Magnus might never forgive her for it, but she had to place his life above that of his young friend. Magnus was the backbone of Sanctuary, despite all its troubles, and if he died it would sever the cord of nerves that kept it upright and functioning to the best of its ability.

He needed to live so his ideals could survive long enough to be realized. She believed that. It was a faith all on its own.

"There are tunnels behind these rooms," Nicoya informed her, stopping at an alcove in the hall meant to provide a place to sit and study or converse in semiseclusion. Daenaira closed her eyes briefly when she realized the bench seat and the entire back wall could be triggered to swing away, allowing entrance into the tunnels that no doubt ran alongside many of the private rooms. "I will watch you from here. It will also keep me hidden from sight in case anyone is alerted to search for me as yet. If you falter or try to warn him in any way, I will march myself to the closest student I can find, whatever their age, and sacrifice them in his place. Do you understand? I will not tolerate deception. If you try and make a fool of me, others will die."

"Relax," Dae said dryly. "No need for drama. One question, though." She continued at Nicoya's nod, smiling wolfishly. "Are you in any particular hurry? Seems such a waste not to get a ride off him after the way you described him."

Nicoya chuckled, looking her over thoroughly. "By all means. Be my guest. I'd love to see him betray his old friend by taking Magnus's precious handmaiden before he dies. How sweet, when he realizes he will burn in Light for eternity as he dies with such a sin on him."

"My thoughts exactly," Daenaira murmured.

"You see, I knew I liked you." Nicoya laughed.

Nicoya disappeared, closing the secret portal tight behind her. Daenaira sighed in soft, silent relief. If Nicoya stayed where she was, at least she wouldn't be out in Dreamscape helping Shiloh fight Magnus or attempting to kill Sagan. The gambit of seducing Brendan would buy her time and, hopefully, the opportunity to make him aware something was very wrong. It made her nervous, knowing Magnus distrusted him even a little, even if it might well have been irrational jealousy. Did he have cause to suspect Brendan of breaking temple law in the past? Honestly, though, this had to be the least of her worries.

Licking her lips, she entered Brendan's rooms, and only after she closed the door and locked it tightly behind herself did she sheathe her sai. She walked through the empty bedroom that had once belonged to Nan, the handmaiden who had died of Crush, Hera had told her, nearly a year ago. The room was connected to the bathroom and then to the priest's bedroom, just like the setup in her and Magnus's suite, only not nearly on the same scale of size. Instead of the spring-fed tub, a simple modern Jacuzzi tub of impressive size had been sunk into the stone floor.

She reached the priest's bedroom and took a moment to look around. In Shadowscape, everything was exactly as it was in Realscape. Objects all remained the same, and anything she did would eventually reflect itself in Realscape as well. If she moved his brush in Shadowscape, it was likely he would pick it up and move it exactly the same way in Realscape eventually. Or a cleaning girl would, or any number of scenarios. The end result would be that both objects would end up in the same place.

But that couldn't help her now. Nicoya was no doubt watching her, and time discrepancy between 'scapes would make anything she did unpredictable or obsolete. All she could do was hope her ingenuity in Realscape would be enough to help her do this.

Daenaira Unfaded and materialized in Brendan's bedroom.

He was singing.

The understanding, as well as the surprising beauty of his rich baritone, made her smile. She realized she was hearing him in the acoustically tiled bath she'd just come through, and she contemplated whether to wait for him or confront him in his bath. She shook out her wet skirt, hiding her sai as best she could, and slowly walked into the doorway of the bath.

Oh my.

She hadn't even noticed the shower. Piped in straight against the wall and drained directly into the floor, it had no doors or curtains or anything like them. Why would there be? Privacy between a priest and his handmaiden was really a moot issue. So she got a fine view of tall, beautifully proportioned male standing under the spray of hot water as soap wound down over the muscles and dark skin of his body.

Also, she never would have thought Nicoya would understate matters, since she seemed a bit of a drama queen, but as Brendan turned and gave her a full frontal view, she couldn't help but wonder what Sagan must be like in order to have Brendan coming in second in Nicoya's estimation.

Of course, nice as all of Brendan was, it only reminded her of the vital, breathtaking man she was trying to save. *I want us both to live long enough to make love again,* she thought fiercely. What they had shared that afternoon had been nowhere near enough.

Daenaira kept that in mind as she began to cross the bathroom and prepared to seduce her lover's friend.

Chapter Thirteen

Magnus curled his hand into a fist, trying to capture the warmth of Dae's body even as she ripped away from him to exit her Fade and the dangers of Dreamscape. He understood why she had done it, and he hoped her gambit paid off. He knew, though, that if Nicoya wasn't lured away by Dae's trick, his handmaiden would return quickly to aid him in another way.

Battle.

He took a slow, deep breath, his body loosening up now that Dae was relatively out of danger. He was still concerned that Nicoya was much older and was, no doubt, far better trained and tempered than his wildfire Daenaira was, but Dae had her third power and her naturally dogged viciousness and stubbornness when it came to refusing to lose a fight. That would go very far for her, and it would be easy for Nicoya to underestimate that.

Magnus had to shed his concerns for her and focus on the here and now. This was too volatile a situation in too unpredictable an environment.

Focus.

He needed focus.

He took a deep breath and threw.

The glave had hung from the back band of Daenaira's skirt, and he had just closed his hand around it when she had distracted anyone watching with her irate performance of betrayal. It only took the flick of a wrist to extend the palmed weapon into rigidity and he sent it flying in a whipping, singing swirl of sharp curves that flew like a boomerang through the Dreamscape air. Even as he followed through for maximum power into the throw, he was drawing his katana and making ready for both retaliation and the return of the glave.

There was a kind of art form to distinguishing truth of locus in Dreamscape, and Magnus had studied it as deeply as he could both during and outside of hunts. He still didn't know exactly where Shiloh was, but he had determined which general direction and almost how distant he really was despite the naked landscape toward the horizons. This was how he forced Shiloh to dive to the ground, his invisibility instantly nullified by the cloud of dust the impact kicked up. The other priest swore vehemently as he found himself victim to a savage Magnus, who bore down on him with all of his strength and fury packed into his first blow.

The clash of sword on sword resonated through the endless air, muscles and bone vibrating with the impact before Magnus grabbed his foe by his collar and yanked him hard from the ground, whirling him a foot and a half to his left. The air whistled sharply right before the glave returned to its master . . . stopping only when Shiloh's upper back provided a sudden obstacle. Catching it hard in his lower shoulder, Shiloh grunted as the impact made him lurch awkwardly against Magnus.

"Oh, you fucking bastard," Shiloh groaned, grinding his feet into the ground and lurching all of his weight against Magnus's center of gravity. Magnus didn't want to be within biting distance of any of his blades, so he roughly rolled Shiloh's weight off himself and backed off. Sweeping the katana artfully around the other man's blade, he caught it in its decorative hilt, and with a hard fling of sharp steel, he ripped Shiloh's sword out of his hand and sent it soaring.

Shiloh knelt crookedly on the ground, ready to rise to his feet, and he chuckled. "Do you know what the best part of all of this is? Hmm?" He stood up, holding out visibly weapon-less hands, but this was Dreamscape and they both knew it. Anything was possible if you had the right control, experience, and imagination. "It's getting to watch and learn how really fucking stupid you are. I mean, all your idealistic bull-shit. What a joke. Now"—he grinned—"I admit you had me there in the beginning. Light and Dark, *Drenna* and *M'gnone*, the cosmic balance of power and action versus apathy and sin. But then"—he shook a scolding finger at Magnus—"you sent me little Nicoya, and everything changed."

Magnus frowned at that, wondering what in Light Nicoya had to do with his sin and madness, other than his having coaxed her into sin along with him. He let the other man talk, however. Shiloh, he believed, didn't realize just how deep the glave had gone into his back, and he was surely bleeding rapidly. The more time he wasted talking, the weaker he would get.

"Now, keep in mind I know you can compel the truth from me," he mentioned as they slowly started to circle each other, "if you get your hands on me."

"Regardless, it was not I who sent you Nicoya. She came to you through the blessings of *Drenna*. You were the one who decided to destroy that gift by corrupting her."

Shiloh chuckled at that. "Yeah. You see, that's the part I like. If *Drenna* sent her to me, then that means anything that happened between us was *Drenna*'s will, right?"

"*M'gnone* lives in the temple as well. We do not speak His name, but we know his influence challenges us every day. It is up to us whether we want to live in Darkness or Light. You are a priest and you know this. Do not stand there like a child and play bargaining games to excuse your wrongdoing. You are an adult with the free will to make your own choices. We allow *Drenna* or *M'gnone* into us and let them guide us as they will. *M'gnone* will give me the ferocity, cunning, and savagery I need to destroy you and your sins; *Drenna* will give me the strength to offer you repentance and pity and whatever else it takes to save both of our souls. I am the one who chooses which will give me impetus and when."

"Hmm. Yes, ladies and gentlemen, he can fight and give sermons, too." Shiloh chuckled. "Is that why you chose to neglect poor Karri for so long? I admit, in the beginning I thought you were like me—"

"I am nothing like you," Magnus hissed sharply, his katana slicing out in sharp warning at the insult, nearly nicking Shiloh's face, but the other priest was strong and quick. He was back out of reach in an instant. Magnus grinned without satisfaction as he stalked after him.

"I thought," his enemy persisted as he continued to back away, "that you were into boys or men. That was Coya's theory for the longest time. Karri thought that could be it, although she liked to convince herself you were physically impotent. After all, even I was in denial for the longest time. I didn't even want to do another man the first time it came up, so to speak." His grin was lascivious. "But you know, it grows on you really, really fast. The dominance. The power of taking someone over so completely that they feel pleasure even though it's the last thing in the universe they want. The look on their face, such a pure mixture of passionate horror and guilty ecstasy. It's better than any drug."

"I hope you are saying all of this because you plan to repent these sins," Magnus spat, his disgust for the other man raw and bone deep. How could there ever be repentance for someone who had purposely used his position to manipulate and emotionally ravage the innocent youth he had been entrusted to guide and protect? What penance could there possibly be for such brutal sin?

If there was one, Magnus would be the one to find it and administer it.

Magnus carefully watched where they were stepping. In Dreamscape, Shiloh's weaponless state was no advantage. He could eventually replace the blade, if he focused well enough. But he seemed to be more intent on talking Magnus to death first. It was always like this. The guilty always talked, either to coax, convince, or, as with Shiloh, to crow. It was his one true advantage because it split the other man's concentration from where it ought to be. Or so it appeared. He took nothing for granted. He simply wanted to put an end to this so he could back up Daenaira.

"Not in the least," Shiloh said with an unrepentant shrug. There was a flash of bright light and a metallic weapon grew from it and seated itself in the priest's hand. It was a heavy battle-axe. Something slow and unwieldy. But as powerful as Magnus's weaponry was, it would never stand up against something so huge in a parry. "Trouble with those light blades," Shiloh noted dispassionately, "is that they're light."

"Only if you depend on them completely. Which I do not. Also, I was curious as to how often you will be able to swing that thing with a hunk of metal grinding around in your shoulder."

There was some advantage to talking after all, Magnus mused as he saw the lash of fury that crossed Shiloh's features. Realizing Magnus was correct, Shiloh sent the thing away as quickly as he had made it. The light flash, while it did not burn the men, did blind them both temporarily, which meant only one thing . . .

"So," Shiloh prattled on, "as Cort and I were fucking your former bitch in every hole she had, it occurred to us that after two hundred years, even a gay man would have found the interest to slake his lust at least once. You know, Karri thought the same thing. Honestly, you should have seen her face the day we showed her the tunnels behind the priest suites on your level. There we were, looking into your rooms, and damn if you weren't having a go at yourself. She watched for an hour, making these little whimpering sounds of abject misery every time you came." He mocked the sounds and Karri's weeping expression. "By the way, excellent recovery time you have there."

"Thank you," Magnus said just as conversationally, in no way revealing the red-hot fury of rage boiling through him. Not because his privacy had been breached, but for the unfortunate woman he had honestly loved in all of her years with him. No, he had not felt passion for her, but he had loved her, and a twisted, sick *bituth amec* like Shiloh had taken her and warped and destroyed a good woman, using her unexpressed loneliness and the needs of her physical body as a way of training her to their heels. But worst was knowing he could count himself as one of those evils that had had a hand in her downfall.

He also did not enjoy the reminder that he had been so remote in his personal interactions with her that he had never intuited her needs. Nor had he ever made it clear to her how much he cared and how grateful he had been to have her by his side all those years. It made him fear. It terrified him to think he would make the very same mistakes with Daenaira. She was so willful and had such a hot nature that she wouldn't put up with him treating her neglectfully. She had already proven that much. On the one hand, he was grateful for it, because she would never let him be dense about it like he had been with Karri. On the other, he was shocked at how terrifying a prospect it was to him that she might leave him for it.

When the first sting of a thorn hit him in the back of his neck, he cursed and hit the ground with all speed. Still, the back of his body burned with dozens of piercing bites as thorns the size of thick needles peppered into him. He hadn't been listening, and it served him right for not paying attention. He heard Shiloh move, and rolled back up to his feet even though it meant stabbing the little drills farther into his skin. He was up and guarding in a heartbeat, waiting until he was certain Shiloh was at a respectful distance before yanking a thorn to inspect the tip.

"What? No poison?" he asked dryly.

"Now, now, you know nothing made of Dreamscape can kill you in Dreamscape. That's the rules. Only the weapons we bring with us can do that. You can be hurt and hurt badly, but no one dies in their dreams. Well, not unless one of us comes to Fade with a sword and hacks their little heads off. Which reminds me—I wouldn't let your new piece go to sleep as long as Coya and I are alive. There are ways, as you know, of damaging a dreamer without the need to kill them, and we promise to hurt her *a lot* the very instant she closes her eyes." He seemed to think on it. "Of course, if I know my Nicoya, by now she's already begun her plans to lure your Daenaira far, far away from you."

The confidence of Shiloh's speculation sent a bolt of burning cold down through the center of Magnus's body. It was so cold that it numbed him completely to the needles stabbing into him. Now, suddenly, he wanted this deceitful bastard to talk his damn fool head off.

"Dae won't go down easy," he said, somehow managing to sound unconcerned as he casually reached to pluck a few more thorns from his body. He never lowered his weapon and never took his eyes off Shiloh.

"Shame, I was hoping she might," he said with a salacious grin. "She certainly has your cock wrapped up tight in her fingers. Has you coming to a whole different tune now. I look forward to testing her out for myself."

Magnus saw red.

Despite his experience and his best intentions, the very idea of Shiloh laying his perverted hands on Dae's precious mocha skin sent infuriated adrenaline screaming through him. With a roar he attacked the other priest. Shiloh barely had time to call up a parrying blade before Magnus was beating him back with violent blows that made the air ring with the sound of scraping, clashing metal. Within minutes Shiloh was panting, stumbling, and weakening, blood loss and the agony of using full-strength overhead parries to keep Magnus off him reminding him of how deeply wounded he was. Shiloh staggered and broke away from him, retreating as quickly as he could as the savage golden eyes of his enemy bored through him. Magnus stalked him, no longer the tolerant, patient man Shiloh was used to. Shiloh had thought he had wanted this, to bait Magnus until he was out of control with temper, but he had meant to give himself advantage by it, not get himself killed by releasing a beast on himself.

"Daenaira *huth a j'vec muli vu bituth amec*!" Magnus spat, letting him know exactly what he thought of the likelihood of Dae ever allowing a vile creature like Shiloh within arms' reach of her body.

"Really?" Shiloh panted, trying to back off a little quicker without falling on his ass. "The chit abandons you in battle and you still don't get that she doesn't want to be near you? She's smart, that one. She won't stay with a sinking ship. Coya's counting on that."

That was the second time Shiloh had referred to Nicoya as if she were playing a more specific role for him than just a sidekick and recruiter. It made Magnus's blood slow enough to force him to think. Perhaps Nicoya was more equally partnered to Shiloh's plans than he had been giving her credit for. Suddenly, that made her seem a lot more dangerous to him.

"Dae has no loyalties to me, you, or anyone else," he said, his voice rasping with the tightness of his still-pumping outrage. "She is loyal to herself, and that alone will keep her on *Drenna*'s path."

"Yeah. She's real law-abiding, that one. She floors four of the city's guards without even flinching, makes no apology to any of them, and all but throws back her head and howls in

delight when she beats her opponents in practice. She lives
for blood and victory. She lives for battle. That she abandoned
the opportunity to fight me with you says a lot."

"Come, Sinner, enlighten me," Magnus growled in low
threat. "Tell me what you know of my Daenaira."

"I know she's a natural redhead," Shiloh sneered.

The reminder of just how intimately Shiloh had invaded
Dae's privacy was as big a mistake as his previous goading.
The entire ground rippled with Magnus's resulting wrath. It
rolled and bucked beneath the other priest, flinging him off
his feet until he landed hard on his back, his second weapon
flying free and the one in his back grinding harder and deeper
into him. Next, he felt a heavily booted heel crunching into
his breastbone so hard that he couldn't breathe. Magnus
leaned most of his weight forward on the rib-cracking foot
and those vengeful golden eyes stabbed down at Shiloh.

"Go on," Magnus coaxed softly as he laid the tip of his
blade under Shiloh's jaw with enough force for the edge to
break his skin. "Tell me more of what you know of my Daenaira."

My Daenaira. It was the second time he had said it in that
way, with such possession and intimacy. Shiloh felt very real
panic flood through his body. He had thought, knowing how
gullible Magnus could be when it came to his faith, that his
life would never be in any real danger so long as Magnus
gave him his standard opportunity of repentance. The priest
was renowned for his enduring lectures to the other penance
priests that there was no soul in any of the 'scapes who was
not capable of redemption, and so it must always be offered.
Of course, he and Nicoya had stopped offering the stupid recourse ages ago, but he knew Magnus believed in it with all
of his soul.

Only . . . he did not look so benevolent just then. In fact,
his hard, dark features looked quite fanatically eager for Shiloh
to push him just one little inch further. Shiloh began to fear

and relish the idea of pushing the prudish priest beyond his values, even though it would cost him his life. No matter what Nicoya's plans for the priest, nothing would destroy him faster than defying his own principles. It would make the victory Shiloh's, through and through.

"I know," he squeaked against the pressure on his lungs, "that she screams for you when she comes like a yowling bitch in heat." The sword popped past more skin as Magnus's rage began to make him shake. "That you made her cry when you—!"

Shiloh gagged on his words when the katana sliced over his windpipe as it switched to the opposite side of his jaw. He now had a thin cut from ear to ear, and the boot on his chest was pushing the blade in his back deeply into him until blackness tickled the edges of his vision.

"I'm sorry, I couldn't hear you," Magnus said with low menace as he leaned over him. "Would you like to repeat that before I shove my sword down your gullet?"

"What? No offer to repent?" he rasped in a whisper.

"Always," Magnus assured him quietly. "Unfortunately, I may not be able to hear your reply if you have to talk around carbon steel. So, I suggest the next words out of that filthy mouth of yours be well worth a final farewell quotation."

Shiloh smiled in the face of the doom and death promised him in the other man's eyes.

"If you kill me, you'll never know the truth."

Magnus paused significantly, even easing his weight enough to allow Shiloh to breathe back the darkness covering his vision. "The truth about what?"

"Sanctuary. Temple. The Senate. Your precious fucking twins. The way your son is going to pay one day for what he's done. For what you have done."

Magnus dropped his foot away and all of his weight fell onto Shiloh via his bent knee as he lowered himself to kneel on his chest. He adjusted the blade against Shiloh's throat to his new position, then reached out and touched bare fingertips to his enemy's bare forehead. Skin-to-skin contact was all he needed. Just a touch.

"Tell me about my son," he demanded.

"Even if you kill me and, in the unlikely instance that you kill Nicoya," Shiloh choked out, compelled to speak the utter truth as Magnus's third power filtered through him, "your son will be destroyed. His wife and child will be murdered sometime after the first two months of the child's life. They will be hunted until they drop and then staked out for your son to find."

"Who arranged this? Who will do this killing?" Magnus spat, his whole world swimming in a sea of horror and fear unlike anything he'd ever felt exposed to before.

"Nicoya arranged it. But she told me nothing else. She knew you would try to compel us if we were caught, so she sent a messenger a choice of twelve assassins' guilds to pick from to arrange the payment. When he returned, she killed him without knowing a single detail. It cannot be recalled. It cannot be stopped. Not unless you find those twelve guilds and destroy every member of every one of them. Good luck. You have what, eight months? A year? Some of those guilds have been hidden for decades. Especially to a priest like you."

"Nicoya arranged it," Magnus echoed, every word Shiloh spoke like a new coat of ice on his soul. "You had your lackey do your dirty work in case of . . . this?" Magnus shook his head, confused. Shiloh, he realized, had gone down far too easily for a warrior of his fame. He had barely tried to manipulate the environs around himself, though he ought to be an expert at it by this point in his career. "What am I missing here?"

"Everything." Shiloh chuckled weakly, his lashes lowering briefly. Magnus realized then how pale he was becoming, and that the blood of his body was pooling wider beneath him. The glave had nicked or severed an artery. He was bleeding out.

"Specifically, Shiloh, what am I missing here?" he barked.

"Nicoya isn't the lackey," he whispered. "I am."

Magnus felt a wave of numbing paralysis washing up over him, locking and stiffening every joint in his body until he knew he couldn't move. His heart thundered in frantic attempt to revitalize him while also trying to manage the tide of emotions flooding through him.

Dae.

My son.

Sanctuary.

The twins.

All of it. Everything important to him was in threat and in danger, and he had been looking in the wrong place at the most crucial moment.

"Who else?" Magnus stammered as he remembered he had to be specific to compel the truth. "W-who else is behind all of this plotting?"

"Coya. Cadia," he replied weakly. He was losing consciousness, and Magnus slapped him hard with the back of his hand to rouse him.

"Who the fuck is Cadia?" he shouted down at him.

"Acadian!" came the rasped reply. "Coya's mother, you dumb bastard! Yeah, that's right. The woman who tortured your son for eleven months is Coya's mother. And you know what? She's been right under your nose all of this time."

"Where? Where is she? Tell me!"

"Right now? I wouldn't know."

It was the truth, of course. Shiloh had been well trained to give the truth against his power without giving any real information. He was buying precious time.

Time to die.

Shiloh's eyes slid closed and Magnus roared with pain and outrage. He grabbed at Shiloh, and straddling his body, he shook the bastard hard. "Wake up! *Wake up!* You will not escape me this easily, you fucking prick! Wake!"

But it was too late. Shiloh lost his Fade at the moment of unconsciousness, and slipped out of Dreamscape. Magnus's mind was reeling, and Dreamscape right along with it. He had to waste several crucial moments calming himself enough to Unfade from Dreamscape and back into Shadowscape. He appeared knee deep in snow, the frigidity of the Alaskan winter biting into him shockingly hard. There, lying in the snow, was Shiloh's dead body. Unlike Dreamscape, once you died in Shadowscape, you stayed in Shadowscape. There would be no more Unfading for him.

Lost for a moment, blinded by his own distress, Magnus raked wild eyes over the terrain around him.

And he saw two sets of footprints walking away, side by side.

"If I know my Nicoya, by now she's already begun her plans to lure your Daenaira far, far away from you . . ."

"Oh gods," he choked out, his voice echoing hollowly in the open night air. Nicoya. The real danger had been Nicoya all along! No. Worse than that. It had been the sadistic woman known as Acadian. Faceless, formless, and unidentifiable even to his son, who had been her captive for nearly a year, except, perhaps, by the nature of her voice. She could be anyone. Anyone. But Trace's torture had taken place some twelve years earlier. In all of that time, wouldn't he have come up against that voice he swore he knew so well that he would remember it until the day he died?

But even Trace was susceptible to the flaws of memory and the damage done to the mind when torture of such a brutal nature was involved. Trauma could blind his mind to knowing the voice when he heard it. Distortion of memory would be enough on its own. As much as he wanted to believe his son would know her from a single word, he knew the mind did not obey the will that well.

But they had thought Acadian was dead.

They would never have suffered her to live unhunted and his son unavenged had they thought for a minute otherwise. When Trace had been rescued from the stronghold of the clan who had hired her for her skills, the place had burned down around their enemies' ears and no one had escaped Tristan's vigilant army. Or so it had seemed. There must have been another escape route.

Magnus sheathed his weapon and began to run after the prints in the snow.

If Nicoya was Acadian's daughter, and if Shiloh was submissive to Nicoya, then that meant that she was the real danger. She could even be leading Dae to Acadian, who was no doubt twenty times as deadly as her offspring. The very thought of Daenaira being led into the clutches of a known and accomplished torturer made him run even faster.

Brendan turned away from the wall after shutting off the taps. He nearly gave himself a coronary as he came face-to-face with the last woman he would have ever expected to find in his bath, regardless of how his fantasies had been tending toward exactly that not too long ago. Ever since he had watched Magnus brush her damned hair as if he were eagerly seducing *Drenna* Herself, he hadn't been able to shed the forbidden craving from his thoughts. Gods, but he was crazy about those beautiful and unusually colored tresses of hers. It had made him realize Magnus had probably been right to be jealous of his intentions in the lecture hall. Brendan had subconsciously been taking advantage of his position in that class to get his hands into her hair.

"*Drenna!* Dae! You just took a decade off my life!"

"It's a good thing we're long-lived, then, isn't it?" she asked drolly, quirking up a pretty little reddish brow as her candid eyes drifted slowly down the length of his naked body. She held up a clean, folded towel, extending it to him generously even as her gaze lingered over his sex far longer than was sanely comfortable for him to cope with. He snatched the towel from her, wrapping it quickly around his hips before she got an eyeful of his response to that heated appraisal.

Uncomfortable and resisting the urge to look for the wrath of Magnus coming down on him, he ran a nervous hand through his wet hair, pushing the jaw-length mop off his face.

"What are you doing in here, Dae?" he demanded as he pushed past her and walked into his bedroom. "This isn't proper behavior."

"Oh, come on, Brendan. I'm a handmaiden. I've seen naked men before," she teased him with a laugh as she dogged his heels. "Look at you, all embarrassed. You had Nan bathing you for what, fifty years? Before Crush took her? What's the difference?"

"The difference is, she was *my* handmaiden. You are Magnus's. Do you know what he would do to me if he found you in here? Gods, you need to go." He paled just thinking about the trouble she could cause him. He had never seen Magnus so possessive and volatile as he was with this woman. This impropriety might mean little to her, but it would be a huge betrayal to Magnus, especially in light of Karri.

"Oh, stop," she brushed him off, trotting in a skip to his bed and landing on it with a flounce. "We aren't doing anything wrong. He's just a bully."

"He's also my boss! Our boss," he corrected.

"*Drenna* and *M'gnone* are our bosses," she reminded him blithely.

"Dae, you aren't supposed to speak His name in Sanctuary unless it is to give a sermon or lecture."

"I just did give a lecture," she pointed out.

Well, she had a point there. She had been correcting him. The realization of a raw maiden correcting a veteran priest was enough to make him chuckle, lightening the mood when she grinned back at him.

"So you have a reason for being here?" he asked her, trying not to eye the way she looked as she sprawled back across his bed, her red-black hair glowing across the violet spread.

Gods, Brendan, you need a new handmaiden, he lectured himself harshly before turning to seek out some clothing from his bureau. Except it wasn't so simple. He had cared for poor Nan very much. It had been hell watching her die a little every day. Slow and excruciating, Crush was the most horrid death known to their kind. Worst was at the end when it suddenly decided to pick up speed and blindsided both its victim and those who had seen her alive, chatty and happy only days before she had been knocking at the door of the Beyond. She had been blind, nearly deaf, and weak, but she had still been Nan until those last days. Then she had been a screaming, ravaged husk of pain that no medication, no herbs, no healers could quiet. To send her to sleep would do nothing because it was obvious that Crush followed its victims into Dreamscape.

It had felt almost impossible to replace Nan before the disease had ravaged her. Once it had wrung through him and clawed her life from her inch by excruciating inch those last few days, he couldn't bear the idea of drawing so close to someone only to lose them so brutally once again. If not for Magnus and Karri being with him every step of the way, he wasn't certain he would have risen from the oppressive gray pall that had weighted him at the sound of Nan's last breath. His relief at her death had been so overwhelming and so unbearably shameful to him that it hurt still to think about it. It had felt selfish, and like a betrayal, but neither would he have wished a single instant's further pain on her.

Brendan bent his head, using his dresser to lean on as he tried to breathe through this sudden tide of emotion he was feeling. He didn't even hear Dae get to her feet. She touched trailing fingertips down his spine, peeking around his biceps and the irremovable band of his office he wore around it.

"Hey, you still here?" she asked gently, her touch following the gully of his backbone between the strong muscles of his back. He was hardly the hardened, massive warrior that Magnus was, but he was still strong and fit, nicely sculpted, with a body he was actually a tad vain about. Her touch, however, felt just a little too good on his skin.

"Yup," he assured with a nod. He straightened up and continued to look for clothes.

"This is unusual," she remarked after a moment, stepping behind him and drawing her fingertips low along the line of his towel.

This time, Brendan was all too aware of how her touch woke up his skin with a blazing fury. Her thumbs smoothed over the low curve of his back and nearly tugged his towel free. That wouldn't have been good at all, because he was quite sure he had the heaviest erection of the year going on beneath it. Brendan grimaced, realizing she was going to take notice eventually, regardless.

"The tattoo?" he asked knowingly, swallowing hard and striving for control. "I know."

"Magnus has one in the same place. Half moon, half sun. *Drenna* and *M'gnone*. Dark and Light. But I don't know if I understand this one." She traced over the image and the delicate green fronds of bamboo decorating it like a frame.

"It's called a yin-yang. The white and black are good and evil, at least roughly, and the dots on opposing sides remind us that we all have a little of each inside of us, no matter what the bigger part of us appears to be made of. Magnus showed it to me long ago, when I became angry because he forced me to allow a man, a Sinner that I despised, the opportunity for repentance. He was a coward who preyed on those weaker than he was, and when faced with Magnus's sword he wanted to swear repentance and take penance. Magnus agreed, although we could both see it was merely a tactic to buy himself time. I was so angry I almost hit Magnus that day. He showed me the symbol, explained its meaning, and then said that he was now responsible for finding

that single speck of goodness inside all of that badness."
Brendan turned and smiled at her. "Then he told me I could
watch him do it as slowly and as excruciatingly as possible.
He kept the bastard in penance for a month until he broke.
Then kept him here in Sanctuary for three years after that,
working his ass off and making him prove he was worthy of
seeing the outside world again one day."

Brendan shook his head in admiration. "That guy eventually volunteered to make amends to every person he had
hurt, no matter how hard it was for him. Magnus had found
a way into him, drew out that speck of good and somehow
made it grow. Now that former Sinner volunteers most of his
time here and helps out the priests who have no handmaidens with the more squirelike tasks; weapons cleaning, a little
housekeeping, helping them pack for migration time, or
making sure we all eat. We forget to do that sometimes."

"That just proves you are all dedicated to what you do,"
she murmured, her hand sliding into the lean cut of his waist
and then across the rigid bumps of his tightening abdominal
muscles. Brendan hesitated moments too long, enjoying the
wicked sensation, before reaching to carefully enclose her
hand in his, trapping her palm against him.

"What are you doing, Dae?"

"Brendan," she said softly, coyly, "surely it hasn't been
that long for you?"

It was a tease, but he found no humor in it. A strange cold
dread writhed through the immediate heat her flirtation also
sent slithering through him.

"Dae," he began sternly.

But she effectively silenced him when she used surprising strength to shove him roughly back against the dresser,
and with a full-bodied press of her flesh, she wriggled up
tightly against him. Her hands began to coast over his damp
skin. She shaped his pectorals, his shoulders and arms, her
breasts and her bare belly pressing into him with electric
contact. The way her hips snuggled up against his, he knew

she couldn't possibly miss the heavy weight of his thickened cock. Brendan closed his eyes as sensation overwhelmed him, and he swallowed back a low, heartfelt groan. It was an effort, but he managed to keep his hands off her, holding them up and out to his sides like a man surrendering.

"Daenaira!" he choked out in a strangled attempt at normalcy. "Quit it! This isn't funny!"

Why in Light would she be doing this? It has to be a joke! For fuck's sake, I can smell Magnus all over her! It was obvious they had been quite intimate very recently. Was that it? She'd had a taste of his friend and now wanted something more? Or was she thinking it was okay to comparison shop? No. There were very basic rules here, and she knew what they were!

"I don't recall making a joke," she observed, her unimpeded hands stroking down his sides and back, sliding softly between the press of their bodies and slowly, inexorably heading below his navel.

When her fingers snagged the edge of his towel, he had no choice but to grab her wrist in a harsh, bruising grip.

"Stop!" he hissed. "There are rules, Dae, and this is sin you are toying with."

"You say that as if you have no sin in your heart," she said softly, looking up at him through her lashes as her free hand slid down to cup his erection into her palm through the terry of the towel. There was no repressing the moan of agonizing pleasure he released. "You're already sinning in your mind."

"Coveting is one thing," he rasped, knowing he should push her away and unable to do so in spite of himself. "Sin of the flesh is another. I won't betray Magnus, Daenaira. Stop!"

"Your body betrays Magnus," she noted, her voice dispassionate even as she breathed hot breath over his exposed nipple. Her deft fingers found the seam of the tucked towel, but instead of pulling it free, she slipped her hand beneath and sought him out.

"Dae!" he gasped as her fingertips brushed against him, the skin-to-skin contact electrifying.

"Shh." She smiled as she reached her other hand up to cover his mouth, concealing his protests. "Just feel me. Pay careful attention and feel me."

She slowly moved her touch over to his leg and spaced her fingertips out across his thigh muscle. Then, with all of her strength, she dug her nails deep into his skin. Brendan shouted a curse beneath her hand, though it was completely muffled, and he tried to throw her off him.

But before he could grab her fully she said, "There now, that feels good, doesn't it? I could make you come just by touching you like this, couldn't I?" Brendan stared at her as if she had lost her mind, groaning a little as she dug in her nails a little further. "Do you like the way I stroke your cock?" she asked him. She dug into him when he blinked dumbly at her, his head dropping back as he released a muffled cry of pain that, he slowly realized, could easily be mistaken for a sound of pleasure. "I bet you'd like me on my knees," she continued to purr, the catch of her gaze turning suddenly meaningful beneath the false allure of her lowered lashes. "You'd love my mouth on you, your hands in my hair as I sucked you to climax. Don't stand here and pretend to be all righteous when I can feel how much I turn you on."

She carefully peeled her fingers away when she was clearly satisfied he was getting the picture something wasn't right. This was some kind of a staged act, Brendan realized. But staged for whom? And who in Light could be listening? Or—he took into consideration how she had carefully hidden her gouging nails—watching? Was someone watching her do this? Relief washed through him when he realized she wasn't really trying to test his fortitude and his friendship with Magnus. But just where in Light could someone be watching from in the privacy of his own bedroom?

Daenaira glanced down Brendan's body, finally satisfied he'd gotten the message. Granted, she'd been a little surprised at first to find him so excited, and she'd felt awful about making an embarrassing moment for him even worse, but she had needed to be convincing from all but the most minute angle of concealment.

And now she had to take it further.

Brendan's towel, staining red against the violet fabric where she'd clawed into him, dropped to the floor, leaving him naked. She guarded the wounds with the shield of her body as she turned him and walked him backward to his bed before dumping him onto it. Then she drew up her skirt and quickly climbed him to straddle his hips.

Being sex to sex with Brendan while he was so aroused was highly disconcerting to Daenaira. Worse, she had to affect having sex with him in a position she'd never tried with only two actual experiences under her belt. The seductress business, she realized, was much harder than she'd thought, even with the proverbial eager male at hand.

Brendan reached for her upper arms, his strong hands closing hard around her as he strangled on a sound of crossing pain and pleasure. Gods, she hated to do this to him! She could feel how furious he was with himself for reacting to her so strongly. His body clearly had no qualms about betraying the trust and faith of a friend, whereas the man himself wanted nothing of the kind. It mortified him, knowing she was in need of help and that he couldn't control himself. But that was okay. She actually didn't want him to control himself. The more realistic this was, the better. They both knew what was in their hearts. She just had to warn him that he was marked to die *before* she actually had to kill him.

"Put me inside you," Brendan ground out huskily, his cock leaping with a heated pulse in agreement although he knew it wouldn't get the satisfaction it wanted so badly. With her skirt spread over him concealing the truth of their acts, she reached between them and pretended to do as he asked. She rose up, and hesitated, seeking help from him. "Slow," he urged her, grabbing her round hips in both hands. "Come down on me so I go in really slow."

He was teaching, she realized, and it made her smile. She mimicked what he asked, and he helped guide her hips in a lusty undulation back flush against him.

"Gods, Dae, you feel so hot. So good," he croaked out. She knew he wasn't lying or acting about that just by the flush on his skin and the need in his voice. "Please, just move. Move on me. I'm begging you . . ."

The desperation in his eyes tore at her heart. She was torturing him. It had to have been a year at the very least since he'd been with a woman, and who knew how much longer before that when Nan had been too sick for them to physically show love to each other? Her body, she knew, was only for Magnus. Brendan was handsome, strong, and a well-muscled specimen of masculinity, but while she admitted to feeling a rather low-key arousal, she felt nothing like with Magnus. Still, when Brendan moved her sex along the ridge of swollen flesh he harbored beneath her, she let him. She figured if she was going to do what she had to do to save his life and her own, she could begrudge him nothing. She leaned forward over him, her hands pressing to the bed beside his shoulders, and she made herself stare down into the torn conscience in his eyes. She lowered herself to his lips, kissing him gently before trailing her lips down his cheek and finding his ear briefly.

"It's okay," she whispered before rising up once more and following the rhythm of his hands on her hips. His fingers dug into her with bruising force as she rode against him. Dae wasn't expecting the rub of their simulated intercourse to stimulate her, but her body was newly awakened to all kinds of sensations and sensitivities because of Magnus, and it responded to the cadence of her clit being steadily massaged by his hard length against her underwear. She flushed, feeling embarrassment of her own as her panties went damp and warm against him. She knew the very instant he felt the change and saw him grit his teeth together as if in excruciating pain. Or pleasure. They were so close it was hard to tell. He dragged her against him, a little harder and a little faster, his hips surging up now with every pull and press.

"Oh, fuck," he gasped, his face flushing bright red, his skin coated in perspiration. "Dae . . . this is so wrong . . . but I can't . . ." He was gasping the words, desperate to make her understand and ashamed of himself for abusing their situation. Daenaira was certain he wouldn't feel that way shortly.

Brendan surged up against her over and over, her heat and dampness rubbing him raw with the need to come. She was breathless herself, his work against her rousing her clit, he knew. But he had to draw the line somewhere, and that meant leaving her to her own devices, whatever happened. He didn't understand fully what she was doing or why, but he did know without a doubt that she didn't want him. It was clear to him in the calm of her amber eyes. When a woman wanted him again, he knew it would be with passion and fire in her eyes, a body craving everything he could give her, and the yearning need to join together at all costs.

These thoughts, these needs, as much as her physical ride against him, were what sent him over the edge. Brendan gripped her hips hard, surged up into her in a long arching of his back, and he came with blinding pleasure and much, much needed release. He was shaking as the orgasm pumped from him, ejaculate spreading over his belly, her skirt, and her thighs. She didn't come, and he was glad. This dishonor would be his and his alone. She was in trouble and he hadn't had the control to temper himself, humping himself to climax against her like some too-eager boy.

Brendan opened his eyes, blinking clarity into them just as the icy cold touch of steel rested against the rib hiding his still-pounding heart.

"Thanks for the ride, handsome," she said blithely right before she plunged the sai into him with all of her weight and strength behind it.

Chapter Fourteen

An inch too low and she would really kill him.

Daenaira had to pray she didn't nick anything else just as important as his heart, but there was no faking this part, and she desperately needed to gain the trust of a crafty bitch so she could save so many other innocent lives. She wished she could have believed Magnus would come in time to spare her this mess, but he hadn't.

Brendan bellowed with shocked agony, bucking wildly beneath her. His tormented eyes found hers and she leaned over to kiss him in an appearance of cold amusement.

"Shame to waste you, stud, but I have my orders. It's okay," she soothed him. "Look at the bright side, at least you know you'll die with a *huge* sin on your head and no chance to repent. Aww, don't look like that," she purred, actually cooing at him as she had once seen Winifred do to Friedlow. "Light won't be that bad, I'm sure. *M'gnone* will eagerly gobble up the soul of a priestly morsel like you, all tarnished and tortured." She met his eyes with total sincerity then. "Are you ready to die?" she asked softly.

He pushed aside the pain to understand she was trying to

save his life by what she was doing. Or somebody's life. He gave her a curt nod. "Do your worst, bitch," he coughed out, blood tart on his tongue and appearing on his lips. He saw her hesitate when she saw it, but this time he dug his fingers into *her* thigh cruelly to force her to act.

"When I pull this out," she noted with an amazing dispassion that did not match her worried eyes, "you will bleed to death in an instant. Any last words?"

"Yeah," he forced out in a gurgle. "Get the fuck off my dick, *k'ypruti*."

She laughed at that, actually. Really laughed. He had meant to crack as wise as he could, the urge to alleviate her emanating guilt so very strong. Brendan watched Daenaira slowly come around from her amusement.

"Don't feel so bad, lover," she all but hummed, her tawny eyes picking his up with incredible specificity of intent. "You'll be in good company today. They will mourn your death beside Sagan's and Magnus's, two of the greatest priests in Sanctuary. They will count you a hero for giving your life in the slaughter that brought them down. Regardless of your shame, no one will remember you that way except for those who find you here. Naked, soiled, and sated."

She paused long enough to blow him a kiss in the air, and then yanked the sai free while dismounting him in a single fluid movement. He thrashed, the pain excruciating, and tried to suck for the breath to scream out, but she had punctured his left lung. Brendan gasped weakly, suffocating in blood, and not needing for a single instant to pretend like he was dying . . .

Because he was.

Dae ran out of the bedroom and into the bath. She fought the urge to wash herself clean beneath her skirts. She was choking on guilt, fear, and emotion, but she could feel Nicoya watching, could feel her gloating, and it made her sick. She had shamed Brendan, and then she had wounded him so badly he might die by her hand after all. She had tried to angle toward his shoulder, but she'd been off and she knew what the blood on his lips meant. Still, she pushed her devastation stubbornly aside. She wouldn't show a flicker of remorse to Nicoya. She simply couldn't afford to. All she could do was pray it wasn't obvious to the bitch how distressed she truly was. Dae knew she would have to be very clever or she would be dead—and so would Sagan, Brendan, and Magnus. This corruption did not end with Nicoya. Someone had killed Tiana while Nicoya and Shiloh were busy elsewhere. That person could help Nicoya in her quest to destroy everything.

And gods forbid Magnus should fail in his battle and fall to Shiloh!

No. She had to have faith that would never happen. Shiloh would not hurt anyone else ever again. She knew Magnus, and even if he were about to die, he would take Shiloh's evil with him. That much was over and done with.

Except the idea of Magnus dying made her physically sick to her stomach. Another emotion she had to swallow down as she paused to wash blood from her hands and the sai. Above the sink was a mirror, and she simply knew that it was one of the viewing portals into this room. She could hear Brendan gasping, growing weaker and weaker, but there was nothing she could do.

Nothing.

She needed to force herself to think of all of the lives that would be ruined if Nicoya got control of Sanctuary. Church and State would eventually go to war as the power-hungry handmaiden tried to rule more than just her roost. She would never be satisfied with Sanctuary if she thought she could have their entire world.

Daenaira ran from Brendan's rooms into the corridor, her hands still wet as she wiped them and her sai against her skirt.

Nicoya appeared moments after she did, her sword sheathed and her eyes shining with delight. She clapped like a child ready to open a gift, bouncing in her merriment.

"That was gorgeous! Did you see the look on his face? I loved it! I must say, disappointing ride for you, wasn't it? Short fused, hmm? Where was all that blessed control these men are supposed to be taught when they are young?"

Daenaira shrugged and sheathed her sai nonchalantly. "I think it's been a while for him, that's all. Nice, fine cock in any event. Rather hated to not give him a second run. But you said we had things to attend to?"

"Mmm, so I did. I am going to go after Sagan. You find somewhere to wait for Magnus. Best wash up, though. He'll smell another man on you and that will be the end of it."

"Trust me, he'll never know," Daenaira assured her. "Are you certain you can handle Sagan on your own? Don't need my help?"

"Oh, I'll be fine. Besides, we're never alone. After all, I have *Drenna* and *M'gnone* on my side, now don't I?" She winked broadly. Then, with a laugh, she turned and lightly ran down the corridor toward wherever it was that she sensed Sagan to be.

Nicoya's third power was Daenaira's curse. She couldn't go back to Brendan or do anything to save his life. She knew as well as she knew her own heartbeat that Nicoya would be tracking her every movement to make certain she didn't betray her in any way.

Fighting the horrible urge to scream and weep all at once, she forced herself to walk away from Brendan's rooms without looking back. There was one thing Nicoya was all too right about. The last thing she wanted was to encounter Magnus while she smelled of another man. She felt suddenly ashamed and dirty for what she had done, the guilt of tempting a good man beyond his tolerances weighing on her like nothing she had ever felt before. She had hurt people very badly in the past—physically, that is—and had never regretted it. This was something else entirely, and she felt it like a stain on her soul. And that wasn't even taking into consideration that she knew he was dying as she left him alone. All she could do was pray that the rapid healing of his body was enough to sustain him until help arrived.

She began to pray.

True, heartfelt prayer with hope and faith she had never felt before poured out of her soul and whispered past her lips. Hera had taught her prayers, and she had learned them, but she had repeated them all by rote, never feeling the passion she had seen in so many others in the temple. But she felt it now. She had to believe with all of her heart and soul that evil could not be let loose so easily on the world of her people. Not when there were those like Magnus and the twin regents who were trying so hard to make it a better place. A place where hidden slavery could be abolished one day. A place where anyone, even the most insignificant woman in the most concealed corner of the world, could suddenly rise up and find a purpose, and yes, even happiness. Before this day had turned so critically wrong, she had been honestly happy.

She rounded the corridor hall and crashed full force into Magnus.

He grabbed hold of her arms, steadying her even as he stared at her. Relief entered his golden eyes, and his entire body seemed to shake with repressed emotion as he suddenly dragged her up against him.

She hugged him as tightly as he hugged her, gratitude and joy at seeing him alive and completely uninjured flooding through her and rushing the urge to sob up on her all over again. She could smell the amazing richness of his skin, dosed with the cold of the outdoors and the thickness of adrenaline. She breathed deeply of him, resisting the urge to weep. She had so much she needed to do before she allowed herself the luxury of falling apart. But something about the sanctity of his arms around her made her feel . . .

Brendan.

The scent of the other priest on her skin rose up to inter-fere with her intake of Magnus's wonderful aroma and sud-denly she lurched back away from him, tearing out of his hold and backing up. Of course, it would do little good unless she went far enough away, but it wasn't about that. It was about touching him, soiling him with the body that now, she felt, had betrayed him. She hadn't had sex with Brendan, but it was as good as—or so it felt. But the worst part was know-ing she had pushed his closest friend in Sanctuary into hu-miliating disloyalty against him.

And Magnus had already been betrayed enough to jade him forever.

"Dae?" he asked, confusion rushing over him as he stepped closer to her. She hastily backed away, holding out a hand to stay him even while she wrapped the other around herself in protective dismay.

"No. Don't touch me."

Her words lashed at him, and she saw ghastly pain fly through his golden irises. She hadn't meant it that way! Gods, there was nothing she wanted more than to be held by him right then. His embrace had such power to make everything seem like it would be brought to heel and calmed just because he was there!

"Brendan," she said in strangled dismay. "He's dying. Magnus, you have to go. Help him! I need to . . . I have to find Sagan."

She needed to back up the other warrior. There was noth-ing she could do for Brendan. Magnus was what Brendan needed. Sagan would need a fighter.

"Dae, what in Light are you talking about?" he demanded.

"Brendan is dying! In his rooms! Please help him!" she cried in a panic, jerking away when he tried to capture her again. Then she was running down the hallway away from him, leaving him with an untenable circumstance.

Brendan was dying?

The words echoed through him with a strange sense of surreal impossibility. What did Brendan have to do with this epic battle? Why would Nicoya take the time to hurt him? Where was Nicoya now?

All these questions and more reeled through him, but he knew he had no choice. He had to let Daenaira go while he went to see if his friend needed his help. Whatever was upsetting her, she was alive and well. She could wait, even if it screamed against every fiber of his being to do it.

Magnus rushed down to Brendan's rooms.

He didn't bother to knock, bursting into Nan's old chamber and cutting through the bath to find Brendan. He was halfway there when the dark tang of blood struck him.

Oh gods.

He broached the doorway to Brendan's chamber and instantly saw his friend sprawled back across his bed, but what he'd heard first was the tortured gasps that weakly attempted to draw air into his damaged body. Magnus had heard that sort of deathly rattle before and knew, even before he reached his friend, that he was almost out of time.

"Brendan! What—?"

Magnus had knelt on the bed and was reaching out toward the wound killing his friend, his instinct to cover the spot where blood was bubbling in mixture with air as it escaped his chest.

But he froze.

He froze because there was the sudden, pungent aroma of sex beneath that rusty odor of blood. And he realized that he could all too easily identify at least half of the combination.

Brendan reached out, grabbing desperate hold of his sleeve, using what had to be the very last of his strength to force Magnus's attention onto him. But the senior priest found himself all but blind with fury, hurt, and utter devastation.

This is why she didn't want me to touch her.

"What did you do," he heard himself snarl out as various unrealized clues filtered into him. The scent of blood and

Brendan on Daenaira. The wound Brendan bore and the two smaller punctures on either side of it that marked it as caused by a sai. The sai *he* had made for her. Daenaira had run Brendan through, mortally wounded him, and it was clear she had done so just after some kind of sexual encounter. She had left him lying there, naked and dying, and had escaped him.

"No," Brendan gurgled when he saw the dawning realization in his friend's gold eyes and the contempt and rage that was bursting up behind it. "Not what you think." Oh, he might die, Brendan thought fiercely, but he would not do so before he made his friend understand Daenaira was not to blame; that she had had no choice. He believed that with everything inside of himself. "My fault," he gasped weakly. "This . . . my fault."

"Then I assure you, it is *exactly* what I think," Magnus growled in vicious threat. "And you should be very glad you are already nearly dead."

Brendan's mind was hazed with pain, muddled with onrushing unconsciousness, but he suddenly understood that Magnus thought he had forced himself on Daenaira. His eyes widened in horror at the very idea, and he tried to push away the feeling of hurt that rushed through him to think his best friend would think him capable of such a heinous act. It was easy enough to do, however, when he knew what he had done was just as bad. At least, it was to his mind.

He shook his head, tightening his grip on Magnus's arm.

"It was an act . . ." he rasped. "Someone . . ."

"An act?" Magnus hissed, leaning over him and baring his teeth as he came within inches of his face. "You smell of my woman and are drenched in your own spent seed. At least one of you was *not* acting."

Brendan could only nod curtly. He couldn't deny that.

"Watching," he finished his original thought. "Someone was watching. Dae . . . no choice. Don't let her . . . blame herself . . . when I die."

Watching. Someone was watching.

The words drilled through the black and red wall of outrage suffusing all of Magnus's senses and thoughts. Alarms rang through him as everything he'd learned from Shiloh resurfaced to combine with his understanding that there had been no sign of Nicoya when he'd found Dae. Somehow, she had managed to free herself from the dangerous and treacherous handmaiden. But how?

He got the overwhelming feeling he needed to think faster, that he was being slow and dumb at the worst possible moment. Grinding his teeth together, he reached and sealed a harsh hand over the wound in Brendan's chest. The other man groaned at the agony, but his next breath came a little bit easier, though it still rattled with fluid.

"The truth," Magnus growled in demand, his contact more than enough to compel the other man. "Did you force her?"

"No. An act. I swear." Brendan's eyes reflected his desperation that Magnus believe him. "I . . . lost control. Not her fault. *Not her fault.*" He sucked for waning breath. "This sin is mine. I beg you . . ." Another weak breath. "Forgive. Absolve."

Magnus stared down at him hard. He knew Brendan spoke with truth and sincerity. The other priest knew he was dying and wanted absolution for the sin he'd committed against his mentor. He wanted to be forgiven by the ones he had offended with . . .

Was it lust? Dishonor? Betrayal? All of those? What in Light had happened between him and Daenaira? Clearly, whatever it was had shamed her because she had forced herself away from his touch. And yet, she had desperately begged him to help save the life of a man she had apparently tried to kill. It made no sense! The only one besides Daenaira who could make sense of it was Brendan, who could barely speak. Magnus reconciled to being left in the dark for the time being. No matter what, Brendan was seeking repentance, and that could not be ignored. It was true, sincere, and everything he knew Brendan to be . . .

He couldn't have imagined how hard it would be to push down the choking territorial wrath that barked and snarled in his head in response to the scent of his woman all over this man, but he managed it somehow and reached for the handset of the telephone without letting go of Brendan's wound. It wasn't until he had finished calling for medical assistance that he remembered one crucial detail.

"Why is she looking for Sagan?" he asked aloud, not even intending to include Brendan in his thoughts.

"Next . . . victim."

He looked down on Brendan with doubt. He made it sound as if Dae were following some kind of hit list. No. He didn't know what had happened here to cause this mess, but he would never believe she was going around picking off priests like ducks in a shooting gallery.

No. Not her.

Nicoya.

"Oh fuck! Fuck me!" He exploded in movement, as if he wanted to run away, but his hand was glued to the chest of a dying man. *That little fool!* She had discarded him and sent him to be nursemaid while she went and fought against a threat which she had no real concept of! He'd been so mottled up with emotions that he'd just been relieved to see her alive and unharmed. Damn her!

Brendan made a sound.

Magnus glared at him when he realized it was a weak little chuckle. Brendan's eyes spoke volumes of amusement as he watched Magnus twist in the wind over this insane, stupid little girl who was going to get herself killed.

"I'm glad you find this so amusing," Magnus barked down at him. "She's going to get herself killed! Nicoya was the one probably watching you both, by the way, and it turns out she has been the one doing all of the penance assignments I was giving to Shiloh! She has turned herself into a warrior and given him the credit for it. Now Daenaira is off chasing her down, thinking she can keep her from causing any more damage!"

Now Brendan's eyes cleared of amusement and rounded with worry. He grabbed Magnus's hand with limp fingers and tried to push him off his chest.

"Go," he croaked.

"No."

Yes!

Magnus frowned. He shook his head when his brain cried out in opposition.

"You'll die if I leave you now, and I know Dae didn't want that," he said. He swallowed thickly. "They'll be here for you soon. She's okay. She's—"

He stopped speaking because suddenly he couldn't breathe. He had never known such overwhelming emotion in all of his life. He felt as if it were too much, that he was on an overload he just couldn't handle. The feeling of utter helplessness and devastation was so alien and so unwanted. How? How had this happened to him? Why had this happened to him? What in the names of both his gods were they trying to tell him? To teach him? What purpose could all of this serve? All of this . . . *fear*?

He was numb and on autopilot by the time help arrived for Brendan. He simply dropped his hand from his peer and turned and walked out without a single word to answer the questions the healers were flinging at him. He had no time for them. For anything. Time, he realized, had run out the moment she had left him in Dreamscape. He should never have let her go. And once he found her, he never would again.

And that, he realized with a strange sense of calm creeping over him, was the lesson he was supposed to learn.

Chapter Fifteen

Leaving Henry with others to care for him turned out to be one of the most difficult things Sagan had ever had to do. The traumatized boy had been terrified to leave his protection, but he had covered it well with some of his usual cheekiness and a man's bravado meant to fool the healers into believing nothing was wrong with him. Mostly, he had been trying to convince himself.

Now Sagan needed to find his peers and help them. The hunt for Shiloh and Nicoya must be made general knowledge, and then he needed to join that hunt more than anything. After spending all of this time trying to help hold together a fragile child, he needed to spill a little blood to avenge the wrong done to him.

"Death is too kind for that pair of—"

"Uh, uh, uh—be nice," a female voice warned teasingly.

Sagan drew to a sharp halt. Without hesitation, he reached for his *khukuri*, the softly swept recurve blade he was famous for carrying and handling with merciless power and precision. Though only fifteen inches long, comparatively small in length to swords like Magnus's katana or the sojourn Nicoya held idly before herself, the *khukuri* was balanced forward in a way that allowed for brutal momentum. As he drew the blade, he was forced to wonder why she had announced herself. The element of surprise was so essential in battle, especially when you knew you were outclassed in weight, size, and skill. Nicoya had always been a proud, vain bitch, but she hadn't struck him as particularly stupid.

"Nicoya," he drawled, guarding as he mentally measured the width of the corridor and glanced around for bystanders. "Something I can do for you?"

"I think dying would work. Wouldn't want to throw yourself on your sword, would you?"

"Not particularly."

"Didn't think so."

Her free hand shot out sharply, flinging a saw-star at his head that a swift duck and parry with the *khukuri* sent reeling off with a spark, but the second star she winged out caught him off guard and buzzed sharply through his shirt and nipped just through the skin of his shoulder.

Nicoya smiled in satisfaction, her blade whipping up readily, her stance beautifully aggressive and not in the least lacking in confidence or, he noted, skill. He shrugged his injured shoulder and narrowed his eyes on her when she smiled with smug contentment, as if she knew something he didn't. He didn't like that feeling, the sensation sitting ill in his mind. Why, he asked himself, would he ever be concerned over the skill of a handmaiden? He was never concerned over anyone's skill when it came to an out-and-out fight. Not even Magnus. But there was a reason for this worry, and he knew it was his third power that caused it. It niggled at him like this when it was crucial to use it.

Sagan opened his mind to the woman across from him even as they began to circle one another. He rarely spoke of his third power, never caring to share it or anything else about himself with others. He hardly cared to use it most of the time, except he refused to leave any skill unpracticed that could help him in battle. Within moments, his telepathic ability had flooded through her mind, and he was astounded by what he began to learn. For the past few months, he had been wrestling with himself over the thought of slowly beginning to scan his coworkers for traitorous thoughts, but there had seemed something invasive and dishonorable to the idea. If there were only three individuals who were evil, but he had to invade the sanctity of eighty minds to find them, then to him it just wasn't worth it. Firstly, he had no desire to know any of his peers with such intimacy. When he opened like this, he mined thoughts utterly, like strip mining left the land naked and fallow. No one should be raped of all their secrets in such a manner, and he despised the ability for what it did.

Even now.

He grimly glanced down at his wound. It stung like any other, but now he knew he had been poisoned by the treacherous woman before him. Just as he now knew who and what she really was. Just as he knew she had coaxed so many others to do her bidding. And he knew who her mother was.

"So, you think to become a queen, do you?" he asked her, turning his grip aggressively as he advanced on her.

There was something familiar to the sound of colliding metal and the accompanying vibration that shuddered through the bones and muscles of the body that gave him comfort. Her poison would take time. Just enough time for him to dice her conniving little ass up into tiny pieces. He outmuscled and outweighed her by at least a hundred pounds, his height and reach both superior to hers, but when it came to Shadowdweller women, their speed and equally remarkable strength made them near matches for some of their advanced fighters when they were this well trained.

However, he was no mere advanced fighter.

"I am already a queen," she said as she came in close and rammed her knee up between his legs. He easily anticipated the tactic, turning his thigh into the blow and using his elbow to belt her hard against her cheekbone. Nicoya staggered back between the blow and not having both feet on the floor. He gave her credit for recovering quickly enough to parry his next few blows. "And I don't have to be better than you," she breathed with feral delight. "I only have to last longer than you do against the poison coursing through your veins. Very sloppy, M'jan, to let yourself be wounded. But you always say, better to let yourself take the light wound than the deadly one."

And she had counted on that. Damn her, she'd used his own training against him. All those times she had lingered in the training hall, all the times she had flirted with him, making him uncomfortable and irritable because he had thought her a tease getting off on fucking with his head; it had all been a distraction to keep him from realizing she was studying his teachings and his skills.

"So let's see who told you that you were a queen," he mused, moving swiftly against her, tiring her overhead parries so she would take the easy low block when it came. He backhanded her as soon as she was open, sending her reeling and sliding over the floor on her ass. "Your twisted whore of a mother."

She rolled with the punch impressively, gliding back up to her feet and shaking off the blow as she licked her own blood from her lips.

"Now, you see, that's what I like"—she laughed, taking a moment to shake the kinks out of her body—"a man who isn't afraid to beat the shit out of a girl. My father had a thing for women who could take a beating. The whips-and-chains type. Until he met my mother, that is. She showed him a whole new way of getting off. Unfortunately, she did it too well. He tried to get her to marry him by knocking her up. She just disappeared on him and never said another word. That man was Adrian of the J'ernnu Clan. Adrian, as you know, was one of the two sole surviving brothers from the royal line. Alexsander, the father of your precious twins, was the other. That makes me his firstborn child. That makes me equal heir to the Chancellery. Of course, after they are dead, it makes me the only heir. And since they were kind enough to reinstate the monarchy for me and have no heirs between them, that means I would ascend in their place."

"I know you believe that to be true," Sagan said with a dirty smile, "but you'll forgive me if I doubt your claim. Besides, the twins aren't dead."

"Yet," she stipulated, lunging into melee.

Sagan fought her off, but he could feel the beginning muzziness of the poison in his body. He had to end this before it struck him down fully. "Oh, and you think you have that figured out, do you?"

"No. I was concentrating on getting Sanctuary and studs like you tightly under me first. Mother is handling all the rest of it."

Sagan had to dodge sharply when she used an acrobatic swing of her leg to tangle him up. His attention was fumbling, a metallic flavor flooding his mouth. The warrior cursed bluish, and Nicoya clicked her tongue at him in admonition. "Sagan," she scolded, "we're in the house of the gods."

"Where more appropriate to strike you down?"

He was on her in a heartbeat, forcing her to use all of her skill and strength until, grudgingly, he had to admit she was as good as the reputation she had earned for Shiloh. Still, that wasn't good enough. Not to his mind. Or it wouldn't have been had he not been weakening so rapidly. Just the same, he staved off the force of the poison just long enough to slip in under her guard once more and slam an elbow so hard into her ribs that he could almost hear a couple of them snap. She staggered under the pain, gasping and looking surprised almost in spite of herself. Now, he knew, he would have her. She was a wicked swordswoman, but she didn't take injury well.

Neither did Sagan take poisoning well.

Just as he was ready to press his advantage, weakness shuddered like a wave of paralysis rushing through him. He faltered, and she saw it, but he was already swinging the vicious *khukuri* for a maiming blow, if not a killing one. He went for her leg as her injured side forced her blade's guard to drop.

But before he could hit, out of nowhere he felt the strike of a violent pain across the whole of his back. He heard a crack and fuzzily hoped it wasn't any of his bones making the sound. His sword arm was suddenly and harshly lashed around the biceps, and he was jerked with amazing force away from the victory blow to his target. The owner of the *vitanno* whip that crippled and bound him was strong enough to jerk even his significant weight of muscle and momentum right off his feet. He crashed to the tiled floor, his head cracking forcefully in whiplash. Sagan, sickened and furious, struggled to free himself and return to his feet. However, before he could make his polluted body obey his commands, he heard two sharp steps and felt the newcomer to the battle shove a hard, booted foot against his chest, forcing him down onto his back.

"Mother! What took you so damn long!" Nicoya hissed. She recovered herself, listing into her injured side as she, too, came to stand over Sagan's prone body.

"Don't speak to me like that," the other woman warned quite calmly, her cool grey-black tourmaline eyes inspecting her victim as if he were some unfortunate road kill requiring her morbid fascination. There was, Sagan realized a bit belatedly, some form of cleat on those heavy boots, the sharp points burrowing into the muscles of his upper chest. However, he was numbed to the sensation despite the blood he saw slowly staining his shirt. "Don't kill him," she said sharply when her daughter thrust the point of her blade into his throat. "I like him. I might play with him." She contemplated him, seemingly measuring her capacity to enjoy him.

"Mother, he's poisoned. He won't survive."

"I think I can fix that. He seems strong enough. He might recover eventually."

"Acadian," he ground out, his dark eyes spitting fury and hatred at the woman above him.

Acadian lifted a delicate brow and bent over him. "Hmm. You told him?"

"No. I don't know how he knows."

"Hmph. Some sort of telepath, no doubt. That could be quite challenging. Bind him for me. Morrigan and Davide are at the end of the hall." She lifted her foot, kicking Sagan over hard onto his face so she could disengage the whip. She no longer needed it. The poison in Sagan's system was quite thickly in effect. For all his power, strength, and skill, he had been defeated with the first cut Nicoya had made. "All that matters is that they lose yet another penance priest. This leaves only Magnus and Ventan."

"And Magnus will be dead inside an hour. You were right about his handmaiden, Mother."

"Of course I was," she said with a rather bored shrug. She wrapped up her whip as her daughter narrowed cold eyes on her.

"Don't act so superior, Mother. You may take credit for your orchestrations in the Senate, but this victory is mine." She knelt to grab Sagan by his hair, pulling his head back to expose his face and unfocused eyes. "Sanctuary is mine."

"You got sloppy and stupid. And don't count Magnus out until you see the bastard dead at your feet. Get him out of here and go find out if that girl is following through. I can't be seen here for this."

She hooked the whip back beneath her Senator's sari, concealing it. Then, without a word, she turned and disappeared down the hallway.

* * *

It took much too long for her to find Nicoya.

Actually, it was Sagan she was tracking down after finding Henry in the infirmary and realizing he couldn't be far away, given how long ago they said he had left. Then again, it was a very big place. Knowing every twist and turn was fine, but you had to know which spot you were looking for first.

Unfortunately, she encountered Nicoya shortly afterward. She was bloodied with a fat lip, nursing her side, and there was fury in her eyes as she approached her.

But there was no Sagan.

Gods, she thought, *she's killed him*. Somehow she had done the inconceivable and had killed one of Sanctuary's finest warriors in a head-on, face-to-face confrontation. Sure, *she* had killed Cort, but Daenaira was damn quick to admit she'd backstabbed him to pull it off; otherwise she wouldn't have been likely to manage it.

"What are you doing here? I told you to wait for Magnus and kill him," Nicoya hissed, storming up to her and giving her a hard shove in her shoulder. The handmaiden was injured, but there was no denying the strength in that powerful push as she staggered back.

"Yeah, well . . ." Daenaira hung her head submissively as she recovered her balance, and Nicoya exhaled in disgust. It was when the other woman was busy rolling her eyes that Daenaira struck up suddenly and palmed her so hard in the nose that her entire head snapped back. On the recoil, Dae snatched her sai into her hands, whirling the hilts outward and laying the center prongs along her inside forearms for a brace. "I guess I changed my mind," she spat as she used the gem-set handle butt to clip her in follow-through up under her chin.

Dae invested all of her pain and fury over Brendan into the blow, trying not to think that she should have done this in the first place. She knew she would never have gotten past this woman's guard without the established false trust she had orchestrated. Plus, Nicoya was injured, and she had to pray that would make all the difference.

Though, seeing she had likely defeated Sagan in spite of those injuries, she highly doubted it. Just the same, she had no other choices anymore. Or she was just too damn mad to think of them.

She gave no quarter to the stunned woman, knowing that to pause and let her recover even for a second could cost her her life. If she failed, she shuddered to think of what could happen to Magnus. The thought fueled her next blow, and she threw all of her body force into smashing her steel-lined forearm into the side of the traitor's head.

"You stupid," she hissed, enunciating each word to follow with a violent strike, "gullible, arrogant, deceitful *k'ypruti*!"

This last was delivered with a kick into the center of the other woman's breastbone, toppling her back onto her ass. Nicoya's supply of saw-stars spilled out of their pouch at the rear of her weapons belt. They skimmed like a fanning deck of cards across the floor, but neither women paid it any heed.

"Oh, bitch," Nicoya growled contemptuously, "you're going to die for that."

"Yeah? Well, sure, after you die for what you did to Henry." She advanced on her and was satisfied when the other woman scurried backward over the floor away from her approach.

"Is that right? And who is going to kill you for Brendan? My guess is Magnus!"

Nicoya's hand touched a star, and grabbing it, she flung it at Daenaira when the cutting remark made the surety in her step falter. Fearless of what she knew was poisoned, she threw up a forearm to block the star, her black steel deflecting it easily. It had been a bad throw in any event. Still, the distraction served. Nicoya was on her feet and pulling her blade free of her scabbard. Black as the metal was, Dae could see the pitting and flawing in the blade from what had clearly been a heavy battle. The blade had been in near-perfect condition when she'd seen it pointed at her during their earlier encounter. It only confirmed her suspicions that, somehow, she had managed to defeat Sagan.

"You stupid, stupid child," Nicoya spat disdainfully. "Don't you see? They've already lost! Magnus is the only one left. Once he's gone, it's all over!"

"Oh, and what about Ventan? You think he'll see he's the only penance priest left to take Magnus's seat and just hand it over to you? Or did you whore all over him, too?"

"Ventan is old and burnt out. Magnus doesn't even give him hard assignments anymore. You think he scares me?"

"I think someone should!" Dae flipped her right sai around, leaving one to guard as she rushed her enemy. Since she had the lighter weapon and was uninjured, she had speed and agility in her favor, but she didn't have Nicoya's experience. The handmaiden's sword punctured her thin skirt between her legs, tearing through the front and rear panel, just missing the insides of both her thighs, not to mention more intimate places. She could only save her skin, literally, by quickly catching the blade in her sai and holding it tight with a twist. Then she was kicking her leg high and "dismounting" the blade as it tore her skirt nearly in two. Sparks flew and burned her skin when Nicoya savagely yanked her weapon free.

Daenaira would hardly recall very much after that because, without realizing just how unwise it was, Nicoya took advantage of her turned back and rammed her into the nearest wall face first. She felt the cold, unforgiving surface hit her forehead and cheekbone above and below her left eye. The pain was sour and sharp as it stung all the way down to her chin and radiated back over her scalp. With a poisoned sword behind her, however, she had no time for being stunned.

But she had plenty of time for a growling wrath to come over her, considering how brilliant and fast it moved. Possessed by another part of herself, she turned to catch the lunge of Nicoya's blade in the prongs of the sai. She deflected it with a hard flinging movement that almost ripped the blade free of her enemy's hand.

Nicoya had found Sagan an exhausting, intimidating contestant with skill and power she would never have been able to match had he been one hundred percent, but she had expected the new handmaiden to be a far simpler target once she'd finally realized where she really stood. However, nothing had prepared her to fight a savage animal. Dae was tireless and relentless, her amber eyes aglow with rage. It was as though the girl had been born to fight as her movements became faster instead of more weary, and stronger, as if fueled by the momentum of her fury. She deflected her every sweep of the sojourn as if brushing away a pesky fly, and advanced. She advanced so much, forcing Nicoya's retreat so far, that they traveled far enough down the corridor to begin attracting an audience of youths. One at a time, eyes began to fall on the epic battle between the women. They didn't entirely understand what they were watching, but they did understand just by watching the scarlet wrath in Daenaira's movements that it wasn't a practice session. No one dared interrupt or intervene, but neither could they bring themselves to tear away from the drama of the mortal combat.

Nicoya was sweating, pain making her nauseous as the other woman forced her to abuse an already abused body. Daenaira kept dodging in under her drooping guard, introducing her sai hilts to her cheek, her belly, her back, and her thigh. Anywhere and everywhere she could target, she battered at her relentlessly. When she landed a critical blow in Coya's already damaged ribs, the pain was blinding and excruciating. Moments later, Nicoya coughed up blood and began to have trouble catching her breath.

She knew she was in trouble.

Chapter Sixteen

He knew she was in trouble.

Magnus had wanted to burst into the middle of the battle the moment he had found them; wanted to rip her out of reach of that deadly, poisonous blade, but he knew that in and of itself could get one of them cut and killed. He found himself pushing past students and their teachers who were wisely trying to keep the curious children back out of harm's way.

"Clear this hallway!" he spat at them.

If any of those weapons went airborne, everyone was in danger. By now, after so much contact, the sai were also coated in the sickness of Nicoya's blade. His heart choked and throttled in his chest as he watched Daenaira fight so damn close to the thing, her fearlessness scaring the hell out of him. It didn't take him long to realize she had slipped into her third power, her berserker fighting fever totally possessing her. When Nicoya finally faltered, coughing up blood on herself and leaning into her injured side heavily, Dae's advance was what truly terrified him. Here, now, was the ultimate danger to her, the trouble he had seen.

Easy, love, easy, he thought desperately as she caught the tip of her enemy's blade in a sai and jerked it safely downward. She slammed her foot down on the flat of it, snapping the sword out of her opponent's hand with a sharp crack against the floor. Then she surged forward with a snarl, both sai swirling into outfacing prongs. She plowed over the senior handmaiden, smashing her back into the floor so her head struck with a sickening crack. She straddled Nicoya's chest with a crush of her full weight on her knees, her shins pinning the other woman's hands and arms to the floor. She raised her sai, ready to plunge both into the target of her throat.

Easy! His mind screamed to her, so aware of his every religious tenet, all the students surrounding this drama who were going to be influenced by whatever she did next, and then, most importantly, the risks to her own peace.

Daenaira jerked slightly as Magnus's voice roared through her mind, commanding her to think before she acted. An outpouring of things she needed to consider flooded her thoughts, crowding out the bloodlust that had possessed her so thoroughly. Angry at the intrusion of conscience and the emotions it threatened to let in, she let out a battle cry as she stabbed the sai down at her target. She pounded them into the tile on either side of her enemy's throat, the crossed prongs barely giving Nicoya room to breathe as they held her throat under their oppressive press.

"Repent," she ground out through her teeth with barely contained ferocity.

Magnus felt something inside of himself completely unravel when she spoke, his whole body loosening almost to the point of weakness—*that* was how relieved he was to hear that single word erupt from her stiff lips.

"Fuck you," Nicoya returned on a rasp, taking the moment to spit blood in her enemy's face. Not the wisest choice, because Magnus was certain Daenaira would not be as calm about such an obvious insult as he would have been.

But she *was* calm about it.

Somewhat.

She slowly lifted the sharp points of the sai from the tile until they were prodding painfully into Nicoya's throat on either side of her windpipe. Baring her teeth in what was a vicious little smile, she said, "I believe you are the one who is fucked, treacherous *k'ypruti*. Now search your black heart, before it beats its very last, and see if you cannot find the smallest speck of remorse within it so we may attempt to salvage it. Repent."

"You have me helpless. If you kill me, you are a murderess under the law—*again*," Nicoya stressed. She was purposely raising her voice. "Just like you murdered Brendan after you seduced him and rode him to exhaustion!" Her eyes lit up with triumph when she heard gasps of shock. "You are the traitor. You have no right to ask me to repent! You are no penance priest!"

"But I am."

Magnus stepped forward, the strike of his boot a hard clipping echo in the suddenly silent corridor. Everyone wanted to see what he would make of this tangle, and Nicoya's accusations, he could feel it in every stare that fixed on him. He didn't much care what anyone thought about himself, in that moment, but he did have other concerns. Concerns about Daenaira. There was blood on his hands and clothes and he knew, despite the dark violet color, it would be seen and scented, and those who knew the younger priest's scent would know it was Brendan's.

For a moment, Nicoya registered fear, but then triumphant glee glowed in her eyes as she saw the tension in his, the blood of his friend on his clothes, and no weapon drawn.

"Daenaira," he said, his voice hoarse with angry emotion, "is my handmaiden and she will always have the power to ask repentance in my name."

Nicoya's victory melted away from her expression, and she began to panic. "You blind fool! Can't you smell it on her?" she screeched. "The seed of another man? She's covered in it! I saw her do it! Then I saw her stab one of these sai into him and kill him!"

Magnus moved forward slowly, feeling the way Dae quivered with emotion but noting how she would not look up at him. She remained fully focused on her prey. Slowly, he stepped behind her and knelt over their traitor as well, pressing his chest to Daenaira's back. She stiffened when he ran gentle palms down her upper arms in what was meant as a reassuring caress, and he felt her panic. He felt how wrong and soiled she felt, the guilt of what she had done making her want to wrench away from him. She didn't want him to touch her while she was stained with her sins.

He ignored that, pushed away all the signs and scents that marked her as murderous and deceitful, trusting that overwhelming sensation of guilt and remorse inside her to tell him who she truly was.

"Tell me the truth," he said in a ringing resonant tone as he touched his fingers to her throat. He felt her swallow against his touch. "Answer one question, before all these witnesses, with my power compelling you, Daenaira." Her eyes finally left Nicoya and swept with alarm to those watching her. He felt her pulse storm beneath his fingertips. Then, he asked very specifically, "Did you have intercourse with M'jan Brendan?"

Her chest heaved with her breath and she tried to see him, but he kept her facing her enemy and said softly, "Yes or no?"

"No," she replied hoarsely.

"She lies!" Nicoya hissed.

"She cannot lie," Magnus bit out harshly, "while I compel her."

"It's a trick!"

"Very well, then," he hissed at the woman beneath him, grabbing her hand where Dae's leg held it pressed to the floor. "Are you or are you not a traitor to this Sanctuary? Did you, or did you not, conspire to kill me and other priests while seducing innocent students into acts of degradation and humiliation?"

He could feel her shaking with fury, her mind racing to find a truth that would mask her fault and blame, but he had been too specific. She was doomed, and it showed in the black rage and trepidation in her eyes.

"Yes! I did all of that!" she blurted out.

"Is there anyone else in this sacred house that follows your scheming, sinful plans to do this and worse?"

She regurgitated three names, fighting his will with every single one, her eyes darting to the crowd watching her with repugnant fascination and growing hostility.

"Where is your mother?"

"In the Senate," she hissed.

"Who is your mother?"

Here she smiled. "Acadian."

It was, after all, the truth. Despite the shock of those around him, he had known this already. He wanted something else.

"Who is she pretending to be?"

"No one."

The reply baffled him. It made no sense. "She is wearing a guise, Nicoya, what is it?"

"None. No guise. None."

Her confident sneer told him that they had somehow prepared for this. He sighed, realizing he wasn't going to get his answers this way. He would have to be satisfied that he had routed out the last of the traitors within his own house. He would have to leave the Senate and the deceptive Acadian to the twins. He already had his hands full in Sanctuary, repairing damage and faith, restoring penance and priests, and most importantly, Daenaira.

"Do you, honestly in your heart, repent any and all sins you have committed as is seen by the laws of this church and this government?" He asked this with grim resignation, his fingers tightening on the woman's wrist.

"No! Never! I will never grovel to you! None of you! You are all—"

"Kill her," he said flatly to Daenaira before finally rising to his feet.

Dae didn't hesitate. She skewered the handmaiden through her throat, crossing through her windpipe and cutting off any more foul speech or mad words. She ran them through until the sharper small prongs punctured as well, and then twisted hard to gouge open the major neck arteries. Then she withdrew from the bucking, thrashing body, backing up right into Magnus. She flinched when he touched her, so he lowered his hands.

"Shiloh is also dead," he informed the others around them. "He was part of her treachery. These others mentioned will be found, and they will either be repentant or they will die for their sins."

"M'jan Sagan is dead," Daenaira whispered to him. "She said she defeated him."

"We will find his body to be certain," Magnus assured her. "*K'yan* Tiana, also a victim in this, must be taken to rest as well." He assigned these tasks to those nearest him, dismissing the students sternly and with the help of their instructors. Magnus held Dae's arm in a firm grip all the while, keeping her closely secured to his body when all she wanted to do was run to find a bath or a hole or anywhere far from him.

It had been wrong, her mind thought in racing circles. It had all been wrong. The wrong choices. The wrong acts. The wrong man.

She was wrong.

He was good, powerful, and honorable, and now he had tied himself to her, a woman who would do such dire things and make such terrible decisions. He had known the truth of what she had done to Brendan. She had realized that when he had been so careful to specifically word his query. But why had he spared her reputation in such a way when she had betrayed him and destroyed his friend? Or was he just trying to save himself from another scandal?

It was quite some time before Magnus was able to leave the area, dragging a reluctant Daenaira with him. She couldn't understand him, couldn't figure out what he wanted. Did he mean to hurt her or punish her? Would she be forced to suffer excruciating penance? Like the Sinner Brendan had spoken of?

Just thinking about the younger priest made her heart ache and her eyes sting, but she refused to show any emotion he might mistake for fear or weakness. Whatever he planned to dish out, he wasn't going to find her a willing target. Wrong or right, she had done her best, and she wasn't going to stand and be beaten like a criminal.

Magnus drew her into their rooms, forcing her to pick up her feet to keep from falling on her face. He slammed her door shut and turned the bolt tightly. Without further pause, he urged her into the bathroom. He finally let go of her once they were beside the tub. Then he crossed to the long mirror that had once been so innocuous. Picking up a jar of the cream she liked to use, he dunked his hand in and proceeded to smear and paint the mirror until it was completely obscured to the view from the other side. She blinked as she watched him, wrapping arms around herself as she felt chill in spite of the damp heat from the bath.

He turned to her, his golden eyes fierce and faceted with strong emotions she didn't understand, but it was as though she could feel them battering at her just the same. Many of them slapped like stinging blows, others confused, and still others made her heart race with hope.

These, she thought bitterly, *are very likely from my imagination*.

The others she had no trouble believing at all. She felt all of her chances at making a better life, a useful life, crumbling around her. She was supposed to serve as his partner and mate, the truest soul for his trust, and to remain pure only to him, and she hadn't.

She watched as he reached to divest himself of his weapons belt. Post battle as they were, it was her duty to do this for him, but she didn't think he wanted her to touch him. He stripped off his bloodied tunic next, baring the wide expanse of his chest and the breathtaking landscape of nut brown skin over muscle that never ended. Dae didn't know why, but seeing him made her entire face sting with the urge to cry. She stepped backward away from him, but he caught her quickly.

"Take off your clothes."

"I don't want to," she whispered.

"Your entire psyche is screaming for the cleansing heat of that water," he said, nodding his head at the bath. "Do I need to compel that truth from you?"

"I'll bathe later. When you're done."

She saw a muscle jump in his jaw. It was the only warning she had before he grabbed hold of her hard and flung her right off her feet and into the water. Plunged unexpectedly into such extreme heat, she surfaced spluttering obscenities. By the time she had stood up and shoved her hair out of her eyes, Magnus was naked and dropping into the water near her. She made an effort to go for the stairs, but he had hold of her again and pinned her between his body and the far wall. Magnus grabbed the wet velvet of her shirt and stripped it almost violently over her head. Then he squeezed his grip tightly around her arms, gliding his hands down after a moment to work free the knives secured at her wrists. Never once did he allow her to look away from the volatile emotions within his eyes. It was so clear he was feeling so much, but she was too upset and too panicked to figure out what those emotions were.

"I don't understand what you want from me!" she cried out as he finished tearing her skirt up to the waistband and snapped it off her body. He simply let the fabric sink or float as it would.

He responded to her dismay by placing himself nose to nose with her and staring hard into her eyes. "What I want— no, what I *need* is to wash the smell of another man off your body so you will let me touch you. That's why you keep pulling away, isn't it?"

She shook her head in quick, repetitive negations. "You shouldn't touch me," she said on a swallowed back sob. "Not after what I've done."

"Tell me what you did, *K'yindara*. Repent to me. Confess your sin and show me your penitence. Show me your regret."

"You wish to give me penance, then?" she asked sadly.

"If I have to, I will." He reached down to grasp her thigh, raising her leg up alongside his until he could reach the fastenings of her sai sheath. He slipped off her shoes as well, again letting them sink into the tub. Soon, she was standing against him in only her panties. He reached to smooth his hands over her hips, his thumbs hooking into them. "Speak to me. This is your chance. Or must I compel the truth from you?"

"Why would you believe me unless you did?" she asked miserably.

"Why?" The fabric slid away beneath the push of his hands and she very obediently stepped out of the underwear, pressing her hands against the wall and still refusing to touch him. "Because I trust you will tell me the truth, Daenaira."

"Why would you trust me?" she asked. "Gods, have you any idea how stupid that is?"

"To trust you? Why? I shouldn't trust you, is that what you are saying?" He cocked a brow, waiting expectantly for her reply as he braced both hands against the wall behind her.

"Why would you trust anyone?" she demanded. "People all around you are turning into black husks of lies, and you are going to be stupid enough to trust someone?"

"I must say, I never trusted Shiloh or Nicoya. In fact, neither knew it, but I removed him from succession two months ago."

Surprise lit her eyes and, Magnus saw, she bit her lip to prevent a wicked twitch of a smile. She was pleased that he had been so wise. Well, good. Then maybe she would see his wisdom elsewhere as well when the time came. He left her only long enough to reach for soap and a sponge. He lathered them together and, after pressing a hand to her chest to hold her still, true to his word, he plunged the sponge below the water and began to wash Brendan's scent from her thighs.

He was watching his own work, his movements in no way harsh against her. In fact, she felt they were rather gentle and thorough. If she hadn't known how unlikely it was, she might have even considered it . . . loving.

Her lips trembled when the thought made her realize how much she had lost because of her night's work.

"I won't excuse my actions," she whispered.

"I did not ask for excuses. I ask for your repentance. I asked for your sin." His tone was clipped but neutral, unfathomable to her. Was he angry or wasn't he? She couldn't read him! She would sense a tide of anger, but then he wouldn't show a single sign of it. Then there was the distracting sensation of the sponge in his hand swirling steadily against her skin. She felt his fingertips at the edge of the sponge and her skin sparked longingly at the simple contact. Her nerves did not seem to realize the difference between their lovemaking this afternoon and his ritualistic cleansing of her stained body. In the end, Daenaira was so confused, she could only do as she was asked.

"I seduced Brendan," she said stiffly, turning her face away so she wouldn't have to see his expression. But he wouldn't allow it. He caught her chin and brought her right back to his volatile eyes of gold.

"You made love with him?" he asked tightly.

"No! I just . . . I didn't . . . I was afraid to take her on by myself! Nicoya demanded I murder Brendan, and I thought if I . . . if I seduced him first, it would buy some time for you to . . ." She raised a hand to cover her mouth, shaking her head as tears filled her eyes. "It wasn't his fault. It just wasn't fair to him. You can't blame him for this. He misses Nan so much! He has been alone . . . and I think I p-pushed him too far. He hated himself for it. For the weakness of losing control. Please don't blame him for this."

"So I should blame you?" he asked softly.

"It was my choice," she nodded, swiping at her eyes angrily. "It was supposed to be pretend, but I must have done something wrong. I should have chosen another position. Something less stimulating for him. But it was the only way I could think of to mask that it was an act. If . . . if I covered him with my skirt . . ."

Magnus's attention had drifted back down to the water, but his gaze snapped up at that information. "You rode astride him?"

She nodded, her burning tears refusing to stop. "He . . . I didn't know how to, really, so he took hold of me and I guess . . . the friction of my panties and . . ." She swallowed.

"And?" he prompted carefully.

"My heat. I didn't expect to . . . but after a while I felt . . ."

"Stimulated," he supplied quietly.

"I'm sorry. I never meant to do anything wrong. I'm so sorry. Please let me go. I'll just leave."

To her surprise, his hand came up and gripped her hard by her chin, forcing her to focus on his fearsome gaze.

"Step out to the right," he commanded her. "Spread your legs."

She warily obeyed, but quickly gasped and surged up on her toes when the sponge dove directly between her legs, hand, fingers, and all stroking over her intimately and thoroughly. The stimulation made her whole body shiver, her nipples tightening into thick points. He washed directly over her clitoris, the hub of nerves screaming to awareness and wakefulness despite the distress and upset of her warring mind and emotions. After several swirling passes, he crowded his body close to hers, his head lowering until his lips all but brushed her mouth.

"Body and mind do not always have to be in agreement to react to such direct touches," he said in a low, calm sort of manner. "A woman can orgasm from simply riding against something. A saddle, perhaps. A man's thigh. Nerves do what they are meant to do, regardless of the desires of the mind, especially in the body of a naturally passionate and sensitive make-up. Do you know the guilt you are feeling is common for women who climax during an act of sexual violence? They feel shame, embarrassment, and they blame themselves. They think they must have invited it or even enjoyed the attentions no matter how horrifying they know it really was."

Magnus closed the final distance between them and kissed her lips very gently. The tenderness took Dae's breath away, just as the sudden flush of hope did.

"Did you climax like Brendan did?" he asked softly. "Is that why you are so determined to destroy yourself over this?"

"No," she said, shaking her head while rubbing her lips across his warmly and wetly. "But Brendan . . . I can't forget the look in his eyes; the distress and his self-loathing as I forced him to feel what he felt was a betrayal of your trust. And of mine. Then I killed him and gave him no chance to make it up to you. Please, believe me. He wanted to make it up to you, to beg your forgiveness."

"He did beg my forgiveness. And I have given it. To both of you."

Her look of utter shock made him smile down at her. He forgot so easily how unused to benevolence she really was.

"But my forgiveness is not even required here, Daenaira. You did what you had to do to try to save as many lives as you could without foolishly throwing your own away. I would rather you have done what you did than die." His thumb reached to brush wetly over her cheek. "It is enough to know both of your hearts were pure and trustworthy." He frowned in the next instant. "But you are never to get that close to another man ever again, do you understand me?" The hand between her legs tightened up against her through the softness of the sponge. "You and all that is sacred to you belong to me now. Just as I will always belong to you." He let the sponge go, leaving nothing to interfere with his touch as he came tightly against her and caught her parted lips.

Daenaira was still trying to conceive of what he was saying, but it was the bare touch of his fingertips over her sensitive tissues that really snapped her out of her shock. She gasped, lifting onto her toes reflexively again. Then his tongue was slipping into her mouth and engaging her in a breath-stealing kiss.

"And while I do not know if he will survive the day," he said softly against her, "Brendan was alive when I last saw him."

"He was?" Magnus saw her tear up again, and her sudden show of sensitivity warmed his heart. She didn't realize it yet, but she had already come to care for her new friends and new home far more than she admitted to. Had he come to mean as much as well? Or was he foolishly asking too much after she'd spent so much time being angry with him?

He probably was.

Magnus decided he would have to be satisfied with her other affections in the meantime.

"Would you like to know what your penance will be, K'yindara?" he asked quietly as he nibbled at her bottom lip, the flesh of it so succulent and sweet that he found he needed to suck on it and taste her. "There should be a punishment, after all, for tempting any other man but me."

She laughed, the little snort as sarcastic as it came. It was perfect.

"If that earns me punishment, then I'm going to be doing a lot of penance. Men are too damn easy to tempt."

"True. I suppose I will have to choose the punishment to

fit the crime." He reached for her thigh, drawing it up to his hip and stepping securely between her legs so she could feel the prodding of his rapidly growing erection. "How about, every time I catch you torturing some poor bastard with your very existence, you have to submit to me in any position I choose?"

"And if I find some woman drooling all over you?" she countered, her hands finally resting to touch his shoulders. The contact was a relief he felt to his very soul.

"Then it becomes lady's choice. But women do not drool over the leader of Sanctuary," he said dismissively. "I am too intimidating to them."

Again, she snorted in laughing disbelief. "Yeah, right. I can name three women right now who want you so badly they cream when you walk by."

Magnus's eyes widened, his brows lifting. "Is that so?"

"Though perhaps I won't tell you, lest you get too fat an ego."

"That sounds suspiciously like a cop-out."

"And that sounds suspiciously like you are fishing with bait."

He chuckled. "Well, I will not believe you unless you give me examples."

Daenaira smiled and began to drop slow, meandering fingertips down along his wet chest. "Greta," she replied. "Even Nicoya knew this. She sent Daniel to her wearing your scent and told him to leave behind one of your shuriken. He took her so she never saw him, and she believed it was you."

Magnus stared at her incredulously. "Greta thought I would do such a thing?"

"She all but sank her venomous teeth into me when I first arrived, she was so hot with jealousy."

He frowned darkly. "I will speak with her. I am insulted she would think me capable of such hypocrisy." He narrowed his eyes on her. "Who else?"

"Condilaya."

"Connie?"

"Mmm." Dae slowly traced the pads of her fingertips down the ridges of his tense belly.

"You are mistaken. Condilaya is a sweet young woman who is much too shy to—Why are you shaking your head at me?" he growled.

"Connie was sitting to the right of us when we were doing the hair-brushing exhibition in Brendan's lecture. Your attention must have been elsewhere, or you might have noticed how she couldn't sit still to save her life and stared at you with stars in her eyes."

His attention *had* been somewhere else. He'd been completely focused on Dae and the glorious sensation of having her hair in his hands. It was unnerving listening to her take note of other women who saw him as a man, rather than as a priest. He had not seen himself in a normal sexual way for so long that he had completely eradicated his notice of it in others, and of others noticing it within him. Until Daenaira had come to him. Now he was taking notice of a great many things. For instance, the feel of her provocative fingers sliding with ghostly sensuality beneath the water and through the thatch of pubic curls at the root of his sex.

"And the third?" he asked a bit roughly, his cock nudging insistently up against her in response. He could feel her fingertips and her sexual heat against his ragingly sensitive skin. He didn't hesitate to nudge himself snugly to her, the thickly swollen head to his shaft finding that nice, cozy notch to her entrance.

"Me," she said softly as she lifted her other leg to his hip, wriggled the angle of her hips until he was about an inch inside of her, and sighed as she began to tighten the clasp of her legs and bring him farther in.

"Is that right?" he asked with a sound between a groan and a chuckle. "Even when you were angry with me?"

"Perhaps especially then," she confessed on a noise quite similar to a purr as she arched upward and offered her delectable breasts to his mouth. "Anger is so passionate an emotion, you know. That, and your ass is quite gorgeous." She reached to caress him over his backside, pressing him deeper inside her at her own pace for her own reasons. Magnus availed himself of a sweetly plump nipple, sucking so hard at her that she contracted around him in her surprise.

"I wear a tunic," he pointed out through nipping, sucking lips that rimmed her large areolas, one after the other and back again. "And a weapons belt. You can't see my ass."

"Oh, yes, I can. And you take your tunic off when you are in the training hall. Then not only can I see you, but I can smell you all the better."

Grasping her hips in hand, Magnus suddenly surged the rest of the way into her, a savage sound of satisfaction stuttering out of him as he threw back his head and let himself simply burn within her. She gasped and moaned at the masterful intrusion, her entire body from hands to legs to pussy reaching to clasp him ever tighter into her embrace.

"The smell of lemon oil, sword polish, and the clean sweat of a hardworking warrior. Your skin," she breathed, her mouth opening against the crest of his neck and shoulder, teeth scraping and tongue and lips stroking, "gleams like glazed toffee, and all I want to do is taste you over and over again."

Magnus had to reach out and brace a hand flat against the wall as his balance was affected by her seductive words and lips, not to mention the heavenly tight heat of her sheathed around him. She was so tight, in fact, that it forced him to remember she was still quite new at this, despite her ability to make him feel like he was in the arms of a well-trained seductress.

"Are you still tender from earlier?" he asked roughly, his entire cock throbbing with eager need for friction as he forced himself to await her answer. He hadn't even properly prepared her . . .

"No. Not at all," she assured with an enticing wriggle that bathed him in wet, wet heat. "Please," she begged softly, her body and hands urging him to move. "Fuck me, Magnus. Hard. Fast. Deep. I need to feel you like that."

"Such language," he teasingly admonished, even as he pinned her tight to the wall and surged as deep into her as he could manage.

"You like it," she countered breathlessly as he began to grind himself against her, the pressure rubbing her clit with maddening results, as it was intended to do. "Magnus!"

"Right. Hard. Fast. Deep," he echoed just as he began to obey her with passionate diligence.

Daenaira simply couldn't believe he was even there. She had thought she would never feel this sacred, stunning connection again. She had feared he would never want to touch her again. But he did touch her, and touched her deeply. Her whole body strained to take him in, to join them as tightly as possible, and the pleasure of it bolted through her in time to her racing heart and the fire rushing over her sensitized skin. It was a raw joining, no preliminaries, and she liked it that way. So did he, by the feel of him, so heavy and thick with excitement inside her. This was absolution, she realized. The glory of this feeling and of having him so powerfully alive and in need of her was the ultimate in forgiveness. But it should be punishing, and it should be hard, and it quickly became both as Magnus's need intensified and his territoriality finally released to rise to the surface.

The civilized man of the gods had kept control, had managed her with logic and exoneration, but the dominant Shadowdweller male would be satisfied with nothing less than a claiming that marked her as his once more.

"I'm yours," she whispered into his ear, her teeth nipping at him hungrily. "None but you will ever have me."

"You're goddamn right about that," he hissed as he shoved himself deep with a crash of pelvises. "You're mine, Daenaira.

Drenna gave you to me and me alone. I'll never share you. I'll never release you." He growled roughly as he began to speed his tormenting stroke inside her.

Dae realized then that it wasn't just a possession he spoke of, but a promise and a commitment. He was flooding every statement with an emotion she'd never heard anyone use toward her before. She felt it resonating through her mind like a clear bell.

I will always need you.

I love you as I love life and my gods.

One day, probably quite soon, I know I will come to hold you above Sanctuary itself.

"Never that much," she whispered against his shoulder. "I would never deserve that much."

"That much and more," he said heatedly, the thrust of his fervent body into hers making them both moan in a deep chorus of surging desire. "Gods, Dae," he gasped, his hands shaping and framing her head and face reverently as he slowed to a lusty, meaningful cadence inside her. Golden eyes bored into hers with nothing short of adoration and painfully undeserved admiration. Daenaira reflexively shook her head, but he held her still and forced her to watch and to feel the raw need and pure love he felt for her.

"Why?" she almost sobbed as he overwhelmed her physically and emotionally.

"For the same reason I have my faith and my devotion to the tenets of my gods and my place on this earth. Fate has demanded it of me, *jei li,* and my heart needs you to complete its will. Don't you see?" He broke off to heed the spiking need rushing through his body, a soulful groan erupting out of him that she felt all the way to the heart of her womb. Every move he made, every passionate word he spoke drove her higher and faster toward release.

But it also drove her into a panic like nothing she had ever felt before.

"No!" She tried to shove against him, even as her whole

body screamed in protest at her disruption of her focused bliss. "Let me go!"

"Never!" he spat in breathless countermand.

"Stop! Stop it!"

With a furious roar of masculine dominance, he turned them, holding her struggling wet body tight until he was climbing the steps out of the bath, every step pounding vibrations into the core of her body until she made a pitiful sound of resisting need. Magnus dropped her back onto the chaise even as he knelt on the floor, never once decreasing the depth to which he penetrated her. She immediately tried to gain purchase, but he easily subdued the attempt by pulling her hips up high to meet him, her knees almost draped over his shoulders as his hands locked to her hips and pinned her for his pleasure.

His next thrust was brutal; without the water to act as a buffer for the impact, it resonated through her every bone and made every muscle quiver. Her head hung back limply over the opposite side of the chaise, the position exposing and submissive in the extreme as she became completely quiescent to his pistoning hips.

"Bituth amec," she groaned, in no way meaning it against him so much as it was meant against the desperate need of her own hungry body. The whole of her flesh tautened, an arching and bowstring tightness snapping her back tighter and tighter as he pumped his beautifully thick cock deeply into her.

"That's right," he all but snarled at her, "you take it, *K'yindara*. Take it all. None of it gets left out, none of it denied. You will not shut me out."

Every word brought him to a harder pitch, until all she felt was the impact of their bodies reverberating through her and the sound of their wet flesh slapping heavily together. His relentlessness stole her will and her resistance in a sweeping wave of uncontrollable release. Her orgasm came through her like a berserker rage, obliterating everything until all she felt was heat and the passion of their struggle against one another. She burst into a fury of spasm and arched high and hard against the chaise and his strong body. He plowed through her as she strangled him in muscular contortion, giving no quarter to her until he thrust her so high into mindless ecstasy that she could do nothing but scream, vibrate, and clutch helplessly in his hold.

She seized so hard, milking his cock so violently that he dove through Light to maintain his control. But even as sweat dropped into his eyes to reflect the agony his denial caused him, he gritted his teeth and forced her to understand that there was no coming down from this particular high. There was no escape. No hiding. Nothing. It was raw and frightening beyond belief, but he wasn't going to pretend it wasn't there just for her comfort.

So he reflected that in the way he controlled her body. He had quickly figured out that she naturally arched her body to bring him across the most sensitive spot within her vagina, and by dropping her back over the chaise he forced her to hold the position to perfection. Now he added the use of his fingers against her tender clit, and she cried out. She tried to push and pull away from the renewed stimulus, but he only used her movements to circle himself around inside her. Soon she was clinging to him so tightly with her legs again that he could feel every tremor and shiver rushing through her. She jerked her hips up to meet his in mindless need, the rhythm setting him so deep he was biting back uncontrolled groans of joy.

Her second orgasm took them both by storm. She gasped in, long and deep, her body bowing back. Her exhale was a sharpening keen of release reflecting the pleasurable agony of where he had forced her to go. This time the wrenching spasms of her walls around him were his total undoing. With a monstrous bellow he pumped himself and his jetting seed into her until they both dripped thick and wet with their combined fluids. His arm locked tight around her hips as he sat back hard on his heels. He dragged her off the bench and sat her straddling his lap, half on and half off the chaise behind her. She was limp and gasping, not caring what he did to her. She had no control over her limbs and didn't want any. She left her body to its own devices as it rushed and shivered in the aftermath of his blissful abuse of her.

Relative silence ensued as they struggled to breathe and recover from the explosions their bodies had endured. Eventually, he cupped the back of her neck into his hand and sat her up tightly to his chest. Now he took the time to properly kiss her, paying a long and loving tribute to her. His sweetness made her heart ache, and she felt ridiculously shy as she raised her eyes to meet his.

"What happened?" she asked, obviously in a bit of awe from the wild tide of her adventurous night. It was almost over, daylight approaching quickly beyond the safety of the buried city, but still they both could sense its presence.

"We had a damn rough night," he informed her on a soft chuckle as he trailed the kiss of his lips over her jaw, beneath her ear, and then with quickly renewing voraciousness, down the side of her throat. He hadn't had nearly enough of a starting taste of her before all Light had burst in on them. Also, they were both very aware that this was their first truly private moment together.

"I meant . . . I can feel you," she said breathily.

He lifted his head and eyed her with amusement. "I should hope so," he remarked.

"In my mind." She laughed, pinching muscle that refused to give under the punishment. "I've been hearing you in my head. I noticed it most for the first time when I was battling Nicoya. You yelled at me." She frowned in consternation. " 'Easy,' you said."

"So I did," he agreed. "It's the Bonding," he realized with no little surprise himself. "I didn't even realize we've only been speaking aloud half of this time. It just came so . . . "

"Naturally," she finished for him. "Does it always happen so quickly?"

"It's actually a rare sort of thing. We speak of it like it is always possible, but we never truly expect it. Hera would know best, but I thought it took time and—"

"And?"

"Love," he said cautiously, remembering how resistant she had reacted when she had realized his mind was flooded with the deep, abiding love for her he had never wanted and never expected to feel. Even now it intimidated him to feel it, just as much as it frightened her to be on the receiving end of it. Even more frightening for him was knowing she did not feel the same way for him. "I mean," he clarified quietly, "reciprocal love."

"Oh," she said on a whisper.

Instantly he felt her rushing anxiety, her desire to break away from him and leave him. Though she could hear his thoughts on occasion, it seemed, he could not shed light on hers. But he could feel the powerful wrenching impulses of her emotions, especially her fear. He tried not to feel stung by it, but it was difficult when she said, "I don't love you, Magnus."

"I did not say I expected you to," he returned with a frown.

"No. But you hope for it. You wish for it." She swallowed as she squirmed uncomfortably in his lap. "But I never will," she told him almost coldly. "I loved my mother, and she is the only one whom I will ever feel so deeply for. If you wish more from me, you will only be disappointed."

Magnus's hands tightened around her thighs, and he re-sisted the urge to shove out from under her. They were still intimately connected and it seemed somehow obscene to him to be having this exchange while he was still inside her. But he controlled the desire, forced aside the injured anger, making himself look into her as best he could with every-thing he could. His eyes, he realized, would have lied to him just as she was lying to him. She cared far more than she admitted to, though it was true she didn't feel the level of consuming love that seemed to ebb and flow through every corner of his existence as he looked at her beautiful features and lying eyes. Despite her claims, he could feel the fear that fueled her denial. What would she do, he wondered, and what would she say, if he were to compel the truth from her and ask her the right questions? What could he force her to admit to herself?

And how much would she hate him for pushing her before she was ready?

"Don't worry. I hear what you're saying, Daenaira," he said, making quite certain every thought remain placid and cloaked in the blankness of neutrality. "I do not expect you to be responsible for my feelings, only that you be open to the benefits of them."

"The benefits?" she asked suspiciously.

"Yes. I won't detail them, but it cannot hurt you to have someone like me love you, *K'yindara*." He drew gentle fingers down over her wet hair. "I will not treat you badly. I will never demand more than you can give."

"You always demand more than I can give," she retorted.

"More than you *think* you can give," he corrected. "Amazingly, I have been right every time I have asked you to stretch yourself." He gave her a rather wolfish grin as he perused her moist, naked skin and began to contemplate the way he would like to really stretch her, making those thoughts as vivid as he could just to see if she was paying close attention.

"Magnus!" she exclaimed a little breathlessly. "People don't really do that—do they?"

"And so much more," he assured her, satisfied she was plenty distracted as the deeper topics were discarded and more carnal ones arose. "Do they frighten you, my thoughts of what I want to do to you?"

He could tell by the blush suffusing her upper body that they didn't, but he wanted to hear what she would say. Daenaira bit her lip and looked down at where their bodies were thoroughly connected . . . where she could feel him recovering his arousal in quickening, thickening increments.

"I don't really think so," she mused, fascinated by the changes she felt happening inside herself. That didn't surprise him. He felt, quite certainly, that she was capable of an enormous and rapacious appetite. All she needed was a little time.

Just a little time and she would reach all of her fullest potential.

Emotionally as well as physically.

He was sure of it.

Chapter Seventeen

Daenaira awoke feeling distinctly sore.

It had been a long, exhausting week.

The whole of Sanctuary, it seemed, was in an uproar. Sagan was missing and presumed dead or worse. Brendan, though alive, remained weakened from his injuries and massive blood loss. The volume of blood he had lost inhibited his natural ability to heal, and it was very difficult to provide transfusions between members of their society.

Magnus, who should have been enjoying a small reprieve and relief from knowing Sanctuary had been gutted of its influence of evil, was instead steadily driving himself to exhaustion as he tried to pick up the shattered pieces of trust all around the city and within the religious house itself. Parents had yanked nearly half the student body out of Sanctuary when rumors of student abuse filtered into the city. Daenaira had watched with devastating sorrow as Magnus had taken each and every instance deeply to heart. But as each child left, he spoke to the families and turned it to his use. *Take them*, he said to each one, *until I am done securing the school once again. When I have implemented safety measures that will assure all our children will be safe with us once more, I will call you back to me.* And, baffled and frightened, the parents would nod and agree, their anger and their indignation dissipating as this man they had all been raised to trust so implicitly made them a promise they knew he would die to keep.

Then there were the three.

Those three names Nicoya had mentioned before her death, who were also betrayers. All had escaped just ahead of justice, and with only Ventan and Magnus alive to dole out penance, there was no one left for Magnus to delegate to. This eradication of his penance priests was, by far, the most devastating effect to ripple through the temple itself. He and Ventan had to pick up the slack of listening to confession of sins, overseeing penitence, and doling out penance. Then, when he wasn't teaching his courses, which he refused to hand over to anyone else, he was out trying to hunt Nicoya's remaining devils.

And somehow, in the midst of all this, Magnus made the time to dwell in the chambers of the female Chancellor, providing her with his guidance and reassurances. They were lucky, he told her, to have finally rid one of the three most powerful bodies in their government of the seeds of deceit growing inside it. The Chancellors were confident that their upper echelon was also free of such deception. Now the Senate was all that remained. This, however, would not be so easy to rectify as it had been to set Sanctuary to rights, and they all grimly settled themselves in for the long haul where this was concerned.

It was another part of Nicoya's legacy that truly kept Magnus in a state of perpetual devastation, and watching him struggle with it had the power to shatter Daenaira's heart. For a week he had agonized over Shiloh's dire prediction of woe and death for his son's family, and he knew of no solution. Had it been in his power, he would have erased the threat completely, allowing his son and his wife to continue on in complete ignorance of there ever being any danger. However, all his initial quests for information had proven to him how fruitless it was to hope for such a thing. Dae knew he was now only waiting for the warrior who guarded the queen, Guin by name, to return so he could plumb his resources in a final attempt. Only after he had exhausted the other man's mind would he relent and finally tell his son and new daughter of the threat that hung so direly over their heads.

And then, long after day broke, he would enter their rooms and seek Daenaira in her bed, climbing in to swallow her warmth and passion like a healing draft. He blanked his mind of his worries during this time, focusing so fully on her and the pleasures they shared that she had little opportunity to help him vent mentally as well as physically. So she allowed him his fierce moments of respite inside her, welcoming his fever and the sense of desperation she knew came with it. He was working so hard to keep everything from slipping through his fingers, and he feared, she knew, that he wasn't going to be fast enough, smart enough, keen enough, or wise enough to rectify all of the damage that had been done.

The previous night had ended in a fruitless hunt for one of Nicoya's henchmen, and he had come to take his frustrations out on Dae's tender body. Oh, he was quite welcome to do so when the result was a chain of orgasms unlike anything they had previously shared, but there was a price to be paid when she let herself be so worn out and slept too little to compensate.

Daenaira looked at the empty pillow beside her and sighed. He had been up before dusk, no doubt, and was already back at work trying to stitch the world together. She picked up the pillow, taking a moment to rub her face against it and inhale his wonderful scent. The thick masculine aroma and the heady scent of sex made her squirm for missing him with a sudden and biting hunger. He had been quite tender and assertive this week, always taking control of their needs for both of them, obsessing over *her* pleasure and *her* passion, that she had hardly gotten in a word or action otherwise.

Not that she was complaining.

She had never realized how addictive her own body could be to her. The roughly awakened sensuality inside her suddenly seemed to permeate her everywhere. Magnus made her feel incredibly beautiful, and she was beginning to believe it for herself. Instead of being insulted by the attention and staring of other males, she took note of it, studied it, and even toyed with the power of it to see what she could create within herself to make her body all the more alluring.

Then she would tentatively test what she learned on Magnus.

But tentative was not working, she realized. Well, it was— just not as she wanted it to. She enjoyed all of the attention she received, she just sensed there was need for something different. Something more. By drilling his focus onto her and her pleasure, he was trying to manage and control her just like every other thing he felt he needed to repair in his damaged life. She supposed he thought if he kept her blindly happy, she would never doubt or question her need to stay or her purpose in being there. It was ridiculous, of course.

But she felt saddened by the fear that motivated him to it. He shouldn't feel so isolated and so starkly alone that he felt he needed to hold the entire world up on his shoulders with perfection. What he needed, what she wanted to give him, was a place and space of reprieve from that. At first she had thought that was what she was doing when they made love, but his controlled, methodical passion was too starkly different from the wilder lust and fervor that had always overcome him before.

It was mildly insulting, actually.

Daenaira sighed, tossed away his pillow, and got up. Well, she wasn't going to help him by lazing around in bed, and it was very clear to her he needed help. Since she was the only one within arms' reach he seemed to trust, it was her responsibility to see to his well-being.

She bathed and dressed, secure in the knowledge as she did so that the mirror back had been painted black and boarded over besides. The tunnels had all been locked or sealed permanently. The only ones Magnus had not closed off were the ones behind the private tutoring rooms. These he had kept secret. He had locked them away to anyone but himself and her, and whenever they passed or had time they would observe the lessons in the rooms to assure that no one was abusing their positions as Nicoya and Shiloh had done.

For Henry's sake, the entire incident had been left without names or specifics. He had been offered a chance to go home, something that wouldn't be questioned with so many others leaving as well, but he had refused. He wanted to stay close to Daenaira and Magnus and the few who knew what he had been through and would understand what he needed when he needed it. She felt bad for the boy who tried so hard to act normally, but his cocky humor was nowhere to be seen now and he had switched to the early lecture, which Magnus had taken over for Brendan, securing a distant place of viewing. Daenaira had attended this week as well, sitting near to Henry and finding that her own naïveté was a calming and disarming influence on the tightly wound student. This was probably why her dry, sarcastic and amusing whispers to Henry had gone unchallenged by the keen-eared teacher who lectured them.

Realizing she was going to be late for the lecture if she didn't hurry, she gave her sai a quick pat of reassurance before dropping her sari into place and dashing out of the room. She ran most of the way to the educational wing, her still-damp hair curling in lazy streams behind her back. She entered the lecture hall and was surprised to see she was, in fact, early. The only ones in the room besides herself were the day's models. Smiling, she went up to them and greeted them.

"Hello. I am Daenaira."

"Hello, *K'yan* Daenaira. I am Sydney and this is my mate Thomas."

"A joined couple? That's so nice," she said with a smile. "We don't see many joined couples modeling here. It seems to be something the single and youthfully adventurous favor." She laughed when she heard her own unintended insult. "Not that I mean to insinuate . . . "

"No, we understand." Sydney chuckled. "And you are right. When you are joined, sex seems to become more insular—unless you are fetishists. But Thomas and I like to challenge each other every so often to put thrills into our routine."

"To what benefit?" Dae asked candidly of Thomas.

"Well," he said, clearing his throat. "I suppose it is a powerful affirmation of the sexual self. Also, the excitement is so jacked up. Mostly, though, it's about making ourselves vulnerable—but vulnerable together. We are exposed, but as a joined entity we can withstand anything. It's very spiritual in a way."

"Loving, too. But I doubt many others would agree with that. Our thrill seeking is different from what the others come here for, I'm sure," Sydney said, with a becoming blush tingeing her cheeks.

"What are you modeling today?" Daenaira asked them attentively.

"Oral sex. I believe the focus is on the male. I wish it had been something more along coitus, but Magnus asked us to do this since he is short models of late."

"Yes," Daenaira said thoughtfully. Her heart began to race as a terrible, awful, and shockingly wonderful idea came into her mind. "Um, could I ask you a huge favor?"

* * *

Magnus sighed wearily as he pushed through the lecture hall's doors. He was barely halfway through his evening and he already felt like he could use another eight hours of sleep. He spared a glance at Henry, who nodded to him, and noticed that Daenaira wasn't in her place near to him. The realization made him a bit tense on Henry's behalf. Considering the topic on the syllabus, he had really been counting on Daenaira to keep close watch on the boy. Especially after her detailed descriptions of his victimization at Nicoya's devious hands.

He had very specifically chosen today's models as well. Sydney and Thomas were a loving and beautiful couple, their tenderness and easy humor perfect for what he needed. They were also very physically different from Henry's abusers, and he thought that would be important as well. He was running a little late, so all of Brendan's students were sitting and waiting patiently. All that were still enrolled, that is. There were maybe ten left out of a class of twenty. Magnus could only hope that within a month it would be back to normal. He had a great deal to prove to some rightfully fearful parents. One of the girls giggled as he passed her, and he almost tripped when he realized it was Condilaya. He couldn't help but notice her crush on him ever since Daenaira had pointed it out to him. Now he rather wished she hadn't done so. Every time he saw the girl, his memory went flying back to the erotic orgasms that bath had produced, as well as the difficult clash of emotions.

It was a little unnerving, actually, to realize Daenaira had developed a far clearer pathway into his mind than he had into hers. There was a particular superiority for her in that. Perhaps this was why, ever since the day he had recognized their cockeyed Bonding, he hadn't had a single moment of honest thought. He couldn't help guarding himself from her notice. His burdens and his emotional torments were *his* to cope with. He wouldn't weigh her mind with any more troubles and he certainly wouldn't make her feel guilty or obliged to him in any—

Magnus stopped short when he realized a stunning blanket of red-black hair was hanging over the edge of the bed. The female attached to it was stretched out on her back, giving him an incredible diagonal profile of large, firm breasts, a fit, flat tummy, and long, long, so very damn long legs accentuated by the playful cock of her knee.

For a very long moment, he didn't know how to react. Then, as if in a surreal painting where he didn't quite fit, he swept his eyes over the room to make certain he was exactly where he thought he was and that he hadn't gotten turned around or wandered back to his rooms where he had left her sleeping in such peaceful, beautiful repose.

Once he was quite certain of where he was, he was able to decide just how furious he should be. The trouble was, there were ten pairs of expectant eyes on him and on the bed. Magnus glanced up at the rotunda ceiling. He was forced to add four more to the count, and he didn't doubt there would be a very large increase as time went on. Daenaira had made herself quite well known, even infamous, with her cutthroat battle to the death with Nicoya. The students had even made up a little song about her epic performance, something about the downfall of the Killer *K'ypruti*. It was rather endearing, actually.

As calmly as he could, he continued forward and stepped up onto the platform that raised the circular bed to optimum height. Without headboard or footboard, it allowed every student a unique and very comprehensive view of the lesson on display. He leaned forward to look down at her face when he reached the edge of the bed and, unable to resist the temptation, his fingertips dove into the thick veil of her hair left hanging over the bedside. She was clothed, thank the gods, but barely so. She was wearing a *k'jeet* made of tissue-thin fabric, the milky chocolate color of it only a few shades darker than her natural skin color. He could see every curve, every shadow, and he could quite easily make out the enticing thrust of her attentive nipples.

The urge to touch her there was just as irresistible as the urge to feel her hair, but with a monumental effort he managed to keep his free hand at his side.

"Dae, would you mind telling me what you are doing?" he asked, actually managing to edit out the wild chains of profanity choking him for the freedom to dwell in that question.

She smiled up at him, that slowly sly grin of a cat.

"Well, your models cancelled for the day. Something came up." The flash of challenge in her eyes dared him to compel the truth from her after so obvious a lie, but he was too afraid to find out what exactly was on that scheming little mind. "So I figured it wasn't anything we couldn't handle ourselves. After all, the students need their lesson."

And what he needed to do was to strangle the wretch. *Drenna*, if she hadn't just made him hard as a pike with that outrageous proposition.

"This is an oral sex lecture," he rasped thickly. "I can hardly lecture and perform at the same time."

"Of course not. That's what makes this so perfect. It's oral sex on the male. Something, by the way, I have yet to learn. I consider this an opportunity to cover many bases at once. The students get their lecture, I learn something new, the models are replaced, and I get to do what I have been wanting to do to you for over a week now."

This last part was delivered on such a low, seductive rasp of her voice that it sought out every raw nerve he owned. Blood rushed through him, his balls aching with the longing of the desire she painted in his mind, not to mention the visual stimulation he was forced to endure as her every breath beneath the *k'jeet* rubbed those darkly visible nipples of hers to firmer attention.

He could sense her excitement and her anxiety. She was

afraid and thrilled at her own daring all at once, and unless his sense of smell was playing tricks, she was wet with arousal from just the idea of it.

The stumbling block here was that he hadn't done this before.

Not just this particular unique situation, but exhibitionism as a model for a class. He hadn't been intimate with Karri, and before that had had no handmaiden. Back then, back when he had raised Trace, it had been more acceptable to be without a female counterpart, and he had spent the first thirty-five years as a priest without a woman by his side. It was, in fact, the basis he had used in his supposition about sex versus his ambitions for Sanctuary. As for before that—well, he had been taught like everyone else, had indulged as any young man might have done, but he had been born to be a priest, and he had stepped into the role immediately after he had graduated from his classes. There really had been no time for adventurous games and experimental daring.

Daenaira watched his thoughts fly through him, heard everything he was thinking, felt the pounding excitement searing through him with every pulse beat. If she weren't breathing so hard, she would have held her breath. It had been a dare, a risk, and a damn treacherous gamble, and it could very well backfire on her. He was so possessive, whether he comprehended that in his own actions or not, and he was also fighting so hard to re-establish dignity to his sacred home. It was possible he might consider this an unseemly thing for the leader of all Sanctuary to do.

Or he could realize what a hypocrisy that would really be, and shed just a few inhibitions.

"Do you really think," he said softly, almost dangerously, as he reached to stroke his knuckles beneath her chin and down along her throat, "that I would want to share you with the world?"

"I think you have a class waiting for their lesson, and I

think this appeals to you more than you would like me to know."

The damn Bonding. That and the fact that the way she was lying with her forehead now bent back to touch his thigh, she could easily see the state of his body. He watched her take a slow breath in through flaring nostrils and his gut went tight as he realized she was drawing on the heaviness of his aroused scent. Suddenly he could so easily imagine the scenario she suggested.

Too easily.

"Class." He had to stop to clear the thick rasp from his throat. Right. Give a lecture like this? "Class is cancelled for the night."

Daenaira jerked herself up into a seated position in surprise, her wild cloud of hair settling messily around her shoulders. The class complained as a whole, but all it took was the scathing stare of golden eyes to push them into silence. When the last pair of dragging feet had finally exited the hall, Magnus reached across the bed and grabbed her under her arm, literally yanking her off the bed and hauling her against him, his stare burning into her.

"What are you doing? Are you so eager to show yourself to the student body?" he demanded. "I would have thought you had had enough exposure after the way Nicoya and Shiloh violated us. What? Have you discovered you like it and miss it knowing the possibilities have been painted over and sealed away?"

"You bastard!" She hauled off and hit him so hard and so fast across his face he never even saw it coming. "How dare you speak to me that way!"

"I dare because you don't think!" he railed back at her. Magnus tongued his inner lip, tasting blood where she had cut him against his own teeth. "If you were anyone else, you would answer for this."

"Oh, well, don't let me stop you," she hissed, her face and

eyes burning with her embarrassment and fury. "By all means, have me answer for it!"

"Is that what you want? Do you want to suffer penance?"

"Gods know it has to be better than this insulated, kid-glove treatment I've been getting lately!"

"Very well. This desire, at least, I can grant you."

Chapter Eighteen

The temple proper consisted of three levels, the first and main level at the entrance of Sanctuary, and two below. Penance occurred in the chambers on the lowest level. Magnus dragged her there by her arm and on the tips of her toes with a furious speed to match his rollicking temper.

But Daenaira wasn't afraid of him. Not in the least. Though his thoughts were hazed in anger, she could hear and feel the subconscious understanding within him that he was overreacting, but that he couldn't seem to help himself. They both knew she had done nothing to earn time in a chamber with him; even the slap was justified in its way and repayable with a long hour of prayer repenting on her knees.

But this twisting need and emotion was what she had lost from him this week. He had so deeply repressed everything he was feeling in order to shut her out of his churning thoughts, trying to bring himself onto an even keel with her because he did not have the same access to her mind that she had to his. He had wanted to level the playing field between them, trying to stop the stinging, slapping reminder the unbalanced Bonding between them gave him of her unreturned feelings of love. Neither did he want to burden her with what burdened him. His worry, his stress, and all of the ramifications of Sanctuary's now-tarnished reputation that he took so personally, he felt these were his concerns and no one else's. This was his penance, to bear up under what he had unwittingly let occur in his own house. Ignorance was no excuse. Trickery was no excuse. He should have been above all of it. Better than all of it.

Daenaira thought he demanded the impossible. Of himself, and now of her. He wanted a partner in his life, but only at his convenience? Did he think that because she wasn't in love with him, she didn't care at all? That she had no feelings of her own? That she couldn't understand what a trial all of this was for him?

That she couldn't help him in any way other than to comfort the hunger of his body in the sharp hours before sleep?

Magnus threw open one of the five chambers, each designed for and by the specific priest that claimed it. He shoved her inside ahead of him, and she stumbled and fell to the floor. When he slammed the door shut in his wake, she heard the crack of his hard-soled boots on the intricate tiles of the chamber floor.

She had never been in a penance chamber before, had never experienced it for herself, and now as she looked around the stark atmosphere of the room, she could understand why it was so effective in quelling sin. The room was designed with a single purpose in mind. Punishment. And while there was an archaic collection of objects like whips and crops settled each in its own place along the wall on one side, there were other, far more creative ways of extracting obedience. Mostly, it came down to a person and a priest, one mind against another, one psyche trained to pick apart a resistant one while there was nowhere to escape to. No way to escape, she noted as well when she saw several ways a penitent could be bound into place.

This made her heart trip into an awkward beat of trepidation. She had not been bound since she had last been in her old life and, while it couldn't be much more than a few weeks since, she had come so far from that stifling and cruel existence that seeing the manacles and chains made her panic with the sensation of being thrown back into what she had once been. She struggled to swallow this all down as she watched from her position on the floor while he paced in a hard, sharp step around her. He was clearly trying to work some of his anger off, but he didn't yet realize that his fury went deeper and further than just her and just this moment and that he would find it inexhaustible unless he purged himself of it the right way.

Or even the wrong way.

Any way. Just so long as he stopped shoving it aside and stopped pretending it wasn't even there. Seeing his struggle reminded her of why she was doing this to begin with, and she tapped into the core reserve of obstinacy and defiance she had always used to frustrate her targets in the past when they had tried to punish her. She couldn't help the absently nervous need to touch the scarring at the back of her neck where the brutality of her collar had left its mark. Most of it had faded to a sightless texture already, having been given time to heal without constantly renewed irritation, but it was still easily felt and much more easily remembered.

Magnus had his hands secured to his hips as he paced, and she watched him warily for a few moments. It wasn't long, however, before she was just watching *him*. It was hard not to appreciate just about every movement he made. He hadn't given her much opportunity to explore his fine masculine body, but she was determined to change that one way or another. He might want to dominate her along with everything else he tried to control in his life, but he was going to find himself sorely disappointed again and again. She had never been easily tamed, and in her opinion the very last thing he needed was a compliant female who left him to his own devices. He had to realize that doing things as he had always done them was absolutely not the answer. Things needed to change for him. He was the crest of Sanctuary. Everything he did filtered down into the rest of his house. Emotional distance had damaged it once already. It was time he felt his passion to all of its depths, whether or not it was returned or able to be controlled. Just like it was time for the Chancellery to assert itself on the Senate and control its power, it was time he brought his focus back to the essence of what this place was meant to be.

It was, in at its core, his heart. When he had let it grow cool and distant, calling it control and discipline, it had allowed weakness and an undermining of the essentials of what it meant to be a warm, living being. If the heart did not feel, then there was no hope for the rest. Feeling was necessary to passion and caring and belief. Faith was more than rote behaviors and acts.

Love was going to be painful as well as pleasurable.

That was simply its nature.

"Why would you do this?" he demanded in abrupt frustration. It so clearly irked him that he couldn't figure it out for himself. Worse, that he couldn't glean it from her senses and thoughts like she could from him. She couldn't help but smile in an irritatingly smug fashion because of it.

No sense in being cautious now, she thought with a shrug.

"Because I wanted to," she replied simply, applying it to her shrug. "And frankly, I don't see what you're so pissed off about! Priests and handmaidens do this all the time."

"Well, *I* don't!"

"Why not?" she demanded. "Aren't you a teacher? An instructor? Are you too good to lower yourself to your own lessons? Because I have to say, I see something very different when you climb into bed with me in the light hours."

"Don't you dare drag our private times into this!" he hissed at her sharply.

"Oh, I'll dare that and much, much more, I promise you. I'm not some obedient little pet that sits, stays, and fucks on your command alone, Magnus. I have a mind, a heart and desires of my own."

"And one of those desires is to perform oral sex on me in public?" he roared furiously, his fists clenching along with all the rest of his body as he stood over her. "Something, as you pointed out, you haven't even tried in the privacy of our own rooms?"

"Not that you'd give me a chance," she muttered crabbily.

"What's that supposed to mean?"

"Oh, figure it out for your own damn self!" she spat. "It's not like you ever ask for my opinion or my help with anything else."

She was going to sit up Indian style, cross her arms obstinately beneath her breasts, but she slowed her temper down enough to realize the sprawl of exposed legs and tightly caught chocolate silk around her higher curves made for much more of an attractive distraction. Since she was determined to disturb him at all costs, she would stay exactly as she was and let him suffer with glimpses at her body's shadows and sweet places that he found so damn hard to resist. Served him right for pissing her off.

So, instead of sitting up, she rolled onto her belly, propped her elbows on the floor, and supported her chin, looking casual and bored with the whole situation. Plus, she had effectively turned her back on him and presented him with a fine view of her backside.

And it was thoroughly appreciated, however reluctantly it might have happened. She felt his distraction and his stare, the struggle to reconcile his anger with the frustration of how she drove him insane with need. The urge to get himself into place behind her and jerk her to him so that delectable backside was rubbing back against his pelvis was nearly as strangling as it was stimulating. It reminded him that he had been very unimaginative in bed with her, restricting himself to a very standard degree of missionary positions despite his crazed desires otherwise. Oh, he would fantasize about having her on her knees, against the wall again, or riding astride him, but each one either reminded him of things he had yet to deal with completely, or—gods, it would just feel too intense and he would feel too exposed . . .

Was that what she meant by "kid-glove" treatment?

"What is it you are trying to achieve here, Daenaira?" he asked harshly. "Just tell me instead of playing games with me."

"You think this is a game?" She rolled over sharply, altering the gorgeous landscape of her body as she leaned back on her elbows and braced a knee. The skirt of her *k'jeet* slid up her thigh, a victim of gravity, exposing delicious mocha skin almost to her hip.

Gods, he was still hard from seeing her in the classroom bed. He didn't need any more stimulation.

"This isn't a game, Magnus. Especially not if you're bringing *me* in *here*." She suddenly rose to her feet in a graceful glide of muscle and silk, drawing up so close to his tense body that she could feel the intense heat of temper and sexual awareness radiating off him. She had half a mind to reach out for him and show him exactly which of them was in control at the moment, and exactly how aware of it she was, but she wasn't trying to make this quick and easy for him. She needed to see just how far he was willing to take this for the sake of protecting himself. "So let's get started, shall we? What's on the agenda? Going to tie me up so I can't run away?"

"The bindings are for violent offenders so I can focus on the mind rather than the physical struggle," he informed her with a frown. He reached to touch her wrist where it bore distinctive scars from her captivity. "And I would never do that to you. I would give you to Ventan if something like that were required, because I could never do it to you myself."

"You might as well," she said, trying not to let how much his tenderness affected her show in her voice. So, he hadn't been willing to go so far after all. "You tie my hands in so many other ways, why not this as well?"

She turned, her heart beating at a rapid thrum, as she surveyed the various methods of imprisonment arrayed before her. Swallowing her fear for his sake, she moved over to a set that would lash the prisoner by wrists and ankles while bending them back or forward over the rounded beam of a gymnast's vaulting horse. It left the penitent exposed, helpless, and vulnerable; stretched to the limits of their endurance, forcing them to trust their priest for everything from punishment to food and drink. She ran a hand over the horse's back, the lambskin padding fresh and new, probably changed after use. How often, she wondered, was a method this extreme even employed? For how long would a penitent be kept in such a manner? If it were someone like Nicoya, she imagined it would be for a very long time.

She realized then how much Magnus must dislike the evils and sins of the world. For a man like himself, one so instinctively tender and caring, so soulfully determined to make things good, to find it in himself to work what was genuine cruelty against those who had been cruel to others . . . It was a very fine line, she thought. A brutal and difficult one to walk. No wonder it had been so easy for Nicoya to lure away two of the five penance priests in existence. Between balancing on such an edge and being required to kill those who would not relinquish themselves to the good of the gods, it was no wonder Magnus sought solace with her. But . . .

But after two centuries of bearing it all himself, solace wouldn't come to him in half-measures. He needed to expose himself to the bone, risk everything, if he was going to be soothed and brought back to the balance she knew he was seeking.

"Would you like to bind me down?" she asked. "Or shall I do it myself?"

"Neither. You'll not be tied down in this session."

She turned around slowly to look at him, and then drew her elbows up to lean back against the horse, the position exaggerating her posture and catching his quick, heated attention along the length of her body.

"What exactly was your plan, then? Did you want me on my knees?" She smiled with wicked mirth. "We could have just stayed in the classroom, then."

Magnus stepped up to her, his height and powerful body quite intimidating—to most. He wrapped a hand that trembled with repressed temper around one side of her throat and neck and bent so they were nearly nose to nose. Golden eyes bored in deep, shimmering with their kinetic emotions.

"Do you think this is a joke?" he exhaled in hot threat against her, the brush of his breath sending a wild chill flashing down the front of her body and stimulating her nipples into tight little knots of flesh.

"I think you are a joke," she retorted. "Mr. Mad Bad and Dangerous to Know. You are so full of shit."

"Excuse me?"

Daenaira could imagine he wasn't used to being spoken to this way. The way his coloring tinged with dark fury reaffirmed the notion. But she was no longer impressed with his volatile temper. It was like a storm that never broke, all grumbling rumbles and ominous threat but not so much as a spit of rain.

She was looking for a deluge.

"Are you going deaf?" she countered. She enunciated every repeated word. "I said you are full of shit."

"Why are you pushing me?" he asked through tight teeth, his hand growing tense around her.

"Am I? Tell me, what am I pushing you toward?"

The answer clearly scared Light into him, because he lurched away from her and began to back up. She decided to stalk him, meeting him step for step and pushing him every inch of the way.

"Tell me. Are you going to hurt me? Are you going to

kick me out of Sanctuary? Will you smack me around a little? Or maybe you will just ignore me for two centuries."

"Daenaira!" he barked in warning. But it was hard to take it as much of a threat when he had just backed up into a chair, sitting down hard when her forward motion screwed with his balance.

Dae braced a hand on either side of him, using the arms of the chair, and leaned in on him until she was pushing him all the way back in the seat under the threat of touching his lips with hers. She didn't kiss him, though, just hovered within a millimeter of doing so.

"What? Am I going too far? Don't want to talk about it? You don't want to talk about anything, do you? You don't want to feel anything, for that matter. You just want to bully everyone around, shuffle them here and there like pieces on a chessboard and make sure they perform just their precisely assigned maneuvers and nothing else. Nothing unique or illegal. Certainly nothing emotional. You play the king, making sure they all hop squares just right, obeying and performing as you will them to, all with their allocated duties so you can create a perfect game and protect yourself all at the same time.

"But before you forget, while you sit stagnant in your little corner of the board, there is one piece that obeys almost no rules and has her own commands. Utter freedom is the way of the queen. She is your most powerful piece, your very best ally, the ruination of your enemy—but only if you utilize her properly, my king. Only if you are willing to do what it takes to plumb the depths of her power to aid you to victory. Just try to win without her, and you'll see you are doomed to failure."

She backed away from him, satisfied with the analogy and the point it made. She turned her back to him, and with the proud grace of the queen she had paralleled herself to, she circuited the room.

"I'm still waiting for my penance, M'jan Magnus," she

said in a singsong tone that taunted him. Then she laughed at him.

"Gods! You infuriating, brassy, *bold* bitch!" he exploded at last, bursting from the chair like an army charging down a hillside. He was on her before she could slip out of reach, both arms wrapped in his punishing grip as he shook her to the point of lifting her off her toes. "I swear, you would test the patience of *Drenna* Herself! For the life of me, I cannot figure you out! I don't know what you want from me! I don't know if you even give a damn about any of this or if it's just all an amusing game, a change of pace from the lifestyle of imprisonment you lived that must have grown so boring when you realized you had defeated those simpletons before you even stepped foot in their door!"

"Oh!" she exploded furiously. "That's right! Every girl wants to dance a game with a madwoman who swings a poisoned blade just to keep from being bored out of her goddamn skull! You fucking bastard! You jerk!" She broke from him with a swift, powerful movement, making herself as slippery as the silk she wore. The fabric itself allowed her to squirm free of him, even as it ripped from her body. His fists clutched tight and she dashed away in the opposite direction.

Daenaira tore away from him, stripped to her skin and the ever-present weapons aligned to her calves. A naked warrior woman, savage in her anger with him, her amber eyes flashing with indignation so righteous he began to doubt the wisdom of his unchecked words. He hadn't meant to say it at all, in fact. She just kept pushing him until he spat words without thinking. Now speech was damn near impossible as he was confronted with what he deemed as the ultimate in feminine perfection. Roughened places and dimmed scars had long ago melted away from his vision of her, and all he saw was smoothness, curves, and brown beauty. Her every muscle stood firm and poised, her darkly tipped breasts proud and tempting. Silk slid between his fingers, escaping his grasp as it fell in a torn pile at his feet. He paid no attention, all of his focus on the awesome female figure he craved in so many wild and ruthless ways.

But if he showed her that unrestrained side of himself, if he tore into her with that unregulated need, he would just as surely lose all hope of her ever learning how to love him. The reasoning was twofold. She had had enough savagery to last her the rest of her life, and she couldn't possibly want to tie herself emotionally to something so volatile, could she? And if he unleashed this one aspect, it would be chained to all of the others he held so carefully under his control. He couldn't be so raw and honest with her in one way and then not in all of them. He would begin to pour his stress into her, weight her with his worries, and use her to vent his frustrations and fears.

No woman deserved such barbaric treatment. He would much rather try to love her sweetly and pay her kind attentions he had not paid to Karri. He would not make the same mistakes as before, leaning too heavily and never giving back in balance. He had to be careful if he wanted to keep her. If he wanted to win her.

Otherwise, she would never love him. That was a thought he simply could not bear. Only if he did everything just right could he possibly expect to earn the love of this difficult woman. His mistakes had almost cost him and his people the blessings of Sanctuary. He couldn't afford to be wrong any longer. Not again. Never again.

"You are such a fool," she whispered with sudden ferocity, bracing her hands on her hips and striking an astounding pose of pride and loveliness. "You just won't listen! What you want to do is impossible! Perfection doesn't exist, Magnus! No one can be perfect, and it is your attempt to gouge out your reality and the flaws that come with simply being a person that will make you lose everything again and again! We don't want an untouchable man! Not me and not Sanctuary! Nor do we want anything to do with a man who will not touch us in return! Who would want to tie themselves to such a cold, unfeeling brute? How could we ever trust you to know and understand what we need, desire, and feel inside when you seem to have no feelings of your own? How can we ever come to you and confess our flaws when you seem so aloof and flawless? We won't ever expect you to understand!

"And how," she demanded, stepping forward as she drew hard for passionate breath, "can I ever believe you really love me when you will not trust me enough to show me all that you are? Of all the people you can show reality to, it should be me! I have swallowed buckets of one of the coldest, cruelest realities our world can dole out. Don't you think I can manage the parts of the one you are trying so hard to navigate alone? And I am not saying that there is no desire in me for sweetness and tenderness, because *Drenna* knows I have seen sore little of it in my lifetime, but I'll not take comfort and solace and mincing lovemaking from you when inside yourself you need to roar and rampage and slake your lust wildly! If you continue to do so, it will be lies upon lies and more deceit than I can bear to stomach! That you treat me like I am such a simpleton, unworthy of sharing the weight of your world—!"

"No!"

Magnus was on her so fast and so hard that their breastbones collided harshly. She reached to catch her balance, and found her hands wrapping around the bulge of mighty triceps as he scooped her head into his hands and dragged her onto the very tips of her toes to meet his descending mouth. She resisted the compelling passion of his kiss, her heart thrumming in consternation at her as it longed to fling itself into the delight of it. But the physical arousal was not enough, she knew. It was powerful and dizzying, more than she had ever expected in her life, but he had already spoiled her and now she wanted more. More of him. All of him. She wanted everything, not just what he was willing to dole out to her on a moment-to-moment basis. And she was afraid that if she didn't demand it now, didn't hold her ground, she would be doomed to a lifetime of stilted, cockeyed reservation and a man who would perpetually dice away parts of himself because he thought sacrifice was the only path to the enlightenment he so hungered for.

Daenaira closed her eyes and went still and lax beneath the press and dip of his mouth. Soon, her lack of response to him drove him to frustration and fury and he shook with his repressed emotions as he gripped her, wanting to shake her apart and make her act the way he wanted her to. But she would much rather act the way he needed her to.

Ignoring the uncomfortable strength of his hold, she lowered her hands to his hips, traced the leather thickness of his belt, and burrowed one hand deep beneath it as the other worked the buckle and let the prized weaponry fall to the floor in a heedless clatter of steel. She was stroking his cock through the fabric she encountered even as she was working open his second belt and zipper.

"Let go of my arms," she breathed out beneath his ear. "If you would have me sweet and gentle on command, then you can have me nasty and dirty as well. If you would have me be your whore, Magnus, I can easily act however you demand I act at any given moment. You need not limit yourself."

Dae had to admit, considering the force of the red rage that bolted through his mind and was streaming into her brain, she was quite shocked that he didn't strike her. She would not have been so controlled, she suspected. She probably would have belted him, had he insulted them both so crudely. Still, he had done that and worse, and she was sick of pussyfooting around the issue.

Of course, she had not expected his hand to come out and lock around her throat, shearing off her ability to speak and half her ability to breathe as he turned her hard around and slammed her back into his chest. He sent them across the room in three hard, lurching steps until her belly hit the horse she had seen earlier, and she found herself being bent forward over it harshly as his grip slid around to the back of her neck—without a word, without even a coherent thought for her to glean from his blackened mind. Then, without so much as a testing touch to see if she was remotely ready to take him, he freed himself from his clothing and with only a single moment's hesitation to aim himself true, he sent his hard cock balls deep into her in a single, severe stroke.

"Is this it?" he snarled savagely. "Is this what you want of me?"

Daenaira couldn't reply. He was so heavy on her back she couldn't afford to waste an ounce of her precious breath. To say nothing of what it felt like to feel him in such a raw capacity, unchecked and unfiltered. It even overwhelmed him, she knew, as he immediately began to rut against her in deep, slamming thrusts. Dae gritted her teeth, drew hard for breath, and felt her body flooding him with liquid arousal. He couldn't know . . . he couldn't understand how much it turned her on to feel him let loose on her with everything he needed and wanted. Civilization melted away from him like a rapid thaw, and she became the resulting deluge. He thought he was being hurtful and violent, but she knew he could never really hurt her. It wasn't in him to do so, no matter how harsh or how rough he wanted to be.

One hand pinned her by the back of her neck, the other raked down the bare track of her spine as he thrust into her with increasingly violent speed. Her wetness eased his way, fired his need as he felt it coating him in hot, alleviating welcome. Control unfurled, and it all narrowed down to just the shoving plow of his cock into her tight, hot pussy.

Raw. Crude. Animalistic. It was all of that and nothing else as it raced from beginning to end in a matter of heart-pounding minutes. Regardless of how he tried to blame her for it, asking if this was what *she* had wanted, there was no denying how quickly he fell apart in his excitement to be fucking her so obscenely. He was hilting into her hard and fast, his ground-out cries tumbling out of him in a crescendo to match the violence of his thrusts. He came with the blinding speed and force of colliding locomotives. Daenaira moaned low and soft as she felt him buck viciously behind her in time to the spurting release he unleashed into her core.

For a long minute, he lay heavily weighted against her back, gasping for breath that misted damply against her skin. Then reality struck him, and his breath locked in his chest. She felt him shove himself off her and out of her, and he staggered back hard. She gripped the horse to steady herself as she turned to see him. She watched as he lost strength in his legs and collapsed to his knees. He cried out, a terrible, heartbreaking sound that shredded her to her soul. Dae quickly fell before him, wrapping herself around him in a hug of solace, refusing his attempts to strip her away from him.

"No! No!" she said fiercely as she fought his strength. "Keep me now. Take me again later in another way entirely. Hold me and shake me and kiss me as you like. This is what I want! This and more! This and everything! All of it. Give it all to me and I promise you'll never regret it!"

"I already regret it!"

"You don't! You only think *I* will regret it! You are afraid I won't be able to love you for everything you are, and I'm trying to tell you I won't be able to love you *unless you give me everything that you are*!"

These words, better than any others, penetrated the haze of his pain and misery. Here Magnus had thought he had just destroyed everything; thrown it all away as he had unraveled and lost control to the most volatile display of his temper and his lust he had ever experienced. The utter perfection of the draining of his tension, the completeness of his sense of total abandonment to what he had truly needed in the instant he had wanted it had been glorious. He had absolutely relinquished all rule, all responsibility, consciousness, and worry, and all of the thousands of other things he was hammered with from a hundred sides all night long, every single night.

And then he had felt her gasping for breath beneath his weight, reason returning to him in an ominous and dreadful tidal flow. In an instant he realized he had destroyed everything. Horrified with how he had used her, how he had torn into her like some animal on a sexual rampage, how he'd taken what should have been held sacred and instead let it be wild and brutally untamed.

So he hadn't understood the wrapping comfort of her arms and body. It had felt profane that she should touch him after what he'd just done. But now, the words she spoke were a balm for his shattering soul. It suspended everything from respiration to reproof within him.

I'm trying to tell you I won't be able to love you unless you give me everything that you are . . .

. . . give me everything that you are . . .

Show me everything, and it's here . . . waiting for you. I can't entrust it to you if you only meet me in half strides. I've never loved anyone before, none but my mother, and I won't allow the first time to be with a man who will not love me or himself enough to just be who he is and stop being so fucking afraid of what others will think of him for it.

The blinding rush of her vehement thoughts through his mind blew him away, forcing an explosion of keen emotion to sting across his features and burn tears into his eyes. His arms were wrapping around her tightly, nearly throttling her as he hugged her to him in brutal joy and need. He sobbed into red-black tresses of silken softness, inhaling clouds of sweet cream and strawberries with every hard breath.

"You said you didn't love me," he said roughly after struggling a while to compose himself enough to speak.

She smiled where she was pressed against his throat. "I don't. Or I won't. Not if you think you're going to bullshit me like I have been watching you try to bullshit everyone else this week."

He frowned at that. "I don't . . . "

"Those parents know their children need to be here. They know the majority of the danger is passed. They do not want to be glad-handed by you and promised moonshine and roses. They want to see you get pissed off. They want to know your indignation. They want to feel your wrath come down on those who dared to threaten their children while they were in your keeping. *Then*, and only then, will they be able to trust you to watch over them again. Don't you see that? You have always been the ultimate symbol of prescience and retribution, and if you show your awareness of your mistakes and then show the reckoning of those who cross you and our gods, then they will see this sacred place in any way you wish for them to see it. Powerful. Benevolent. Merciful. A house of trustworthy shepherds eradicated of the insurrection of poison and now made stronger because of it.

"*Jei li*, we are so easy to please, those who are common in our species. We want our larger-than-life heroes, it is true, but we need our down-to-earth ones as well. Let them be in awe of Tristan and Malaya for their perceived perfection and power. But let them come running to you because you will admit to feeling as they do, stumbling as they do, and erring as they do, all the while empowering them as you seek justice for them, instill the fear of the gods in them to guide them, and all the many things you do every single time you dress yourself in these clothes and these weapons."

He heard her. He really and truly heard her this time, and understood what she had been trying to tell him all along. Whether it was because of how she had broken him down, or because once she said the words "*jei li*," he would always remember every single spoken word of that day, it didn't matter.

The point was that he understood.

He loosened his grip on her slowly and gently, turning her in his lap and in his arms until she lay with her cheek cradled against his biceps of his left arm and her bottom snug against his thighs. He brushed her hair into order with tender fingers as his golden eyes shimmered smiles down onto her.

"I wonder," he said after a long time of simply watching her face, "if it is your youth that makes you see things so much more clearly than one of my age and supposed wisdom."

"You are very wise, M'jan," she assured softly, reaching to stroke her fingers along his strong jaw. "But time has inured you to poor habits that no one would notice unless they were close enough. I think *Drenna* is quite clever and knew so very well what she was doing for her servants when she sent us to one another. First you saved me . . . so that I could then save you. Now together, truly together," she repeated with intent warning in her amber eyes, "we can make a partnership of priest and handmaiden that will inspire Sanctuary to become as close to your ideal as is possible on this earth. This place has become very important to me. I see the good it does and the potential for more, especially now that it is free of Acadian's influence and rotted offspring."

"And I will not have blind faith in my people any longer," he said a bit grimly. "That faith is still blind, when it comes down to it. There is a place for faith and trust, and a place where the reality is that sin does exist even in what appears to be the hearts of the best of men."

"And women."

"Yes. And women. I feel one lesson I have learned in all of this is the power and value of women among us. We have never had a woman dole out penance before—not officially, anyway—but perhaps it's time we considered changing that. Sex shouldn't make a difference in the ability to acquire the skills needed. You broke me down, a trained master at psychology, in less than an hour, Daenaira. Granted, you had an inside track, but I see the potential in you. You are as clever, stubborn, and as superior as is needed, but you have a woman's mercy and softness. You are unexpected and ruthless. Even at the highest heat of your fighting rage, you still tempered yourself enough to ask the vilest creature to repent. You need a great deal of training, and I may never send you into the field alone without me, but one of these rooms could be yours."

"Mmm, but does that mean now *you* have to give *me* ritual baths after battle?"

"I already have," he reminded her, slowly rolling her to the floor beneath him as he stretched the length of her body. She squeaked and arched up into him when the cold tile met her naked skin. "Damn, woman," he complained, "how in Light am I going to get you into my bed when you've nothing to wear for the walk through the temple?"

"I could wear your tunic," she pointed out.

He frowned. "Do you know what that would look like? Me bare-chested and you—"

She covered his mouth with her fingers, stopping him. "What of it?" she asked of him. "You preach the freedom and joys of sex, but you are such a prude. We are as man and wife, Magnus. Whatever it is called, it is a Bond that allows us to be with one another. It even allows us to love one another. It's clear that love is what really creates the Bonded connection between priest and maiden. It's a gift, I think, from our benevolent goddess. I think it pleases Her to see us open ourselves completely to the mate she chooses to send us."

"I think *M'gnone* has had a hand in this particular mating as well," he said, kissing her fingertips as they lay lax against his lips. "Our tempers and our need to fight carry out the will of the gods as much as our mercy and our love does." He smiled at that. "And it is *our* love, isn't it?"

Yes. I do love you. Does this not answer that question?

"It does, *K'yindara*," he said softly. "But I should like to hear you say it to me aloud. You hurt me very much when you denied me that day, and it would go a long way to soothing that."

"I am sorry. I was very afraid of you that day. I didn't want to be responsible for how you were feeling. But this past week as I watched you struggle so hard to maintain the picture of gliding on an even keel, I began to realize that I was always going to bear responsibility for you and your emotional well-being. It is impossible to be a handmaiden of any effectiveness without it. I am meant to be solace and comfort to you, the one place you can turn to and be a man instead of a priest; the one soul where you should be able to find unconditional love in a physical being. I am representative of *M'gnone*, who caters gladly to the will of the goddess so she may sit resplendent. But he rules over the land of Light and Sinners with an iron determination to see they pay for their crimes forever. I may be your servant, M'jan, but I am also here to keep you true to your path as sternly as I need to."

"And I assure you, you are a screaming success, *K'yan*." He bent to kiss her mouth in slow, thorough tastes before abruptly lifting away. "Damn me if you didn't weasel out of saying you love me!"

She giggled. "That's what you get for forcing me to lie on a cold, hard floor. Bring me to a warm, soft bed and make love to me as wildly as you dare, and I shall think about gracing you with those words."

"Done!"

Epilogue

"*Jei li*, my son is due to arrive any minute." Magnus groaned softly, figuring she probably couldn't care less. Frankly, as warm and sucking wet as her mouth was on his achingly hard cock, he didn't much care either. The door at his back was locked, and Trace would wait until he bid him in.

But having Daenaira on her knees before him had a way of wringing him out. Ever since she had first taken his lessons on how to perform effective fellatio on him, she had discovered she not only had a talent for it, but a voracious appetite for the effect it had on him. Some saw the act as one of female submission, but she had proven it to be a woman's domain of dominance. Just the starting flick of her tongue was all it took to drive away all of his thoughts of duty, responsibility, work, and any other damn thing he needed to attend to. She didn't just like that power, she thrived on it.

And she loved the taste of him. He could hear the cravings in her thoughts, the desire to feel him burst on her tongue in hot, salty gushes. Just listening to the music of her seductive mind drove him to the brink of orgasm.

For the third time that night.

And the night wasn't even half over yet.

Magnus gripped fistfuls of lush red-black hair, looking down to see himself gliding past her lips as they made mutual effort at it. The wicked flutter of her tongue drove him to distraction, the rushing surge of his pulse in his ears deafening him to the knock that sounded at his back. When Daenaira released him from her lips so very close to his crest, he hissed in pained denial.

"One moment, please," she called out to Trace, gifting Magnus with her signature sly smile before using her tongue to draw him back into the darkness of her mouth.

Knowing Trace was close enough to hear them, she took that as her cue to pit herself strongly against Magnus's desire to control himself into silence. She stroked him now as she drew on him deeply and quickly, her free hand scraping and tickling against his ball sack, especially just behind where she knew it drove him crazy. Magnus ground his teeth to nubs, trying to breathe in desperate draws as quietly as he could even as she became more and more relentless.

Culmination thundered over him so suddenly and with such blinding power, he forgot all about silence as he roared out from the start to the finish. He swore a blue streak, called her name, and growled with masculine satisfaction as he pulsed his release into her eager, sucking mouth. She licked him quite thoroughly clean and then sat back on her heels to smile up at him with the satisfaction of a cat. The scent of her sharp arousal wafted up to him, and he grinned down at her.

"Payback's a bitch," he reminded her gruffly.

"Yes, yes, and so am I," she pointed out with a laughing sigh. She rose to her feet, straightened her sari, and watched him right his clothing as well. "I had meant to finish before he arrived," she offered. Daenaira felt it was important he know she had not been out to purposely embarrass him in front of his son.

But he had known that. It had been clear in her thoughts.

If he had spent less time uselessly resisting her, she would have had her way. It was his fault. Besides, his son was a grown, married man. He could certainly cope with the fact that the man who had raised him was having a sex life of his own.

The unfortunate part of the visit would come afterward, when he had to warn Trace that his wife and future child had been marked for death.

And as if that were not horrible enough . . .

Daenaira sat on a sofa, her legs tucked beneath her bottom, her body poised and dignified as Magnus opened the door to the royal vizier. Trace, of course, looked thoroughly amused as he greeted his parent. He nodded a greeting to Daenaira as well, his eyes sparkling like polished onyx with his humor as he gave her a wink. His attitude toward her had thoroughly changed since the battle with Nicoya had become known. The depth of risk she had taken to fight for his father's cause had made him understand that the very things he had feared her for could also be a fearsome protection in his beloved father's life as well. Knowing the lengths she would go to for the sake of Sanctuary, and realizing there was something quite deeply emotional between priest and handmaiden that had his father happier and far more satisfied then he'd even known him to be, had made all the difference.

Of course, Trace didn't doubt after what he'd just heard that the satisfaction came from things other than emotion as well. Had he been stone deaf, only the high flush beneath Magnus's coloring might have given him away. The two looked as innocent as angels.

Almost.

"M'jan, *K'yan,*" he greeted. It was so tempting to rib his father a bit, but he would wait until the coupling between them was not so new. In a new relationship for himself, he knew how delicate things could be before familiarity settled in.

"*Ajai* Trace," Magnus returned, settling back behind his desk and looking very relaxed and comfortable. Trace made an effort not to chuckle. "How is Ashla?"

"Better. I think. Stronger. Getting a little plumper, I'd say. And about damn time, too." He looked at Dae. "My woman is too damn thin, especially to be breeding. She was sick for a long while."

"I have heard. The baby will certainly round her out. I am glad she is feeling better. I know it unnerved you to see her so sickly."

Trace lifted a brow. "It did. I suppose my father told you that?"

"No. I overheard Killian say something about you avoiding her. Once I learned who you were, I figured if you were anything like your father, you couldn't bear to see someone you love in pain. Which is why this is going to be such a difficult visit for us today."

Gods, talk about a segue, Magnus thought grimly as he watched the bemusement fly from his son's features and alarm replace it.

He is no child, and a warrior at heart as his father is, he will want the truth and quickly, she returned.

"Trace," he began.

"What did she mean by that?" Trace asked simultaneously.

Magnus very carefully and quietly explained to Trace about Nicoya's plan to harm his wife and as-yet-unborn child. The vizier went blank with fear and then colored with fury.

"Of course, we will do everything to intercept this before it happens, son," Magnus assured him.

"But, Trace, you should know something more," Daenaira segued for Magnus once more, giving the impression that they were both talking from the same mind, which in essence they were.

"Nicoya was the daughter of a Senator. One who, as it

turns out, is a very old enemy. I am afraid I must tell you that Acadian is still alive."

Trace exploded from his seat with an oath that even made Dae wince.

"You've known this for how long now, Father?" he demanded with sickly understanding. "It's been almost two weeks since Nicoya was killed! Did it not occur to you Acadian might seek revenge for that?"

"I have no doubt that she will. However, she will not target those she considers to be dealt with already. I expect Daenaira and I will be made to pay for her daughter's death one day. But Acadian was ever the patient creature, and she is also quite busy plotting within the Senate. It will take time for her to come around to us. Meanwhile, we will fortify ourselves within Sanctuary and live with caution, though not paralysis. The only way to stop Acadian now is through the acts of the twins and via you. You must search yourself and your memories of your captivity and find some clue to her identity. Sagan is missing, Trace. I do not dare presume him dead while that creature walks this earth and was so very close by when he disappeared. Perhaps if we had found signs of blood or death somewhere—but we did not. We made the mistake once when we thought you had been killed, and you suffered for it cruelly as her prisoner for a year. At this point, you are Sagan's best hope of recovery. The best hope for your family will, no doubt, be Guin. He has knowledge of assassins that we don't. If anyone can draw an end to this threat, it will be him."

"Our fortune," Daenaira said quietly, "rests solely on the time we have been given. The longer your mate carries, the more time we have."

"And if she miscarries?" he spat, his sturdy frame shaking in a fine tremor under his rage. "She is half human, frail and small. Gods, she may not even survive the birth. Don't you think I've seen how taxing this is on her? Don't you see

how much I despise myself for impregnating her so reck-
lessly, however much it was a strange twist of physical laws?
She cannot know about the rest of this. The stress would kill
her."

"I think you underestimate your woman," Daenaira said
gently, and then held up a hand at his furious glare. "I know.
Who am I to talk? But we women are often stronger than we
appear to you males. Even the frail ones. She will sense you
are keeping something from her if you are not up-front."

"You are Sainted," his father reminded him grimly.

Sainted. Similar to the Bonding, yet different. There did
not need to be love for the Sainting to occur, only the intent
of ultimate sacrifice. But Ashla could wend her way into Trace's
thoughts all the same, plucking at his worries and making
him confess them to her. It would be a terrible way for her to
learn of these threats. Besides, Trace wouldn't take for granted
that Acadian was wholly satisfied with her daughter's plans.
He would need to protect her, and that alone would raise Ashla's
suspicions. Thank *Drenna* they lived in the royal palace.

"Guin is not yet returned. He is a week overdue. Malaya
worries," he said a bit numbly.

"Guin will return soon. I intercepted him before his return and redirected him to begin the search for the assassins.
Do not speak of it to Malaya. He prefers she think he is still
off 'having a sulk,' is how he put it. I tell you only because I
want you to know the search is already begun. I would never
fail you in this. We will find this treachery in time. You have
my word on that."

"Then my heart is at ease," Trace said with sudden and
calm sincerity as he met Magnus's steady golden gaze, "for
you have never lied to me and you have never disappointed
me. Your wisdom brought Ashla safely to me, and I will trust
it again to keep her as safe as I will try to do."

"Watch yourself, Trace," Dae added with concern as she
sat forward on the sofa. "Nicoya was pure poison, the fruit

of a black womb. You know well enough the woman who birthed her. She is equally capable of anything."

"I know. Trust me," he said grimly.

Daenaira watched sadly as he left a short time later, her heart going out to him. "He should be headed home, but if he is anything like his father, he will divert somewhere and blow off a little steam first. He won't want to go to Ashla in a temper."

"He is a great deal like his father," Magnus said, the mixture of love and pride so very evident that it made her smile. "So I imagine you are right." He got up from his seat and came to her, squatting down before her as his hand curved possessively around her thigh beneath the fall of the sari. "There is threat to you, *K'yindara*, and it distresses me. I take comfort in your fighting heart and third power, but I need to ask you to keep close to me as much as you can until the twins can resolve this battle within the Senate. Until Acadian is made to repent for her crimes, none of my family and no part of this society is safe."

"Keeping close to you," she said with soft affection as she leaned close enough to brush warm, fairy-light kisses against his cheek, "is something I find I am growing a happy talent for."

"Mmm. It's a wonder I get anything done of late," he scolded with a gentle chuckle.

"And yet, you have already selected a new penance priest, welcomed back much of the student body, and delegated new staff to all the classes left abandoned by Nicoya's failed insurrection."

"It helps that you have been writing my sermons for me. You have a very grounding touch. I feel as if I am connecting to others in a whole new way. Thank you for that." He reached to nuzzle warm, wet lips into her neck, a hand arriving quite suddenly at her breast. He burrowed beneath the sari and the velvet hem of her blouse until his fingers were pinching her

lightly in a tease. "Not to mention I have never been so relaxed throughout my nights as I seem to be of a sudden."

"You see? Change can be a good thing," she reminded
him with a pleasurable murmur.

"In the case of recent events, I wholeheartedly concur.
However, I know one thing that will never change, *K'yindara.*"

"Payback is a bitch?" she breathed hotly as he began to
gather her forward against him.

"Mmm," he agreed as he lowered her to the floor. "In
many ways. My faith is in *Drenna*, Dae. She will bear us
through the trials to come and see that Acadian gets what she
well deserves."

"The question is, will it come in time to keep your loved
ones safe," she said, speaking aloud his worries for him. He
sighed as he took a moment's comfort in the sweet cream
aroma of her skin.

"Is it asking too much to want all that and be blessed with
you as well?"

"Never. Good intentions and goodwill can never be over-
abundant."

"My gracious gods"—he chuckled, pulling back in affected shock to look at her—"you actually sound like a handmaiden."

"Imagine that." She giggled.

He paused to rub a gentle, loving thumb against her temple, simply absorbing her presence in his life for a moment.
"I want you to be happy here with me. I want to keep you
protected and to love you well. Never let me forget how to
treat you and never let me neglect what we need."

"Never, *jei li,*" she promised softly. "Because you know,
if you do . . ."

"Mmm?"

"You're totally fucked."

Can't get enough Jacquelyn Frank? Don't miss the
NIGHTWALKER SERIES.
Start the journey with JACOB . . .

Since time began, there have been Nightwalkers—the races
of the night who live in the shadows of the moonlight. Love
with humans is absolutely forbidden, and one man makes
certain to uphold this ancient law: Jacob, the Enforcer . . .

**For 700 Years, He Has Resisted Temptation. But
Not Tonight.**

Jacob knows the excuses his people give when the madness
overtakes them and they fall prey to their lust for humans.
He's heard every one and still brought the trespassers to justice. Immune to forbidden desires, uncontrollable hungers,
or the curse of the moon, his control is total . . . until the moment he sees Isabella on a shadowy New York City street.
Saving her life wasn't in his plans. Nor were the overwhelming feelings she arouses in him. But the moment he holds
her in his arms and feels the soft explosion of her body against
his, everything changes. Their attraction is undeniable, volatile,
and completely against the law. Suddenly everything Jacob
has ever believed is inflamed by the heat of desire . . .

Bring on the night.

GIDEON is next on the list . . .

They're called the Nightwalkers—proud, ancient beings who live in the shadows, existing just beyond the human world. But there are also dangerous humans who hunt them—necromancers who use the blackest magic to manipulate them. And for a Demon named Gideon, the battle against these evil forces will soon be all too personal . . .

As A Healer, He Knows Her Body. But It's Her Heart He Wants.

For a thousand years, Gideon has healed his people. And as the oldest surviving male of his race, his wisdom has always been respected without question. But Gideon knows that even he is vulnerable to the powerful, primitive desires that befall his kind during Hallowed moons—and nine years ago that truth was hammered home when he found himself claiming Magdalegna, the Demon King's sister, in a wild embrace. Horrified by his lack of control, he left her wanting and furious—and then exiled himself for the better part of a decade. Now, with necromancers threatening his people—and Magdalegna nearly their victim—Gideon must face another truth. He and the beautiful, stubborn Magdalegna are destined to be together, to share a love as deep and old as time itself. But first he needs to regain her trust. Then he'll have to save her life . . .

Every night holds secrets.

And keep the magic going with ELIJAH, the sexy Warrior Captain . . .

They are called the Demons, one of the elusive Nightwalker races living in shadow and struggling for survival against their human enemies. Their proudest warrior is Elijah, a man who bends for nothing and no one . . . until one woman brings him to his knees . . .

Some Feelings You Just Can't Fight.

He is known as the Warrior Captain—a master of every weapon, a fierce soldier sworn to protect his kind. Powerful, relentless, merciless, Elijah has always won every battle he's ever taken on—until now. Ambushed by necromancers, he is left for dead only to be discovered by the woman who could very well deliver the final blow . . . Siena, the Lycanthrope Queen . . .

With three centuries of warring, little more than a decade of uneasy peace has existed between the Lycanthropes and Elijah's people. Now, after a lifetime of suspicion, the warrior Elijah is consumed with a different battle—winning Siena's heart by giving her pleasure beyond all boundaries. What starts as attraction and arousal soon burns into a passion with consequences that will echo through the ages for both their people. And as would-be enemies become inseparable lovers, another threat approaches, one with the power to destroy them all . . .

Surrender to the night.

The story continues with DAMIEN,
available now from Zebra . . .

They are the Nightwalkers, mysterious beings who dwell in
the shadows of our world, and Damien, the Vampire Prince,
is among the most powerful of them all. But one woman will
tempt him with a desire unlike anything he has known, and
together they will face a terrifying and relentless foe . . .

**He'd Never Loved.
But She Was Irresistible.**

As reigning Vampire Prince, Damien has tasted every pleasure the world has to offer—consorting with kings and queens
and delighting in sensual adventure. Now, tired of such pur-
suits, he devotes his energies to protecting his people. The
war between human necromancers and Nightwalkers has es-
calated, and when the enemy makes a daring move, kidnapping
Syreena, a Lycanthrope Princess, Damien boldly follows.
He succeeds in rescuing her, but is unprepared for the erotic
longing her lush sensuality awakens in him . . .

Gifted with rare abilities, Syreena grew up in a cloistered
setting and was forbidden to form attachments to others, yet
the connection Damien feels with her is immediate, intoxi-
cating, and impossible for either to resist. But claiming Syreena
as his mate could have shattering repercussions for every
Nightwalker—and leave their enemies more dangerous than
ever before . . .

Temptation tastes sweetest at night.

And finally, the Demon King, NOAH, gets his story . . .

The Nightwalkers have lived in the shadows of our world for centuries, gifted with abilities few humans can comprehend. For Noah, duty is all—until he meets the woman who is his destiny . . .

She Will Take Him Beyond His Wildest Dreams.

As Demon King, Noah is dedicated to protecting his kind from their human and Nightwalker enemies. Yet for six months he has struggled with vivid dreams that threaten his very sanity. Every night he's tormented by images of a woman both achingly real and tantalizingly beyond his grasp. And his bone-deep need leaves him no choice but to force her to leave the life she's known and enter a world beyond her imagining . . .

Every day, Kestra risks her life in perilous missions that veer just shy of the law, but she instinctively knows that the imposingly sensual figure before her is a danger unlike any she's ever faced. Kestra has sworn never to trust or need another man, but Noah's lightest touch scorches her with fevered desire, branding her as his mate, blinding them both to the terrifying truth. For within the ranks of their own people lies an adversary growing in number and power. And nothing and no one will be safe again . . .

Desire awakens at night.

Try the SHADOWDWELLERS series from the beginning!
It all starts with ECSTASY . . .

At one with the darkness, the mysterious Shadowdwellers must live as far from light-loving humans as possible in order to survive. Yet one damaged human woman will tempt the man behind the Shadowdweller throne into a dangerous desire . . .

Worlds Couldn't Keep Them Apart.

Among the Shadowdwellers, Trace holds power that some are willing to kill for. Without a stranger's aid, one rival would surely have succeeded, but Trace's brush with death is less surprising to him than his reaction to the beautiful, fragile human who heals him. By rights, Trace should hardly even register Ashla's existence within the realm of Shadowscape, but instead he is drawn to everything about her—her innocence, her courage, and her lush, sensual heat . . .

After a terrifying car crash, Ashla Townsend wakes up to find that the bustling New York she knew is now eerie and desolate. Just when she's convinced she's alone, Ashla is confronted by a dark warrior who draws her deeper into a world she never knew existed. The bond between Ashla and Trace is a mystery to both, but searching for answers will mean confronting long-hidden secrets, and uncovering a threat that could destroy everything Trace holds precious . . .

And get excited about Jacquelyn's newest book,
the third in the SHADOWDWELLERS series,
coming in January 2010.
Turn the page for a sneak peek!

"Guin!"

Malaya's scream came so suddenly, a blood chilling shriek of desperation. Guin was armed and through the door in an instant. His eyes swept the room and she screamed for him again. Malaya was sitting upright in her bed, arms outstretched, fingers grasping as her beautiful whiskey eyes stared sightlessly up at the ceiling.

"Guin! *Guin!*"

She'd have the whole household on them if she continued to scream so disturbingly. Knowing so well how she hated rousing from a vision surrounded by people and afraid of how she had been unwittingly behaving, he hurried into her bed and filled those reaching arms as he gathered her up close and tight to himself.

"Shh," he soothed her, trying to give comfort when his heart was racing with fear and adrenaline was blasting through him. *Gods*, he thought in a cold flash of realization, *how can I ever leave her?* It was moments like this when he believed he would hear her screams for help anywhere in the world, no matter his distance away from her, and that he would never escape his seemingly instinctive calling to keep her safe. "I'm here, my honey," he whispered thickly against her ear. The smell of her overwhelmed him, the clawing of her grasping nails into his bare back tearing him up in more ways than one.

She wasn't crying, and he never knew if that was a good thing. Sometimes it meant she was terrified beyond something like tears, other times it meant they weren't called for. But she rarely screamed out like this. He'd heard her wake with a raw gasp often enough over time, but this vision held her entrapped and he was helpless until it chose to let her go.

"Guin," she rasped again, her hands so desperately holding him close, their restless grasp continuously searching for the best and tightest hold on him.

"Yes, I'm here," he assured her, crushing her lithe body to his in the tightest of hugs so she could feel him as much as possible. He heard Rika in the doorway, but as usual she returned to her room when she realized Guin was in control of the situation. He found that funny, because he couldn't have felt more out of control if he had tried.

"Guin . . . my Guin," she breathed as her fingers threaded up into his hair at the back of his neck.

His reaction was instantaneous and brutal. Guin felt every muscle in his body clench tight at the stimulus of her touch, but more from the impact of her verbal claim. Oh, she'd referred to him this way before, but each time had been a light and affectionate toss of words. There was deep intensity for him feeling her say it like this. Feeling her against him while she did. The smell of her sleep-warmed body and the feel of it under the slide of the silk tissue of her *k'jeet*. And the touch of her hands reminding him of how she had recently pulled him down to taste her.

Guin closed his eyes and tried to take rein of himself. She would awaken soon and he was not going to be in a state of sexual excitement when she did. It would be a thrice-damned perverted betrayal. She despised her vulnerability and inability to control her actions and she would despise him for getting off on it. Gods, he didn't mean to! He fought it with everything he had, but for some reason it wasn't enough anymore. It was as if she'd opened a flood gate and his strength wasn't enough to close it again.

He needed help.

More by Bestselling Author
Fern Michaels

__About Face	0-8217-7020-9	$7.99US/$10.99CAN
__Wish List	0-8217-7363-1	$7.50US/$10.50CAN
__Picture Perfect	0-8217-7588-X	$7.99US/$10.99CAN
__Vegas Heat	0-8217-7668-1	$7.99US/$10.99CAN
__Finders Keepers	0-8217-7669-X	$7.99US/$10.99CAN
__Dear Emily	0-8217-7670-3	$7.99US/$10.99CAN
__Sara's Song	0-8217-7671-1	$7.99US/$10.99CAN
__Vegas Sunrise	0-8217-7672-X	$7.99US/$10.99CAN
__Yesterday	0-8217-7678-9	$7.99US/$10.99CAN
__Celebration	0-8217-7679-7	$7.99US/$10.99CAN
__Payback	0-8217-7876-5	$6.99US/$9.99CAN
__Vendetta	0-8217-7877-3	$6.99US/$9.99CAN
__The Jury	0-8217-7878-1	$6.99US/$9.99CAN
__Sweet Revenge	0-8217-7879-X	$6.99US/$9.99CAN
__Lethal Justice	0-8217-7880-3	$6.99US/$9.99CAN
__Free Fall	0-8217-7881-1	$6.99US/$9.99CAN
__Fool Me Once	0-8217-8071-9	$7.99US/$10.99CAN
__Vegas Rich	0-8217-8112-X	$7.99US/$10.99CAN
__Hide and Seek	1-4201-0184-6	$6.99US/$9.99CAN
__Hokus Pokus	1-4201-0185-4	$6.99US/$9.99CAN
__Fast Track	1-4201-0186-2	$6.99US/$9.99CAN
__Collateral Damage	1-4201-0187-0	$6.99US/$9.99CAN
__Final Justice	1-4201-0188-9	$6.99US/$9.99CAN

Available Wherever Books Are Sold!
Check out our website at **www.kensingtonbooks.com**

Thrilling Suspense from
Beverly Barton